INVADING HELL

THE OCULUS GATE SERIES

BOOK ONE: HEAVEN CAME DOWN
BOOK TWO: INVADING HELL
BOOK THREE: MY SOUL TO TAKE
BOOK FOUR: ON EARTH AS IT IS IN HELL
(BOOK FOUR RELEASE - APRIL 15, 2023)

INVADING HELL

BOOK TWO IN THE OCULUS GATE SERIES

BY

BRYAN DAVIS

MOUNTAIN**BROOK**FIRE

Invading Hell
Published by Mountain Brook Ink under the Mountain Brook
Fire line
White Salmon, WA U.S.A.

The website addresses shown in this book are not intended in any way to be or imply an endorsement on the part of Mountain Brook Ink, nor do we vouch for their content.

This story is a work of fiction. All characters and events are the product of the author's imagination. Any resemblance to any person, living or dead, is coincidental.

ISBN 978-1-953957-02-3

Published in association with Cyle Young of the Hartline Literary Agency, LLC.

The Team: Miralee Ferrell, Alyssa Roat, Cindy Jackson
Cover Design: Indie Cover Design, Lynnette Bonner

Mountain Brook Fire is an inspirational publisher offering worlds you can believe in.

Printed in the United States of America

Chapter One

Trudy aimed her flamethrower at the metal door. The barrel nearly touched a warning sign emblazoned on the front—Angel Hive: Authorized Personnel Only.

"Jack," she shouted. "Found it. Basement. Northeast corner."

Jack's voice filtered through her earbud. "I'm thirty seconds away, Sis. Don't burn the place down without me."

"No promises. If you want in on the party, you need to get here on time." She adjusted the fuel tanks on her back and gazed down the empty hallway. As expected, her call aroused no guards. Angel headquarters appeared to be abandoned, no dangers in sight. Yet, with so many valuables lying hidden within these walls, who could tell if a door might lead to a trap?

Loud footsteps thumped on the carpeted floor. Jack's athletic form appeared as he jogged around a corner, a flamethrower gripped in both hands and his own tanks strapped over his camo uniform. When he arrived, he pushed his hair back, his dark curls dampened by sweat.

Trudy punched his arm. "Tough day at the gym?"

"I was on the top floor, and these tanks weigh a ton."

"Cry me a river, muscle man." She adjusted her earbud. "Kat? Did you hear? I found the hive room."

"Got your position," Kat said through the bud. "I'll unlock it." A click sounded from the door.

Jack offered a tight-lipped nod. "Having the angel queen's face and fingerprints is like the ultimate skeleton key."

Trudy smirked. "She'll milk that advantage all day long."

"That should do it," Kat said. "It looks like the hive room has a separate computer control system, not accessible remotely. Be careful."

"Will do." Trudy touched the door's latch. "Leo? Iona? How goes the city flyover?"

Iona's voice punched through. "Already done and on our way to HQ. The thermal sensors say plenty of warm bodies are in the temple, so it won't be an easy nut to crack. We'll be there to pick you guys up in a little while."

"Thanks." Trudy looked at Jack as he drummed his fingers on his flamethrower, his angular face tense, obviously anxious to charge into the hive room. But he could wait another minute. "Kat, what's your status?"

"Ben and I are in the computer vault downloading the angel databases. I used the data key I already had and found where the other key is hidden, locked in a bank in the city. When the download's done, we'll meet you out front."

"Sounds good. Keep an ear to your buds. If the intel's wrong about fire destroying the hive, we might need help."

"Copy that."

"We're going in." Trudy gripped the latch. When Jack gave her a nod, she pushed the door open. A hiss sounded—air pressure releasing.

Jack stepped past the threshold, Trudy following. Inside the warm, humid room, a pale-yellow glow washed over them. A honeycomb-like structure arched over their heads, creating a low tunnel with thumb-sized octagonal holes embedded within the walls, maybe the cells for the spawns. A scarlet light pulsed from each hole, perfectly matching the cadence of the others.

Trudy whispered, "Their hearts are beating as one."

"A hive mind." Jack raised his flamethrower. "Shall we test the intel?"

"Cool your jets, cowboy. We're not in a hurry." Trudy scanned the tunnel's curved walls, about ten feet long and eight feet high, arching over a four-foot-wide concrete path running through it. The hive cells appeared to be divided into six-inch squares with a shallow indentation marking the boundaries.

"Trudy. Check this out."

She pivoted toward Jack. He pointed at a missing square in the hive matrix near his shoulder. "Think the angels moved a spawn somewhere?"

"Looks like it." Trudy peered into the hole. The recess, about an arm's length deep, held only empty air, though markings on one side, written in the language of the angels, likely identified the former occupant.

She stepped back and spread her arms. "This means we still have phony angels, hundreds of them. Kat's theory was true."

"Yeah. The force that drew the implanted angels to Chantal didn't penetrate this pressure-sealed vault." Jack readied his flamethrower. "Time to dispatch them."

A buzz sounded. The surrounding light flashed. A voice emanated from somewhere unseen. "Temperature falling to critical level. Open access door detected."

The door began closing on its own. Jack shouted, "Keep it open! I'll raise the temperature!"

Trudy dropped the flamethrower, leaped to the entry, and slid into the narrowing gap, her fuel tanks against the jamb and her hands on the door. As it pushed, she pushed back, grunting, "Torch it!"

A stream of fire spewed from Jack's flamethrower toward the rear of the tunnel. He waved the gun in an arc, igniting every inch of the honeycomb as he backed toward the door. Within seconds, an inferno engulfed the entire tunnel.

The door's pressure eased, allowing Trudy to push it the rest of the way open and retrieve her gun. They stepped out, closed the door partway, and stood in the corridor at a safe distance. Squeals erupted from the hive along with accompanying pops and sizzles.

Jack grinned. "I love the sound of angel bacon frying."

"Behave yourself." Trudy elbowed him but couldn't suppress a smile of her own. For the first time in a while, they had accomplished a mission without botching it. "Let's check in with Ben and Kat."

"We've been listening," Kat said. "It sounds like a spawn is missing."

Within the tunnel, the flames roared, sending intense heat into the corridor and forcing Jack and Trudy to back away several more steps. Fortunately, since the vault was lined with metal, it would probably contain the blaze. "Right," Trudy said. "Any theories?"

"I have a vague memory. While Laramel possessed me, I carried a box through a roomy chamber with stacks of crates, like a big warehouse, but in the memory, everything's blurred. No labels on the boxes or any other details."

Jack shrugged off his harness and set the fuel tanks on the floor. "I'll bet it's a spawn safe house. Laramel wanted to keep at least one of her little devils locked away in case something happened to the hive."

"Sounds reasonable," Kat said. "Laramel was always kind of paranoid, especially about the force she wanted the Refectors to help her neutralize."

Trudy removed her tanks and laid them near Jack's. "And we still have no idea what that force is."

An explosion erupted from the hive room. The door flew off its hinges and hurtled through the corridor, propelled by a comet-like ball of fire. Jack shoved Trudy out of the way. The edge of the door smacked his hip and threw him against her, making them both crash into a wall and fall to the floor.

The door tumbled end over end, and the flaming sphere exploded. Fiery debris scattered and ignited the walls and ceiling, some of it pelting Jack and Trudy.

Trudy batted smoking embers from her hair as she climbed to her feet. The fire continued roaring in the hive room, maybe ready to blast another barrage, and flames crawled closer to the fuel tanks. "We'd better bolt."

"I'll second that." Jack reached a hand up. "Give me a lift. Not sure if my legs are working."

She grasped Jack's wrist and pulled. As he rose, he grimaced, then stood on one leg. When they took a step to run, Jack faltered and nearly fell. Trudy pushed a shoulder under his arm. "Lean on me."

They hustled toward the stairwell, Jack limping heavily while Trudy hauled him along. Another explosion sounded behind them, louder than the first. The building shook, and the corridor's drop ceiling collapsed in front of the stairway door. Trudy pulled the knob, dragging debris as the door opened. The gap allowed Jack to hop through on one foot. She called over the fire's roar, "Ben. Kat. You'd better bug out. This building's going up in flames."

"Got it," Ben said. "We're on our way."

While Jack and Trudy hobbled up the dim stairway toward the first floor, Iona's voice broke in. "Headquarters is in sight. The fire's spreading across the lower level. If you're already in a stairwell, hightail it to the roof. We'll pick you up there."

They struggled together up the next flight, two away from the roof. "We'll be on top in a couple of minutes," Trudy said, grunting. "Don't leave without us."

"We're standing in the parking lot," Ben said. "Pick up Jack and Trudy first, then land here."

"On our way," Iona replied. "Punch it, Leo."

At the parking lot, Ben and Kat stood in the late afternoon's chilly autumn breeze and eyed the roof of the main HQ building, the central four-story unit in the country-club-like campus. Leo and Iona had landed the angel cruiser and were helping Jack and Trudy into the side hatch. Since the luxury, propeller-driven drone could hold ten passengers, they had plenty of room.

The smoke forced Ben to rub his eyes before looking again. Although the fire drew closer to the rescuers, they seemed to have plenty of time to escape. No worries.

He curled a hand into a fist. The dreaded headquarters complex was burning to the ground. Good riddance. Now it was time to plan the next step—get the second key from the bank and take over the city temple. But who would be the best choice for completing each mission?

Kat touched his tightened hand. "I know that pose. You have a plot cooking."

He turned to her and smiled. Her sparkling green eyes seemed able to see straight through him. "You're right." He ran a hand through her dark hair, recently cut to a pageboy style for the new mission. "I'm thinking about the two of us storming the temple while the others sneak into the bank to find the second key."

Kat nodded. "That works as long as—"

"Good," Iona said through the earbud. "Sneaking is my specialty."

Leo piped in. "Truer words were never spoken. The sneaky sniper should be registered as a lethal weapon. A small one, perhaps. Poison in a pill bottle."

Ben mentally cringed. Accidentally leaving the earbud turned on could someday lead to trouble. He covered the error with a laugh. "I'll bet Iona doesn't like that description."

"Hard to tell from here. If she kicks my shins, I'll let you know. But she might have to stand on a stool to kick that high."

"Now you've guaranteed a shin bruising." Ben glanced at the roof. Leo was boosting Jack, apparently hobbled by an injury, into the cruiser. Smoke billowed, blocking the view at times. Seconds later, the cruiser lifted off and quickly glided out of the plumes of smoke.

"Leo," Kat said as she eyed the drone. "Fly around in a safe area until you hear from us again."

"Will do."

"How's Jack?" she asked. "He looked kind of gimpy."

6

"Trudy's checking him out. She thinks it's just a nasty bruise, but she wants to make sure."

"Good. We're going silent for a little while." Kat removed her earbud and turned the microphone off, then motioned for Ben to do the same.

When he complied, he gave her a questioning look. "What's up?"

"Well …" She flashed a tentative smile, the kind she always used when she was about to say something he might not want to hear.

Ben stayed quiet. He probably needed to hear it. After escaping implantation by an alien only two weeks earlier, his wife, Katherine Garrison, also his counselor and confidante, had returned, a blend of warrior and techno-geek in a lithe but powerful package. "Go on. I'm listening."

She took a deep breath. "You know I trust your judgment. It's always been spot on." Her smile widened. "Well, almost always."

"Go ahead. Spill it. I'm ready."

"It's Iona. You're thinking about making her the point person for the bank mission, aren't you?"

He shrugged. "Well, like she said, sneaking is her specialty."

"No argument on that point." Kat sighed, her brow bent at a sympathetic angle. "I know you think the world of her. And so do I. But remember, she's only sixteen. She's got the heart of a lion. As brave as Trudy was at that age, and that's saying a lot."

"True, but I sense a big *but* coming."

Kat nodded. "Iona is impetuous. Impulsive. Both with her mouth and her actions. No governors on that young woman's tongue. She's a great infiltrator, but she's also a powder keg. She could blow up a mission if she's not careful."

"Yeah. I know." Ben pushed a hand into his pocket. "She needs … well … a good coach."

"Or a father?" Kat set a hand on his cheek. "Like you?"

Ben looked down as he slid the toe of his shoe along the ground. "You see through me like a wide-open window, don't you?"

"You hide it well from others, but I know your heart. I mean, what you really want." Touching his chin, she lifted his head, making eye contact again. "You've never even hinted at blaming me for losing our baby, even though it was my fault. You warned me not to go out on that drill when I was preg—"

"Stop." He pressed a finger against her lips. "Not one more word. Like I told you then, forgiveness is forever."

She guided his hand out of the way. "Right. And I love you for that. Always have. But since I can't ever have any children, I'm probably the last person who should warn you about your feelings for Iona. And you do have them."

He averted his eyes from her ever-piercing gaze. "Yeah. You nailed me, as usual. I can see her as a daughter." He shrugged. "I guess I want to give her a chance to shine, like most dads want for a daughter."

"Dads also want to protect their daughters from harm, like you wanted to protect me and our baby. You were right then, and I think you'd be right now to keep Iona in check until she's ready."

He regained eye contact. Tears sparkled across her emerald irises. "Sure, but we're talking about infiltrating a bank. It's not like spying behind enemy lines. Danger is winding down, not up."

"I'm not so sure." Kat set her computer pad on her palm and pointed at an icon on the screen. "Remember I told you that I found a message from Commander Barks?"

Ben nodded. "An encrypted file for you and me."

"Well, I used the usual password and decrypted it. It's a video, and I think we should watch it together."

"Now?" Ben glanced at the sky. The angel cruiser flew in a slow arc nearly overhead. "They're waiting for us."

"They can keep waiting. Unless your back's hurting and you need to rest in one of those cushy lounge chairs."

"You make resting sound like a bad thing." Ben stretched his back. The burn scars inflicted by a plasma sphere still stung, but not enough to be crippling. "I'm all right."

8

"Good." She tapped on the icon. A new image filled the screen. Commander Barks sat with his hands folded on a table, facing the camera. Based on the lack of a scar on his jaw from an injury he suffered three years earlier, this recording was at least that old.

Barks removed a patrol cap and ran a hand through his gray crewcut hair. "I'm ready."

"It's running, Roland."

Ben looked at Kat. "Was that Doc?"

She nodded. "He was always more tech savvy than Barks."

"Good." Barks gestured to the side with his head. "Now get your butt out of here. This isn't for your ears."

"It's leaving, and the rest of my body's going with it."

After a door closed, Barks focused on the camera again. "Ben and Kat, not to be dramatic, but since you're watching this, I assume that I am dead. You likely discovered this recording in the firebox among my other personal effects with instructions not to view it unless I kicked the proverbial bucket, which means that I am speaking to you from beyond the grave."

He pressed his thumbs together, his lips tight, as if nervous about his next words. "It's confession time. You see, I am one of the reasons the angels came to Earth. It's a long story with many unimportant details, so I won't bore you with them. Suffice it to say that I played an instrumental part in the angels' arrival, though I strongly objected to their implantation in humans. Since then, I have done everything in my power to make amends for my mistakes, including a pledge to die for the cause. I can only hope that when you hear this, the angel scourge will have been wiped out."

Ben whispered, "Wiped out in the nick of time."

"Right," Kat said. "But probably not the way he expected it to happen."

Barks raised a finger. "There is one issue I haven't discussed with anyone, not even the good doctor, because it sounds like something out of a horror movie." He picked up his hat and fumbled with the bill. "I suspect there is a great evil behind everything that has happened. The angels didn't put Hell's Gate in the sky. It preceded them, and it was always a mystery to them. Someone else put that portal in the sky. Someone else called those parasitic tyrants into our world. Someone else concocted the entire sinister scheme with a more devilish goal in mind. Yet, I don't know who, and I don't know why.

"We have theories, of course, but none answer the overriding question. How could it all happen unless someone wanted it to happen? Cookies don't magically appear from an oven. A baker has to come up with a recipe, mix the dough, grease the cookie sheet. There is intelligence behind the entire process. In short, no baker, no cookies. And the coming of the angels is far more complex than any baking process.

"As I mentioned, I had a part, as did a physician named Dr. Elder and a scientist, Dr. Harrid, an eccentric fellow who disappeared not long after I worked with him."

"Harrid," Ben said. "First time I've heard that name."

Kat nodded. "Same here."

"But we were role players," Barks continued. "The grease. The oven. The dough. Someone else was the baker. And I'm sure you're asking who this baker is." He shrugged. "Frankly, I have no idea, which is why I never talked about it. But I do know that he or she must exist, as surely as I know that a creator God exists. As you realize, this world did not come into existence by itself. It, too, had a baker.

"I tell you this in case you're pondering the same questions I have. Simply put, even if the angels have been eliminated, it doesn't mean our mission has been fully accomplished. The evil baker might still be lurking." Barks looked upward as if wondering what else to say. "That's all. I hope I don't sound like some mad fool." He leaned close. "I should be able to figure out how to turn this blasted thing off without Doc's help. Ah. Here's the switch."

The screen flickered and went blank.

Ben and Kat stared at each other as they let the message sink in. After a moment, Kat turned the pad off. "I agree with Barks."

"You mean there's a great evil lurking behind the scenes?"

"Exactly. And he, she, or it won't give up just because we eliminated the angels. Someone smart enough to pull this off has to have backup plans, you know, Plan B and C. Or maybe the angels were expendable, and Plan A is still going on."

"True. A lot more is going on besides the angels coming here. The alien Refectors replaced them, and somehow they knew they were supposed to live in human bodies with purged souls."

Kat pointed at him. "And don't forget the other force Laramel was worried about. Obviously, the angels weren't the ones in charge."

"I'm with you. There has to be a grand scheme designer. But the reason you showed me the message now was because of Iona's mission. How are they related?"

Kat attached the computer pad to her belt. "A brilliant schemer would see Iona as a vulnerability, an easy target. She's smart and brave, but not seasoned and wise. With this schemer still lurking, the bank mission might not be as easy as you imagine. Maybe danger isn't winding down at all."

Ben glanced at the cruiser again and imagined Iona watching them. Knowing her, she probably wished she could hear every word of this conversation. "Are you saying she shouldn't be part of the mission?"

"I think she can go to the bank. But as a role player. Let's come up with a way to use her talents alongside Leo, Jack, and Trudy. As a learner, not a leader."

"Don't you think giving her more responsibility will help her mature?"

Kat shook her head. "Too soon. Baby steps. I want to see some growth first. Less swagger. More caution."

"Fair enough. We'll work it out. But if the time comes when I need her to step up, I'm giving her the lead. She's already proven that she can carry a huge weight."

"Like you said. Fair enough." Kat ran a hand through his hair, copying his earlier gesture, though his crewcut probably felt like a scrub brush, unlike her soft tresses. "You'll make the right call." She winked. "Dad."

The word pinched hard but sounded like sweet music at the same time. "If only. But she might be too independent to look up to me. I'm barely old enough to be her father."

Kat rolled her eyes. "My husband. Super soldier. Planner extraordinaire. A kind-hearted warrior who can't see what's obvious to everyone else."

"Can't see?" He cocked his head. "What do you mean?"

"Trust me. Iona looks up to you. Adores you. Give her time. She'll let you know in her own way."

Warmth surged through his body. Maybe Iona could never be a real daughter, but knowing that she looked up to him really helped fill the void. "Thanks. I appreciate that." He grasped Kat's hand and interlocked their thumbs. "Ready to go for a ride?"

"Ready." Kat turned her earbud on and reinserted it. "All right, Leo, or Iona, or whoever isn't too injured from shin kicking. Sail that cruiser down here. Let's go kick some alien butt."

Chapter Two

Bartholomew padded down the steps toward the castle's lower level. Although the air was cooler here, it carried the usual odor—the stench of sulfur infused with the aroma of death. All of hell smelled that way, impossible to escape, as was hell itself, or so it seemed to most condemned souls. He, however, had a sliver of hope, and pretending to be an ally to the so-called queen of hell was a small price to pay for that sliver.

"Bartholomew." Alexandria's voice rode the air from below as if part of the foul odor. "That ward-breaking ring I gave you was not an open invitation to come to my abode. Unless you have significant news to report, leave at once. I am occupied with an important issue."

He grasped the ring and turned it on his finger. Even this bauble felt like part of his ball-and-chain commitment to the self-absorbed queen. The drop of human blood suspended in the ring's jewel did allow him to come and go as he pleased, but it signified her power and his lack of it.

Summoning his usual act, a blend of stately gentleman and reluctant advisor, he strode down the rest of the stairs and turned toward the courtroom. "I do have news, and it's more than merely significant."

At the end of the passageway and elevated on a stage, Alexandria sat on a throne, her ebony violin and bow leaning against the throne's side. In front at floor level, near her black-booted feet, a transparent, rectangular basin held her collection of soul energy, a pool that appeared to be nothing more than water. A misty aura hovered over the pool, swirling slowly like fog in a twisting breeze.

A woman stood trembling next to the throne. Her height, perhaps six and a half feet, made her look like an oversized adult, but her youthful face revealed the aspect of an older teen. A thick, dark braid of hair lay across the front of her torso, dangling past her waist. Wearing buckskin leather from neck to feet, she looked like a prop for a museum of ancient western culture, though her torn clothes, quaking frame, gasping respiration, terror-filled eyes, and bloody gashed cheeks made her look more like a victim of horrific torture.

One of Alexandria's furry beasts clutched the woman's arm with a humanlike paw, its pig-like snout oozing green mucous, as usual. Standing two heads shorter than its prisoner, it flexed its muscular arms as if to compensate for its height disadvantage.

Alexandria rose slowly, anger in her silvery eyes as she aimed them at Bartholomew. "Your reason for interrupting my"—she glanced at her prisoner—"my counseling session had better be a good one."

"My news can wait." Bart waved a hand. "By all means, finish what you were doing."

She glowered at him for a moment before tossing her blonde hair back from the shoulders of her leather jacket, open in front to reveal a form-fitting white T-shirt, a typical gesture when she wanted to show off her motorcycle-tough persona as well as her never-aging form. "Perhaps it's for the best." She turned toward the prisoner. "Our new arrival can be a witness to my mercy toward you, Lacinda."

Lacinda's trembling eased, and her breathing steadied. "Mercy?" Her voice was deeper than expected, like a low contralto, though still feminine. "What is that?"

"Mercy means to give you relief. Rest from your work." Alexandria lifted Lacinda's braid in her palm. "You suffered greatly in the abyss while trying to accomplish the task I assigned you."

Lacinda blinked. "A ... accomplish? Suffered?"

"To accomplish a task means to do something. To suffer is to hurt. You hurt a lot while doing what I asked."

Lacinda nodded, blood dripping from her chin. "Yes. Yes, I did. I hurt. Many times."

Bartholomew cocked his head. English was obviously not this woman's native language, and her facial structure seemed off somehow. Maybe she wasn't even human. That would explain her height as well.

Alexandria dropped Lacinda's braid. "Before I decide what to do with you, I want you to see the importance of the task you failed to accomplish."

Lacinda's brow knitted, but she stayed quiet, apparently not understanding but fearful of asking for an explanation.

Alexandria turned toward the mist as it continued spinning above the pool. She picked up the violin and bow and played a few measures of a classical requiem by Mozart, if Bartholomew remembered his music history correctly.

As if blown by the tune, the mist cleared, replaced by a rotating globe—Earth floating in space. She lowered the violin and pointed with the bow. "Bartholomew, the pace of events on Earth and Viridi is accelerating. On Earth, the angels have been destroyed, which is no setback, of course. They were merely my advancing pawns." She leaned the violin and bow against the throne. "What is surprising is the ragtag team of rebels that defeated them, a pathetic little party that has dwindled to only six survivors, and one of them is a teenager."

Bartholomew closed in and stood within reach of the globe. "Then they won't be obstacles to the next part of the plan."

"Not obstacles at all. Assets. We can employ them to our advantage." She used both hands to expand the globe, as if drilling down to a more detailed map. After passing through several layers, the image settled on a thirtyish woman with brown hair cut in a pageboy style, her facial features animated as she seemed to be talking to someone. Alexandria pointed at her. "Yet, one of them,

15

Katherine Garrison, might be trouble. Her intellect is high, and she is not easily fooled."

"What do you care?" Bartholomew asked. "They're on Earth, and we're here in hell."

Alexandria's lips curled into one of her twitching smiles. "That will change." After waving the guard away, she stepped over to Lacinda, set a hand on her shoulder, and pushed her down to her knees, then lifted her braid again and wrapped it around her throat. Lacinda closed her eyes and wept, her head bobbing.

When Alexandria halted, she stood at Lacinda's side, still holding the end of the braid. "Although Lacinda is alive and not a disembodied soul, I suspect that her lack of being human contributed to her failure. Therefore, I need living humans to come here, and not just any humans. They must be capable and motivated to a maximum level, and members of that angel-killing team might fill that need nicely, but ..." She gave the braid a light tug, prompting more shaking from Lacinda. "They also have to stay completely unaware of my ultimate goal. In order to keep Katherine from figuring it out, I will have to flood her mind with emotional upheavals."

Bartholomew resisted the urge to wince at Alexandria's sadistic drama. Any negative gesture would make the situation worse. "And how do you plan to do that?"

She nodded toward the image of Katherine. "By drawing her husband here first. Then she will come, armed for bear, as they say. I will use her fury against her."

"I see. Then she will be your vehicle out of hell, and her husband will be mine?"

Alexandria slowly tightened the braid around Lacinda's throat but not enough to shut off her air passage. Her breathing accelerated, but she stayed quiet.

Ignoring Lacinda's travail, Alexandria shook her head. "No. Those two are too psychologically mature. We need someone more naïve, more volatile, less experienced. I have a pair in mind, but I have to watch them for a while to see if they're good candidates."

"As you should. Considering what we want to do to them, a mismatch would be unsustainable."

"Exactly." Alexandria smirked, a tight smile that looked like the grin of a Cheshire cat, a deceptive feline ready to swipe with a claw. "When we rise like a Phoenix from the ashes, we want to emerge in the perfect vehicles."

"Like a Phoenix?" Bartholomew rolled his eyes. "You're so funny."

"I thought so." She set a hand on Lacinda's cheek. "I apologize. The Phoenix reference is an inside joke. You wouldn't understand."

The girl nodded in a fast cadence, her entire body tense.

"And now for the next step." Alexandria threw Lacinda down to her stomach, set a knee on her back, and pulled the braid, harder and harder. Lacinda flailed—gasping, choking, retching, too bruised and beaten to fight back.

While the poor girl's travail continued, Bartholomew glanced at the guard. Saliva dripped from its gaping mouth. It knew where its next meal was coming from. When Bartholomew looked again at Lacinda, she lay limp and motionless.

Alexandria released the braid and patted Lacinda on the head. "That was my version of mercy. You don't have to go to the abyss again." When she rose, she looked at Bartholomew. "What's your news?"

He shifted from foot to foot. Questioning her "mercy" might result in getting a dose of it himself. "As you asked, I have been interviewing souls who recently entered hell. The newcomers always try to climb out of the abyss, so it's easy to spot them."

She motioned for the guard to take Lacinda. When it lifted her limp body and carried her toward the stairway, drool dripping on her clothes, Alexandria waved the image of Katherine away and sat again on her throne. "And?"

"The most recent keeper died. He confessed that he extorted the remaining funds, and there is now no money for fueling your preservation capsule and no replacement keeper to watch over your body."

She shot to her feet. "What?"

"Like I said, he confessed—"

"I heard you!" She paced on the stage, her black leather pants swishing. "Did he say how much time my body would last without anyone taking care of it?"

"The system is in automatic mode, but that won't last long. Two weeks, at the most."

"And when did he die?"

"The best I can tell, about a week ago. As you know, time passage becomes rather skewed when death—"

"Of course I know." She halted and stared at him, her face a mask of seething wrath—every feature taut and downturned. "We'll have to accelerate our plans. We need the Refectors to deliver the souls to the network at once, even if the giants are not yet eliminated from the area. We can afford to lose a few Refectors to the giants' ravenous appetites."

"Will you make contact with them in the usual way? Transmitting through the Oculus Gate is not always a fast option."

"With the proper incentive, my surrogate will act quickly. A threat to Lacinda's safety will work."

"But Lacinda is—"

"I know, you fool, but I can mimic Lacinda with no trouble at all." Her eyes glinted with a metallic sheen. "You should have learned by now that knowledge is power, and knowing more than my adversaries has always been my key to victory. And, of course, deception that comes with my acting prowess. Even overacting at times has its benefits."

"Indeed, which is why I sometimes wonder if you really intend to take me with you."

She set a hand against her chest in mock surprise. "Oh, Bartholomew, would I lie to you?"

"A hundred times a day. Without flinching."

"Which is why you are wise to keep the location of my body a secret. As long as I need you, you have nothing to fear."

Bartholomew tried to read her face for any hint of dishonesty, but, as usual, it proved to be an impossible task. Yes, he did know where her body lay preserved on Earth, and it had been his leverage to become part of her escape plan, but something in her manner gave him pause. She would eventually betray him, but how? He would have to be on the alert. "Now that you have my news, what's the next step?"

She pointed toward the staircase. "Go to the entry forest and wait for the arrival of the one who will be the catalyst for the team's invasion into hell. He will be alive, which means you can use his blood to allow him to break my forest's warding and enter without delay."

Bartholomew nodded. "Understood."

"And since we will soon have company …" She spread her arms. Her leather jacket and pants transformed into a silky black gown fit for a queen, though her motorcycle-style boots remained. She retrieved the violin and bow again. "It's too bad I can't take this lovely instrument with me to Earth. Its power would be quite useful."

"It would raise too many questions?"

"Without a doubt." She tucked the violin under her chin. "And now I must send one message to the Refectors and another to a certain giant who will do whatever it takes to keep his family safe."

"Then I will take my leave." Bartholomew pivoted and strode to the stairway. Once he had ascended out of her view, he retrieved the metal box from his pants pocket and set it on his palm. No doubt she would eventually betray him, but as long as he had this in his possession, he could defeat her, though with difficulty. Her only vulnerability wasn't well known. Only he and the other keepers of her body were aware of it, and they were all dead, their souls wallowing in the abyss.

19

He pushed the box back into his pocket. While it was true that the violin would raise questions, a nondescript box in his pocket likely wouldn't. No matter what happened, when the resurrection vehicle was chosen, he had to be ready to transfer the box to the new host's body. As a real, physical relic, that was the only way it could leave hell and arrive safely on Earth.

Chapter Three

Ben leaped out of the angel cruiser, his grip on the parachute's ripcord. The cold air nearly sucked his breath away, and the landing zone lay far below, out of view in the pre-dawn darkness. Jumping from a lower altitude would have made the stealth attack easier, but noisy propellers could alert someone guarding the city's angel-worship temple.

His arms spread in freefall, he called into the helmet's built-in microphone. "Kat? You with me?"

Her voice crackled in the speaker. "Look up." Above, Kat copied his spread-eagle pose, almost invisible in her black, ninja-like outfit. "Race you to the temple."

"Nope. We have to start steering now. Let's deploy. You first, since I'm below you."

"Aye, aye, Captain." She pulled her cord. Her chute billowed and sent her zooming upward, at least in Ben's perspective.

Ben pulled his cord. His parachute expanded, caught the air, and slowed his plunge, allowing him to get a better look at the ground, now in view. The temple's spires, well off to the left, appeared as a trio of silvery lines.

As he manipulated the toggles to turn in that direction, the gusts buffeted his body, and the rifle and flashlight attached to his belt whipped against his thighs. He glanced back. Kat floated less than three seconds behind. Her own weapons and gadgets, including the computer pad she acquired at HQ, swayed on her belt.

When they neared their target, Ben scanned the area. As expected at this hour, no one occupied the well-lit temple grounds, either in the parking lot or the expansive lawn between the building and a small lake in front of the main entrance.

"Ben," Kat said, "I saw someone run into the temple. No obvious weapon, but they might have an arsenal inside."

"We'll assume the worst. No telling how aggressive the angel sycophants might be."

"Especially if they're infused with a violence payload."

"Right. I know how strong that stuff is, and I got only half a dose." He gave the sky a quick scan. The cruiser was no longer in sight. "Trudy, when you drop Jack off at the bank, don't hover around and wait for him. Leo and Iona will probably have hellfire on their heels, and they might need evac. You can pick Jack up when he's got the key."

"Yep," Trudy said. "Already planned on that."

"Should've known. Over and out."

The temple's spires now loomed immediately below, seconds away. Ben pulled a toggle once more, the parachute narrowly avoiding one of the sharp points. He landed feet first on the central building's flat roof and ran out his momentum. Seconds later, Kat landed a few steps away.

Without a word, they removed their helmets, shrugged off their packs, detached rifles from their harnesses, and set everything on the roof, then reeled their parachutes into tight wads and stuffed them into the packs. Leaving the skydiving gear on the roof, they inserted earbuds, scooped up their rifles, and strode to a metal trap door. Kat pulled on the handle, but the door stayed put. "Locked."

"No surprise."

Kat unfastened the computer pad from her belt and tapped on the screen. Two seconds later, the door emitted a click. She grabbed a flashlight from her belt, flicked it on, and aimed it at the entry. Ben flung it open, revealing darkness below.

A steep staircase descended to a concrete landing next to a door that likely led to a corridor. Farther down, more flights of stairs switched back and forth into darkness. All clear so far.

Rifle in hand, Ben hustled down, Kat following after closing the roof access. When he reached the landing, he pulled the door open a crack and pushed the rifle's barrel through as he peered out. In the dimness of a single ceiling light, the carpeted hallway appeared to be vacant.

"No one's coming." Staying in the stairwell, he closed the door. "Where are we on the map?"

Kat showed Ben the building's layout on the screen and touched a room near the middle. "Here. Directly above the control center. It's at basement level. Three floors below us."

"Good. Secure this door."

Kat tapped the screen. The door clicked. Ben pulled the handle—locked. "Perfect."

Guided by Kat's flashlight, they jogged down the next flight of stairs to another landing and stopped at the new level's door. Footsteps pounded closer on the other side.

Ben whispered, "Secure it."

"On it." Kat tapped the screen once more.

Just as the door clicked, a man shouted from the hallway. "It's locked."

A woman called, "Punch in the code."

As beeps sounded from the other side of the door, Ben and Kat scrambled down. "No worries," Kat said directly behind Ben. "I locked all stairway doors on this side of the building and changed their access codes."

He smiled. "You're making this too easy."

"It's my job. After all, I *am* the brains in this duo."

Ben lifted his brow. "Really? And all this time I thought I brought you along as eye candy."

"Careful or I'll program your earbud to play a two-year-old saying *why* every time you speak."

"Ah, my wife. Brains, beauty, and bite. Gotta love it."

"You'd better, Mr. Buff and Brave. We're a matched pair."

When they reached the basement level, they stopped at a single wooden door leading out of the stairwell. Kat unlocked it and pulled it open. Their heads low, they skulked into a hallway, illuminated by fluorescent ceiling lights, some flickering and buzzing. A tiled floor led to a dead end on the left. To the right, the hall widened into an open area with tables and chairs, enough to seat at least a hundred people. Vending machines lined one wall, and a counter with a few microwave ovens and coffee makers lined another.

Directly across the hall, a massive metal door stood with a wheel at the center, much like the vault door at angel headquarters that led to the Oculus observation room. Ben leaned his rifle against the wall, grabbed the wheel with both hands, and tried to turn it, but it wouldn't budge. "What's up with this door?"

Kat slid a finger across the pad's screen. "It has multiple layers of security. I'm past the first one. Working on the second. Not sure how many more are behind it."

At the far end of the open area, a door banged open, splinters flying. Two men and a woman barged into the corridor, barefoot and wearing black flannel pajamas. One man carried a broken table leg, and the others each held a kitchen knife. When they saw Ben and Kat, they marched toward them at a slow pace, their weapons raised in tight hands, twenty steps away.

Ben grabbed his rifle and aimed it at the trio. "Halt, or I'll shoot!"

Unflinching, they continued their steady march—fifteen paces away.

He whisper-shouted toward Kat. "Get that door open!"

She furiously tapped on the pad. "Second stage unlocked. One more. I think."

The three drew ever closer, their blank stares making them look like zombies. Ben fired at the leg of one of the men. The bullet smacked into his thigh and zipped through, striking the carpet on the other side. He halted, dropped the table leg, and stared blankly as blood pooled at his feet.

"It's like he feels no pain." Ben fired at the other man, this time aiming at the body. The bullet ripped into his chest, making him stagger back and fall. Screaming, the woman lunged with her knife. Ben dodged, flipped the rifle around, and bashed her in the head.

The blow knocked her against a wall. Her eyes rolled upward toward her bleeding brow, and she slid to the floor, likely dead.

A dozen more men burst into the hallway at the far end, most carrying shotguns. Dressed in military camo, this group was ready for battle.

"Kat," Ben said with a sharp whisper, "it's now or never."

"Got it." The vault clicked. Kat tucked the pad under her arm and shoved the wheel counterclockwise, face tight, muscles straining. "It's opening."

Ben aimed the rifle at the charging men and squeezed the trigger. A hail of bullets mowed down three in front, but the others tromped over them.

Kat heaved the door open. "Go!"

A gun sounded. Ben and Kat dove through the opening as buckshot pelted the metallic door above their heads. Ben leaped to his feet, reached back into the hall, and pulled the massive door closed just as a shotgun blasted another round. Darkness reigned except for the glow from Kat's computer pad as she slid a finger across the screen and Ben turned the inside wheel. When another click sounded, she breathed a sigh. "Single-level lockdown. Let's hope they can't override it."

Something pounded on the door, followed by a garbled shout and the sound of thudding footsteps fading down the hallway.

Kat bent her brow, barely visible in the screen's aura. "Think they're soulless? Guarding the place instinctively?"

"Yeah. They seemed kind of haphazard." Ben looked at the dark ceiling. "Can you get us some lights?"

"Probably, but first things first. I'm triple locking this door with new passcodes."

"Good thought." Ben touched his earbud. "Jack? Trudy?"

"Here," Trudy said. "Jack's busy hovering this flying beast to drop Leo and Iona off. We're still learning this ship's tricks. Besides, it's windy out here."

25

"Okay. Just letting you know we're inside the temple. Locked in the central computer vault. Three people attacked us, then a second wave. Maybe ten or twelve. They all seemed like mindless zombies."

"Any weapons?" Trudy asked.

"The second wave had shotguns. And the first three were in pajamas. No firearms."

"Pajamas? Are you saying alien creatures dwelling inside soulless humans wear pajamas?"

"Exactly." Ben grinned. "We can take a set of PJs off a corpse in the hall if you're interested. She's your size."

A laugh rode Trudy's reply. "Only if they're bloodstained. I want to look like I earned those sleepers."

"I can arrange that."

"Speaking of corpses …" Her tone turned serious. "This place is a ghost town. Not a soul on the streets. By this time in the morning, we should at least see delivery people running around."

"What do thermal scans of the buildings show you?"

"A few warm bodies here and there. That mass exodus we monitored yesterday must've included ninety percent of the population."

Ben drew a mental picture of zombies marching out of the city while the unaffected citizens hid in dark rooms. "So everyone who stayed behind is holed up. That's not a good sign."

"We'll figure it out soon enough. Leo and Iona have boots on the ground now, and they're moving into position near the bank's front door. Jack and I will land on the roof in about thirty seconds."

Ben eyed Kat's fingers as they continued racing across the computer pad. "Do you have a scan of that building yet?"

"Yep. One warm body. Probably a security guard."

"Good. If the plan works, it won't matter how heavily armed the guard is. Then Jack can go in alone to get the key while you keep an eye on Leo and Iona. Make sure they're safe."

"We already agreed to that, Mother Hen, but thanks for the advice."

Ben let out a huff. "Mother Hen? Now you're sounding like Leo."

"Good guess. He called you that before we dropped him off. And he's listening in, by the way. So's Iona. Remember, if we detect someone hacking our frequency, we can switch to our version of Morse code."

"But Leo and Iona don't know that code."

"Iona does. Barks taught it to her when he commissioned her as a spy for us. She said she'd teach it to Leo. If he knows traditional Morse, it won't be hard to switch."

"Yeah," Ben said. "Should work. They need to be in the loop for everything."

"Agreed. We're all family now. Gotta go. My turn to fly this angel buggy. See you soon."

"Yeah. See you, Sis." Ben blew out a sigh. Indeed, they were all family now. And sending them on a dangerous mission felt like leaving his own children on a minefield with sharpshooters all around. But they weren't children. They were warriors. If only he could picture them that way all the time.

"Got it." Kat made a louder tap on the screen. "We're triple-locked in. But no light controls. They must be manual."

"Then we'll do this the old-fashioned way." Ben snapped a flashlight from his belt, turned it on, and scanned the wall with the beam until it swept across a bank of switches. He walked to the wall and flipped them on.

Ceiling fixtures flashed to life, revealing a massive chamber with a concrete floor. A giant screen hung on the far wall, and a long desk stood in front of it, as well as a trio of computers and wheeled chairs, much like the vault control stations at angel headquarters.

Kat withdrew her master access key from a pocket and strode to the desk's central computer. "Let's check the first level and see what we're up against."

While she booted the computer and tapped on the control station's keyboard, Ben scanned the walls adjacent to the huge s

Thousands of books and other media weighed down shelves from the floor to the twenty-foot-high ceiling. This place was probably a repository for temple information, or *esoterica*, as Iona called it, before they transformed the place into a computer room.

The big screen turned on, displaying hundreds of squares. Each showed a different city scene within its frame, early morning sun making the details clear. "Camera views?" Ben asked.

Kat nodded. "The first level is a security monitoring system. Looks like the angels installed cameras all across the city."

"Any idea how deep into the system it will let you go without the second key?"

"I'd say ankle deep. It's not budging." She leaned closer to the monitor. "Wait. There's a square for a thumbprint." She pressed her thumb against the screen.

A voice emanated. "Access granted for Queen Laramel. Enter security key for further access." A new scene filled the wall display, the dawning sky with the familiar eye-shaped ring of stars.

Ben whispered, "The Oculus Gate."

Kat nodded. "Too dim to see with the naked eye, but it's still out there, like you suspected."

"That means they were monitoring it here as well as at HQ."

"At least Laramel was when she visited the temple." Kat's eyes darted as she studied the smaller monitor at her station. "I see lots of readings. Looks like brightness of each light, signal variations, color fluctuations, etcetera. And by the looks of the data, the focal points are strengthening. Not fast, but it's noticeable. The same thing happened when the Refectors were getting ready to come through the gate."

"Just what we need. Yet another alien species invading Earth to destroy us."

"Or possess us." Kat tapped on the keyboard. "Let's go back to the cameras and see if we can find Iona and Leo. Maybe we'll get a clue to what the Refectors are up to."

"It won't be hard spotting Iona's fiery red hair. She's wearing pigtails again for her innocent-little-girl persona." The screen switched back to the matrix of camera feeds. Each displayed a three-digit numeral in the corner. Near the middle, two figures moved. "There." Ben pointed. "Number zero, nine, six."

"Got it." After a few more keystrokes, that square's feed filled the screen. Iona, dressed in oversized military camo, crept toward a marketplace square with Leo at her side. As usual, the tall huntsman wore a long cloak as dark as his thick hair.

Kat settled back in her chair. "Let's see what they find."

Chapter Four

Iona peeked around the end of a brick wall. Across a vacant plaza, the three-story bank stood between a delicatessen and a drug store. She pulled back and looked at Leo as he leaned his tall frame over to keep his head below the top of the wall. After a shave and a collar-length trim of his normally unruly mane, he looked presentable, at least for a trail-weathered huntsman. "Are we sure this is the right bank?" she asked. "It's a small branch."

"Positive." Leo set his plasma rifle against the wall and peered over the top for a moment before looking at Iona again. "Hiding a valuable key at an offshoot branch is more secure. Who would think to steal it here?"

"Apparently we would." Iona scanned the sky. The hovercraft flew in a slow orbit a few hundred feet in the air, probably waiting for them to make their move. "Does your superpowered nose detect anything?"

Leo inhaled. "I smell humans. No one close, though."

"Good. Let's notify air support."

Leo touched his earbud and spoke softly. "Jack. Trudy. We're in position."

"Roger that," Trudy said. "We're seeing three warm echoes inside now. Stay safe."

Leo picked up his plasma rifle. "I'll go first."

"Wait." Iona grabbed his arm. "Better if I go." She flipped one of her pigtails. "If I get spotted, I'm not as likely to raise an alarm. It's worked before."

He nodded, his hair whipped by the strengthening breeze. "Good point. A ginger pixie isn't as scary as a big ugly huntsman."

She cracked a smile. "Your words. Not mine."

"Never fear the truth." Leo turned the rifle on, energizing the plasma spheres. "I've got your back."

Iona peered around the end of the wall again. The bank's front glass door opened. A young man and woman walked out, each wearing a bulging backpack, their heads low and their eyes darting as if expecting to be pounced upon by an unseen predator.

"Two adults," Iona whispered. "Really shifty, like they robbed the bank. It's too early for it to be open for business."

Jack's voice came through her earbud. "Maybe they incapacitated the guard. That would make things easier."

"Could be. If they got vaccinated, then they're soulless zombies with a violence payload."

"And maybe possessed by Refectors," Leo added.

Iona waved a hand. "Not all of them are possessed. I think the Refectors guided the mass exodus, like shepherds leading everyone else out of the city. I mean, the city's population is about a hundred fifty thousand. I doubt that many Refectors came through the conduit. Not enough time."

"Is that so?" Leo narrowed his eyes. "How many Refectors can fit through a cosmic conduit, and how fast do they travel?"

She frowned. "Okay. So I was guessing. Now shut up. When the thieves take off, we'll check on the bank guard."

"All right, Diminutive Despot, but if you'll listen to my advice—"

The wind gusted, cutting him off. At the plaza, a dust devil swirled slowly behind the couple, as if stalking them. They halted next to two bicycles near the plaza's edge. As they mounted the bikes, the dust devil drew closer and closer. Its particles swelled, some dark and some light, a few glimmering in the muted sunshine.

When the outer edge of the particles touched the thieving couple, they gasped, then laughed, as if relieved that it was only wind. A moment later, the swirl enveloped them. The particles adhered to their bodies and forced them into the spin. They screamed, but as the swirl rotated faster and faster, the wind's roar drowned their cries, and their bodies blurred in the rotation.

Money flew everywhere, an eruption of paper bills that flew into the sky and floated down all across the plaza. After several seconds, the swirl slowed and the particles drew together, congealing. When the spin halted, a tall, dark-skinned woman with short, curly hair stood where the couple had been. Dressed in black pants and an angel-logo sweatshirt, she set a hand on her stomach, swollen by the thieves she had apparently consumed. She then swaggered toward the bank with a satisfied smile.

Iona gulped. "So ... um ... Leo. What's your advice?"

Peering around the corner with her, he whispered, "Stay away from that woman."

"No kidding." Iona eyed her as she strutted into the bank. Had she set a trap for the robbers, like a spiderweb to catch wayward flies? "So, let's say she has a Refector inside. Obviously it gives her the power to break up into a ... well ..."

"A gluttonous gale. Let's call her Gale."

"That name works." Iona studied the door again and listened to the sounds of the abandoned city. The breeze kicked up a canopy over a window at the delicatessen next door. Otherwise, all was quiet. "I say we stick with the original plan. Lure Gale out to give Jack a clear path and shoot her only if we have to. She might not be as dangerous after feeding so recently."

Leo nodded. "Getting information by talking is your specialty. You are the Goddess of Glib."

"Thanks, I guess, but just in case, be ready to shoot her. And to run."

He lifted his rifle. "Trigger finger and legs are ready."

"Then let's go. Jack. Trudy. We're executing the plan now." Iona stepped out from behind the wall and strode toward the bank. As the breeze whipped her pigtails and camo shirt, she shivered. The air was cold enough to raise a chill, but this march also felt like a journey into the jaws of the spider from hell, or a swarm of devouring locusts.

As she walked with Leo close behind, memories of Chantal came to mind—her courage, her passion, and her fateful words. *I'm your spy, Commander.* Her heroic qualities led to her death, a glorious, sacrificial death that saved the entire planet. She was amazing.

Iona clutched the cross hanging around her neck, a gift from Chantal. She could do this. She had to do this. The planet needed saving again, and only she, Leo, and the Garrison family were left to get it done.

When they arrived at the entrance, Leo stepped behind a portico support column while Iona opened the door with a confident tug and looked inside. The place had the typical layout—a line of teller windows against the opposite wall, offices on one side, and a closed vault on the other. Polished floors reflected a high ceiling with recessed lights. She resumed her confident stride and scanned the interior, but no one stood in sight.

"Okay, Fire Plug," Leo said through her earbud. "I'll be listening to every word. Call me if you need me."

"In a heartbeat," she whispered, "but if I have to talk my way out of a tangle, don't provide commentary."

"Got it. Going silent."

Iona called, "Hello?" Her voice echoed in the vacant room. She strode to the side of the teller stations and peeked behind them. No one hid there.

She backed to the center of the room and called again. "Hello? Is anyone here?"

The vault door opened slowly. Gale peered out, then walked toward Iona, smiling. "Are you lost, little girl?"

Steeling herself, Iona spoke with her preteen voice. "Not at all. I was told to come here by our leader."

Gale stopped just out of reach and chuckled. "Our leader? We have no leader. At least not on Earth, though she will arrive soon."

Iona folded her hands at her waist. One mistake already. Time to backpedal and try again. "I meant the leader who's not on Earth yet."

"She told you to come here? My, my, aren't you the important one?" Gale walked slowly around Iona, looking at her from all angles. She spoke a few phrases that sounded like gibberish.

Iona moved her eyes to keep track of Gale's orbit. "If you don't mind, I would like to refrain from using our language. I'm trying to master the local human dialect."

"Very well. Then answer my question in the local tongue."

Iona resisted the urge to swallow. "I don't know the answer."

"You don't know? How unusual." Gale halted in front of Iona and crossed her arms. "At least tell me why you're here."

Iona covered her mouth and coughed while whispering, "Leo, I'm crashing. Be ready."

His voice filtered in through her earbud. "Closing in. You're in view. When you hit the deck, I'll fire."

Iona looked straight into Gale's eyes. "I'm here to find a certain item in this bank."

"And what item might that be?"

"A key to gain access to a high-security data area in a computer system."

"Interesting. That is exactly what I was assigned to protect. Our leader would have sent me a message if she wanted me to give the key to someone."

"Consider this your message." Iona dove to the floor. A plasma sphere zipped over her and slammed into Gale. She slid back, erupted in flames, and fractured into a thousand pieces. Then, spinning in a fiery frenzy, the particles flew at Iona.

Leo hoisted her to her feet. "Run!"

They dashed out of the bank and across the plaza, their shoes pounding on the bricks. "Jack!" Iona called. "The vault's open. You're clear!"

"I dropped him off," Trudy said. "Do you need extraction?"

Iona ran abreast with Leo on a sidewalk next to a two-lane street. "Yeah. Hurry."

34

"I lifted off the roof a second ago. I don't see you in the plaza."

Leo shouted, "Because a spinning spawn of the devil is chasing us, and we're running for our lives!"

"And she eats humans," Iona said, panting. As she ran, she searched for a street sign in the midst of dingy, multi-story apartment buildings, but her rapid footfalls made her vision bounce. "I don't know where we are. Looks like a rundown residential area. Not slummy, but close."

"Can you see the temple's spires?" Trudy asked.

Iona scanned the sky over the building rooftops. After a few seconds, they passed a shorter building that allowed a glimpse of the spires. "Yeah. I see them."

"Head toward them. I'll find you."

"This way!" Iona careened around a corner onto a side street, Leo next to her. She glanced back as the tornadic inferno twirled around the same corner, now only seconds behind. A half mile ahead, the temple loomed. A grassy park and a lake lay in front of it. Gasping, she spoke through the earbud. "Water might be our only chance."

Leo nodded. "Let's douse that demon."

Ben and Kat watched Leo and Iona on the wall display, Kat touching her desktop screen to alter the camera views when needed. When the two ran onto the temple grounds, she switched to a camera mounted on a spire and zoomed in on them as they raced toward the lake.

The fiery swirl roared and closed in, now nearly on their heels. When they reached the lake, they ran to the end of a dock and halted. The swirl rushed toward them, closer and closer. They leaped into the water and submerged, and the swirl tumbled in as well.

Ben touched his earbud. "Trudy, do you see them?"

"Yep. I'm on it. Gotta figure out how to hover in autopilot so I can fish them out."

Steam shot from a violently swirling eddy as it edged closer to Leo and Iona. They swam furiously toward a ladder attached to the dock. Iona climbed it, then spun and held a hand toward Leo. The moment he stepped up, a human arm pushed out from the eddy. The hand grabbed his wrist and jerked him back into the water.

Leo thrashed, punching and kicking. Iona leaped into the midst of the fray and clawed at the beast like a wildcat. Splashes flew and veiled the scene.

A rope ladder dropped from the sky. Leo snatched the bottom rung and began to rise, his other hand locked on Iona's wrist. Soon, they both lifted well above the surface as water droplets fell from their clothes into the bubbling lake. Within seconds, they rose out of the camera's view.

"I got 'em," Trudy said. "Looks like they're okay. Just wet and cold. No serious injuries."

Ben eyed the lake. The surface continued settling—no sign of the bizarre monster. "What happened to that … thing?"

"Not a clue, but I can hardly wait to hear Leo's spin on this tale."

Ben rolled his eyes. "Spin. Very funny."

"I thought so."

"Well, when you finish laughing at your wit, take another scan of the temple to see if the Refectors brought in reinforcements. We haven't heard a peep from them since we locked ourselves in."

"Already did the scan, and I dropped Leo and Iona off on the temple's roof. They're on their way down, so be ready to let them in. Now I'm heading out to get Jack. Haven't heard from him, but he should be waiting on the bank's roof by now."

Ben looked up, imagining Trudy studying the cruiser's screen. "What did the scan show?"

"Not a single warm body anywhere in the temple. That's why I decided it was safe to drop them off."

"You can't even see us?"

"Nope. I'm guessing you're in a shielded room."

36

Ben eyed the ceiling. It appeared to be metallic. "You're probably right, but that means there's either another shielded room, or the zombies vacated."

Kat typed on the keyboard and looked at the smaller monitor. "Vacated is my guess. I have detailed building specs here. No other shielded rooms that I can see."

"Ominous. I can't imagine they would give this place up without a fight."

"True, but flushing us out of here won't be easy."

"Then we should be safe for now. When Jack brings the key, we can take some time to research."

"And not a bad place to be." She touched an on-screen schematic. "According to this, we have a weapons room, showers, cots, a kitchenette, and a food cache. It's like a survivalist bunker."

Ben looked over her shoulder at the drawing. "The showers are community style. Trudy said we're all family now, but I don't think we're ready for that."

Kat huffed. "You got that right. I'm a team player, but only with my uniform on."

Leo's voice entered Ben's ear. "Two wet warriors await permission to enter."

"Trust but verify," Kat said as she searched the big display's security feeds. She locked on a camera outside the vault and expanded the view. On the screen, Leo and Iona stood in the hallway, hugging themselves and shivering. "I'll unlock it."

Ben hurried to the entry. The moment the lock clicked, he turned the wheel and gave it a shove. Leo and Iona shuffled in, their clothes dripping.

Ben pointed toward a side door. "According to the floor plans, the locker room's that way. I don't know how well supplied it is."

Leo halted. "I heard what you said about community showers." He gestured with a hand. "Ladies first."

"Thanks." Iona walked through the side doorway, calling back, "If I find any towels, I'll toss you one before I shower."

Ben heaved the door closed. "Trudy, we've got Leo and Iona. What's your status?"

"I plucked Jack off the roof, and he's got the key. Mission accomplished."

"Super. Let's convene here and see what the computer has to tell us."

"Landing on the temple roof in two minutes. We have a lot to talk about."

"Right," Jack said. "I'll wait till we're all together to tell my story, but I'll say this much. The mysteries keep getting deeper."

Chapter Five

"And that's the short version of the story," Leo finished, sitting cross-legged on the floor with a towel around his neck. He took a drink from a flask of angel tea and recapped it. "Unless the glib-tongued grappler has something important to add."

"Let me think." Iona pulled a brush through her damp hair, a mess of tangles after her pigtails unraveled in the shower. A few droplets fell to her lap, absorbed by the black pajamas she had found in the bunker's locker room. "Nope. You pretty much covered it."

"No complaints about the name I called you?" Leo pointed at her. "You're getting to like those names. Admit it."

"Well ..." As she averted her eyes while sneaking a glance at him, she concealed a smile. His beaming face raised memories of her father's approving gazes, the loving looks that coaxed her to attempt the seemingly impossible. Leo had the same effect. "Some of the names are okay. I kind of like *grappler*."

"You deserve it. You fought that she-devil like a warrior." Leo turned toward Ben and Kat, each sitting in a desk chair. He rolled up his wet sleeve, revealing a bloody gash on his forearm. "When that monster turned fully physical again, it sunk a pair of fangs into me and pushed me under. I couldn't breathe. That's when our stout-hearted half-pint jumped in, clutched her throat, and wouldn't let go. Drowned the beast. I wouldn't have survived without her."

Iona pointed the brush at him. "*Half-pint* is not on the approved-name list."

"I didn't ask for your approval." Leo climbed to his feet and lifted his legs in turn. Watery footprints marred the concrete. "My turn for a shower. Any dry clothes in this bunker?"

"Yep." Jack, standing with Trudy at the side door next to a pile of rifles and weapons belts, gestured with a thumb over his shoulder. "Lots more pajamas in there. Not sure if they have extra-long, though."

Leo huffed. "I said *clothes*. I meant real clothes. I've never worn pajamas in my life."

Iona touched one of the long sleeves. The dark shade brought back so many memories, some good, some bad. "They're comfortable. We priestesses wore them to bed all the time."

"Priestesses?" Leo spread his arms. "Do I look like a priestess?"

Iona grinned. "You look sort of like Priestess Laura. Except she's more masculine. Thicker beard."

He shook a finger. "Lying doesn't become you, Tater Tot. And I don't care if that name's on your approved list or not."

"Suit yourself, Bean Pole." Iona set the brush on the floor and picked up a camo helmet. "The choices are stay wet, go naked, or wear pajamas."

Ben raised a pair of fingers. "And option number two's not allowed."

Leo stalked toward the door, muttering, "I suppose a dry bean pole is better than a shriveling prune."

As he left Trudy called after him, "Iona strung a line in the locker room. Hang your clothes next to hers. There's a heater blowing hot air on them. They'll dry in a flash."

Leo's voice echoed from beyond the door. "Yes, dear."

"Now that he's gone." Iona put the helmet on. "Check this out. Found it in the weapons room. Great for warrior mode."

Jack snorted. "While wearing pajamas? A warrior in your dreams, maybe."

She rolled her eyes. "I was hoping to avoid Leo's snide comments."

"I'm his snidely surrogate." Jack touched the helmet's goggles. "Actually, it's pretty cool. Kind of swallows your carrot-top head, but you do look menacing. Like a ginger Pekingese."

"Oh, yeah?" She whipped the helmet off and threw it at him.

40

He caught it with both hands. "Whoa! The ginger snaps."

"Speaking of snaps." Ben snapped his fingers toward Jack. "The key?"

"Sure. Just a second." Jack gave the helmet back to Iona. "Actually, you do look like a warrior in this. No kidding. Wear it with pride."

"Thanks." She set the helmet in her lap and ran a finger along its smooth surface. It brought a sense of protection, strength. "I will."

Jack slid a hand into his pocket, withdrew the access key, and set it in Ben's palm. "Are we in a hurry?"

"No red lights flashing, if that's what you mean, but the zombies know we're here. No sense delaying."

"Then let me give you a quick version of my story, and then you can fiddle with that key." While speaking, Jack pivoted in place to address everyone. "When I found the safety deposit box, I drilled through the lock and pulled the box out. The access key was inside. I thought it was a done deal. Easy stuff, right? But there was also a safety deposit box key without a number to tell me which box it belonged to, and there were dozens of boxes. Then an alarm went off and gas started hissing into the vault from a ceiling vent I couldn't reach. I guessed it was poisonous, so I held my breath and started shoving the key into box after box, but it didn't work on any of them. When I couldn't risk it anymore, I gave up and hightailed it to the roof. Figured I could go back when the gas clears."

Ben nodded. "Laramel was hiding something else. Interesting." He looked at Kat. "Any ideas?"

She shook her head. "I'll probe that part of my memory, bruised as it is."

"Take your time, but for now ..." Ben handed the access key to her. "Let's fire it up."

She plugged the key into a port next to the other key. The wall display and desktop screen cleared, then showed a message. "Thumb scan required." The screen drew two boxes under the message.

Kat pressed a thumb inside each box. "In case someone stole the keys, I guess."

A light blinked under the boxes. The screen cleared again, and the image of two eyes appeared with the words "Retina scan."

Jack snorted. "In case someone stole your thumbs."

"I'm wondering if a brain scan's next." Kat leaned toward the desktop monitor and set her eyes close. After a bright flash, she settled back in her chair.

The display cleared once more. Three spheres appeared on a black background, like a trio of planets hovering in space, an Earth-like one near the left edge and two grayish ones near the right. An eye-shaped cluster of bright dots occupied the center area, like a divider separating the lone planet from the other two.

"It's a map," Trudy said, pointing at the lone planet. "That one's Earth. And the Oculus Gate is in the middle."

Iona stepped closer to the wall and studied the displayed orbs. Part of the array seemed pretty easy to figure out. "One of the other two planets must be where the angels came from. Maybe the third is the Refectors' world."

On the desktop monitor, Kat touched one of the planets to the right. A caption appeared underneath. "Asketelean. Sentient Population – 0. Conduit Level – 0."

She touched the other mystery planet. Another caption appeared. "Viridi. Sentient Population – 800. Conduit Level – 0."

Kat read the captions aloud in a slow cadence as if searching for clues. "Since Chantal destroyed all of the angels, Asketelean is probably their world. No one made it home. Zero population. The Refectors were Laramel's name for the beings from the other world. Maybe that's Viridi. She didn't know much about them. I suppose some kind of scan revealed how many occupy each planet."

Ben gestured toward the screen. "See what it says about Earth."

Kat touched the leftmost planet. "Earth. Sentient Population – Approximately 2,000,000,000. Conduit Level – 6%. Too Weak for Transport."

"Ah," Leo said, now standing at the side door, wearing black pajamas that didn't quite reach his ankles. "The conduit still exists. Chantal's bomb didn't destroy it completely."

"Wait." Trudy pointed. "Wasn't the level six percent a minute ago?"

Ben leaned closer. "Now it's showing seven percent. It's increasing."

"Which probably means," Jack said, "someone is rebuilding it."

"Let's try to get more info." Kat touched the Oculus Gate.

A caption appeared under it. "Generating Conduit Profile—3:00 minutes." The numerals began counting down—2:59, 2:58.

Kat sighed. "Looks like we have to wait."

"While we're waiting," Jack said as he tapped on the computer pad, "check this out. According to the temple's records, they did only one hundred vaccinations. Even took photos of the privileged few. No explanation on why they stopped."

"Maybe people weren't showing up?" Kat asked.

Iona shook her head. "Not a chance. I was here that morning and saw the line of people myself. It went outside and all the way around the lake. The media did a good job scaring people into believing a third plague was coming. Bunch of cowardly sheep out there."

Kat wheeled her chair toward Jack. "Let me see the photographs."

"Sure." Jack handed her the pad. "Got an idea?"

"Facial recognition. I'll program the cameras to let us know if any of these people show up in the city."

Ben rotated his chair back and forth, apparently in thought. "Strange. Only a hundred vaccinated. I wonder what they told the others."

The computer beeped. Kat spun her chair and typed on the keyboard. "We got a facial-rec hit. I'll bring it up."

A camera view filled the wall display. A man wearing a dark topcoat and fedora stood at the center, walking closer, a few wrinkles on his pale, round face giving away his fifty-something age.

Kat pulled up another screen on her desktop. "Damien Collins. He has a PhD in chemistry and top-level security in the angel database." Her eyes darted as she continued reading. "Oh. Now that's interesting. He actually created the vaccine. And according to the vaccination records, he was the first to get the injection."

"He would know what was in the vaccine," Jack said as he retrieved the computer pad from Kat. "That means the stuff the first hundred got was safe, probably without the soul-purging component or the violence payload."

On the screen, Damien glanced up and looked straight into the camera. His eyes widened, and he dissolved into a plume of smoke.

"What in the name of—" Ben wheeled closer. "Where did he go?"

Kat splayed her hands. "He went poof."

"Poof? People don't go poof."

"Damien did. In a puff of smoke."

"Could that be a Refector power?" Trudy asked. "Going poof?"

"Only way to explain it." Kat restored the planetary map to the wall display. "We'll let the facial-rec engine search some more. The three minutes are up."

Under the map's Oculus Gate image, the caption now stated, "Conduit Profile Generation Complete."

Kat touched the new caption. The display shifted Earth to the center and moved the Oculus Gate above it to a position near the top of the screen. A line ran from the middle of the gate to a point on Earth at a northern latitude, then more lines appeared, running from the same point on the Gate to different points on Earth at or near the Arctic Circle, four in all. "It looks like the conduit is rebuilding over the North Pole," she said, "but I have no idea why."

Trudy nodded toward the display. "One of the connection nodes is in Alaska. Is it the closest node to us?"

Kat shook her head. "The one in Canada is closest. And Siberia is the farthest."

"But the Canada site is in water. The Alaska node is the most accessible."

"I'll see if I can get a satellite view." Kat typed once more. The map zoomed in toward the northern part of Alaska, redrawing itself and adding more details with every change in zoom level. Within seconds, it showed an area of bare, icy terrain with a small building and a tower with a lattice frame and a pair of antennas on top.

"A transmission tower," Ben said.

Leo pointed at the screen. "Those antennas are old technology. That tower's been there for years. Decades. Probably long before the angels came. Unless it was built recently using castoff materials."

"Then maybe the tower's not a factor." Ben wheeled his chair close. "Now check Siberia."

Kat switched the view to northern Russia. When the computer locked on the location's coordinates, the map magnified the spot, showing a similar building and tower. "Looks identical. Building, tower, terrain, everything."

"Except," Leo said as he leaned toward the display, "I see a person standing over to the side."

Ben squinted. "You're right." He tapped Kat's shoulder. "Can you get a read on how tall the tower is?"

"Maybe." Kat touched her desktop screen with two fingers. Lines crisscrossed the wall display, and an axis appeared from the top of the tower to the base. "Now to correct for the zoom level and angle." She made a final click with the mouse. "The tower's about one hundred twenty feet tall."

"Now measure the person."

Kat went through the same procedure with the human figure. "That's weird. He's around ten feet tall."

"A statue?" Leo asked.

Ben firmed his jaw. "Let's hope so. I don't like the alternative. A living, ten-foot-tall person."

"One way to find out. I'll fetch an earlier photo." Kat again worked her computer magic. After a few moments, the screen flickered and showed a new image. "This one was from a week earlier."

Iona studied the scene. Although the image was shifted slightly to the left, the important portions were still in view—the tower and the surrounding terrain. The person was gone.

Leo huffed. "Unless the angels erected a statue in one week, we're dealing with someone bigger than Goliath."

Kat switched to a new window on her desktop screen. "Let's do a database search on Alaska, maybe get some clues." Several messages popped up, each in its own window. "This is interesting. Vaccine shipments. Huge ones."

"To Alaska?" Ben asked, leaning closer.

"There and to the other three nodes on our conduit map. Well, to the closest towns. Some of those spots are in the middle of nowhere."

Ben crossed his arms. "Okay, now it's coming together. Vaccine shipments to the Arctic Circle and a mass exodus from the city. Gather the people at the conduit-generating sites. Vaccinate them. Purge their souls. Make them hosts for more Refectors coming through the conduit. Warm bodies, special delivery."

"But," Jack said, "the locations are absurdly inconvenient, which means the polar cap is the only place they could rebuild the conduit, probably for technical reasons."

"Such as?" Ben prompted.

"Such as ..." Jack walked over to his pile of weapons near the side door and picked up a rifle. "The solstice is nearly here, so it's dark at the circle almost twenty-four hours, so maybe they need darkness and extreme cold, which means we'll need winter gear."

"Why so?"

Jack ejected the rifle's ammo magazine and checked its bullets. "How else are we going to survive our trip to the Arctic?" He focused on Ben. "I mean, that's what this is all leading to, right? It's the only way to figure out what's going on there."

"True." Ben slid his hands into his pockets. "I need to choose our teams. Two per team, one conduit site each. Since Alaska is the most accessible, one team will go there."

"And Siberia." Jack wagged his thumb between himself and Trudy. "We both know Russian pretty well. Send us there."

"Wait." Trudy walked toward him. "My Russian's as rusty as an old roof nail."

"No worries. We probably won't see anyone there. And if we do, I'll do the talking."

"If you say so." Trudy fastened on a weapons belt of her own and slid a handgun into one of the pouches. "But, like you said, we need winter gear. No clothes in the bunker will be warm enough."

Kat pointed at the smaller screen. "We have access to the temple's bank accounts. Plenty of funds. And the stores in the city are mostly abandoned. We can see what's in their inventory."

Ben sat on the edge of the desk. "Great. So Jack and Trudy will go to Russia, while Leo and Iona go to Alaska."

Iona rubbed her hands together. "Awesome. Going undercover. Infiltrating the Refectors. I'm perfect for the job."

Leo snorted. "Perfect to pretend to be a mindless, soulless zombie? I'm not touching that statement with an eleven-foot pole."

She grinned. "Smart man."

Ben forked his fingers at them. "I've been noticing that you have a lot of camaraderie for two people who aren't related and have almost nothing in common."

Iona drew her head back. "What do you mean? We're both dedicated to the cause, ready to die to save the world. What more *in common* could you possibly want?"

"Let's see." Ben stroked his chin. "How experienced are you in military maneuvers, espionage tactics, and battlefield surveying?"

"Well ..." Iona drummed her fingers on her helmet. She could mention her spying successes, but they would sound puny compared to what Ben had accomplished. No need to make herself any easy target. "Not much."

"And, besides, you're a teenager, and he's a … well … a mercenary, for the lack of a better word. You two shouldn't be traveling alone. Together, I mean."

Leo crossed his arms. "What exactly are you trying to say?"

"Yeah." Iona copied his pose. "What *are* you trying to say?"

Ben's ears turned red. He opened his mouth, then closed it as if not knowing how to answer. "I'm saying that you're both inexperienced. You need a specialist to go with you." He tapped himself on the chest. "Me."

"Oh?" Iona uncrossed her arms. "Then that's great." She looked at Leo. "Right?"

He nodded vigorously. "By all the stars, of course. We need an expert planner."

"And Kat …" Ben set a hand on her shoulder. "She'll stay here and hunt down the missing hive section. No one else can access Queen Laramel's secrets."

Trudy walked toward the main door. "Now that that's settled, let's go, Jack. We'll lock this building down and see what we can find for our road trip while Kat arranges our transportation."

Jack grinned. "Shopping with the sis could be the greatest adventure." He followed her to the main door, an obvious limp in his gait.

She looked back, her brow creased. "Hip still hurting from the hive blast?"

"Not much. I'm limping because I attached a switchblade to the inside of my boot. It's pinching a bit. I'll have to readjust it."

Trudy rolled her eyes. "Paranoid, as usual."

"Prepared." Jack looked at the computer pad. "I'll unlock the door."

"Wait." Iona put the helmet on and grabbed a rifle. "I'm coming. I know the temple from top to bottom."

"Wearing pajamas?" Trudy asked.

Iona looked at her body, still dressed in the black silk. "Oops." She jogged into the locker room and felt her camo clothes as the heat fan flapped her pajama sleeves. The shirt wasn't quite dry enough. She set the rifle and helmet down on a bench and tugged her pants off the line. The force shook Leo's cloak, and it dropped to the floor.

She picked it up and ran a hand along the coarse outer material, still somewhat damp, then the softer inner lining, much drier. A familiar aroma rose to her nostrils. She drew the cloak closer and inhaled deeply. A blend of pipe tobacco and angel tea entered— Leo's distinctive scent. She smiled. The sensation raised memories of home not so long ago. Her father sometimes smoked a pipe, and before he died, he drank angel tea now and then. It seemed that, in some ways, Leo had taken his place, Leo's silly names replacing her father's lame jokes that would make her groan, though she secretly loved them.

After rehanging the cloak, she breathed a sigh. Leo had turned out to be a great ally, almost like an older brother or an uncle. Of course, as a confirmed lone wolf, he could never be a father. Probably wouldn't want to be. Which was fine. An older brother would do.

Iona threw her pants on and fastened them. Now to find a shirt. She grabbed her helmet and rifle and rushed to the weapons room. At one wall, tactical vests hung from a rod along with suitable shirts to wear underneath. She chose a vest and shirt combination in her size, stripped off her pajama top, and put the new gear on along with her helmet and a pair of cool shooting gloves she found on a shelf.

Iona touched an empty holster hanging at chest level on the front of the vest. No use leaving it that way. On an adjacent wall, a multi-tiered rack held at least thirty handguns. She grabbed a nice Toger 45 semiautomatic, loaded a magazine from a shelf, chambered a round, and pushed the gun into the holster. Much better.

When she hustled back to the main room, Jack's eyes widened. "Now *that's* warrior style." He pushed the door open. "Let's go, Helmet Head and Siberian Sister."

Trudy shook a finger as she stalked out the door with Iona. "No Leo labels, or I'll make your face look like a bruised banana."

Ben watched as the door swung closed behind Jack, Trudy, and Iona. Kat again began typing. "Since the angel cruiser won't fire up without my thumbprint, it has to stay with me, so I'll set up transportation for everyone else. With so many people migrating to the colder climes, I'm not sure what'll be available."

"While you're doing that ..." Ben looked at Leo and gestured with his head. "Show me the locker room. I haven't been in there yet. And your clothes might be dry by now. Iona's were."

"Uh ... yes. Of course." Leo led the way to the side door. Ben glanced at Kat and gave her a wink. She offered an I-know-what-you're-doing smile and continued working.

Ben and Leo walked through a corridor and entered a room with at least a dozen lockers lining one wall and a long bench sitting in front of them. A standing floor fan with an orange light at the center blew desert-like heat. Next to Leo's clothes, his cloak hung doubled over a line that stretched between two adjacent walls, swaying in the arid breeze. Ben leaned against a locker while Leo felt his cloak, looking at Ben, his bushy eyebrows high. "Is something wrong?"

"Relax. I just want to ask you about Iona." Ben pushed away from the locker. "With all that playful bantering, you two seem to have grown really close."

"Ah." Leo nodded in a knowing way. "And you're taking the protective father role. Am I right?"

"Being a father is a role I would cherish, but ... I never ... I mean, we ..."

Leo waved a hand. "No need to explain. Few men get everything they desire in life. And sometimes, at least in my case, it's best that we don't. Speak your mind, Ben. I'm all ears."

"Okay. Well, it's about Iona. As you know, she's only sixteen, and ..." Ben cocked his head. "How old are you? Thirty?"

"I am thirty-five, and I know where you're going with this. You needn't have any fear of impropriety." Leo took his shirt off the line and looked it over while talking. "Iona is the same age my sister, Lorelei, was when she passed away. Besides Iona's red hair, they could be twins. I used to banter with Lorelei in the same manner." He shed the pajama top and slid his arms through his shirt sleeves. "I've told Iona about her. She knows our banter is all in fun." As he fastened the buttons, he focused on Ben, his expression sincere. "Perfectly innocent, I assure you."

Ben pulled the cloak from the line and draped it over his arm. "I believe you."

"Good." Leo exhaled heavily. "That's a relief."

"But I'm still going to Alaska with you."

"Of course. Of course. We need a leader." Leo pulled his pants on over the pajama bottoms, maybe because he wanted an additional layer for the cold destination, or maybe he liked the silky feel and didn't want to admit it.

"You don't consider yourself a leader?" Ben asked.

"Only if the team is tracking down a fugitive." Leo zipped the pants, sat on the bench, and began putting on his socks and boots. "When it comes to infiltration, Iona would be the better choice."

Ben raised his brow. "Really? A teenager?"

Leo tied a boot. "If I had to choose a leader for a stealth operation, between her and me, I would choose her every time. No question. She was born to spy."

"Interesting. I'll keep that in mind." When Leo finished tying the second boot, Ben lifted the cloak. "Ready?"

Leo rose from the bench. "If your trust in me is restored."

"Not restored. Confirmed." Ben handed Leo the cloak. "Let's go to Alaska."

Chapter Six

Ben stopped the SUV at the top of a snowy ridge and looked out through the frosty side window. Amidst the sea of snow at the lower elevation, a few islands of trees stood out, mostly snow-laden evergreens.

Iona, sitting in the front passenger seat and wearing thick gloves and a furry-hooded parka, touched the GPS map. "One-point-two miles to go."

"Right." Ben lifted his foot from the brake, turned the SUV toward the closest tree island, and guided it down the slippery slope. "We'll hide the vehicle and go on foot the rest of the way."

"Have you decided on footwear?" Leo asked from the backseat, his parka and gloves at his side. "Skis or snowshoes?"

"Both. We'll start on skis and take snowshoes with us. See what the terrain looks like."

"I'll stow a pair in each pack." Leo turned around and reached over the back of his seat into the cargo area. "Won't take a minute."

After Ben parked the SUV under a canopy of snow-covered tree branches, he shut off the engine and looked at Iona. "Ready for your role?"

She nodded, intensity in her eyes. "Born ready."

"That I believe."

Leo, now wearing his winter gear, passed a pack forward to Ben, then to Iona. A pair of snowshoes had been pushed behind the netting at the back of each. "Change of clothes. Extra batteries. Handgun with five ammo magazines. I have tranquilizer cartridges in my pocket in case we need a quieter weapon. We also have backup ham radio if the earbuds can't communicate with the satellite relay unit we set up." He gestured toward a ridge to the rear about half a mile away.

Iona rolled her eyes. "I still say we could've trusted the phone system. These Refectors have been here, what, two weeks? They don't know squat about our technology. No way they'd track a phone. Now you have to lug that extra unit around."

Ben opened the driver's side door. "True. We count on the earbuds and leave the radio here for now. It'll be close enough if we need it." When they had all exited and crunched through the snow to the back of the SUV, Ben opened the rear hatch. "But we have to remember the other force, the one Laramel was worried about. Whatever that is might be tech savvy, able to listen in on our conversations."

Leo pulled out three pairs of skis and poles and set them on the snow. "Unfortunately, I can't track this other force if I don't know what it smells like. I'll just have to detect anything that's not a tree, but that won't be easy. The evergreens around here have a strong aroma."

The trio spent the next few minutes strapping on the skis, loading the guns, and fastening them to their belts under their parkas. When they finished, Ben looked at a computer pad. After synching the pad's positioning map with the receiver, he pushed the pad into the parka's pocket and adjusted his earbud. "Comm check. Kat, are you there?"

"Here," Kat said, her voice marred by static. "You're coming across fuzzy. Maybe you should've used the phones."

Ben winked at Iona. "Yeah, my local nag already told me that."

Iona put her helmet on. "Don't worry, Kat. I'll keep him honest."

"I'm sure you will. But we'd better not be nags. I mean, it would be nagging if I told him that Jack and Trudy are using phones, and they're working fine."

"Trust me." Iona elbowed Ben's side. "I won't breathe a word of it."

"Good," Kat said. "Hold on a second, and I'll patch them in. You'll all be connected."

After a quick static spike, Trudy's voice came through clearly. "Ben, can you hear me?"

Ben adjusted his earbud. "Was that Jack or Trudy? And what about deer meat?"

"Don't be a pain in the butt," Trudy said. "Listen, we're about two miles out from the tower, and we need to keep moving or we'll be popsicles in about ten seconds. We'll keep you up to date on the fly."

"No flies here." Ben closed the rear hatch. "But, sure, get whatever you need. You like grape popsicles, right?"

Trudy clicked her tongue. "Ever since we rescued Kat and killed the angels, your old humor's come back. It's cornier than Grandma's toes, but I love it. Over for now."

"Talk to you soon." Ben dug his ski poles into the snow and pushed off. "Let's go."

They skied single file out of the trees and up a slight incline, lifting their skis and pushing with their poles. Ben looked back. Iona plodded at the tail end of their line, puffing clouds of white vapor. With only half an hour of training at the Fairbanks store where they bought the ski equipment, she was doing really well. Leo pushed forward like a pro, pausing every once in a while to sniff the air, but he also likely wanted to give Iona a chance to catch up.

When they reached the crest of a hill, they stopped and took a breather. Downslope on the other side, a treeless expanse of snow spread out for miles. In the distance, a tower stood atop the next hill, much higher than the one they were on. A single-story building sat next to the tower, a small hut that looked like it held only one room.

"That's probably the conduit site," Iona said, breathing heavily through a scarf that left only her eye shield and protruding red hair visible. "If we go straight there, anyone inside that little shack could spot us coming a mile away."

"You're right. That shack is likely the station's outpost, so there's a good chance it's occupied." Ben withdrew the computer pad and looked at it. "The map shows more trees at the far side of the hill the outpost's on. We can take a long route around and keep to the trees."

Iona took a deep breath and exhaled a long stream of white. "I'm game."

"Problem is, we've got only about an hour of sunlight left, then we'll have a couple of hours of twilight before it'll get dark and super cold, so no wasting time. We have to get back to the SUV—"

"Wait." Leo pulled his scarf down and sniffed the air. "I smell something strange. Well, not really strange. Unexpected."

"What?" Ben asked.

"Buttered popcorn. And it's fresh."

"Coming from the outpost?"

"Without a doubt. Breeze is from that direction."

Iona lifted her skis in turn. "I don't think Refectors eat popcorn. And maybe they haven't even had time to get here with the mass exodus." She waved a hand toward the snowy expanse. "Look. No tracks, either from SUVs, skis, or snowshoes. Some outpost guy is probably just kicking back in front of a woodstove, watching a movie while eating popcorn. It should be safe to go there, and since we're short on time—"

"No woodstove." Leo inhaled deeply. "But I smell smoke from another source. A diesel generator is running somewhere."

"Okay," Ben said. "We'll check it out."

Leo lifted his skis in turn, probably to keep them from freezing in place. "Maybe your brother and sister know what's going on at their site by now."

"Good point." Ben looked upward. "Jack. Trudy. Update?"

A garbled voice came through, filled with static.

"Hey," Ben said, "you're breaking up. Seriously. No joke."

Static continued, this time without a voice.

"Kat, are you getting a signal from my sibs?"

"No. Their transmissions stopped a few minutes ago. They've had time to get to their conduit node."

"Like we expected, we have a communications tower of some kind at our site, but we're still pretty far from it. Maybe their tower is interfering with their signal. If so, our signal might get zapped when we get close."

"Understood."

Ben turned toward Leo and Iona. "No use taking chances, so we'll go the long way around. Quick and quiet. Let's go." He pushed the poles into the ground and shoved off toward a path that would lead them around to the outpost, Iona and Leo following. As they glided, all remained quiet except for the swishing of skis and pantlegs along with an occasional grunt. The sun, close to the horizon, provided enough light to blaze a trail but only a little warmth to fend off the chilly air.

When they arrived at the outpost building, a one-story structure about the size of a residential bungalow, they passed a large generator at a windowless side of the building. As its engine chugged, smoke puffed from a pipe at the top.

Ben skied around the corner, stopped at the front door, and tried to look through a window, but a coating of frost kept the inside veiled.

Leo and Iona slid to a halt behind him. Leo inhaled deeply, then whispered, "Popcorn. The aroma's strong now. It's definitely coming from inside."

"Then someone must be home." Ben grasped the knob, but it wouldn't turn. Maybe it would be a good idea to put whoever was inside at ease, avoid scaring him. He whispered to Iona, "Ready to be a lost little girl?"

She squinted, her voice low. "Seriously? Little Bo Peep lost her sheep at the Arctic Circle?"

"Call for help with a girlish voice. At least that'll get someone to open the door."

"If you say so." After the trio removed their skis and set them to the side, Ben and Leo stood behind Iona while she took her helmet off, tucked it under her arm, and knocked on the door. "Is anyone home? I'm freezing out here."

Something bumped. Seconds later, a click sounded, and the door opened a crack. Iona peered through the gap, then turned and spread her hands. "I don't see anyone."

Ben stepped past her and pushed the door fully open. At the opposite wall, an electric heater radiated next to a rocking chair. A side table held a ceramic bowl filled with popcorn and a portable communications radio with a handset microphone. No one sat in the chair, and the one-room building appeared to be vacant. He called, "Hello?"

The chair began rocking slowly on its runners. "If you're coming in," a man said, "then be quick about it. This little heater's no match for the winds of Alaska."

Ben waved Leo and Iona inside and closed the door. "Where are you?"

"Sitting right in front of you." A popcorn kernel lifted from the bowl and disappeared. "Can you see where I am now?" His voice seemed muffled by chewing.

Ben took a step closer. Another Refector? First, a woman who could turn into a man-eating tornado, then a man who transformed into a puff of smoke, and now this? "You're invisible."

"Observant, aren't you? I assume you're the detective in the group."

"But you're eating popcorn and rocking the chair. You must be physical."

"As if physical can't be invisible." The man chuckled. "A detective, but not exactly Sherlock Holmes."

Ben strode to the chair and grasped the space above the arm. His gloved fingers wrapped around something solid. When he pulled, a human-shaped figure rose from the chair, no more than a shimmer of light that vanished as quickly as it had appeared.

An electric shock sent Ben staggering back. Leo caught him, preventing a fall. When he set Ben upright, he looked him over. "I smell burnt leather."

Ben opened his hand. A singe mark ran horizontally along his smoking glove. "I think he's made of pure energy."

"Not quite pure," the man said as the chair began rocking again. "Some physical matter to allow the enjoyment of eating popcorn, among other activities."

Ben squinted, now able to see the man's nebulous outline. "Who are you, and why are you here?"

The chair stopped rocking. "Since you're the intruders, I thought you might want to introduce yourselves first."

"I'm Benjamin Garrison."

"Ah. Thought so. Some rumblings about you in the airwaves. Supposedly you expelled the angels from the planet."

Ben nodded. "We did."

"And now you're here. Maybe you're a good detective after all."

"Because this place is connected to the Oculus Gate?"

He waved a nearly invisible hand. "Finish the introductions. I don't know who your two companions are or why you're here."

Ben gestured toward Iona. "Go ahead. Secrecy doesn't matter anymore."

She set her helmet on the floor. "I'm Iona Macklin."

Leo cleared his throat. "Leo. Not my real name, but it's the only one I use."

"We're here," Ben said, "to investigate some strange goings-on that are focused on your outpost and a few other places."

The chair began rocking again. "Well, well, well. It's refreshing to hear someone telling the truth. It's not the whole truth, but at least it's the truth."

"It's often not wise to tell a stranger everything you know," Ben said.

"On the contrary." The bowl of popcorn rose from the table and floated to the floor. "Have a seat there, and I will tell you whatever you need to know. As you can see ..." He chuckled again. "I am completely transparent."

Ben looked toward the door. "We don't have much daylight left, so—"

"That's not a concern. You're staying here."

"Staying here?" Ben glanced around. No sign of any other transparent people. "One man can't hold us prisoner, even an electrified one."

"I don't need to hold you. You simply have nowhere to go. I saw you when you stopped at the top of that hill back there. Then when you started on a long route to my cabin, I hustled to your vehicle, hotwired it, and hid it. If you try to leave on foot, you'll find that it's more than a hundred miles to the nearest shelter. You'll surely freeze to death."

Leo opened the door. "I'll check on the SUV."

Ben tossed the key fob to him. "Hurry back."

He snatched the fob out of the air and stealthily touched his ear, a sign that likely meant he would try to contact Kat.

When Leo left, the invisible man chuckled. "He won't find it. It's too well hidden."

"You don't know Leo." Ben sat cross-legged on the floor next to the bowl and scooped a handful of popcorn. Iona remained standing, her arms crossed and her brow furrowed as she edged sideways toward a wall. Ben focused on the man. Letting Iona do the scouting while their host was distracted might be the best plan.

Ben tossed a popcorn kernel into the air and caught it in his mouth. "All right, whoever you are, what's going on at this outpost?"

The chair runners scraped the wooden floor as they turned toward Ben. "First, my name is Elliot Quincy Patterson, but you can call me Quince. Second, I assume you want to know why I am invisible."

Ben watched Iona out of the corner of his eye. She had made her way behind the chair and was now tiptoeing toward the radio. "That question did cross my mind."

"I am one of a group of visitors to your planet. The angels called us Refectors because we have the ability to transform the physicality of our hosts, a renewal of sorts, hence the Latin word Refector coined by the queen of the angels. Some of us can become a vaporous mass, others a consuming swarm or one of several different end-result forms."

Behind the chair, Iona picked up the radio and looked at its settings. Hoping to keep Quince from noticing her, Ben gestured with his hands as he spoke. "Yeah, I guessed that you're a Refector, and I noticed the differences in abilities. Do you have labels that describe the different powers?"

Quince pointed at himself. "I am a Radiant, in effect, a capacitor. I alter my host's cells into miniature panels that absorb and house energy that stays in an excited state, thereby making them transparent. In essence, I am a power source myself."

"Then why do you need a generator?" Ben asked.

"I have to preserve my energy for a different use, but don't bother to ask what it is. My transparency goes only so far."

Iona set the radio down and looked at Quince, then at the heater's power cord leading to a wall outlet, then at Ben with a questioning expression. Her question was easy to guess. Should she test Quince's power capability and maybe drain it?

Hoping to signal Iona, Ben nodded in an exaggerated way. "Okay, so back to the other Refectors. Is it true that souls are purged because the Refectors can't live in bodies with souls present?"

Iona inched toward the wall outlet, not making a sound. Her stealth skills were every bit as good as Leo advertised.

"That was the pretext. In the vernacular, it was a big, fat lie, but it's a long story that I don't care to tell."

Iona crouched at the outlet, her hand on the cord. Since the heater sat to the side of the chair, it was out of Quince's line of sight. Yet, if she unplugged it, he might not notice the change in temperature immediately.

"Okay," Ben said as he tossed back another popcorn kernel. "What about your host's soul? Is it still inside?"

"No. He didn't receive the vaccine, but I possessed him anyway because we needed access to this tower, and I purged his soul myself with my internal energy."

Ben hid a tight swallow. This *capacitor* was a monster that needed to die. He cast a stealthy glance at Iona as she unplugged the heater and, carrying the cord, approached the chair from behind. Ben continued focusing on Quince. "What's this tower supposed to do?"

"The detective asks far too many questions." Quince sighed. "Very well. It won't hurt to satisfy your curiosity. The tower is one of four that communicates with the portal you call the Oculus Gate. Because of the collapse of the conduit between our world and this one, we Refectors were not all able to come."

Iona set the plug close to Quince's neck, exposed through a gap in the back of the chair. She looked at Ben as if waiting for a signal.

"We suspected that," Ben said.

"And it doesn't matter that you know. You'll be dead before the night's over." The chair stopped rocking. "Is it getting colder in here?"

"Now!" Ben shouted.

Iona shoved the plug into Quince, reached through the gap, and grabbed his throat, holding him in place. His body lit up. Sparks flew. Iona groaned, clenching her teeth as smoke shot up from the radiant humanoid in the seat.

Ben raced around the chair. Just as he lunged to take over for Iona, Quince exploded in a splash of arcing sparks that cascaded to the floor and sizzled on the wood. Iona flew back and slammed against the wall. The cord still in hand and her hair frizzed, she blinked at the plug and whispered, "Wow!"

Ben hustled to her. "Are you all right?"

"I think so. Just ... um ..." She licked her cracked lips. "Shocked, I guess."

"Your sense of humor's still intact. That was a whale of a jolt." Ben extended a hand. "Think you can get up?"

She nodded, grasped his wrist, and rode his pull to her feet.

The moment she stood upright, the door opened. Leo walked in and sniffed. "Is something burning?"

Iona pinched a few strands of her frazzled hair. "Me."

"And our host." Ben ran a boot across a few remaining sparks on the floor. "Iona drained his power until he exploded."

Leo closed the door. "Then I assume he was a threat, not merely a popcorn eater."

"Without a doubt. He expelled his host's soul, and he said we would be dead before the night's over." Ben firmed his jaw, trying to convince himself as well as Leo that killing Quince was the right thing to do. "Maybe I could've gotten more information out of him, but we had an opening, so we took it."

Leo looked at the window. "The sun is setting, so we'd better use the two hours of twilight to figure out how we're supposed to die." He lifted a hand, pinching a key fob. "Or, now that Quince is dead, we could announce *mission accomplished* and make a getaway in the SUV. Our toasted host hid it out of sight, but not out of smell."

"The mission's not accomplished until we figure out what the tower is supposed to do." Ben stroked his chin. No matter what the Refectors' goal was, it couldn't be good. They were aliens, an invading force that had to be stopped. "Or maybe we should sabotage it. Try to shut it down."

"Did you get in touch with Jack and Trudy?" Iona asked. "Maybe they learned something about their tower that can help us."

Leo touched his earbud. "I was able to update Kat, but static flooded in when I got close to the tower again. And Jack and Trudy have gone silent. Not even modified Morse code taps."

Iona pointed at the portable radio. "Maybe that'll get a transmission out."

"What frequency is it set on?" Leo asked as he drew closer to the radio.

"Twenty-something, but I don't know if it's kilohertz, megahertz, or whatever."

Leo looked the radio over. "It's a ham unit, similar to the one we left in the SUV. The shortwave signal travels long distances, especially at night. Considering our location, Quince's contact was probably far away."

Ben stroked his chin. "Interesting. Maybe he was supposed to talk to his contacts at the other towers after dark, and since we're at the solstice, the signal would be enhanced around the entire Arctic Circle."

"Which means," Iona said, "adjustments could be made to the towers. Otherwise, why station someone here with the ability to communicate to the other towers?"

"And if Quince could make adjustments, so can we." Ben pointed at the radio. "Try to call Kat with that ham unit while Leo and I figure out how to shut the tower down. She's supposed to be scanning those channels. Tell her what's going on."

"Okay, but ..." Iona picked up the radio and sat in the rocking chair. "She probably can't hear me until after sundown back home."

"We're farther west, so it's already close to sundown there. We can give it a try."

Iona lifted the handset. "I'm on it."

Ben began pacing. "Okay, let's think about this. Quince was here because of his electrical powers, maybe as an energy source to transmit the signal. But they had a generator, so that idea doesn't fly."

"Right," Iona said as she turned a radio dial. "He didn't emit much power. A little heater drained him. I wasn't sure it would work, but it did."

Leo's brow lifted. "I smell diesel, and I hear engines. Getting closer."

"Let's bolt." Ben waved at Iona. "Bring the radio."

They jogged outside. Several sets of headlights broke the dim surroundings, and loud engines rumbled as large vehicles parked about a hundred yards from the outpost.

Leo gathered the skis into his arms. "Follow me. Our tracks will be obvious, but it can't be helped."

They trudged through the snow, lifting their feet high to wade through the drifts. When they passed a line of trees at the edge of a forest, Leo halted at a tree where the SUV sat nearly completely hidden under snow-laden boughs.

All three leaned against the vehicle, breathing heavily as they watched the outpost from the forest. Leo set the skis on the ground. "Let's hope they weren't paying much attention."

Iona's scarf muffled her words. "If I weren't on this mission, would we be hiding?"

Ben stared at her. Barely visible in the moonlight, her serious eyes seemed both inquisitive and accusing. "What else could we do?"

"You didn't answer my question." She lowered her scarf, revealing tight lips. "But I think I know the answer. If the vulnerable little girl had stayed home, you and Leo would still be at the tower trying to disable it. Am I right?"

Leo snorted. "Don't be so full of yourself, Ego Elf. This isn't about you. Sometimes it's better to watch and learn what a grizzly bear's going to do than to charge at it with a broomstick. And we don't even have a broomstick."

Still looking at Ben, she half closed an eye. "If you say so."

Ben concealed a sigh. "I didn't say it. Leo did. But he's right. We probably would watch to see what's going on. Still, I won't lie to you. If the situation called for us to stay at the tower, I don't know if your presence would make a difference."

She firmed her jaw. "It shouldn't. I can handle it. Just give me a chance to prove myself. You treat Kat and Trudy like soldiers. Why not me?"

"Because you're a teenager."

She huffed. "A teenager who can put a bullet through a donut hole from fifty paces."

"Point granted, but this is no time to argue." He gestured toward the radio, still in her grasp. "For now, try to call Kat while Leo and I get a little closer. If it doesn't work, try the one in the SUV."

After eyeing Ben for another moment, Iona lifted the handset to her lips and spoke. "Kat, it's Iona. Can you hear me?"

While Iona continued calling, Ben walked to the edge of the forest, Leo at his side. They stood in darkness as hundreds of flashlights approached the outpost, the beams bobbing with the gaits of their carriers.

Leo inhaled deeply. "Humans. No surprise, but I smell something else—another creature of some kind."

"A grizzly bear, maybe?"

"No. Smelled them a few times. This is different. Something new to my nose. And they're not the ones holding the flashlights. I think they're farther away, but they're definitely getting closer."

"I guess we'll know soon."

Leo lowered his voice. "Think these are the first wave of people to get their vaccinations?"

"Maybe. That would mean they have doctors or nurses with them to—"

"Ben," Iona whisper-shouted from behind them. "I've got Kat."

Just as he set his foot to turn, a shout burst from the approaching crowd. They stampeded toward the tower, snow flying into their flashlight beams.

Leo whistled. "If something can scare a group that big, it's got to be worse than grizzlies."

A line of enormous men and women, maybe ten feet tall, came into view behind the crowd, swords raised as they ran. When they caught up with the stragglers, they began swinging their blades, hacking and slicing the humans. A few humans broke apart into locust-like swarms and attacked some of the giants, but the giants fended them off with great swats from their meaty hands that split through the swarms and forced them to scatter.

A new shout came from the tower. "Quince!" A parka-covered man stood partway up a ladder, a hand cupped around his mouth. "Quince Patterson! Has anyone seen him?"

Ben whispered, "So they do need Quince. No surprise. But for what?"

The man called out again. "Do we have any other Radiants here?"

"I'm a Radiant." A shimmering woman began climbing up the tower, glowing and semitransparent. One of the giants grabbed her ankle, but when sparks flew from the contact point, the giant jerked away. The giant swatted the parka-covered man to the ground and began hacking him with a sword while the Radiant continued climbing.

Ben took his parka off and gave it to Leo. "Stay with Iona. I have to stop that Radiant. She's doing Quince's job."

"You're going to plow through those crazy, sword-swinging giants alone?"

"No choice." Ben pulled a handgun from his belt holster. "Whatever that Radiant is up to might kill us all."

"Listen, Farmer Jones. You best put aside that protect-the-little-girl chivalry. You need help from both of us. And you'd better get something from the SUV that's more powerful than that popgun."

"Okay. You're right. Get Iona and bring the artillery. But I'm going now. That Radiant's already halfway up the tower, and I can run faster without a rifle." Ben dashed from the forest, again lifting his legs high. With sword-swinging giants and man-eating cyclones ahead, this might be the craziest suicide mission ever.

Chapter Seven

Jack dug his boots into the slope of an icy ridge and peered over the crest with infrared binoculars, Trudy at his side. Near the Siberian tower, a huge woman, maybe ten feet tall, paced in front of the outpost building's door. Wearing a caped cloak, open in front over a medieval tunic, and carrying an enormous sword, she looked like a blend of warriors from a variety of eras.

Jack took a step back and shone a flashlight at Trudy. "She's still there. No sign of changing the guard."

"I wonder how long her shift is." Trudy adjusted her hold on her automatic rifle and looked toward the eastern horizon. "Nights are forever here this time of year."

"And cold."

Trudy shivered in spite of her thick parka. "Right. It's gotta be way below zero already."

"Ten below Fahrenheit. Negative twenty-three Celsius." Jack showed her his wristwatch, the numerals glowing. "My body temperature probably skews it warmer a notch."

Trudy lifted her rifle to her shoulder, stepped higher on the slope, and aimed toward the woman for a moment before stepping back down. "I could take her out from here without a problem."

"Assuming a bullet could take her out. And what if she's on our side? Remember, Laramel was worried about another force. She might be a member of that force."

"Good point, but ..." Trudy craned her neck. "Do you hear that?"

"What?"

She pointed toward the south. "Look."

From that direction, dozens of school buses drove across the frozen tundra, their headlights making them easy to see. Jack trained his binoculars on the closest bus. It appeared to be packed with passengers. "Vaccine supply, maybe? Or people who are coming to get vaccinated? Or maybe they already got vaccinated."

"It might be a zombie supply," Trudy said as she watched with her own binoculars. "Soulless humans or humans who are about to be soulless."

When the buses parked behind the tower's one-room outpost hut, the warrior woman raised her sword as if ready to attack. The moment a man deboarded, she swung her sword and lopped his head off, then decapitated the next passenger with a backswing. Yet, the passengers continued tromping down the bus stairs, apparently not caring about the headless corpses lying on the ground in front of them.

Just as the woman swung toward another victim, five passengers from a different bus leaped on her and knocked her to the ground. They transformed into swarms of insect-like creatures and covered her body. Several seconds later, they lifted away, leaving only their victims' torn clothing behind, and transformed back into humans.

"I guess she was on our side," Trudy whispered.

"Or not on either side." Jack lowered his binoculars. After being inhabited by an angel, skyrocketing to a celestial version of hell, and helping rescue the souls of his departed wife and daughter from that terrible place, it seemed that nothing could get any stranger, but these human locust tornadoes might top all the competition. He shed his parka. "We can blend in with the other humans. See what's going on."

"Without our coats?"

"They're not wearing coats."

Trudy shivered again. "All right. If we have to, we have to."

By the time Jack and Trudy stowed their parkas and weapons, except their belt knives, in the nearby SUV, the newly arrived humans had gathered around the tower, facing it in a multi-ringed circle.

Jack led the way toward the gathering, first jogging parallel to the ridge, then through a gap that opened to an icy path leading to the buses. With the big yellow vehicles and the outpost building between them and the crowd, they strode on the crunching ice, hidden from sight. When they drew close, they skulked around the building and halted in the ring of people farthest from the tower.

Illuminated by the tower's blinking lights, a man climbed a few rungs on the ladder and looked out into the crowd, his face obscured by shadows as he spoke with a loud voice. "The time has come. As promised, you will soon be infused with power from on high. You saw what we Refectors did to our enemy, a giant from Viridi, and you will have similar powers, some even greater than the consuming cyclone you witnessed."

Jack leaned close to Trudy. "That means Viridi isn't the Refectors' home. The giant came from there."

"And only one giant? There must be more. No one can be on sentry duty forever."

"Really odd." While the Refector droned on about having courage to face the changes, Jack glanced at the surrounding higher elevations. More giants could easily be hidden, waiting for the right time to attack. The lone woman might have been a scout or maybe a sacrificial lamb to make the Refectors think they had the upper hand. If so, then anyone in this crowd would be a sitting duck for a horde of ten-foot-tall attackers.

"Trudy, I think we should—"

Jack's phone vibrated in his pocket. He pulled it out, held it to his ear, and gestured for Trudy to draw close. When she did, he spoke in a low tone. "Kat. Both of us are listening. What's up?"

"I heard from Iona on a shortwave frequency. She said a lot, but here's what you need to know in quick bullet points. As we expected, both of the conduit sites we're investigating have a transmission tower. A Refector said Iona, Ben, and Leo would all die tonight, but he didn't say how. Ben suspects the tower has something to do with it, so he and Leo are trying to figure out how to shut theirs down.

You should do the same for yours. Right now, it's pretty much total chaos where Ben is. I'll give you an update when I can."

Jack nodded. "We copy. We'll update you as soon as we can." He terminated the call and slid the phone into his pocket.

Trudy drew back. "How in blazes are we supposed to knock the tower down?"

"No way we can barge through this crowd." He pivoted. In the higher elevations all around, spots of firelight appeared, moving toward them. "Torches. We're surrounded."

"More giants?"

"Probably. Looks like a bunch of them. If they take these zombies by surprise, they'll make mincemeat out of them."

"And us."

"Maybe we can sneak out of here under the cover of darkness and try to come back when the coast is clear."

Just as they began backing away, red lights strobed in a line from the base of the tower to the top.

"In less than one minute," the Refector said, now invisible in the darkness, "we will send the signal to our other towers and create the network that will capture the Earth and hold it for continuous passage between our worlds."

"Scratch that," Jack said. "We're taking the tower out now."

"How?"

"Not sure yet." Jack grabbed his knife from its belt sheath, showed her the blade, then slid it back. "It's got to have a power cable somewhere."

Trudy drew her knife. "Cutting it might bring a jolt, but it beats the alternative."

"We'll sound the alarm that more giants are coming, cause an uproar, then run to the tower and climb toward the top. Get out of reach as fast as possible."

Trudy shoved her knife back to its belt sheath. "Got it."

Jack clenched a fist. It was time for warrior mode. "Here goes." Just as the torches drew within a hundred yards, he took in a deep

70

breath and shouted, "The giants are coming from the hills! Lots of them!"

Everyone turned that way. The Refector called out, "Windstorms, attack! The rest of you stay. I will send the tower signal." He vaporized and streamed toward the outpost building.

"Let's go!" Jack charged ahead, Trudy at his side. They pushed their way past some people, weaving and dodging others. When they reached the tower, they grasped the crisscrossing lattice and climbed to a height of about fifty feet. Jack called, "Stop."

Each hanging on with one hand, they drew their knives. The center of the tower's main support pole lay within the lattice cage about an arm's length away. Below, shouts rose along with the ripping of flesh and fabric. Tower lights blinked here and there, providing brief glimpses of the carnage at ground level, swords hacking and body parts flying.

"I don't see a cable to cut," Jack said, steeling himself against the frigid breeze. "Everything's encased in metal."

"Then we'll have to take out the antennas at the top somehow. Kick them over if we have to."

"It's the only plan we've got."

"Better than getting hacked to death."

They re-sheathed their knives, climbed around the lattice to the tower's stepladder, scrambled to the top platform, and hoisted themselves onto its wooden surface, a flat board about twenty feet long and ten feet wide. Two antennas protruded near each longer edge.

Hugging herself and shivering, Trudy slammed her heel against one of the antennas, but it didn't budge. "It's solid. Maybe both of us kicking at the same time."

"Let's try it."

Jack and Trudy stood together in front of the antenna. Just as they each lifted a foot to kick, a light flashed below. A radiant man climbed up the lattice at a rapid clip. Jack pointed. "Whatever that thing is, it can't be good."

"Kick!"

They pummeled the antenna with their heels again and again. The glowing man climbed to the platform, bypassed them, and stood at the center between the two antennas. His body elongating, he reached over their heads and grasped each antenna with a hand.

Static electricity crackled in the air, sending painful stings across Jack and Trudy. Jack grabbed her arm and rolled with her on the platform until the sensation ebbed. His skin still tingling as the odor of scorched hair assaulted his nose, Jack sat up with Trudy and looked back at the man.

A trio of blue, snaking lights surged from both antennas, met within the man's neck, and radiated through his eyes and out the back of his head, one set of three lights to the east and one to the west, wiggling like agitated sine waves. As the man stood in place, he wailed in agony.

"We have to stop him!" Jack leaped to his feet and tried to tackle the man. The energy knifed through his arms and stiffened his body. Trudy joined him, but she, too, stiffened, her entire frame flashing as she gritted her teeth and held on.

A jolt sent Jack flying. His feet flailed but found no place to land, only empty air. Time slowed to a crawl as the electrified man's guttural scream spewed from his gaping mouth and Trudy's tight grimace pulsed nearby. It seemed as if she flew with him, somehow tethered, though his numb hands failed to register a connection.

As the tower rushed away, Jack grasped for something, anything to stop the furious flight. Another hand grasped his. Trudy's hand. He held on tightly as they fell together toward the bloody melee below, though a competing upward pull seemed to slow their plunge. At the moment of impact, pain spiked, and blackness flooded his mind.

Iona attached the microphone handset to the radio. From the edge of the forest, Leo ran toward her, puffing heavily as he kicked through snow.

"I updated Kat," she said as he arrived with Ben's parka in hand. "What's going on out there?"

"Nothing good." Leo glanced at the tower, then at Iona. "Ben's gone solo with a handgun. Going to try to climb the tower to stop a Radiant, a female Quince. We're Ben's backup."

Iona set the radio on the SUV's hood. "Stealth or guns blazing?"

"Both. I'll handle the blazing while you do the stealthing." Leo yanked the SUV door open, threw Ben's parka inside, and grabbed an automatic rifle and ammo magazines. As he thrust the magazines into belt pouches, he looked toward the tower. "I'll cause the biggest distraction in Arctic Circle history while you figure out how to help Ben at the tower."

"Sounds good." Iona stripped off her outer garments down to her military gear, pulled a plasma sphere rifle from the SUV, and turned it on, making its engine hum. "It's time to fry another Radiant."

Leo shed his parka but left his long cloak on. He charged ahead, leading the way out of the forest as he shouted, "I'll shoot high. You duck low."

When they drew within a stone's throw of the tower, Leo halted and set the rifle to his shoulder, aiming at the chaotic fighting. "Go!"

He began shooting rapid-fire. Iona ran past him and bent low under the hail of bullets, carrying the rifle at her chest. Ahead, the ammo slammed into giants and humans, making the humans topple while the giants fled with bleeding wounds in their arms and sides.

The way now clear, Iona focused on the tower. The Radiant, a shimmering semi-transparent woman, stood on a platform at the top, stretching her arms beyond their normal length as she set a hand on each of two antennas while Ben climbed a ladder about twenty feet below her. Ben fired his handgun twice, but the bullets plunged into the Radiant without harming her.

When Iona neared the base of the tower, she dropped to her knees and slid across snow as bullets zinged overhead. The moment she stopped, she set the Radiant in her scope's crosshairs, trying to steady her aim, but wind kept buffeting her weapon. She had to wait for a split second of calm. A wild shot might hit Ben.

Light energy surged from the Radiant's body and flowed into the antennas. A brilliant aura swelled around her, almost too bright to look at.

Ben climbed onto the platform, shielding his eyes from the blinding light. Twin lightning bolts shot from the Radiant's mouth. Ben ducked. One bolt missed him, but the other stabbed his shoulder. He dropped to his knees, an easy target for the Radiant's next assault.

Iona set her finger on the trigger and exhaled. It was now or never.

She fired. A plasma sphere rocketed from the barrel and smashed into the Radiant's chest. She absorbed the energy, growing bigger and brighter than ever. The Radiant screamed but stayed put, shimmering wildly.

The ground trembled, maybe an earthquake. Iona lowered the gun and scanned the area. Body parts littered the bloody snow. The surviving humans fled toward the trees, the giants in pursuit, though everyone stumbled and staggered as the quake worsened.

Leo grasped Iona's wrist and hauled her to her feet. He pointed toward the tower. "I think those lights are causing this earthquake."

Iona set the plasma rifle to her shoulder again. "Maybe another shot will make her explode."

"No." Leo pushed the barrel down. "Ben's too close."

At the platform, Ben struggled to his feet and charged at the Radiant. He slammed into her and shoved her off the platform, breaking her connection with the antennas. The Radiant plunged while Ben hung onto the edge of the platform, dangling by one hand more than a hundred feet in the air. The Radiant crashed into the tower's support lattice, grabbed the frame with her glowing arms, and began climbing back up. Flames burst from the lattice and crawled upward ahead of her.

Leo sprinted toward the ladder, wobbling as the quake continued. He shouted back at Iona. "Shoot her! I'll help Ben!"

Iona again took aim at the Radiant, though tremors shook the scope's crosshairs. Not waiting for a perfect shot, she fired. The ball flew through the air, sizzling and sparking, and splashed against the Radiant's legs. Again she swelled, becoming three times her previous size until she exploded in a massive eruption of glittering arcs.

As flames continued creeping toward Ben, Leo climbed the tower's ladder. Gunshots rang out from ground level. Bullets zinged past Leo, some smacking into the tower's framework, one next to his head.

Iona scanned the area. No gunman stood in sight. She dashed to the ladder and began scrambling up the rungs, still clutching the plasma rifle as the tower swayed in the quake. When she reached the halfway point, she stopped and looked down. A man stood at a corner of the outpost building, reloading a rifle with a fresh magazine.

As she took aim at him, timing the tower's sways, she muttered, "You're a lousy shot and slow to reload." She fired. The shimmering ball rocketed out and blasted the man square in the chest, blowing a hole straight through. He collapsed in a flaming heap.

She looked at Leo as he climbed onto the platform. "You're clear, and I'm on my way." She fastened the rifle to a back strap and hustled up the ladder.

When she leaped onto the platform, she ran to the edge. Leo lay on his stomach, holding Ben's arm with both hands. Ben's other arm dangled loosely as if unusable. In the distance, one of the giants ran toward the tower, a quiver of arrows on his back and a bow in hand, the glow from the tower making him easy to see.

Iona prostrated herself and reached down toward Ben. "A few inches higher, Leo, and I can grab him."

With a grunt, Leo hoisted. Iona clutched a handful of Ben's shirt, and the two heaved him upward until Ben braced himself with his good arm fully on the platform.

"I got him," Leo said, now holding Ben's belt. "See if you can shut off those antennas."

"Will do, but watch out. One of those giants is coming, and he has an archery bow."

"I see him. I'm more worried about the fire."

While Leo helped Ben the rest of the way onto the platform, Iona rushed to the twin antennas and looked them over, shivering hard as she hugged herself in the buffeting gusts. The antennas stood more than ten feet high and eight feet apart, facing each other with a foot-wide dish perched on top. A trio of squiggly bluish-green lines radiated from each dish and joined at a point halfway between them. At the intersection, two similar trios radiated horizontally at ninety-degree angles and traveled out of sight over opposite horizons, undulating over the Earth's curvature as if following a set path.

Iona knelt at the base of one of the antennas, grasped the central metal pole, and shook it, but it stayed put. She rose and looked at Leo as he helped Ben sit cross-legged on the platform. "It won't budge."

"Maybe I can persuade it." Leo climbed to his feet. "That fire's getting close. We've got less than a minute."

"And don't forget the giant." Iona shivered again.

"No worries at the moment. He's just standing down there like he's waiting for something. Maybe for more of his kind." Leo grasped the center rod of the other antenna with his gloved hands and shook it, his face straining, but, as before, the antenna wouldn't budge.

From his seated position, Ben called over the sound of the whistling wind, "Try shifting a dish."

"Good idea." Leo stood on tiptoes and reached upward, but his fingers groped well below the dish's lower edge. "I'll try jumping."

"No," Iona said. "You won't have leverage. Let me stand on your shoulders."

"Yeah. You're good at that, you acrobatic imp."

When Leo crouched, Iona climbed aboard, set her feet on his shoulders, and spread her arms for balance as he straightened. The moment he rose to his full height, she reached up and grasped the dish. Her gloves provided some protection from the frigid surface as she held tightly to keep from toppling in the gusts. The triad connecting the two antennas wiggled only inches over her head, casting light all around.

"Okay. Here goes." The moment she flexed to push the dish upward, someone shouted from below. She jerked her head in that direction. An arrow whizzed up and struck her pants at the waist, piercing her belt and lodging in her hip.

Pain knifed in. She yelped. Her feet slipped off Leo's shoulders, and she dropped, still clutching the dish. It arced downward and brought the triad of light with it. The stream burned into the platform, and the wood burst into flames. The other triad struck the dish, bounced off its curved surface, and radiated into Leo and Iona.

In a brilliant flash, everything disappeared.

Chapter Eight

The explosion of light dissipated. Half-blinded, Ben blinked at the two antennas. Leo and Iona were gone. Disintegrated.

Ben struggled to his feet on stiffened legs, every muscle cramping. Between him and the ladder, the two streams of light continued burning into the platform. Flames erupted from the wood. There was no escape.

He scanned the area. The light couldn't have completely annihilated Leo and Iona. No energy was that powerful. In his blindness, he must not have seen them fall. Maybe they were still hanging on somewhere.

Battling the cramps, he staggered to the platform's edge and looked down. A giant stood at the base of the tower and looked up at him, an arrow nocked in his bowstring. Ben raised his hands. "Don't shoot!"

The giant, dressed in loose buckskin garments and leather boots, called, "Repair what you have broken."

Ben looked at the two dishes, still askew and shooting triads of light energy into the platform. Flames crawled his way. Soon they would force him to climb down the lattice. "I have to find my two friends. Have you seen them?"

The giant released the bowstring. The arrow zinged past Ben's ear. "Repair what you have broken." He nocked another arrow and pulled back the string. "I will not miss again."

Ben swept his gaze across the tower's surrounding framework. Leo and Iona were nowhere in sight. Could he have been blinded long enough for them to climb down? They wouldn't have left him behind.

The flames crawled closer, creating a crack in the platform and making it sag under his feet. Just as he bent his knees to leap over the fire, an arrow pierced his boot. The platform gave way, and he plunged. He crashed into the latticework, breaking a fire-blackened board, and continued plummeting. He slapped at another support section, but his cold, stiff hands slipped away.

Seconds later, he crashed again. Pain stabbed everywhere, and darkness overtook his mind. A frigid bobbing sensation followed, as if he were floating underwater in an icy river. With each rise to the surface, he gasped for breath, unable to open his eyes.

After a few minutes, heat flowed over his body, and the bobbing stopped. Warm liquid passed between his lips, and a soft, feminine voice crooned, "Try to awaken, human. You seem to have no broken bones and no sign of internal bleeding. I think Caligar softened your fall sufficiently."

Ben blinked his eyes open. Firelight danced on a huge woman sitting cross-legged on a flat carpet, a bowl in her hand. Dressed in pioneer-style leather, much like the giant man he had seen earlier, though barefooted, she seemed to come out of a storybook, much larger than life.

The walls and ceiling appeared to be rock or hard dirt, overlaid by wooden support boards, and a tunnel led into darkness. A table stood next to the tunnel's arched opening with a pair of simple stone mugs and dinner plates on its surface. Flames licked at a pile of logs in a fireplace. Smoke rose into a flue, leaving only a tang of odor in the air.

He checked his body. Everything seemed intact, though a bandage wrapped his bare foot, the victim of the giant's arrow. His back scars still stung from the recent angel encounter, but not too badly. His boots sat on the floor nearby, along with his belt, gun, and ammo.

Images of Iona and Leo crashed in. What had happened to them? If this woman knew, maybe it would be better to figure out if she was a friend or an enemy before asking.

His body aching, Ben managed a weak, "Who are you?"

"Ah. You are awake. Good." Smiling, she scooted toward him, as if looking forward to a conversation. As she leaned closer, the firelight illuminated her tawny, flawless skin and the thick, braided black hair draped over her chest. "My name is Winella, Caligar's life mate."

Ben studied the woman's face—youthful, small nose, larger-then-normal eyes—humanlike but different enough to bring her species into question. "Are you native to this planet?"

"Before I answer," Winella said, "my understanding is that the rules of politeness bid you to provide me with your name."

"You're right. I apologize." Ben struggled to a sitting position and faced her. "My name is Benjamin Garrison."

"I am pleased to meet you, Benjamin." She set her hands on her knees. "To answer your question, we are not native to Earth. We are from Viridi, a distant planet that cannot be seen by your telescopes. We arrived through the Oculus Gate portal. We were called giants by the natives here because of our physical ... um ... stature relative to yours, but we consider our size to be normal. And that size proved to be a benefit for you. Caligar saved your life by catching you when you fell. He is extremely strong, but you were also aided by an antigravity pull on your body provided by the tower's energy, which would take too long to explain."

"I'm thankful for the rescue." Ben shifted to a cross-legged position, though every muscle ached. "Your use of my language is excellent. How did you learn it so quickly?"

Her smile widened. "We are strangers in this land, so we made language education a priority. I studied American English for many months before I could converse with any ... What is the word? Proficiency?"

"Yes, that word is perfect."

"I am also somewhat familiar with three other Earth languages. As you can imagine, we had no one to practice with except between ourselves. We are able to watch human language teachers in video media on battery operated devices, but that is …" She raised her brow. "Narrow?"

"Narrow is a good word. You might mean *limited*."

"Yes. Limited is better."

Ben smiled. This woman seemed so friendly and open. "Well, trust me, your ability is far beyond most native speakers. You have done very well."

She smiled again. "Thank you. Your words are satisfying. Or maybe gratifying."

"Either word works." Ben looked at the ceiling. "I assume we're underground to be protected from the weather."

"Underground, yes, but more to avoid …" She firmed her lips. "Detection."

"Good point. Humanoids your size are easy to spot. You could probably be seen in satellite images."

She folded her hands tightly in her lap. "I apologize for my ignorance, but what is a satellite image?"

"It's a photograph, a camera picture, taken from the sky in a manmade spacecraft."

"Oh. I see. Such an ability would harm privacy. Yes?"

"Indeed, it would." He gestured upward. "Speaking of the sky, how did you get through the Oculus Gate?"

Winella glanced toward the ceiling. "It is a long story that I prefer not to tell in detail, but I will say that when the Oculus Gate opened, some of us were drawn into our sky."

"That must have been terribly frightening."

"It was." She laughed softly. "I screamed like a child. And our entry into this world was even more … um … troubling. Or perhaps traumatic is a better word."

"How many of you traveled here?"

"Ninety-seven. That is approximately ten percent of our people."

More questions stormed in, but the one demanding to be asked could be delayed no longer. "I was on the tower platform with two people, a young woman and a man about my age. Taller than me.

There was a blinding flash, then they were gone. Do you know what happened to them?"

Winella shook her head. "Caligar is investigating. When he comes, you can ask him. While that incident happened, I was chasing the vile devils the angels called Refectors. If they had taken over the tower network, all would have been lost."

"I assume, then, that the Refectors are not your allies."

"Only in a sense. We had an agreement, of sorts. A fragile one. We both hoped to restore the conduit. Their goal is to bring more of their kind here. Ours is simply to go home. And tonight is our opportunity to leave. Our network will lock this planet in place relative to the Oculus Gate, and that fusion will create a draw that we will need to lift away, much like we did from our own planet."

"But what would this fusion do to Earth? Will it draw anyone else away? Disrupt our orbit?"

"I do not know enough about the mechanism to tell you what might happen to your planet. You would have to ask Caligar about that. I do know, however, that any life forms north of your Arctic Circle will be drawn away unless some kind of anchor hinders them. Our research indicates that no one has lived in the area since the first plague."

Ben nodded. "Every species is gone except for fish and migratory birds. We have a few polar bears in controlled habitats, but they're extinct everywhere else."

"Then at least the drawing away will take no unwilling passengers with us, save for some birds, though this time of year I think most are far south. And the duration will be short, a brief burst, which means that even birds would not come if they were to simply resist the pull by flapping their wings."

"Then it shouldn't be a problem." Ben looked at the tunnel. "When are you expecting your … uh … life mate to return?"

"When he—"

"I am here." A giant walked in from the tunnel, a quiver of arrows on his back and a bow in hand. "I have been close. Listening."

"Caligar!" Winella rose and smiled. "Greetings, my love. Were you able to repair the tower?"

Caligar set the bow on the table, his gaze steady on Ben. "I was."

She clapped her hands. "When do we leave?"

"Soon." Taking a long step, he joined her and rubbed her nose with his in a show of affection. His hair matched hers, a long thick braid as black as coal nearly reaching his waist.

Following Winella's example, Ben climbed slowly to his feet, still stiff from the electrical jolt and the fall.

Caligar raised a hand. "No need to rise, Benjamin, my friend. I know you are suffering pain."

Ben straightened and looked up at the ten-foot-tall man. "You call me friend, but you shot me with an arrow."

"Just as you might slap a toddler's hand to keep him from touching a hot stove. I hoped to correct your behavior."

Ben bristled. "My behavior? I was just trying to—"

"I know what you were trying to do, though you have no idea what you were actually doing. You nearly ruined plans to save both your world and mine, and in the process, you lost your two companions. Your rash actions were appalling."

Ben eyed the huge man once more. Although his words stabbed deeply, his expression gave away no anger, only disappointment. It was time to swallow a bit of pride and go along with him. "Okay, Caligar, I know I'm in the dark. So inform me. But let's start with my friends. Do you know what happened to them?"

Caligar glanced at Winella before focusing again on Ben. "They likely traveled into the newly established conduit. Whether or not they survived, I cannot determine. I am concerned that the lasers might have burned them, but perhaps not fatally. The greater danger lies in their journey. Since the energy streams were knocked out of line, the passage to my world was interrupted. It is possible that they died in an airless void. They wore no suitable protection for that scenario."

Ben shuddered, then steeled himself. "Okay. How about when you transported to Earth? You had no protection, right?"

"Correct, but the process took only seconds. Our landing was painful, but Winella and I survived without much injury."

Winella pointed toward his foot. "You broke a bone."

"A metatarsal. It was minor. Others suffered more. Several perished."

"How many survived?" Ben asked. "And where are they now?"

"Eighty-nine. At one time, we were all here, but living together was not feasible, so we divided ourselves into tribes, and three tribes traveled to the other tower locations. Winella and I stayed here along with twenty others. You probably saw them battling the invading humans. Even as we speak, they are still defending the tower or chasing the invaders away, though one of our kind perished in the fight."

"Do you know if the Refectors came through the conduit? Are they here now?"

"They came. And they have possessed many of the invading humans. Unfortunately, it seems that someone has guided the humans into the region north of the Arctic Circle. I turned the conduit's draw to a lower setting until we can chase them south again."

"Because you don't want the possessed humans flying to your world."

"Correct. At the moment, the tower network is maintaining a lock with Earth, but the draw is not powerful enough to pull a human at the current setting."

Ben imagined the humans swarming into the liftoff zone. Why would they go there, apparently guided by the Refectors? In the mental image, the souls of the humans left the bodies, purged by the vaccine.

"Caligar, do you know what would happen to expelled human souls in the area north of the Circle at the tower's current energy setting?"

"That is beyond my knowledge." He narrowed his eyes. "What is your suspicion?"

"More like a wild hunch. The Refectors are up to something sinister. Based on the information I've put together, the people were likely injected with a toxic vaccine right before the buses arrived, and their souls are being purged, if not right now, then soon."

"And you're wondering if the souls could be drawn through the Oculus Gate."

Ben nodded. "In the recent past, some kind of evil force created a blockade that kept souls from entering heaven, and instead they went into the Oculus Gate, or maybe somewhere beyond it. I'm not sure. But one of my team members destroyed that place and released the imprisoned souls. Anyway, if something is trying to collect souls, this might be another opportunity."

"An interesting theory." Caligar stroked his chin. "I have a theory of my own, but I will not speak it yet."

"Why not?"

"Because it is incomplete and might generate dangerously inaccurate speculations."

"From you or me?"

"From you."

"Which means you don't trust me."

"When you earn my trust, you will receive it. At this time, I see you as a well-meaning though impetuous human who tried to destroy a tower when he didn't know its purpose. I assume you conjured a purpose from your ill-informed speculations, and I hope to avoid a similar disastrous result."

Ben balled a fist but kept his voice under control. "Protecting Earth from an invading alien force was not impetuous. It was the right thing to do."

"You think so, but you had no idea that my people were using that tower for another purpose. Trying to destroy something that you are ill-informed about is, indeed, impetuous."

Ben thumped his chest with a finger. "This is *my* planet, not yours. Whatever your purpose is, it's secondary to my purpose—to save Earth from invaders."

When Caligar opened his mouth to speak again, Winella let out a shushing sound. "Arguing is not … um … profitable for anyone. We should focus on what we agree upon and work toward those ends."

"And what do we agree upon?" Caligar asked.

"I assume that we all want to stop the Refectors and for us to go home. And compassion demands that we help Benjamin find his missing friends."

Caligar sighed. "You are a wise woman. We and Benjamin do share similar goals and enemies. And I must admit that he has revealed a potential scheme on the part of the Refectors that I had not considered. We can and should work as a team."

Ben bowed his head briefly, hoping to copy the giants' manner of speaking. "Thank you, Caligar. And I apologize for assuming too much. I knew nothing about you and your people, and I acted in haste. I hope we can forge a strong and effective alliance to accomplish the lifesaving goals we both cherish."

Caligar's expression stayed serious, though his tone softened. "Well stated. Perhaps I misjudged you."

"I assume," Winella said, "that the highest priority is to expel the Refectors from the region north of the Arctic Circle. If they are depositing souls in the conduit, their eternal lives are in jeopardy."

Caligar looked upward. "I agree. We have no idea how to search for Benjamin's colleagues, so that quest has to be subordinate."

Ben resisted the urge to let his shoulders sag. He couldn't argue with Caligar's reasoning. For now, he had to put Leo and Iona on the back burner. "You're right. Maybe we'll learn more about my friends along the way, but I have another question. Winella said to ask you about the tower network's effect on Earth. Might it cause problems? Quakes? Orbit issues?"

"There would be no orbit anomalies, but earthquakes are likely if the network is operating to its capacity, which is another reason I reduced the power to a safe level. Any use to transport people must be quick and guided by an on-ground expert who knows exactly when to turn the mechanism off."

"And if full power continues, how bad could the quakes get?"

"A catastrophic level is possible, but we will be sure to avoid such an event."

"That's not very comforting."

"It should be comforting to know that when I make an attempt to go to my world, Winella will be my ground-based support, and I would not want anything to happen to her." Caligar scanned Ben from head to toe. "You appear healed enough. Are you willing to join me on my quest?"

"More than willing. I'm anxious to go."

"Good." Caligar turned toward Winella. "Collect our needs while Benjamin and I secure the tower. We will meet you at the boundary of the danger zone."

Chapter Nine

Trudy opened her eyes. She sat on an oversized wooden chair, her wrists and ankles bound and her head leaning against Jack as he sat on a chair next to hers. Ropes wrapped around their waists, fastening them to the thick wooden frames. Every limb ached, and a spot on the back of her head throbbed. Somehow they had survived the fall from the tower, maybe by landing in a snowdrift or on a corpse. Either way, this new situation might be even worse. They had apparently jumped from the proverbial frying pan into the fire.

With stone all around, they seemed to be in a cave, maybe twenty feet square and ten feet high. Embedded in a wall alcove, a fire crackled under a huge black pot. Steamy vapor rose into a flue, and a savory aroma wafted by in the otherwise vacant room.

Trudy nudged Jack with an elbow and whispered, "Jack! Wake up!"

"Huh?" His head wobbly, Jack opened his eyes. "Sis?"

"Yeah. We're in hot water. Maybe literally in a few minutes." She nodded toward the pot. "Looks like soup's on."

Jack blinked as if trying to focus. "You think we're the main course?"

"Or stew meat. The way those giants were chopping people up, they looked like experienced butchers."

"Then why didn't they chop us up?"

"No idea." Trudy eyed the pot. The flames dwindled. Someone would probably come soon to feed the fire. "Whatever the reason, I don't think we have much time to escape."

"Have you tested the ropes?"

"Not yet."

Jack thrashed and jerked his hands and feet. The rope around his waist loosened a bit, but the others held fast. "Nope. I think that's as much slack as I'm going to get."

Trudy glanced at her belt, then at Jack's. Their weapons were gone. Someone had even taken his watch. "Do you still have that switchblade in your boot?"

"Maybe." He closed his eyes and concentrated. "Yeah. I feel the sheath. It's still there."

"No way you can reach it, though."

"Right, but maybe you can. I've got a little slack now." He twisted and hoisted his legs up to her lap, his upper body bending away and his feet near her hands as he grunted, "On the right side of the right boot. Can you reach it?"

"Maybe." She inched her fingers inside the boot, but the gap was too small.

"Hurry. The rope's squeezing my guts out."

"Suck it up, Jack. I'm trying, but your laces are too tight." She leaned forward, the rope pressing against her stomach, and strained toward the boot, her lips within an inch of the closest lace but still too far. "Can you nudge it closer?"

"I'll try."

Grunting, he shoved his legs. The boot smacked her in the face and began easing back down. She chomped on the lace with her teeth and held on. As the boot edged away, the laces loosened. She grabbed the boot with her hands and pushed her fingers deeper until two fingertips touched the sheath. "I feel it."

"The sheath's attached. You'll have to unsnap it and pull the knife out."

Trudy scowled. "Wouldn't want to make it easy, would you?"

"Now who needs to suck it up?"

Biting her lip, she pushed her index finger under the snap and popped it off. "Got it."

"The knife?"

"No, the snap. Hang on." She pinched the end of the knife with her middle and index fingers and slid it closer to her palm inch by inch. "Almost. Just another—"

Something thudded, and footsteps thumped toward them.

Jack thrust his legs off Trudy's lap. The knife flew from the boot and landed on her knees.

A giant tromped in from a side passage, wielding an axe and carrying a bundle of wood. A long braid of dark hair draped his back, swaying as he walked, his head nearly touching the ceiling.

Trudy pulled her knees apart, let the knife drop to the seat, and quickly closed the gap.

Wearing buckskin from neck to ankles that made him look like he had stepped off the set of an old western film, he gazed at them. "You're awake," he said in Russian. "Good." He dropped the wood next to the pot's alcove and tromped closer, his brow deeply creased as he continued speaking in Russian. "Ropes loose. Why?"

"What did you expect?" Jack asked, also speaking Russian. "For us to just sit here like good little prisoners?"

"Quiet!" The giant slapped Jack with the back of his hand. Jack's head jerked to the side, and the chair teetered with the blow.

Trudy cringed. That had to hurt.

The giant loosened the knots and retied them. The rope around Trudy's waist tightened, pushing her breath out. Resisting the urge to grunt, she bit her lip again. She glanced at Jack. Although he glared at the giant defiantly, his chin trembled, dripping blood that drained from a cut in his swollen, bruised cheek.

The giant looked them both over, then opened their hands. Satisfied with the search, he returned to the alcove, crouched, and pushed a few pieces of kindling into the fire, stirring the embers to ignite the new wood.

While he worked, Trudy pushed her hands between her knees, pinched the switchblade, and drew it into her hand. The moment she covered the knife with her forearm and repositioned her hands in her lap, the giant rose and walked toward them.

He halted a step away and crouched, eyeing them as he stroked his short salt-and-pepper beard. "You have souls. How?"

Jack spoke in an even tone. "Do you mean how did our souls survive the vaccination?"

The giant nodded.

"How do you know we've been vaccinated?"

"Blood test."

"Ah. We both have antibodies for the contagion."

He nodded again.

"I see. And I assume you have an AngelScan to see our souls."

The giant withdrew a disc from his pants pocket, then slid it back in. He gestured toward Trudy. "Her soul weak. Injured. Yours strong. Healthy. Why?"

"It's a long story."

The giant lifted his hand as if ready to strike again.

Jack sucked in a breath and spoke quickly. "But if you want to hear it, I'll be glad to tell it."

The giant slowly lowered his hand. "No matter. Changes nothing. More vaccine might not work. Did not work before."

"Why do you want to purge our souls?" Trudy asked.

He gestured with a hand toward the pot. "Eating humans with souls not allowed. Get cursed."

Trudy furrowed her brow. "Is that a commandment? Like from some kind of code of ethics where you come from?"

The giant grunted. "Stupid code. Human meat tastes good. Soul or no soul."

"So," Trudy said, "let me get this straight. If we didn't have a soul, you would be allowed to eat us? According to your code, I mean."

"Yes. Eat rabbits. Eat deer. Eat cattle. Any animal with no soul."

"Okay. Great. But now you know we have souls. You won't eat us. You can let us go."

The giant smiled, revealing yellowed teeth. "I do not obey code. Curious about your souls."

"But you'll be cursed, like your code says."

"Already cursed. Caligar was a fool to try to change. Now stuck on this planet."

"Caligar? Who is he?"

The giant lifted his chin and half closed his eyes as if mimicking snobbery. "Our leader."

Trudy eyed his face. Apparently, these giants had studied humankind for quite a while to be able to copy that expression so well. "What did Caligar do?"

"You no need to know." He walked toward the fire. "Dead soon." He picked up a poker and stirred the embers. The flames grew and licked against the pot's sides.

Trudy flicked the switchblade open and began sawing the rope binding her wrists. The sharp blade cut the tough fibers pretty well, but it would take several more seconds to slice all the way through, if only the giant would stay turned toward the fire long enough.

Jack whispered in English, "I have an idea. Hide the knife for a second."

Trudy squeezed the blade back in place and covered the knife.

"Hey," Jack said, switching back to Russian. "What was that loud noise?"

The giant turned toward them. "What noise?"

"That bang. Like a motor backfiring."

"Yeah," Trudy said. "It was loud. I guess the crackling noise masked it. You were so close to the fire."

The giant looked toward a door on the left-hand wall. "No motors here."

"Uh, right." Jack said. "Then don't check it. Really. It's probably nothing."

"I check." After grabbing his axe, the giant trudged toward the door, opened it, and slammed it behind him.

Trudy flicked the knife open and sawed the rope again. Fibers snapped, several at a time.

"Faster," Jack hissed.

"Hush. You're not helping." The final threads popped. Trudy jerked her hand free and sawed into the rope around her waist. "Just a few more seconds."

"I hear footsteps."

"One more second." The rope gave way, freeing her body. "Now my feet." Staying seated, she bent over and began cutting the rope around her ankles, constantly checking for the giant.

The door banged open. The giant stomped in, the axe against his shoulder. "I saw nothing." He looked at Trudy, blinked twice, then charged toward her, his axe ready to strike.

She cut through the final thread, tossed the knife to Jack, and rolled under the swinging axe, crashing into the giant's legs. As he lurched forward, she thrust herself upward and lifted his body. He face-planted on the floor in a splash of blood.

Trudy rushed over to Jack. "Give me the knife."

"No." He sawed with the serrated edge through his wrist rope and broke free. "Get the axe. I got this."

She hustled to the giant where he lay writhing and groaning, the axe still in his grip. She grabbed the handle with both hands, but he held on tightly, still groaning.

She stomped on his wrist and pulled again. The axe jerked free and sent her backpedaling. She collided with a wall and banged her head. The jolt sent a shockwave through her spine. The axe fell to the floor with a clatter, and she slid down the wall to her rear. Black spots flooding her vision, she blinked and wagged her head, trying to stay conscious.

The giant pushed himself up and climbed to his feet. His legs wobbled as he shook his head.

"Hang on," Jack said. "Got the waist rope cut. Feet next."

Trudy groped for the axe. When her fingers came across the handle, she grabbed it. The giant lunged toward her. She shifted to roll out of the way, but he grabbed her by the hair and lifted her off the floor.

She swung the axe against his ribs, embedding the blade. The giant roared and staggered back, dropping Trudy. When she fell to her feet, her knees buckled, and her legs gave way. She crumbled to a sitting position, every limb paralyzed.

The giant jerked the axe from his ribs and raised it, ready to swing at Trudy. Jack leaped from his seat, flew at him, and slammed into the huge body. They crashed to the floor, Jack on top of the giant.

Trudy blinked. The room spun. In seconds she would black out for sure. It looked like Jack was pounding on the giant's head, but blackness and fog veiled everything.

Jack's face appeared. "Let's go! Hurry!" He slid his arms around her, hoisted her to her feet, and propped a shoulder under her arm as he half walked and half dragged her into a dark tunnel.

To the rear, liquid splashed. Metal clanged. The giant roared and cursed. Trudy's numb legs moved in a stepping cadence, though they barely touched the ground.

Jack's voice filtered into her ear, seeming far away. "I've got you, Sis. Just keep walking. That's it. Another step. One more."

Dim light appeared ahead. Cold air breezed by. "We're almost there. Hang on."

The giant's roar echoed in the tunnel, drawing closer.

"Is he ..." Trudy swallowed. "Is he chasing us?"

"Yeah. Kind of. But don't worry about him. It's the other giants we have to worry about."

Colder air whipped against her face, snapping her awake. Ahead, a cave opening loomed, an arch about twenty feet wide and just as high with a lantern embedded in the wall at each side. Jack halted at the cave entrance and scanned her. "You're looking better. Can you run?"

She nodded. "I think so."

"Good." He flicked a bloody knife closed and slid it into his pocket. "Our chef won't find us with his eyeballs cut out, but, like I said, I'm worried about the other giants."

"What other giants?"

"This cave is like a beehive. Little dens everywhere. If they hear our giant caterwauling, we'll be in a stewpot before you know it."

She looked back into the tunnel. "Are you sure they're in there?"

"Not in the slightest. Haven't heard a sound except that oaf spilling his stewpot. They might be napping after chowing down on the people they chopped up."

Trudy inhaled deeply, drawing in the cold air and clearing her brain further. Outside, snow and ice covered the small area within range of the lantern light. Yet, a brighter light shone clearly, maybe half a mile away. Wiggling streams of bluish-green light radiated from it in opposite directions. "Jack, the tower's not far. We could go there. See what's going on."

"Not right away. We'll find a place to hide and try to call Kat, get oriented. Then we'll decide the next step."

The giant's roar drew closer. He shouted and raged in an odd language. Another voice joined his, then two more.

"That's our cue." Jack grasped Trudy's arm. "Ready?"

"Ready."

An arrow zipped past Jack's ear. "Run!"

Chapter Ten

Iona plunged, Leo at her side, both spread-eagle. "Leo!" she screamed. "What do we do?"

"First ..." He took in a deep breath. "First, settle down. Like I'm trying to do right now. We won't survive if we panic. Something strange is going on. We're not falling as fast as we *should* be."

Iona scanned the ground below. Although it was impossible to guess the distance, it didn't seem to be closing in quickly. "Okay. Okay." She took a deep breath of her own. The dense, wet air smelled strange, like a blend of rotten eggs and saltwater. "I'm settling. Really." A shudder shook her body from her boots to her helmet, and her cross flew out of her shirt and batted her face. She pulled it down and stuffed it back into place. "Trying to settle, anyway."

"Good." He pointed downward, slightly to the side. "See that greenish blob?"

Iona looked in that direction. Everything appeared green, as if plants covered the entire surface. "Which greenish blob?"

He thrust his finger again. "The blob that's greener than the other blobs."

She spotted the area. "Yeah. What about it?"

"It reeks of sulfur. It's either water or a volcanic pool."

"So?"

"If it's water, we might survive if we fall into it. A pillow for our plunge."

"And if it's volcanic?"

"We'll boil alive."

Iona gulped. "Boil alive!"

"Like lobsters. But we certainly won't survive if we hit the ground at this velocity."

"You're the one who said we're not falling that fast."

"Not as fast as we should be. I've done plenty of parachute jumps in my time, and we're falling too fast. Unless we hit that pond, we're done for."

"Okay. How do we hit it?"

"Angle your body. Do what I do." Leo shifted his arms and glided toward the green blob.

Iona copied the move and fell in line behind him. When they were directly over the water, Leo straightened and grabbed Iona's wrist, flattening her arc. "At the last second, we'll pivot to feet first, then bend our knees and roll into the impact. Close your eyes and cover your ears. Understand?"

Iona nodded, tight lipped, trying not to shiver. The crazy plunge felt like a nightmare, but somehow Leo's calmness chased the terror away. She could do this.

"I'm guessing ten seconds to the pivot," Leo said. "Nine. Eight. Seven. Okay, maybe ten now. Nine. Eight. Seven. Six. No. Wait. Maybe twenty."

"Stop the countdown! I'll pivot when I'm ready!"

Leo shrugged. "All right. Have it your way."

As the greenery drew closer, Iona practiced turning her body. The air's thickness made shifting pretty easy. Directly below, their target took shape—liquid of some kind, maybe water covered with algae. Now it really was less than ten seconds to impact.

She called out, "I'm pivoting."

"Agreed." Leo began his turn. "See you in the soup."

Iona shifted to vertical, covered her ears with her hands, and closed her eyes. The moment her feet struck, she bent her knees and rolled into a warm, syrupy mass with a dull sploosh. As she submerged, the liquid slapped her helmet, making it and her head jerk to the side. Her ears popped, and the concussive blow throbbed in her skull.

Something grabbed her arm and hoisted her upward. Her face now above the surface, she blinked away the greenish goop. Leo stood next to her in chest-deep liquid, his hair matted. Green slime coated his face.

He spat a stream of goop. "Tastes like cabbage."

Iona licked slime from her lips. It really did taste like cabbage, maybe with a hint of carrots. "It's like this pond is a big bowl of soup."

"Warm enough to be soup." Leo inhaled deeply. "Yep. Cabbage smells like rotten eggs when it's cooked. Hydrogen sulfide. And cabbage soup is one of my favorites. I should have identified it before we splashed in."

"But if this is soup ..." Iona scanned the area. Tall evergreens with low, bushy branches surrounded the pond with a bench at the edge, much like an oversized park bench with varnished wooden slats for a seat and wrought iron arms. Her imagination drew a giant man sitting on the bench and stirring the soup with a huge wooden spoon.

She shuddered. "Let's get to shore. Remember, we saw giants chopping people into bite-sized bits before we started falling."

"I see your point." Still holding Iona's arm to keep her face above the surface, Leo waded through the mass. When they reached a shallower area, he lowered her to her feet. Under her shoes, the pond's bed felt hard, like stone instead of dirt.

An odd noise buzzed in her ear. A stinging sensation followed. She pinched her earbud and pulled it out. Blackened and covered with the slime, it was obviously ruined. "Earbud's dead." She dropped it into the soup. "Yours?"

Leo withdrew his bud and looked it over. "Without a doubt." He let it join Iona's in the green mire.

After trudging to the shore and shaking off as much of the soup as they could, Leo set his hands on the bench and vaulted himself to the seat. His legs dangled, nearly touching the ground.

"How tall are you?" Iona asked as she unstrapped her helmet. "More than six feet, right?"

"Six feet plus four inches. Or one hundred-ninety-three-centimeters, if you prefer a measurement in that system. Why?"

"Two reasons. One, judging by the fact that your feet don't reach the ground, the giants are quite a bit taller than you. Two, since they're so big and they want to eat us …" She leaned close and whisper-shouted, "Why the blazes aren't we running away like jackrabbits?"

"It's a trade-off. If we scamper into the wilderness, we might run into greater dangers or even into the cabbage soup chef. Here, we can rest, look, listen, take inventory, and get a sense of the area. At the proper time, we will run if we must." He reached a hand down. "Better view from here, Short Stuff."

Iona brushed soup from her helmet as she scowled. "That is definitely not an approved name."

"All right. How about Mini Maid?"

"Worse." She batted his hand to the side, climbed onto the bench, and sat next to him, her clothes squishing with every move. From this vantage point, the pond looked more like a bowl than ever, almost perfectly round and bubbling near the center.

Leo pointed toward the bubbles. "Geothermal heat source. Good thing we didn't splash down there."

"Right. Instant stewed meat." Iona set her helmet at her side and withdrew the gun from the vest holster. Without a thorough cleaning, it probably wouldn't shoot.. "Speaking of taking inventory, I still have my belt and this worthless Toger handgun. But no other weapons except a knife in a sheath." She shoved the Toger back to its holster. "You?"

"I also have a knife, but no guns. And I have a few items in my cloak pockets. I'll check later to see if they're too gunked up to function."

"Yeah. The soup's already drying and stiffening." She scanned the trees for any sign of the cook. "Where do you think we are?"

"Well, we're not in Alaska anymore. That's certain. Since they were trying to reestablish the conduit to the Oculus Gate, I have to think that we went through it."

"That means we got transported to the giant's world. Maybe it's Viridi, like we saw on the map."

"That's my guess. Some kind of traction mechanism snatched us off that tower, zapped us into this atmosphere, and kept us from falling too fast. You know, pulling back on us somehow."

Iona looked up. The sky appeared darker blue here, and the Oculus Gate spanned half the expanse, brighter and closer. "I guess the traction mechanism isn't strong enough to pull us back."

"Apparently not."

"So we're stuck here."

"Seems that way."

Iona put her helmet back on and fastened the strap. "Not exactly Mr. Optimistic, are you?"

"Mr. Realistic. Unless you have a series of towers with a Radiant at each, I'm assuming we're here for the duration."

She narrowed her eyes. "The duration?"

"Until we die or until someone on Earth figures out how to pluck us back through the Gate."

She pulled off a boot and dumped soup from it to the ground. "Then we're definitely on Viridi till we die." She put it back on and slipped off the other. "No one even knows we're here to pluck."

"Ben has to know we disappeared. He'll put it all together. That's certain."

"If he's alive, you mean." She put the second boot back on and tied it. "That's far from certain."

"True, which means we'll have to figure out a way to send a signal ..." Leo sniffed. "I smell a giant."

A rustling sound came from the forest in a walking cadence.

Iona whispered, "And I hear one."

"Until we know whether or not the newcomer is friendly, it's better to hide than to make like a jackrabbit." Leo dropped to the ground and pulled Iona down with him. They ducked under the bench seat, Iona's back against Leo's chest as they peeked out.

"Leo," Iona whispered. "We dripped soup on the bench seat."

"Too late to worry about that. He's almost here. If you want to talk, switch to that code you taught me."

A giant man walked to the edge of the soup bowl, cradling a drone-like device in his palms. Shaped like a storybook flying saucer, the drone lifted from his hands and flew to the center of the bowl. As it lowered toward the surface, an egg-beater-like prong descended from its belly into the soup. With a loud whir, the prong spun, churning the soup.

The drone moved around in widening circles. When it finished stirring the entire pot, it flew back to the giant and let some of the soup drip into his hands.

He licked his palms, smiled at the drone, and spoke in a language that sounded like a blend of bestial grunts and bird chirps. The drone pulled the prong back into its body and flew into the forest.

Iona tapped a finger on the ground, spelling a message in code. *Call to dinner?*

Leo nodded and tapped a message of his own. *Sneak away. I will distract.*

No, Iona tapped. *Let me—*

Leo covered her hand with his, his grip firm as he tapped with his free hand. *Trust me.*

Iona resisted the urge to roll her eyes, then nodded.

She crawled from underneath the bench and stayed low while Leo rolled out, straightened, and walked toward the giant. She skulked away while watching Leo, her line of travel perpendicular to his. Only a few steps more, and she could get to a tree and watch the action from a good hiding place, though it felt cowardly to do so. Still, Leo had a lot of experience. Maybe he knew what he was doing and going solo was his best shot at pulling off his secret, trust-me plan.

Leo passed to the side of the giant and kept walking at a casual pace toward the forest, his hands in his cloak pockets.

The giant cocked his head and followed, saying nothing. Iona ducked behind a tree and peeked around it. Leo passed the tree line about fifty feet away and walked deeper into the forest and out of sight. The giant continued following and also disappeared from view.

Seconds later, shouts and grunts erupted from that direction, then all fell silent except for the bubbling in the soup cauldron.

Iona bit her lip. The silence was maddening. Regardless of Leo's orders to trust him, it was time to investigate.

Just as she extended a leg to step out of hiding, Leo burst into the clearing and ran toward her, his cloak flapping. He grabbed her arm and pulled her deeper into the woods. After passing several trees, he stopped behind one of the biggest and pressed his back against the trunk, breathing heavily.

"The giant grabbed my arm," he whispered, "but I jerked away and faced him. You know, trying to read his intent."

When Leo paused to take a deep breath, Iona lifted her brow. "And what was his intent?"

"To put me on a barbecue spit. He was literally drooling."

"A cannibal?"

"Technically, no. I don't think he's human." Leo peered around the tree, his voice still low. "Anyway, earlier, while I was walking into the forest and baiting him to follow, I was secretly opening the tranquilizer cartridges in my pocket. After I gauged his intent, he lunged at me. I dodged him and jabbed a tranq cartridge into his buttocks. That just made him mad. When he came at me again, I dropped to my back and hit him in the calf with another tranq. It ended up taking all four cartridges to put him down."

"No wonder. He's huge. But why did it take you so long to get back?"

"When I hit him with the fourth one, the big oaf fell on top of me. Obviously, I couldn't call for help. All I could do was squirm my way out from under him as quietly as possible. I thought about using a smoke bomb to hide my tracks, but since I didn't see any other giants, I decided against it."

Iona brushed a piece of cabbage from his cloak, one of many clinging to the soup residue. "I guess he saw you as a breadstick, dipped and ready to eat."

"Which means …" He plucked a fragment from her hair and tossed it away. "If they have any sense of smell at all, we won't be able to hide unless we find a place to wash."

"Can you locate water with that nose of yours?"

"Not likely. Pure water has no odor, but an artesian source has a strong one. Unfortunately, it's the same odor as cooked cabbage. Difficult to track when I reek of it myself." He inhaled through his nose. "Got a good whiff of that giant, though, and the others are coming."

Iona scanned the forest—nothing but huge evergreens in all directions. "Which way?"

When Leo opened his mouth to answer, a shout burst from the soup cauldron area, deep and masculine. Then chirps erupted, as if a hundred birds had descended. He looked toward the sound. "I think they found their chef."

"Then we have to scat."

Something rustled in the trees nearby. Iona spun toward the sound. A boy dressed in animal skins dropped from a limb and waved with both hands. "Come," he said, his voice urgent. "Come. Or die."

Chapter Eleven

"Leo," Iona whispered. "Look."

When Leo turned, his eyes widened. "He's human size. Most likely seven or eight years old."

The boy waved more frantically, now with both hands.

"I say we follow him," Iona said.

"Agreed."

The moment Leo and Iona started in the boy's direction, he took off in a dash, forcing them to accelerate as he weaved through the trees, hopped over roots, and leaped across gullies.

Along the way, something moved in the underbrush to their left, then ducked out of sight. Iona touched Leo's arm. "Did you see that?"

"I did. Human shaped. Maybe another small one like the boy we're following. We'll keep watching."

"Yeah." Battling fatigue, she forced herself to breathe evenly. "No telling what's in these woods."

After a few minutes, the boy slowed to a halt and turned toward them, relief in his eyes as he heaved a sigh.

Iona stopped within arm's reach and pointed at herself. "Iona." She shifted the finger to Leo. "Leo." Then she pointed at the boy and lifted her brow.

He touched himself on the chest. "Bazrah."

"Bazrah," Leo and Iona echoed at the same time.

Bazrah walked away, waving a beckoning hand.

Leo and Iona followed. "At least now we know his name," Iona said.

"It's a start. I get the impression that he's smarter than the soup chef. We'll learn more soon enough."

"Speaking of soup chef, do you smell the giants?"

"Just the drool on my cloak. I think we're safe for now."

Soon, the sound of tumbling water filtered through the trees. Bazrah led them to a clearing where a waterfall dropped from a rocky ledge about twenty feet above. The cascade splashed into a shallow pool and ran down a creek bed that meandered through the forest and out of sight.

He pointed at the waterfall and rubbed his arm, as if washing it.

Leo nodded. "I think he doesn't want our odor to lead the giants to his people."

"Hundred percent agree." Iona took her helmet off, walked into the knee-deep pool, and stopped under the waterfall. The heavy torrent pounded her head with plenty of force to shed the residue from her hair, like getting a tub of never-ending bathwater dumped on her. Although it was warm enough to be comfortable, something stung her skin. "It's kind of caustic."

"Acidic?" Leo asked.

"Maybe, but it's not too bad. Since Bazrah led us here to wash, it's probably safe."

"Works for me." Leo waded into the pool, stood under the falls, and used his hands to strip the soup from his sleeves. "It comes right off."

Iona shifted and let the water pour down her shoulders and back. "Good thing. We were walking odor factories."

Leo shed his cloak and moved it under the flow. As he scrubbed the sleeves, he gazed into the forest. "Speaking of odors, I'm trying to keep my nose tuned for the giants, but the aroma of minerals in this stream is strong. Even if we strip away the stench, anyone could follow our trail of broken underbrush and dripping soup."

"Good point." She cleaned the Toger thoroughly and slid it into its holster. It badly needed oiling, but that would have to wait. After rinsing her helmet, Iona stepped out of the falls and waded toward the edge of the pool, her hair and clothes dripping. "Whatever added that stinging sensation helped. It was like a scrub brush. My skin's red, but it's clean."

Leo joined her. "Agreed." As he twisted his cloak, water pelted the stony creekbank. "It reminded me of a lye soap bath."

Iona tucked her helmet under an arm as she wrung out her scarf and tied it in place. "Ready."

Bazrah waved a hand. "Come now." He broke into a jog, following the creek.

Leo and Iona ran abreast, their shoes squishing and clothes dripping. After a minute or so, Bazrah halted and raised a hand. Leo and Iona stopped behind him. He stared straight ahead, the creek to his right, flowing on through the forest.

"Strange," Leo whispered, pointing. "Past where he's standing, the water's flowing in the opposite direction, coming toward us, but where the two flows meet, there's no splash, like the water goes underground."

Iona studied the scene. The trees ahead appeared to be mirror images of ones around them. "I think it's a reflection."

"Then why don't we see ourselves?"

"Good question."

The reflection shimmered. Bazrah pushed a hand into it, making his forearm disappear. When he withdrew it, he looked back. "Come. Slow." He walked through the reflection and disappeared.

Iona felt her mouth drop open. "What on earth?"

"Far from Earth, I'm afraid." Leo put his cloak on and marched forward. "When on a strange planet, do what the strange planet's natives do." He stepped through the reflection and vanished.

After taking a deep breath, Iona steeled herself and followed. As she passed through the reflective boundary, a slight electrostatic buzz ran along her skin, raising goosebumps.

A strong hand grasped her wrist. "Don't take another step," Leo said.

She opened her eyes. Three feet away, the stream plunged over a precipice and into a chasm. Bazrah hung feet first over the ledge,

Bryan Davis

holding to a knotted rope ladder that led downward. With the agility of a monkey, he climbed out of view.

Leo stepped to the edge of the precipice and looked down. "My guess is about a thousand feet."

Iona joined him. Below, the water fell into a narrow canyon, and three huge, black birds flew lazily over the canyon floor. "Vultures?"

"Most likely. If a giant fell here, he would feed a good lot of them."

"Then this trap must have worked recently," Iona said. "The scavengers wouldn't be down there for no reason."

"Come," Bazrah called. He stood on a ledge about fifty feet below, the end of the ladder dangling next to him.

Leo lowered himself to his hands and knees and grasped the ladder, his feet close to the ledge. "Good thing I'm not scared of heights."

"Neither am I." Iona gave the ladder a skeptical stare. "But we're both a lot bigger than Bazrah. That rope isn't very thick."

"It's probably thin to keep giants from using it. And you're no giant, so don't be such a worrywart."

Iona put her helmet on and strapped it with a hard tug. "That's *not* an approved name."

"It's your name until you prove me wrong. But I'm going first. If I make it, you'll make it." Leo climbed down and out of sight.

Iona leaned over the chasm. Although the ladder shook and sagged, it held firm. When Leo joined Bazrah on the ledge, she took a deep breath and copied Leo's moves, taking care to avoid looking down as she descended. While it was true that she had no fear of heights, at least mostly true, it never helped to stare at a potential crash zone.

Soon, her line of sight drew even with Leo's. Beyond him lay a dark cave carved into the cliff face. Trying to appear confident, she leaped off the ladder, landed next to Leo, and brushed her hands together. "Not a problem."

Leo snorted. "Now you're a pretentious princess."

107

"Am not." She set a fist on her hip and glared at him, though a cabbage fragment on his chin forced a grin. She plucked the fragment and tossed it over the ledge. "Okay, Cabbage King, so you busted me. No more pretending. Just don't call me any more stupid names."

"Deal." They shook hands. "No stupid names."

As she drew her hand back, she narrowed one eye. "You don't fool me. I get to decide which names are stupid. Not you."

Leo smiled. "We'll see about that, Your Highness."

She pointed at him. "That one's safe. Keep it up."

Bazrah blinked at them as if mystified. Then he shrugged and walked into the cave.

Leo followed with Iona trailing. As their surroundings dimmed in the low, narrow tunnel, he scraped the top of his head on the ceiling, forcing him to bend forward. "Giants would have a hard time getting through here, I think."

"True. But that doesn't mean it's not a trap. Smell anything strange?"

"Lamp oil."

Iona sniffed the air. The odor of fuel was getting pretty sharp. "Giants and tall Earthlings would have a hard time, but short people like me don't have a problem."

"I'm not touching that line. We made a deal. Stop baiting me."

"Not part of the deal. I am fishing all I want. But you can borrow my helmet if you need it."

"Nope. I would never stoop that low."

"Oh, very funny."

Ahead, a flickering glow appeared. A lantern protruded from a side wall at Bazrah's eye level, its wick alive with a low flame. He picked up a lantern from the floor and lit its wick from the burning one, then continued walking deeper into the cave.

As Leo and Iona followed, the path sloped downward at a sharp angle, forcing them to lean back to keep from slipping or tumbling.

After about a hundred paces, the floor leveled and the ceiling rose, allowing Leo to walk upright.

Soon, they came upon another burning lamp embedded in the wall. Bazrah blew his lantern out, set it on the floor, and walked on. Ahead, a brighter light shone through a hole in the ceiling, painting an aura on the floor and illuminating the tunnel's dead end.

Bazrah stopped at the center of the circle and looked up, blinking. He called out several nasally syllables that sounded like gibberish.

A rope ladder dropped, the bottom rung slapping the floor. Bazrah climbed it and zipped through the hole and out of sight.

Leo walked into the circle and looked up, squinting. "Can't see anything. Too bright."

"I'll go first this time." Iona grasped the ladder and began climbing, the light above making her blink. As she ascended, her eyes adjusted. The surrounding wall, a cylinder about four feet in diameter, appeared to be plaster instead of rock, as if she were climbing through the inside of a manufactured silo.

About thirty rungs up, the cylinder ended at an opening to a chamber. The light, no longer as bright, allowed a view of the Oculus Gate, though much bigger and brighter, as if something had magnified it.

When she reached the top, she set her arms over the lip of the exit hole, hoisted herself into the chamber, and sat on its wood-planked floor, her legs still in the hole. A window of curved glass capped the room, like a transparent observatory dome. A telescope-like tube stood on a tripod, pointing directly toward the Gate, and an empty stool sat nearby, apparently a seat for whoever wanted to look through the tube.

"Are you all right up there?" Leo called.

She scanned the rest of the room. Bazrah was nowhere in sight. A door stood open at the end opposite the telescope, most likely his exit.

"Yeah." Iona withdrew her legs from the hole and stood. "I'm fine. Bazrah left, though. I'm going to look for him."

Leo's voice drew closer. "Maybe you should wait for me. 'United we stand' and all that rot."

"Like when you took off to drug that giant?"

He grunted as he spoke. "We didn't have a choice then. Now we do."

"You told me to trust you. Isn't that a two-way street? Or can't you trust a female?"

"Cut the feminist crap." His head rose above floor level, his wet mane glistening in the brightness. "All labels aside, I'm your number-one fan." He rested his arms on the floor, most of his body still out of sight as he gazed at her with a puppy-dog expression. "I believe in you, Iona."

She rolled her eyes. "Now who's slinging crap?"

"Me. With a big shovel." Grunting again, he tried to climb up, but his foot slipped on a rung, making his chin hit the floor.

Iona bent and extended a hand. "Come on, Number One Fan."

He interlocked wrists with her. She set her feet and leaned back as she pulled, her wet boots sliding as he climbed into the room. When he stood upright, his clothes dripping and adding to Iona's puddle, a new voice entered.

"Welcome, strangers."

Iona spun in the puddle. A gray-haired woman wearing a white apron over a blue house dress stood at the doorway, a hand on Bazrah's shoulder.

"Oh." Iona took her helmet off and tucked it under her arm. "Thank you."

The woman's thin lips and lack of facial creases beyond normal wrinkles gave away no hint of concern about the newcomers. "May I ask your names?"

Iona pointed at herself. "I'm Iona." She jerked her thumb toward Leo. "This is Leo."

Leo gave her a nod but said nothing, his eyes wary.

The woman smiled. "Oh. Are you two related in some way?"

"We're friends," Iona said.

"We're allies," Leo said, nearly at the same time.

The woman chuckled. "I was wondering, because there is a resemblance." Her response seemed to die in the air, and the silence grew awkward as she stared blankly.

Leo cleared his throat. "And what's your name?"

She smiled again, though her lips tightened. "Melinda." She paused once more, seeming neither patient nor impatient as she continued staring.

Iona took a step closer and eyed the strange woman. Something was off about her. What was it?

"Do you have any other questions for me?" Melinda asked in a friendly tone.

"Several," Leo said. "How do you speak our language? Are you from this world or a different one? Are you and Bazrah the only non-giants here? And ... well, I guess that's enough for now."

Melinda chuckled in exactly the same cadence as before. "One question at a time, young man."

"All right. How are you able to speak our language?"

"Oh, that?" Melinda waved a hand. "Learning your language wasn't hard, but how we learned is not something that I am at liberty to tell you. I can tell you that Bazrah speaks your language quite well, too." She patted his back. "Don't you?"

He slid behind her, clutching her apron. "Not really."

Melinda smiled. "He's not used to being around strangers."

Leo tapped a finger on his thigh, spelling words while he spoke. "My second question is, which world are you from?"

"This one," Melinda said. "Viridi. The planet you're standing on."

Iona read the coded taps. *I knew he was hiding something.*

Leo nodded. "Okay. Are you and Bazrah the only non-giants here?"

She chuckled once more, again with an identical cadence. "You really are confused, aren't you?"

"What do you mean?"

"Well, Bazrah *is* a giant, as you call their kind. He is smaller than they are because he is still a youngster, though he is taller than an Earthling would be at his level of physical maturity. Regarding myself, I am not a giant, and I am the only one of my kind."

Iona held her helmet at her waist. "If Bazrah's a giant, why isn't he with the others?"

Melinda stared for another quiet moment before answering. "I don't answer *why* questions, young lady. I am not a philosopher. But I can tell you that he is where he belongs. With me. This observatory is his home."

Iona studied the pair. Something was way, way off. Why would Bazrah hide his ability to speak more than a few words of English? And if he was really a giant, what was he doing here? "If this is his home, it's strange that we found him in the forest near the giants' soup cauldron."

Melinda cocked her head as if confused, but the pose seemed forced. "The soup cauldron?"

"They were making cabbage soup," Leo said, gesturing with a thumb toward the forest. "The cauldron has a geothermal heating source."

"Oh, yes. I know the place." Melinda turned toward Bazrah. They spoke in the same language he had used earlier. When Bazrah finished with a nod, Melinda refocused on Leo and Iona. "He was scouting, trying to find his parents and sister. He was separated from them a while back. I have told him many times that they must be dead, but he insists that they're alive. He is a tenacious boy. He will never give up looking for them."

"How old is Bazrah?" Iona asked.

"In Viridi years, he is fifty-two."

Leo whistled. "Fifty-two years old? He's a middle-aged man!"

Bazrah puckered and blew a whistle that perfectly copied Leo's.

Melinda patted Bazrah's head. "Our years differ from yours. As you can see, he is very much a little boy. But he is a smart one. His intelligence surpasses that of most humans."

"Why does he live …" Iona cleared her throat. "I mean, what brought him here to live with you?"

"Survival. The other giants would kill him."

Iona drew her head back. "Kill him? Why?"

"I do not answer *why* questions."

Iona resisted the urge to roll her eyes. Her brain begged to ask Melinda why she couldn't answer why questions, but that would be pointless. "Melinda …" The second Iona uttered the name, something glinted in Melinda's eyes, as if responding to the word.

"Yes?"

Iona stepped closer and studied her face. "Melinda …"

Her eyes glinted again.

"I am listening," Melinda said. "Do you have a question?"

Iona took one more step and drew within reach. "What are you?"

"I am Melinda, Bazrah's attendant."

Iona gazed into Melinda's steely eyes. She waved a hand and blocked some of the light. Melinda's pupils expanded, making a slight click. "I mean, are you … a robot?"

"Not precisely." Melinda met Iona's stare. "The closest word in your language is android."

"Android?" Iona stepped back. "Then you're a machine. A machine with realistic skin."

"Oh, I am much more than that." Melinda patted her hips with her hands. "My body is mechanical, to be sure, but I also have an embedded artificial intelligence engine that mimics a human soul. I am able to make decisions based on ethics."

Iona blinked. "What? How can a machine do that? Everything you say and do is programmed."

Melinda chuckled yet again. Now it sounded more like clucking than a laugh. "I can't describe the process to you, my dear. I am not the inventor."

Leo tapped, *She is annoying.*

"Then who is?" Iona asked.

"Bazrah's parents worked with a scientist they know. They created me to look after Bazrah in case something were to happen to them. His sister, Lacinda, is old enough to watch over him, but that would be quite a burden for a young person."

Iona scrunched her brow. "Are his parents the only ones who can explain how you got an artificial soul?"

"I think that's likely. They never mentioned others being involved in the process."

"If they're giants, and Bazrah's a giant, then why would they create an android who's human sized?"

"I don't answer—"

"*Why* questions. Right." Iona heaved a sigh. "Okay, maybe it would be easier if you just give us a history of what's happened since you were created, then we'll try to put the pieces together."

She chuckled yet again. "Iona, I will be glad to tell you part of the story, but I'm sure you understand that I have security features. I can't tell you everything I know. Some of it is secret."

"I understand. But are you sure that what you can tell us will be true? I mean, is it possible that your memories have been altered?"

"If my memory has been altered, then I wouldn't know that, would I?"

Melinda opened her mouth and poised her face as if ready to chuckle once more, but Leo leaped to her and covered her mouth. "If you laugh again, my head will explode."

She spoke into his palm, her voice muffled. "Well, we wouldn't want your head to explode, would we? I will refrain from laughing."

Bazrah laughed out loud, then covered his own mouth.

"Good." Leo lowered his hand. "I apologize for being so forceful."

"No need to apologize. You have to protect yourself, though I have no data suggesting that a human's head could explode from laughter. I will have to remember this new information."

"Yes, well, regarding that—"

"Hush, Leo," Iona said. "Let's just listen to the story."

Melinda waved a hand and turned toward the door. "Come with me. We have comfortable seats, and I'm sure I can find suitable snacks for humans." As she walked away, her voice faded. "Bazrah likes batter-fried fish eyes. Do you enjoy those?"

Leo and Iona stared at each other, both cringing. Iona gestured toward the door, giving him a coy smile. "Your turn to go first."

Chapter Twelve

Ben and Caligar stood facing north, each wearing skis and carrying a shoulder-strapped rifle. To their left, at the tower's base, Winella began climbing the ladder, a computer pad attached to her belt. At the top, the light streams emanating from the antennas brightened the area, allowing a view into the icy terrain for at least a mile.

Wearing a parachute pack and holding his ski poles in one hand, Caligar stared at a computer pad in his other. A cord fastened the pad to his wrist. "According to these readings, the conduit's draw is quite strong, and the data history shows a spike at the moment your friends disappeared."

Ben leaned on his own ski poles and looked at the pad. "Strong enough to pull them through the Gate?"

"Yes, but I cannot tell if they survived. The power surge would have delivered a temporary shock, but I cannot judge its intensity."

"Would the Gate have taken them to your world? To Viridi?"

"I don't know. During the event, the conduit was forming and locking the two worlds in place. Whether or not they were in sync at the moment of the spike is impossible to determine."

Ben gestured toward the pad. "But they're in sync now."

"Yes. The connection is complete. Soon, Winella will increase the tower network's power to lift us and then regulate the pseudo-gravitational force to guide us to a safe landing in my world."

Ben gazed at the glittering Oculus Gate, imagining a pair of humans flying through it. How could anyone survive such a trek? Yet, others made it through. Maybe there was still hope. "You said my friends were drawn through by a spike. That means the force decreased afterward. What do you think happened to them?"

"The force did decrease, but I cannot guess the speed they fell through our atmosphere, assuming they arrived there at all. The force's residual pull would have slowed them somewhat, but if the pull dropped too quickly to its earlier level, they would have struck the ground at a lethal velocity."

A new image crashed into Ben's mind—Leo and Iona colliding with the ground. Their bodies smashed, their limbs shattered, and their necks cracked, then they lay impossibly contorted in dead silence. He sucked in a cold breath, his fists tightening. It couldn't be true. They had to be all right ... somehow. He shook his head, casting the image away. "But we don't know that."

Caligar exhaled in a long plume of white vapor. "No. We don't. Hope remains."

Ben relaxed his hands. "Back to the procedure. How would Winella know if a person in your world is falling too fast and figure out how much to adjust the reverse pull?"

Caligar showed Ben his pad's screen. Several windows displayed ever-changing numerals. "Winella and I each have a computer. With the conduit in place, data can pass through. In fact, on Viridi I have a station from which I can send many different types of signals through the Gate. For our purposes, once we are falling in my world, I will transmit descent data to her from the pad, and she can make the necessary adjustments."

"But you're not certain it will work, are you? That's why you brough a parachute."

"Correct. And after we complete our journey, Winella would make an attempt to go through the Gate herself, and I would control the towers from my world."

"What about the rest of your people? How will they return to your world?"

Caligar's lips thinned, maybe from annoyance at the question. "Winella will leave instructions for them to gather within the Arctic Circle, and we will draw them to our world at an appointed time, though we will not be able to guide their fall to Viridi because at full

117

power, the danger to Earth will be great. The entire operation must be quick and without adjustments."

Ben touched Caligar's backpack. "Do they have parachutes?"

"We have given them instructions on how to construct their own parachutes. Whether or not they follow those instructions, I cannot guess. Many are lazy. All are stupid."

Ben cocked his head. "Why do you call the rest of your kind stupid? It's obvious that you and Winella are highly intelligent."

"I am thankful for your evaluation of our mental abilities, but the others are not *our kind*. They devolved into a different species, and I do not wish to explain how or why that happened."

Ben waved a hand. "Okay. No problem."

Caligar lifted his skis in turn, finally showing discomfort with the bitter cold. "In any case, the process will be quick in order to minimize earthquakes. When everyone has been transported, we will reduce the power. Then, if we find your friends and transport all of you back to your world, we will disable the conduit permanently."

"And I can destroy the towers."

"If you wish, but you still have to deal with the Refectors. The Oculus Gate is the only way to send them back to their source, and the towers are the only means to maintain the conduit."

As cold seeped into his gloves, Ben flexed his fingers to keep the blood flowing. "And getting the Refectors to come to the Arctic Circle without letting them know why won't be easy."

"I am sure it will sound callous of me to say so, but that will be your concern, not mine. I had nothing to do with bringing them here, and I never wanted to come to your world in the first place."

"Okay, I get that, but who made it all happen? Where did the Oculus Gate come from?"

Caligar turned his head and gazed northward. After a moment of silence, his reply came in a sigh, puffing out in a new plume of white vapor. "The queen of hell."

"The queen of hell?" Ben's own white vapor shot out like pressurized steam. "What are you talking about?"

Caligar shook his head. "I have already said too much. She might hear me."

"Hear you? From hell?"

Caligar looked skyward. "She is powerful and has ways of communicating through the Oculus Gate. Whether or not she can hear me while I am on Earth, I do not know, but I wish to avoid any further risk."

"Does that mean you communicated with her on your planet? Why would you do that?"

Caligar's huge eyes narrowed. "I am not in league with her, if that is your concern. Far from it. She is my sworn enemy. And I have nothing more to say on this matter. Kindly refrain from asking further questions about it."

Ben stared. Questions pummeled his brain, too many to process, but one pushed to the forefront. Was this queen of hell the great evil that Commander Barks had theorized in his farewell message? If Caligar suspected that she was responsible for the Oculus Gate, maybe so. But a queen who reigned over a place of condemnation seemed more like superstition than reality

Caligar looked at the tower. "Winella is in place and has signaled her readiness."

"Good." Ben planted his ski poles firmly in the snow and fastened his rifle strap to his belt in case it slipped off his shoulder. After testing the rifle's scope light, he looked at Caligar. "And I'm also ready."

"I assume you will not change your mind about accompanying me. The danger level is unknown, but I suspect that it is quite high."

Ben stared straight ahead. "No offense, but I'm sure I have more passion to find my friends than you do."

"No offense taken. I understand your passion, but passion will not help if our drawing mechanism fails after we pass through the Oculus Gate. Therefore, remember to stay close so that you can hold to me if necessary. Mine is the only parachute besides the one

I left for Winella. She was making another but did not have time to finish it."

"Understood. Let's go." Ben shoved off into the dim, icy flatlands.

The sound of Caligar's skis swished to the rear. When he caught up and glided to Ben's left, Ben scanned the area. To the north, the landscape turned darker. Soon it would be impossible to see any tracks in the snow. "Caligar, if any of the Refector-possessed humans are still around, I assume they will be sucked into the Gate with us, right?"

"You are right, but I think none remain in the area. The devolved giants were instructed to hunt for any stray humans and herd them south."

"But isn't it possible they missed some?"

"Possible, but not likely. The humans leave prints, and they are slow, especially in such cold weather. They are easy to track, even by fools."

"True, but do your people have any incentive to be thorough? Why chase a wayward human deep into this wasteland?"

Caligar pushed hard with his poles and accelerated, forcing Ben to do the same to keep up. After a moment of silence, Caligar sighed. "They are incentivized."

"How?"

"By their appetites."

Ben's stomach churned. "They would hunt the humans for food?"

"Yes, and they would have eaten you had I not been the one who caught you."

"Eating humans is part of their devolution?"

"I have nothing more to say about that." Caligar turned and skied backwards as he gazed at the tower. "We are approaching the liftoff zone."

Ben turned as well. At the tower, the streams of light pulsed between brighter and dimmer as they circumvented the Arctic Circle.

"We will soon be lifted," Caligar said. "The farther north we go, the greater the pull will be."

"Will snow and ice come with us?"

"Perhaps some. Most is frozen to the surfaces, while we are not." Caligar halted. "Let us station ourselves here."

Ben slid to a stop at his side. "Any particular reason?"

Caligar fastened his rifle strap to a loop on his parachute pack. "I want to remain as close as possible to where your friends left Earth. Perhaps we will arrive on my world in the vicinity they entered."

"Agreed." Ben planted his poles in the snow. "While we're waiting, I'm going to try to contact my base commander again." He touched his earbud, making sure it was turned on. "Kat, can you hear me?"

Only random static replied.

"Kat, in case you can hear me, I'll add to what I told you before. I'm with Caligar, and I am going to try to go with him to his world through the Oculus Gate. That's where we think Iona and Leo are. When I return, I'll give you a report as soon as I can. Also, if you contact Jack and Trudy, tell them to stand down on destroying the Russian tower. I haven't been able to get a hold of them myself, but it's critically important that they stand down for now." A cold shiver ran along his spine, probably a sudden realization of the coming danger. "And if I don't come back ..." He swallowed hard and glanced at Caligar, who quickly turned his head. "Kat," Ben continued, "just know that I love you. With all my heart. Somehow I'll find my way back to your arms. Or I'll die trying."

After letting out a long sigh, Ben propped himself with the ski poles. "I'm ready."

As they waited, the tower's luminous triads grew brighter and brighter. The pulses quickened. The surrounding light grew. Tremors shook the ground, rising into Ben's legs. "A quake's starting."

"Not unexpected. It should remain local." Caligar unfastened his skis. "You do the same, Benjamin. We will not need them on my planet."

Ben bent over and took his skis off. The moment he finished, he began lifting from the ground. He clutched Caligar's parachute pack to keep from flying away. Then, Caligar floated upward, constantly studying the numbers on his pad.

While they ascended, the tower lights continued to brighten. "Now that we're airborne," Caligar said, "Winella will increase the power sharply to make us fly through the Gate as quickly as possible."

"To avoid too much time in the airless environment."

"Correct. We could not survive there for more than a minute or so."

As if on cue, they accelerated upward. Cold air beat against Ben's clothes and chilled his skin. It seemed that his body stretched out, and the light streams below shrank away, now a circle around Earth's crown.

Then all fell dark.

The wind eased to a perfect calm. His skull throbbed, the worst headache ever. His lungs pushed air out, but nothing came back in. His entire body felt like it was about to explode. Dizziness flooded his brain. Soon he would faint and lose his vise grip on Caligar's pack.

A few seconds later, light appeared far below. A breeze returned. Ben sucked in a breath. Air had never tasted so good. The headache ebbed, and everything came back into focus. He and Caligar were falling toward the ground, a greenish expanse that seemed to be thousands of feet away, though their downward speed was impossible to gauge.

"Caligar," Ben shouted. "Does your pad tell you how fast we're falling?"

Caligar stayed silent, his face toward the ground and his body spread-eagle. The computer pad glided near his hand, the cord keeping it close.

"Caligar?" Ben pulled on the pack and looked at Caligar's face.

His eyes were closed. He was either unconscious or dead.

Chapter Thirteen

Leo picked up a batter-fried orb from a plate in his lap. Sitting cross-legged on a wooden floor with Iona in a similar position to his left and Bazrah to his right, he inhaled through his nose. The sphere smelled like river eel, pecan oil, and red pepper. "Fish eyes, you say?"

Bazrah nodded while chewing, the crunch loud enough to hear.

Iona set her helmet at her hip and laid her vest on top, the gun still in its holster. "Don't be a coward, Leo. It won't bite you."

"I'm no coward, but the pepper is similar to cayenne. If I try one, it will overwhelm my senses. My nose will be no good for hours."

"Suit yourself, but I think we're safe." She popped one into her mouth and chewed. After a few seconds, she gasped, fanning her face. "Oh! That's super spicy!"

Leo chuckled. "It bit you pretty hard, I would say."

Iona reached for a flask on the floor, but Bazrah grabbed it first. "No."

"Why?" Iona continued fanning. "I'm dying, here."

She leaned farther and reached again, but Bazrah swung it farther away. "No. Hurt you."

"Hurt me? How? You're drinking it."

Melinda walked in and sat opposite Leo. "Bazrah is trying to keep you safe." She took the flask from him, dropped a tablet in, and swirled it around. "Now you can drink it."

"Good." Iona grabbed the flask, guzzled water, and wiped her mouth with a sleeve. "Whew! That's better."

"Was it worth it?" Leo asked.

She nodded. "Really tasty. I haven't had anything that good in a long time."

"Well, then ..." Leo bit into one and chewed. Something slimy oozed out of the half still in his hand. Maybe his fish eye wasn't fully cooked, but, as Iona had said, it carried an excellent flavor—the expected pepper along with curry and cinnamon.

When he swallowed, a burning sensation crawled across his tongue toward the back of his throat, increasing by the second. He picked up the flask and took three hefty swallows before setting it back down. He smacked his lips. "It's not like our water. It tastes ... fruity, I think. Like a peach. And it's slippery. Does it have oil in it?"

Melinda nodded. "The tablet I added made it feel slippery. The ingredients protect your throat. Bazrah's throat is not as sensitive."

"Interesting. We washed in a waterfall earlier. It caused some redness but no burns."

"Rainwater is more caustic, which we collect in a cistern for Bazrah's drinking source. A stream's water would have gathered minerals that somewhat neutralized the acidity. Those minerals also have healing properties."

"Ah. I smelled them in the stream. It all makes sense."

Iona looked at Leo's plate. "Aren't you going to eat the rest of it?"

Leo inhaled through his nose. The odors now seemed dull, muted. The pepper had definitely affected his senses. "I'll skip it. I need to get my nose back as soon as possible."

"You're right. We need that valuable nose." Iona turned toward Melinda. "How did you know to put the tablet in the water? It's not like you've had other Earthlings visiting you, right?"

"You are not the first, but I cannot say more about that."

Iona glanced at Leo with one of her familiar distrustful expressions. Knowing her, she wouldn't rest until she figured out what Melinda was hiding.

"Well ..." Iona blinked in an innocent fashion and shifted to her more youthful voice. "It's a good thing, then, that we aren't the first. I pity the unfortunate Earthling girl who was the first to drink your water. She probably nearly died, right?"

Melinda's expression stayed perfectly slack. "The visitor was not a girl, and he did not suffer more than minor burns. Caligar was quick to concoct an antidote."

Iona nodded in an exaggerated manner. "Oh. Interesting. It's good that you had an antidote for any Earthlings who came between his visit and ours."

"There were no other …" She stared straight ahead, her mouth partially open.

"Melinda?" Iona waved a hand in front of her eyes. "Are you all right?"

Bazrah crawled behind her and pushed his fingers into her hair. Something clicked, like a switch being toggled.

"Rebooting her brain?" Leo asked.

Bazrah nodded. "Not working."

A new voice entered the room. "Because I switched her circuits off."

Everyone turned. A man stood at the doorway leading to the observatory, holding a huge rifle. With a short antenna that protruded from the top of the barrel, it looked like a prop from a science-fiction movie.

"We don't want any trouble." Leo rose slowly to his feet, sniffing to check for anything unusual. But nothing entered, not even the man's scent. That blasted fish eye had done its dirty work.

"If you don't want trouble," the man said, waving the rifle, "then I suggest you stay where you are."

Leo looked him over. With badly shorn gray hair and beard, it seemed that he had visited a blind barber. About five foot ten and wearing torn denim jeans, a ragged button-down long-sleeved shirt, and sneakers with floppy soles, he was definitely from Earth. "I will stay here," Leo said. "What do you want?"

The man tucked the rifle under his arm and scratched through his scalp, grimacing, either nervous or battling a skin problem. "I want ..." He lowered his scratching hand and regripped his rifle. "I want Bazrah to come with me to ... to find something."

Leo stepped between the man and Bazrah. "Why?"

"I need him to ...." The man rolled his eyes. "Look, I don't have to explain myself. I'm the one with a gun. You have to do what I say. Got it?"

Leo eyed the man again. He held the rifle away from his body, as if it were a dreaded object. Maybe he would shoot, and maybe he wouldn't. Charging ahead to disarm him was too risky. "May I offer a peaceful solution, uh ... what did you say your name is?"

"Harrid. Dr. Carson Harrid."

"May I call you Harry?"

"No. Dr. Harrid." He scratched his head again. "What is your peaceful solution?"

"Allow me to accompany you. Once you find what you're looking for, I will bring Bazrah back with me."

Dr. Harrid scanned Leo, his eyes moving up and down. "I don't trust you. The second I'm not watching, you could grab me and beat me to a pulp."

"I am big enough to do that, Dr. Harrid, but with the boy's caretaker out of commission, it is my duty to see to his safety. I wouldn't risk—"

"Oh, Leo," Iona said as she stepped to his side, "stop being so polite with this ignoramus. He's threatening a kid. He's a cowardly cockroach."

Dr. Harrid's eyelid twitched. "Don't ... don't call me an ignoramus. I have an IQ of one-ninety-seven."

Iona whispered, "But he didn't mind cowardly cockroach?"

"Intellect is a hot button," Leo quickly scanned her. She had put her vest on again, and the Toger was now behind her waistband at her back, but would it fire after all it had been through? Maybe she was hiding it there as a last resort. "We can use that to our—"

"Stop whispering!" Dr. Harrid fired the rifle. A tiny, bright light shot out, zipped past Iona, and sizzled into a wall.

Leo whistled. "What kind of ammunition do you have in that gun, Sir Shoots Amiss?"

"Sir what?"

"Never mind. Just grumbling about you shooting at the little miss."

"That was a warning shot. I won't miss again. Regarding the ammunition, they are photon pellets." A proud smile emerged. "I developed them from the elements on this vile planet. And the rifle is modified from a weapon I borrowed from Caligar."

"Borrowed." Leo nodded. "I see."

Dr. Harrid's face reddened. "Don't patronize me. It's Caligar's fault I'm stuck here. It's only fair that I use some of his hardware to help me go home."

"You're right," Iona said, her hands folded in front as she switched to a more conciliatory tone. "And I want to help you get home."

"You do?" Dr. Harrid scratched his head again. "Why?"

"Because Leo and I are from Earth. If you can get home, then maybe we can follow."

Dr. Harrid shook his head hard. "No. Once I'm in the air and traveling through the Eye, you'll turn the energy off, and I'll fall to my death."

"Then send us first. If we all go, Bazrah can find his way back here."

Harrid glanced up for a moment as if calculating before re-fixing his stare on Iona. "The conduit won't last long enough. The degradation will occur before we could complete the process."

Iona started rolling her eyes but quickly halted the gesture. "Then we'll all go at the same time. We can work it out."

"I still don't see any advantage for me. Why should I let you come?"

Leo gestured toward Bazrah. "The little rascal might give you trouble if we're not there. He could lead you into a trap. He's really smart like that." Leo stepped to the side and motioned for Bazrah to come forward.

When he stood between Leo and Iona, Dr. Harrid looked him over. "You make a valid point. He is rather impish."

"Then you'll take us along?" Iona asked.

"Perhaps, but I need to check something. Stay here." Dr. Harrid pivoted and retreated to the observatory. Leo crept to the door with Iona and looked out. Dr. Harrid sat at the stool and looked through the telescope, frequently glancing at the door. "I told you to stay."

Leo raised a hand. "Staying right here, as commanded."

"Well, you'd better." He continued looking through the telescope. Iona whispered to Leo, "I could shoot him. I think."

"Don't try it. If that gun doesn't work, we're dead."

Harrid cursed. "No! I can't believe it! It's impossible!"

"What?" Leo and Iona said at same time.

"He's coming. Here. Now."

"Who?" Iona asked.

Dr. Harrid faced her, his cheeks aflame. "Caligar, you idiot! And someone's with him. A human male. I don't know who."

"Maybe I can identify him."

Dr. Harrid scowled. "Out of a billion men on earth, you think you know him?"

Iona set a fist on her hip, her own cheeks reddening. "How do you think I got here, you mental midget? My friends are probably trying to find me."

He aimed the rifle, his hands shaking. "My intelligence dwarfs yours. I am a brilliant scientist."

"Then you need a nametag with *brilliant scientist* written under Carson Horrid. Otherwise no one will be able to tell how brilliant you are."

He screamed. "It's *Harrid*, you stupid little troll!"

"Yep. That's it. I'm a troll. And I'm pushing your buttons like a pro." She set both fists on her hips. "Now are you going to let me see who's falling from the sky before it's too late?"

Breathing rapidly, he glared at her. "All right. It's not too late. The scope is tracking them, and they're falling slowly." He stepped away from the stool and motioned with the rifle for Iona to enter. "Hurry."

Leo took the handgun, pretending to give Iona a push, and slid it into a cloak pocket. With Harrid watching her closely, she hustled to the stool, sat, and looked through the scope. After a few seconds, she stood and turned toward Dr. Harrid. "He's not who I thought he was. I have no clue who he is."

"Well, thanks a lot for wasting my time."

Iona frowned at him. "My pleasure, Dr. Horrid."

"It's *Harrid!*"

"I know your name. You don't have to shout."

"Then use it." Dr. Harrid blew out an exasperated sigh. "All right. Here's what we're doing. First toss that android down the hole. I want Caligar to think she and Bazrah are on an outing. Then you and your hairy brother will go next."

Iona's eyes narrowed to slits. "He's not my brother."

"Then whatever he is. I don't care. When you get down there, wait for me, whether in the tunnel or out at the ledge. Again, I don't care." He gestured with a finger. "Bazrah, come here. I need you next to me to make sure the two Earthlings do what I say, and I have another task for you later."

Bazrah gave Leo a questioning look.

"It's all right," Leo said. "He won't hurt you. He needs you."

Scowling, Bazrah shuffled to Dr. Harrid's side.

"I'll get Melinda." Iona strode back into the room, whispering as she passed Leo, "Ben's coming. We need to signal him somehow."

Leo joined her at Melinda's side, his voice low. "I assume you mean a calling card of some sort."

Iona nodded, grabbed her helmet from the floor, and set it on her head without fastening the strap. She and Leo each grasped Melinda by an arm and lifted. Her legs straightened, and she stood on her own.

"She's responding to her innate programming," Dr. Harrid said, watching from the door with the rifle pointed at Bazrah's head. "My shock impulse disabled only her AI command response engine. If you guide her, she should be able to walk to the exit."

"How do you know so much about her?" Iona asked.

"I helped Caligar build her."

"Really? How long were you with the family?"

"You don't need to know. Just get going. We're in a hurry."

Iona turned Melinda and shifted behind her. As Iona prodded, Melinda walked slowly forward. Dr. Harrid stepped back from the door, tugging Bazrah along.

Iona whispered to Leo, "I thought of a calling card. You got one?"

"Maybe." Leo reached into his cloak pocket and fingered the items within until he came upon his foil bag of smoke bomb spheres. "Yes." He shifted behind Melinda and slipped a smoke bomb into Iona's hand.

She pocketed the bomb. "When we get to the telescope room, do something to distract Dr. Horrid. I need five seconds to hide our calling cards."

"You got it, Sister Sneaky." Leo winced. "Oh. Sorry."

"No problem. I like that one."

When they reached the exit hole, Leo set his ear close to Melinda's mouth. "What did you say?"

Dr. Harrid furrowed his brow. "She's talking?"

"Quiet." Leo curled a finger. "Come closer. You can listen. She's saying something about a secret escape passage."

Dr. Harrid took a step, then stopped. "No, no. You can't fool me. You'll grab my gun."

"That thought never entered my mind." Leo backed several paces away from Melinda. "Listen for yourself."

His expression skeptical, Dr. Harrid crept close and set his ear next to Melinda's mouth. While he listened, Iona skulked to the telescope and crouched at its base.

"I don't hear anything," Dr. Harrid said as he drew back. "What are you trying to pull?"

Leo blinked. "She stopped talking? How odd."

"This is a trick." Dr. Harrid turned toward Iona. "Get away from there!"

Iona shot to her feet and bumped her head on the telescope, knocking it askew. Her helmet toppled off and rolled toward Dr. Harrid. As he bent to pick it up, she used her foot to push something into a hole at the scope's circular base, sliding it out of sight. She pivoted toward Dr. Harrid and rubbed the back of her head. "Now look at what you made me do."

"*I* made you? You're not supposed to be over there."

"I was just trying to figure out how to adjust the telescope. I couldn't see the falling men anymore."

"Because they've landed by now." He tossed the helmet into the exit hole, then, prodding Bazrah with the rifle barrel, he walked with him to the scope. "Get out of my way, troll."

When Iona moved, Dr. Harrid shifted the telescope to its former angle and looked through the eyepiece. "They're gone." He scanned the floor where Iona had crouched. "What were you doing stooped over like you were?"

"I had a cramp in my calf. I was rubbing it."

"Whatever." He prodded her shoulder with the gun. "You and your goon drop Melinda down the chute."

While they walked back from the scope, Bazrah stayed behind and knelt at the base for a moment, pulling something from the hole enough to expose it. Then he hurried to catch up.

From behind Melinda, Leo lifted her and lowered her legs through the hole. "Sorry about the next step, Miss Machine." He released her, and she plunged into the chute.

Iona looked down, then crouched, grimacing as she massaged her leg. "Ow! The cramp! It's awful!"

Dr. Harrid swatted the back of her head with the gun barrel. She fell prostrate on the floor and rubbed her scalp as she moaned in pain. "There! That'll make you forget your calf cramp."

Leo lunged toward him, but when Dr. Harrid set the barrel at Iona's neck, Leo backed off.

"You're a coward," Leo growled.

"Call me what you wish, but I'm going home, and I'm not allowing for any further delays. Or tricks. Caligar will be here soon, and I don't want to be present when he arrives." Harrid nodded toward the chute. "Go down. Both of you. Bazrah and I will be along in a few minutes."

"A few?" Leo asked. "Why the delay?"

"That's not for you to know." Harrid prodded Bazrah in the back with the gun barrel. "Go to the other room." They walked single file through the side door.

Leo helped Iona to her feet. "I'll go first," he said as he looked at a bleeding welt on her head. "That way, if you fall, I can catch you."

She dabbed her scalp wound with a corner of her scarf. "All right, but go all the way down before I start."

"Why?"

She withdrew her knife from its belt sheath. "I think Bazrah will have an easier time with a single rope than Dr. Horrid will. Maybe he'll be able to shinny down fast, and we can escape together."

"Or you might just antagonize the mad scientist and make him even madder."

"We're risking our lives, not Bazrah's. Like you said, Dr. Horrid needs him. Besides, I want to make him mad. I've been baiting him on purpose."

"I noticed. To force a mistake?"

132

"Exactly. I've learned when you deal with brains-only twerps like him, you have to throw them off. Get them flustered. Then look for an opening and make a move."

"Let's hope he doesn't move first to the trigger finger." Leo set a foot on a rung and climbed down. When he had lowered himself fully out of the room, Iona knelt at the edge of the hole and set the blade against the right-hand support rope, waiting.

As he neared the bottom, he scanned the rocky floor to keep from stepping on broken robot parts, but the surface was clear—no Melinda and no helmet. How could that be?

Above, Iona began descending, pausing at each rung to cut it loose from the left-hand support rope. The right-hand support, already cut at the top, now dangled, the end drawing closer to the ground as she continued slicing rungs.

When she came within reach, Leo grasped her by an arm and helped her settle to the ground. "How's your head?"

"Smarts like the dickens, but I'll be okay." She cut the final rung and began reeling the right-hand support rope over her shoulder in loops. "Waste not, want not, my father always used to say."

"Sounds like a wise man." Leo eyed the bloody tangle of hair on her scalp. Her bravado was no act. She was as tough as they came. "We've got another problem. A rogue robot. Melinda's gone."

"Yeah. I know. When you dropped her, I saw her grab the ladder and let herself down. That's why I cried like a banshee about the cramp, to cover up for no crashing sound. I didn't want Dr. Horrid to know."

"She must have some kind of self-preservation programming. No telling where she went."

"Right." Iona continued looping the rope. "And she knows you dropped her, so you might be in her crosshairs."

"Good point. I'll keep a wary eye for the Android Avenger. Strangely enough, she probably also has your helmet. I couldn't find it."

"That's weird." Iona pulled her scarf over her head wound. "I could've used it a couple of minutes ago."

Leo picked up the lantern Bazrah had left, the wick still burning, though dimmer than before. "I assume we should go to the chasm." Iona finished looping the rope. "Right. If Bazrah manages to climb down in a hurry, he'll know where to run. Then maybe we can climb to the top of the cliff outside before Dr. Horrid shows up."

As they walked abreast at a fast pace, Iona sighed. "It'll take a miracle for Ben to find our calling cards. I had to push them pretty far into a hole at the telescope base to keep our favorite sinister scientist from seeing them."

Leo held the lantern out at arm's length, allowing its glow to wash over their path. "I have some good news about that. While neither you nor Dr. Brilliant were looking, Bazrah pulled something out from the hole a little ways. It looked like a string of some sort."

"That's a relief." She touched the top of her sternum. "My cross. He must've pulled the cord partway out."

"Ben will find it." Leo withdrew the Toger from his pocket and gave it to Iona. "He's meticulous. Doesn't miss a thing."

"True." She slid the gun back to its holster and smiled. "He's pretty amazing."

He eyed her contented expression, like a schoolgirl admiring a rock star. "I agree, but you make me wonder if he's impressed you in ways I don't know about."

"Yeah. One time, for sure." She looked straight at Leo. "Remember when you carried Kat out of the tea bunker?"

"Definitely."

"Well, Ben and I were the only ones left in the missile-launch room, and I had just shot his brother. On purpose. He could've slapped me. Cursed at me. But he didn't even raise his voice. He just told me not to say another word, that we would talk later, and he walked out. Then, when we did finally talk, do you remember what he said?"

"Maybe. Refresh my memory."

Iona's voice cracked. "He opened his arms and said …" She swallowed hard. "He said, 'Welcome to our family.'"

As the memory replayed in Leo's mind, warmth rose into his cheeks—a good, satisfying warmth. "Ah, yes. Then the family embrace, and Trudy invited me to join in. It was a tender moment that I will cherish for years to come."

"Then you understand why I admire Ben. He accepted me in spite of my … well …"

Leo raised his brow. "Shoot-first mentality? Whether from a gun or your mouth?"

She averted her gaze, again smiling. "I guess that's pretty accurate. But I didn't shoot Dr. Horrid. I controlled myself."

"Good for you. But maybe you should test that Toger. It might help us."

"When I get a chance. Too risky to make noise right now."

Soon, they exited the tunnel and stood near the precipice. Below, carrion birds flew lazily over the river, likely taking in the odor of something near the shore. Leo set the lantern down and shielded his eyes with a hand as he scanned their surroundings.

Upstream, the river wound into a forest, while downstream, it fed a rockier landscape of scattered, low mesas. Something glimmered beyond one of the mesas, perhaps a lake fed by the stream. Melinda was nowhere in sight. "It's clear that Caligar is Bazrah's father, and since Ben's with him, he'll be on our side." He patted his cloak pocket. "I'll keep the other smoke bombs handy and use them if needed. With Melinda in the wind and our allies coming this way, the situation could change quickly. Surprises are guaranteed."

"Right. The biggest surprise would be if we don't have any surprises." Iona touched her nose. "Has your schnoz recovered?"

He inhaled deeply. One clear aroma drifted in—Iona's minty toothpaste and strawberry jam on wheat toast that her toothbrush didn't quite cleanse. The odor of blood mixed in, the only disturbing scent in the area. "It's working for close-range smells. It might take a few hours to get my long-range detector back."

"It would come in handy for finding Melinda or knowing if Ben's getting close."

"Agreed. I'll keep sniffing for both. Ben's farm-boy scent is pretty easy to pick up, so we can hope."

Iona looked back into the tunnel. "I wonder what's going on in there. I was hoping Bazrah would get here right away."

A shout reverberated from the tunnel. "You fool! Why did you do that?"

"Speak of the devil," Leo said.

Iona leaned toward the cave. "Dr. Horrid's mad at Bazrah about something."

"Maybe he thinks Bazrah cut the rope."

Iona drew the Toger and hid it behind her back. A few seconds later, Harrid, Melinda, and Bazrah walked into the light just inside the tunnel entrance. Harrid carried the strange rifle, and Melinda, wearing Iona's helmet, held Bazrah's wrist. Her gray hair, tied in a bun, made the helmet tip forward, partially covering her eyes.

Leo whispered to Iona, "She must've been hiding in the dark somewhere. My defective nose missed her scent."

Iona scowled. "And she took my helmet. It looks like a turtle shell with a rabbit tail sticking out the back."

When Bazrah saw Leo and Iona, he jerked free from Melinda, leaped to the ladder, and scampered toward the top of the cliff.

Harrid aimed the rifle at him. "Come down this instant, or I'll shoot."

Iona whipped her gun to the front, aimed at Harrid, and pulled the trigger. When it clicked without firing, she hid it again.

Bazrah kept climbing, now fifteen feet up. Harrid fired. The proton pellet struck Bazrah's foot, and he toppled off the ladder.

Leo rushed underneath and caught him. "Got you." He set the boy down gently. Iona rushed over, knelt at Bazrah's side, and examined his wound while stealthily checking her handgun, her actions blocked by Leo.

"Why did you shoot the kid?" Leo glared at Harrid.

Harrid sneered. "Well, if it isn't obvious to your tiny brain, he was trying to escape. Not only that, he sliced through every rung in the rope ladder. I don't know the reason yet, but he's up to some sort of trick."

"Here's a trick for you." Leo lunged, snatched the rifle away, and punched Harrid in the nose. Blood splashed, and Harrid fell flat on his back. Leo flexed his stinging knuckles. "I should've done that a long time ago."

Iona looked up from her kneeling position. "Good job. Now we're in charge. And Bazrah's all right. Just a nick in the ankle."

Harrid sat up, pinching his nose. "Fools." His voice squeaked. "Do you think I'm so stupid that I don't have a backup plan?"

"Yes," Iona said. "Plenty stupid. Mind-numbingly stupid. Your smarts are measured by the font size on your diplomas."

"Well, aren't you the witty one." Harrid climbed to his feet and brushed off the seat of his pants. "You think having my gun puts you in charge, but I'm still the only one who can get you home."

Leo set a finger on the trigger. "And you can't get home without our permission, which means we need each other. That plus a gun does put us in charge."

Harrid smiled. "Except for one factor you neglected to consider." He released his nose and called into the tunnel. "Melinda, disarm this intruder."

She removed the helmet. A pistol fell from the top of her head, and she deftly caught it out of the air and fired it toward Leo. With a loud pop, a photon pellet zipped from the barrel and struck Leo's thumb. Pain knifed up his arm, and the rifle flew from his grasp.

Iona dove toward it, but Harrid snatched it as she slid near his feet. She grabbed his leg and bit his bare ankle. He let out a yowl and shook his leg, but Iona held fast like a vicious bulldog.

Harrid thumped her head with the butt of the rifle. She let go and fell limp. Leo charged, tackled Harrid, and pummeled him with his fists, blow after blow to his face.

"Melinda!" Harrid screamed between punches. "Stop him!"

Another pop sounded. Pain ripped into Leo's skull. He toppled to his side and flopped next to Iona. As he writhed, she slid her hand into his, whispering, "My Toger still doesn't work. We have to stay down."

He compressed her hand and whispered in return, "No ... choice." After taking a deep breath, he closed his eyes and blacked out.

Chapter Fourteen

Kat watched the wall screen as the computer monitored hundreds of communications channels. Numbers in a massive array of data cells displayed signal strengths and saw-toothed sound waves from faraway radios, though the ham frequency Ben planned on using if the earbuds failed showed a flat line. Maybe both the earbuds and the backup ham radio weren't transmitting for some reason.

She glanced at the computer pad on the desk next to the keyboard—no messages and no security alarms. After two days of searching building schematics for a possible location of the missing hive cell, would this day turn out the same? Eventually, she would have to forget about the communications and search for the cell in person. Of course, she could take the pad along, and it would relay alarms from the main computer, but it couldn't receive ham radio signals or transmit using those frequencies.

Something beeped. On the big screen, a red light flashed next to one of the numbers, and its sound wave line spiked with wildly fluctuating amplitudes.

Kat tapped on the signal's icon. The box that held the data expanded and filled the screen with a map of the signal's origin and a pulsing red dot on the conduit site in Alaska. A smaller dot blinked nearby. On her desktop screen, she touched the tiny dot. An information box appeared, showing the frequency and signal strength.

"Ben?" She opened the channel and listened. Static crackled from hidden speakers, then a garbled voice. "And if I don't come back ..."

The voice died. Kat turned the volume up and applied a static filter. "Kat," Ben said, his voice weak and interrupted by gaps, "just know ... I love you ... my heart ... I'll find ... back to your arms. Or I'll die ..."

His voice fell silent.

Kat's heart raced as she spoke into the screen's embedded microphone. "Ben. It's Kat. What's going on?"

The speakers emitted only static.

"Ben?" With a trembling hand, Kat pushed a screen slider, shifting her transmission strength to maximum. "Can you hear me?"

No one answered.

She clenched her fist. "Ben!"

A new voice broke in. "Yelling won't help."

She spun her chair. Damien Collins, the Refector-possessed scientist, stood at the doorway to the residence area, an automatic rifle in hand and his fedora still on his head.

Kat rose slowly. "How did you get in here? We secured the building."

"A simple matter." He spoke with a calm, professorial demeanor, though a slight eyebrow tic interrupted his otherwise relaxed face. "I can transform into a gaseous state along with whatever I have with me."

Kat crossed her arms over her chest. "What do you want?"

He walked within a few steps and halted. "To take control of this room. The resources are far too valuable to leave in your hands."

She nodded toward the rifle. "You could've shot me in the back. Let me guess. You need my biometrics. What? A thumbprint to access something?"

"I am not here to chitchat." He raised the rifle to his shoulder. "Either acquiesce or die."

Kat eyed Damien and the rifle. Although the safety was turned off and his finger wrapped around the trigger, his uneasy stance and slight tremble in one hand communicated nervousness. He wasn't ready to shoot. "I'm not buying it. You need me alive or you would've shot me already. What are you looking—"

Damien fired. The bullet ripped across Kat's upper arm and smacked into the wall. Pain knifed from shoulder to fingertips. She grabbed the wound and glared at him, a hand braced on the desktop as blood dripped to the surface.

"Now that you know I'm serious." With a quick step, he closed the gap and set the barrel an inch from her forehead. "You have another chance to choose."

Trying to breathe without gasping, she ignored the pain and focused on his expression—cold and stern. Obviously, he needed her alive, but for what? Could she take a gamble on that leverage? She had guessed wrong before. Guessing wrong again could be fatal. Now was the time for action.

She swatted the barrel, kicked him in the groin, and punched him in the nose. She grabbed the rifle and jerked back, but he held on and fired again. The bullet zinged past her ear and smacked into the ceiling. She kicked a leg out from under him and gave him a hard shove. He toppled and thudded onto his back, still holding to the rifle as he slid away.

Kat scooped the computer pad from the desk, ran into the residence section, and slammed the door, darkening the area, then set the lock and flattened herself against the adjacent wall. Gunshots rang out. Bullets riddled the door. Splinters flew, and shafts of light knifed into the room.

When the barrage ended, Damien called, "There is no way out, Katherine."

Keeping her back to the wall, she slid to the arsenal room and turned the doorknob, but it wouldn't open. She tapped the pad's screen, found the door on the schematic, and entered her security code to unlock it. No sound came from the lock. She tried the knob again, but the door wouldn't budge.

Damien shouted, "I can guess what you're doing. I locked that door from the inside with the security bolt. Your pad won't open it."

Kat rolled her eyes. Whoever designed that room probably hoped to protect someone holing up inside, a good idea unless a Refector like Damien lurked nearby.

She scanned the area. There had to be another weapon somewhere. A baseball bat? A pipe? Wait ... no. The sleeping quarters. Knowing Trudy, she had probably stashed a weapon there.

"Katherine," Damien called. "I am able to shoot this door open, and I will take what I need from you, dead or alive. You still have a chance to survive if you surrender."

She groaned. "All right. I'm coming. But I took a bullet to the leg. I'm hobbled." Kat skulked around a corner and into the sleeping area where eight cots sat in two even rows. She hurried past her cot and stopped at Trudy's. A blanket and sheet lay atop in a jumble. She reached under the covers and felt for ... Yes! A rifle.

She grabbed it, checked the ammo magazine, and quietly chambered a round, then tiptoed back into the hall.

"Katherine, I now know where your husband went. Come out, and I will tell you. I am certain that he will need your help to return home alive."

Kat gulped. He had to be lying, but pretending to believe him might make him drop his defenses. "I said I'm coming. You try walking with a bullet in your calf."

As she crept toward the riddled door, Damien stood only a few feet away, easy to see through the bullet-hole mosaic. He had lowered his weapon. He was vulnerable. Maybe. Only one way to find out.

She took a knee, set the computer pad down, and aimed the rifle. Ignoring the pain in her arm, she fired in rapid succession. The bullets ripped through the door, adding to the spray of holes. New splinters exploded. Thuds and clanks erupted on the other side and echoed in a cacophonous frenzy.

After firing twenty rounds, she lowered the rifle and looked through the holes. Nothing moved. She rose, padded to the door, and opened it an inch. The hinges broke off, and the door fell over with a thud. Air billowed out, sweeping dust and splinters across the computer room.

Kat stepped in and looked around. No one stood anywhere in sight. At the air vent near the ceiling, the tail end of a cloud of mist streamed out and disappeared. Damien was gone.

She retrieved the pad and set it on the desktop next to the keyboard. On the surface, a blood smear ran along a six-inch path— her blood. Damien had taken some of it, probably because he needed her DNA to access something. But what? And was he gone for good? Did he need the master computer in this bunker anymore?

Damien's words returned to mind. *I now know where your husband went.* The *now* seemed to hang in the air. Why did he include that word?

She looked at the wall display. The planetary map filled the screen. The white band between the Alaska point and the Oculus Gate held a scattering of red dots within. That had to mean something important.

The white beam exiting the Gate from the other side and attaching to Viridi also contained red dots, though none of the other bands held any. Maybe Damien learned something new from this map. If so, he might have been telling the truth.

A chill crawled through her body. Could Ben have traveled from the Alaska tower to Viridi? If so, how could she help him get back? By locating Damien? Or should she first search for the missing hive cell? Either way, she would have to leave.

As the chill transformed into a cold sweat, she scanned the chamber. How could she abandon this facility with all of its benefits—a computer filled with knowledge and secrets, a weapons storehouse, and lodging, complete with food? Of course, with Damien able to come and go in his gaseous form, this room's security was now filled with holes, literally. Considering the treasures here, he would probably return to take possession of them. It was time to leave, but not before collecting what she could, especially weapons and data.

Her arm throbbed, the first spike of pain since the initial gunshot, probably delayed because of numbness or surges of adrenaline. Blood dripped from her sleeve, now soaked. She had to find a first-aid kit and treat the wound. Otherwise, she might not get very far.

The rifle in hand, she rushed to the weapons room, stood back from the door, and fired three times at the lock. When it broke away from the shattered jamb, she entered, found a shelf filled with computer supplies, and plucked a thumb-sized data drive from a bin.

A computer-pad box sat next to the bin, the top torn open. Kat glanced inside—empty. Damien probably took the pad. Now he might be able to use the main computer to give the pad access to all of the security in the building. If so, the security here wasn't simply compromised—this place would become a death trap. Maybe she could program the main computer to lock him out. Since he had to rematerialize himself and the pad at a safe distance before he could make changes, she might have time.

She ran to the desk, set the rifle, pad, and drive next to the keyboard, and typed madly. First step—lock his pad. She pulled up a building schematic on her small screen that showed the pad locations—a flashing red dot in the computer room and one in the lobby near the building's entrance. The second one had to be Damien's. She tapped on the dot, but a message flashed—access denied.

Kat banged a fist on the table. Now Damien could control every door in the building, but he had to override her locks one at a time. What should her next move be? He was probably working on gaining control of the main access doors to let his cronies in, but the portable pads couldn't override the main computer's security system remotely. She could password protect nearly everything, but that would take a lot of time.

Maybe instead she could change the startup password and lock the entire system down, but the first priority had to be getting a data download, a dump of all the angels' secret files.

After changing the system's startup password, she inserted the data drive into the side of the computer screen and started a complete download of the secure portion of the database. That would take a few minutes.

An alarm beeped. On the big screen, a message flashed—main door open.

Kat scowled. Damien's people were on their way. She scooped up the rifle and ran with the pad to the weapons room. After grabbing an empty backpack, she stuffed it with ammo magazines, grenades, poison-gas bombs, tranquilizer darts, and anything else that might be useful.

She whipped on a weapons belt, complete with a plasma handgun in a holster, a back harness for a rifle, and crisscrossing ammo straps in front. She loaded the straps with more magazines and fastened the rifle to the harness.

Her wounded arm throbbed. Trying to shore it up would have to wait. She grabbed a first-aid kit from a shelf, stuffed it into the backpack, and zipped the pack closed.

With the pack hanging by its strap to one shoulder, she hurried out of the weapons room, tapping a message on the pad as she whispered, "Dear Damien, you are welcome to join me in the computer room. I have a surprise for you."

She sent the message and set the pad on the desk. That should keep him at bay for a while. She checked the screen. The data download had finished. She snatched the drive and stuffed it into her pocket.

As she imagined an escape route, the angel luxury cruiser came to mind, parked outside where anyone could get to it, though only she could start it. Damien's goons were probably on guard there, which meant she would have to call for a different flying taxi. She tapped on the pad once more and summoned a drone from HQ, drawing a path to the temple roof. Fortunately, the garage that housed the drones survived the fire, and one taxied out onto the launchpad safely. Flying at top speed, it would arrive in about fifteen minutes. "Time to shut the system off." She started the computer's power-down sequence and waited while watching the drone's progress on the pad's map. Damien's forces had to be closing in, maybe arriving within moments. The computer could shut down without her, but escaping without the drone might be impossible.

She whispered to the pad, "C'mon, drone. Hurry up. You're killing me here."

The map showed ten minutes of flight time remaining. Still too much. Of course, she could engage the enemy, fight back, but they might charge with overwhelming force. It wouldn't be smart to do battle against an army, even if they were zombies.

The computer shut down with a loud beep, and the room dimmed. Kat nodded. If she was looking for a signal to tell her when to leave, that beep would have to do. She used the pad to open the vault door. When the lock clicked, she checked the exit doors on the pad. All were locked with no way to override them. Damien was obviously trying to trap her inside. Yet, the roof hatch was still accessible. Maybe he didn't think that door was a priority—not a likely escape route.

With quick fingers tapping on the pad, she pulled up the current weather conditions—stormy with high winds. Not great for a rooftop drone pickup, but nothing could be done about it.

She withdrew a spherical poison-gas bomb from the backpack and jerked the ignition pin out. She opened the vault door, rolled the bomb toward the computer desk, and walked out. As she shoved the door in place and spun the wheel, a hissing sound emanated from the other side. The bomb was already unleashing a huge volume of poisonous gas, and it would soon infiltrate the air vents and spread into the rest of the building.

Her arm aching, she opened the stairway door. Several guards dressed in camo and carrying rifles burst through the doorway at the far end of the hall. She ducked into the stairway, set the pad on a step, and jerked the rifle out of its harness. If these goons were mindless zombies, they might be easy targets, too stupid to get out of the way. A surprise attack might work.

She leaped out and fired several rounds. Two men and one woman at the front dropped, but the others marched ahead followed by twenty more entering the corridor, all lifting their rifles, way too many to defeat.

Kat ran into the stairway again, grabbed the computer pad, and hustled up the steps. When she reached the roof door, she unlocked it with the pad and lifted it with her shoulder, peeking out. No guards.

She pushed the door higher, crept through the gap, and let it fall closed. As she stood on the roof, she engaged the lock and tried to change the password, but the system wouldn't allow access. Damien would be able to unlock the roof door for the guards, and she couldn't stop them.

Looking up, she searched the cloudy skies for the drone. Gusty winds tossed her hair and beat against her clothes. She checked the map. The drone was about two minutes away, likely being pummeled by the winds. The guards might arrive before it did.

Near her feet, her parachute still lay bundled under its pack. Maybe it could serve as Plan B, though jumping from only a few floors up wouldn't give the parachute much time to slow her plunge.

She set her load down, unfurled the parachute, and put it on. As the canopy billowed and tried to drag her across the roof, she retrieved her items and looped the rifle strap over her shoulder.

Dark clouds drew close. Gusts swirled. She gave in to the parachute's tug and backed to the edge of the roof, five paces from the roof's trapdoor. She glanced down at the grassy yard at the rear of the temple. No one stood anywhere nearby. A jump would be dangerous, ending in a certain crash landing. Death was not out of the question.

The trapdoor flew open. A muscular, crew-cut man stepped out, a plasma rifle in hand, then a wiry woman wearing a military patrol cap, carrying handcuffs and a pistol. As the man aimed his plasma rifle at Kat, the woman called out, gusts tossing her shoulder-length locks. "Damien prefers you alive, but he'll take you dead if necessary. One way or another, you're coming with us."

Kat studied her face. She seemed lucid, probably not a zombie. Maybe taking down these two was possible, but how many more might be waiting below the hatch? Kat shouted to overcome the wind. "Why do you need me? Damien got what he wanted, didn't he?"

"We're not answering any questions." The woman tossed the handcuffs, making them land at Kat's feet. "Put them on. Now."

"Okay. Okay." As she bent toward the cuffs, she looked at her pad. The drone was twenty seconds away. She touched the map on her side of the roof, directing the drone to that spot. It would be close, but maybe not close enough.

She picked up the cuffs with one hand and withdrew an earbud from her pocket with the other and inserted it.

The woman aimed her pistol and barked, "What are you doing?"

Kat fastened the pad to her belt. "Saying goodbye." She leaped back. As she fell, the wind grabbed the chute and drove her away from the building. At the same time, she dropped, much too quickly for a safe landing.

The drone zoomed in. It collided with the chute lines and began sucking them into the propellers under the fuselage, drawing Kat upward toward the whirring blades as it zoomed away from the temple.

Kat tapped on the pad's screen. "Let me go, you mindless beast!"

The prop blades, clogged by parachute line, sputtered to a halt. Kat plunged, as did the drone, momentum driving them farther from the temple. They would crash in seconds.

Chapter Fifteen

Trudy ran with Jack through the snow. Although they still had boots, the giant had taken their parkas. They escaped with only the clothes on their backs and Jack's switchblade—no phones, no earbuds. As they hurried toward the tower, guided by its flashing lights, Trudy's head throbbed, and her vision wavered as if tossed by a storm at sea. That crack on the head might have caused a concussion, but this was no time to rest and recover. They had to escape the giants, and though the cold air jabbed like icicles, they couldn't afford to stop and search for shelter.

"Is that an earthquake?" Trudy asked. "Or is a hammer pounding my head that hard?"

"Feels like a quake." Jack pointed toward the cabin next to the tower, visible in the pulsing glow only a quarter mile away. "First stop."

"That's the most obvious place to hide," Trudy said, puffing. "The giants are sure to look for us there."

"I know. I'm just hoping we can find something warm, like a coat or a blanket. Then we'll bug out and find another hiding place."

"What about the tower?" Trudy asked. "Should we try to shut it off?"

Jack blew clouds of white vapor as he spoke in gasps. "That's the standing order. I don't see any reason to change it, do you?"

"Nope. Either the Refectors or the giants set it up. Maybe both. They're all out to kill us, so it's an enemy asset."

"And one group wants to eat us. Ben said if in doubt, take it out, so I vote for trying to disable it."

"Then it's unanimous."

When they arrived at the cabin, the tremors continued, consistent, neither strengthening nor ebbing. Jack tried the door, but it was locked. He kicked it open and hustled inside with Trudy. Although no lights burned within, the tower's beacon provided plenty of illumination.

Trudy spotted an axe leaning against a corner next to a pile of chopped firewood. "The tower has a wooden framework. What do you think?"

"Hours of chopping." Jack picked up the axe and tested its weight. "But bashing those antennas at the top might work."

"Who gets the honor?"

"Which honor?" He withdrew his switchblade from his pocket. "Knocking down the antennas or fighting off hungry giants with this?"

"It's your blade." Trudy snatched the axe and strode outside, calling back, "Don't hurt them too badly."

"Yeah, Sis. Sure. And I'll start a fire and grill a steak."

"You do that." Trudy grasped one side of the ladder with her free hand and clambered up the rungs. Although cold air continued knifing through her layers of clothes, focusing on the target above shook the chills away.

When she reached the top, she climbed onto the platform and looked down as the tower swayed, both from the wind and the trembling ground. Jack stood at the cabin door with a hand at his brow, the tower's bright pulses illuminating his face with rhythmic strobes. In the direction they had come, several giants trudged through the trail in the snow their human prey had recently blazed.

"Jack!" Trudy shouted. "I count five bogeys! Probably less than a minute."

"Then stop yacking and get it done."

"On it." Trudy staggered to the closer dish antenna, reared back with the axe, and swung at the throat of the support rod. The blade bent the rod and made the antenna shake. The streams of light continued shooting at each other, though the connection point sizzled, as if they were no longer locked in place. Yet, the streams that emanated at ninety-degree angles and traversed the Arctic Circle seemed unfazed.

She slammed the axe's head against the rod again and again. The rod cracked, exposing a thick wire. She whacked the wire with the axe's sharp edge, severing it. Sparks exploded in a wild splash. An electric jolt sent her flying back, and the axe spun through the air.

She landed on her bottom, slid to the edge of the platform, and fell off. With a mad lunge, she grabbed the edge with both hands and muscled up until her arms rested on the platform.

At the antennas, the stream shooting toward the opposite dish died, and the other stream struck the bent rod, burning it until it toppled and crashed into the other antenna, breaking its support rod. Both fell to the platform, and the remaining stream burned into the wood. The platform could ignite at any second.

"Hang on, Trudy!" Jack shouted. "I'm on my way!"

Trudy grunted. "Sure. Right. Hanging on." She looked at the ladder, attached to the platform about ten feet away. She slid her arms toward it, making her body sway and her arms slip, but she managed to hang on. A flame erupted where the jagged stream struck the wood and expanded at an accelerating crawl.

Jack hustled up the ladder, now halfway to the top. At the base, a giant stood with five others and shouted in Russian, "You have nowhere to hide, humans."

Trudy slid closer to the ladder, now six feet away. Soon, she would be able to swing her legs to it. Maybe.

Jack climbed within twenty rungs. "Almost there, Sis! Almost there."

The lead giant began stomping up the ladder, followed by another, then a third. Trudy shouted, "They're coming, Jack!"

"One crisis at a time." Jack leaped up the final steps and crouched at the edge. He grabbed her under her arms and hoisted her to the platform. They rose and stood together as flames crawled toward them from the fallen antennas. Below, five giants climbed closer, each wielding an axe.

Jack breathed heavily. "Stay here, and we're cooked. Go down, and we'll get chopped into pieces."

"And then cooked." Trudy swallowed, her mouth dry. "Got any ideas?"

He turned toward the antenna dishes. A stream of light still emanated from one, shooting through a hole in the wood and burning into the ground near the tower's base. "Maybe, but it's crazy dangerous."

"Crazy dangerous is better than certain death." She looked at the dish and its lightning-like stream. "Wait. Are you really going to—"

"Yeah. Before I change my mind, and before the platform collapses."

"Let me. I'm lighter." She began tiptoeing toward the antennas. "You slow the giants down."

"How?"

"I don't know. Use a bluff of some kind." She stepped gingerly on the boards as flames crawled around her boots. Wood bent and cracked, forcing her to choose other boards. Fortunately, the flames failed to ignite her fire-retardant pants, though her legs grew hot.

At the ladder, Jack shouted in Russian, "If you come up here, you will die. The … uh … place is on fire."

The giants continued climbing, now only seconds away.

When Trudy reached the dish, she grabbed its rod and pulled it upright, the stream still shooting. "Jack! Take cover!"

He dove to the platform. Trudy angled the dish and sent the stream toward the top of the ladder just as a giant appeared. The light shot into his head and burned a hole straight through. He collapsed and tumbled off.

Trudy twisted her body and shot the stream in a safe direction. "What are the other giants doing?"

Jack rose to all fours and looked over the platform's edge. "They stopped. They're staring at the one you cooked."

"We can't let them retreat and regroup." Trudy aimed the stream at the bent support rod. It broke loose, freeing the dish from its moorings. Grunting at the weight, she walked with the dish toward the ladder, its power cord dragging behind her as she again stepped carefully on the scorched wood, though the flames had diminished.

"Hurry." Jack pointed downward. "They're retreating. About halfway to the ground."

"Let's make them drop faster." Trudy stood at the top of the ladder and focused the stream on the giants. It struck the highest one and bored into the top of his head. When he fell away, the stream hit the next giant down, then the next. After several seconds, all five giants lay on the ground in a smoldering pile.

"Great job!" Jack patted Trudy on the shoulder. "Now what're you going to do with the dish?"

"Not sure. I cut the wire on the other one, but I lost the axe. Any ideas?"

"Maybe." He withdrew the knife from his pocket and flicked the blade open. Using the point, he turned a screw on the back of the dish. When it loosened, one of several attached wires dropped away, and the stream died. "That should do it."

"Phew!" Trudy set the dish on the platform. The tower no longer swayed. "I stopped the earthquake."

"Yeah. Good job saving the planet." Jack smiled and tousled her hair. "Don't get a swelled head."

She batted his hand away, unable to hide her own smile. "I'll go on an ego trip later. We have to bug out."

He nodded toward the pile of huge bodies. "But let's see if we can salvage some weapons and warmer clothes."

As if summoned by the words, a cold gust buffeted their bodies. Trudy shivered hard. "Sounds good. I don't want to be a popsicle treat for the giants."

Ben shook Caligar's shoulder. "Caligar! Wake up!"

The giant man continued falling without a flinch. Ben drew his ear close to Caligar's mouth. He was breathing.

A gust slammed them, nearly breaking Ben's hold. Using his free hand, he caught the computer pad and read the screen. A data box indicated that they were falling at a rate of four feet per second, a slow, safe rate, maybe too slow. The draw from the Gate was still strong.

A message in a box at the center popped up. "Waiting for adjustment commands."

Ben brought up the keyboard. No time to tell Winella about Caligar's condition. He typed, "Decrease Gate pull by 10%."

After a few seconds, a new message appeared. "Benjamin? Is Caligar unable to instruct me?"

As Ben lifted the pad to type a response, another message came through.

"Something is wrong."

They plunged, much faster than before. Ben looked at the pad. The feet-per-second reading changed far too quickly to read, but it was already in triple digits. Whatever had gone wrong, it had to be catastrophic. Now their only hope was the parachute.

Ben shifted himself below Caligar's prostrate body, stretched his arms and legs as far as he could around him while avoiding both rifles, and grabbed the ripcord. After shooting a quick prayer toward heaven, he held his breath and pulled.

The parachute spilled from the pack and billowed, catching the air and shifting Caligar to a vertical position. Their plunge slowed drastically, like slamming on the brakes. Ben held on with all his might. Inertia forced his own body into a downward slide, but catching hold of Caligar's belt halted the movement.

Soon, they slowed to a gentle descent. Greenery below clarified into leafy trees—a huge forest that stretched as far as the eye could see. With no sign of a clearing, they had only one choice—drop into the branches.

Several seconds later, they passed between two trees and broke through the canopy. The parachute caught the branches and snagged in place, making the two men bounce like a yo-yo. Then, the branches gave way, and they dropped into thick underbrush, Caligar first, Ben on top of him.

The giant let out a loud, "Oof!"

Ben rolled off, climbed to his feet, and knelt at Caligar's side. "Are you all right?"

He winced tightly. "I am in pain, but I think my injuries are relatively minor."

"Good." Ben unfastened his rifle's strap from his belt, freeing it for use. Who could tell what dangers might be lurking?

Caligar opened his eyes. "What happened?"

"I'm not sure." Ben unfastened Caligar's rifle as well. "When we passed through the Gate, we were falling slowly, but you were out cold. Winella sent a message to your pad saying something was wrong. Then we fell like a couple of boulders."

"One or more of the towers must have failed." Caligar sat up and looked at the torn parachute. "I am glad you had the presence of mind to deploy the safety measures."

"Yeah. Same here." Ben handed Caligar his rifle. "Survival instinct played a part."

Caligar grasped the rifle's stock and scanned the forest. "And now survival continues taking a crucial role. We are in an area where we might encounter hostile forces."

"Enemy territory?"

"Correct."

"How do you know? All I've seen is forest."

"My enemies live in the forest. My abode is underground, though I also have an observation tower."

"Then we shouldn't stay here." Ben extended a hand. "Do you feel well enough to get up?"

"I do." Caligar wrapped his hand completely around Ben's forearm. Ben leaned back and pulled as the giant rose. When he stood upright, he peeled his parachute pack off, slid his rifle's strap over his shoulder, and looked at his computer pad. "I need to analyze the data."

"While you're doing that ..." Ben pulled his earbud out and made sure the microphone was on. He reinserted it and spoke at a low volume. "Leo. Iona. Can you hear me?"

Caligar glanced up from the pad's screen. "What is the range of that communications device?"

"Without a signal booster nearby, no more than a mile. I was hoping maybe Leo and Iona were close."

"Possible, but highly unlikely, even assuming they're here and alive." Caligar ran a finger along the screen. "The rate of fall we experienced when we first entered this atmosphere indicates that the towers were working perfectly, but I see that the strength readings from the tower in Russia began dropping, then suddenly stopped completely."

"Russia? That's where my brother and sister went. We were investigating two towers to see what was going on."

"Come with me and stay close." Caligar fastened the pad to his belt and began walking, clearing a path as he tromped through forest undergrowth.

Ben caught up and walked in his wake. The noise from the giant's steps was loud enough to signal any nearby enemy, but it couldn't be helped.

Caligar spoke at a volume barely loud enough to be heard over the crackling din. "Do you think your siblings might have instigated the signal's demise?"

"Maybe. If they thought the tower was a threat, they would try to disable it. That was their standing order."

Caligar glanced around, obviously wary of being seen. "If they disabled it in a simple manner such as cutting a power cord, Winella could repair it quickly, but if the trouble is the result of a more thorough destructive act, the damage might take much longer to repair, if it can be repaired at all. And she would have to travel to

Russia to do so, which, as you might imagine, is an arduous journey for several reasons—darkness, weather, and other factors, including her conspicuous size."

"I can imagine. And I have no idea how much damage my siblings might have done to the tower, if they were really the reason." An image rose in Ben's mind—Jack and Trudy toppling and burning the tower. Although their success likely put him in a bind, he couldn't suppress a smile at their zeal. They would do whatever it took to get the job done. "I tried to tell them to stand down, but I don't think my message got through."

"I heard you attempt that transmission, but as you say in your world, too little, too late. You should not have given them orders to destroy something they knew so little about."

Ben gritted his teeth. "We knew enough. Earth is my world, not yours. If you try to trap Earth in an interstellar net without telling us what's going on, we'll burn the net every time. Got that?"

Caligar stared straight ahead without a word or a gesture to indicate he was even listening.

Ben fumed. As heat coursed through his body, he slowly curled a hand into a fist. The moment he opened his mouth to erupt, Caligar spoke.

"I informed Queen Laramel, the leader of your world at the time, and she blessed my efforts to create the tower network."

Ben growled, nearly shaking as he kept his voice in check. "The angel queen? The invader who subjugated my world to her tyranny? The alien who possessed my wife's body and kept her in a mental prison for months? The mass murderer who killed my comrades with a toxic vaccine? That Queen Laramel?"

"I know your questions are rhetorical, Benjamin." Caligar glanced back, his pace unabated. "But what did you expect? A personal call from me? I requested permission from the only authority at the time. I knew nothing about you until the moment I caught you as you fell from my tower."

Ben sighed, trying to force his fury to subside. What good would it do to antagonize his only ally in enemy territory? "All right. Fair enough. But if my siblings destroyed your tower, you get no apologies. Laramel was an invader, and so are you."

"I expect no apology. I am home. You are not. Your siblings' efforts have hurt you more than they have hurt me."

"Except that your people are trapped on my world."

Caligar stayed quiet for a moment as he altered his route to go around a tree before returning to the earlier heading, now on a two-person-wide path that seemed to be well traveled. "I will eventually get my life mate home. Regarding the others, who are no longer my people, my world would be better off without them."

"So would mine. We can't let them stay there."

"No. You can't. That's why it would be best if you kill them."

Ben halted. "Kill them? Why?"

Caligar pivoted back. "Benjamin, they are animals. Ravenous beasts who would kill and eat you without a second thought."

Ben narrowed his eyes. "And you wouldn't?"

"Of course not." Caligar winced, as if he had bitten into something sour. "Eating humans is forbidden, and I never partake in what is forbidden."

"Then why do they?"

"I will speak no more about this. We have to find my home without being accosted. The more we talk, the more likely we will be discovered. Our rifles will help, but in a dense forest, our lack of numbers will put us at a great disadvantage. We will not be able to shoot our way out of trouble." Caligar marched on, his long-legged stride leaving Ben behind.

Ben hustled to Caligar's side and matched his pace with a slow jog. The two continued in silence for several minutes until Caligar stopped. With a furrowed brow, he scanned the trees for a moment, then whispered, "I recognize where we are now."

A savory aroma wafted by. Ben inhaled deeply. It smelled like some kind of stew. "Home cooking?"

"Not the kind you would want to eat."

They walked on until they broke into a clearing dominated by a huge circular lake filled with green liquid that bubbled near the center. Several giants stood at the opposite side of the lake, some carrying buckets and two crouching as they dipped their buckets into the liquid. One pointed and shouted something in an odd whistling language.

Caligar grasped Ben's arm and pulled. "We must run. Now."

Chapter Sixteen

Iona blinked hard, trying to stay conscious. Her head pounded. Everything spun. Leo lay next to her, their hands still clasped, his eyes closed and a bloodless hole at the side of his forehead—the wound from Melinda's attack.

Heat surged within her. A wave of desperate energy flowed. She squirmed close to Leo and set a hand on his neck, feeling for a pulse. Nothing.

A spasm erupted, a sob trying to burst forth. No. Not now. She couldn't lose control. She had to help Leo.

Forcing the gut-wrenching pain down, she pushed her hands under him and heaved him over to his back, then crawled up and sat on his stomach, her legs straddling him, one hand covering the other over his sternum. Using all her weight, she shoved down on his chest again and again. "Come on, Leo! Come on!"

After several shoves, she checked his pulse but again felt nothing. The sob burst through. Crying in spasms, she joined her fists and pounded with all her might. With each blow, she grunted. "Leo … don't … die! … I … need … you!"

She felt for his pulse again. Still nothing.

She laid her head on his chest and wept. "Oh, Leo! Why did you have to attack him? I know you did it for me. I know you hate seeing people hurt me. But why? You barely know me. I'm just a punk kid who can't control her stupid mouth. I'm the one who ticked him off with all my sassing. It's my fault. All my fault."

The image of Leo rushing to defend her flooded in, then his many nicknames followed, echoing in her mind—Ginger Cat, Fire Plug, Half Pint, Glib-tongued Grappler—each delivered with a twinkle in his eye.

Yes, he would do anything to protect her. But why?

No matter the reason, she had to do anything to help him. Anything.

She rose and, clenching her fists again, repeated the chest pounding, screaming, "Leo! ... Don't die! ... You can call me ... anything you want. ... Just ..." She rose to her feet and punched his chest once more with all of her weight. "Don't die!"

Leo gasped. His body heaved. Then he settled, breathing with a rasp, his eyes still closed.

"Leo?" Iona laid an ear on his chest. His heart thumped, steady, though weak. Biting her lip, she knelt next to him, sniffing back her tears. "Okay, Leo. I'm here. I'll take care of you. I promise. First, I'll—"

Thunder rumbled. Iona twisted toward the sound. A dark cloud, tinted green, rolled toward them like an ocean wave. It would arrive in seconds.

She looked at the tunnel, only a few steps away. She rose to her feet, her head still dizzy. After steadying herself, she grasped Leo's wrists and began dragging him toward the arched opening, grunting as gusts of wind whipped her hair. "You're not fat enough to be this heavy. What do you have in that cloak? Anvils?"

When she drew within a step of the entry, Leo pulled a hand away. "Stop," he said hoarsely.

"Leo?" She let go of the other hand, rushed to his side, and knelt. "I have to get you to shelter. A big storm's coming." A thunderclap punctuated her warning.

He blinked, then gazed at her steadily. "What about Bazrah?" He licked his lips. "We have to save him."

"I know. You want to do hero stuff. Save the kid and all that rot. But ..." She touched his skin near the wound and raised her voice. "You have a freaking hole in your head, Leo!"

"True. I think the pellet must have shocked my system into cardiac arrest but did little other damage." He interlocked wrists with her. "Help me up. We'll argue while I test my legs."

"Are you sure?"

"About arguing? Absolutely. About my legs? Not even close. But help me up, anyway."

She stood and, leaning back, hoisted him to his feet. He wobbled, but Iona slid an arm around his waist, steadying him. "Can you walk?"

"I have to. Should be downhill. I can manage."

"I know it's downhill. I saw the path. But it'll get slick when it rains. Besides, the storm will keep Harrid from doing whatever he's planning. We'll have time to pin our hero badges on later."

"You have no idea if that's true." Leo pushed his thick mane back, wincing. "And don't go on bad-mouthing being a hero. You don't believe a word of it. Besides, we have to get home, and Dr. Brilliant is our only hope for doing that."

"All right. All right. We'll go." After she found the Toger on the ground and holstered it, the rope she had cut caught her attention, lying in a stack of loops nearby. "We should take the rope in case one of us slips on the path. As gimpy as we are, it could happen."

He eyed the rope. "True, but it'll add to our load."

"Not much. Besides, like I said before, waste not, want not." In the midst of a swirling wind, she picked up the loops and hoisted them over her shoulder, then grasped Leo's hand and set it on the loops. "Hold the rope in place and lean on me at the same time. And don't worry about hurting me. I can take it. I'm stronger than I look."

"I'm sure you are, Gorilla Girl."

When he added weight to her shoulder, she smiled. "Let's take a step together."

As they walked slowly toward the path, he chuckled. "You kind of like that name, don't you?"

She turned her head, trying to squelch her smile as she guided him down the path. "Nope. I mean, seriously, what girl wants to be called a gorilla?"

"Whatever you say, Princess Prevaricator. I'll avoid any further simian references."

"Good. And I'll resist the temptation to throw you into the chasm."

"Fair trade."

Thunder clapped again, drawing closer. Iona strained to keep her back stiff, battling Leo's weight. His pain had to be worse than he was letting on. She couldn't give in to her own pain. Too much was at stake.

With her back bent, she glanced at her chest where her cross usually dangled, but it wasn't there—left behind on the floor, a prayer for help. As she imagined it around her neck, Chantal's sacrifice returned to mind, her determination, her grit, her courage, qualities that reflected the symbol of the cross she had bestowed to a rookie spy. And now that raw recruit had to live them out for herself, for Leo, for everyone.

She gritted her teeth and pressed on. *God, help me. That's all I ask. Just ... help me.*

Ben and Caligar sprinted along the lake's shore and back into the forest. Shouts erupted behind them. After about half a minute, Caligar slowed to a jog. Ben ran abreast. "Why are we slowing down? Are you hurt?"

Caligar gave Ben a quick glance. "I am well. I want them to follow."

"What? Why?" Ben slid his rifle strap off and chambered a round. "Do you want to try to shoot our way out after all?"

"No. I have another solution. You will see."

The shouts grew louder. An arrow thumped into a nearby tree. Another zinged by Ben's ear. "They're getting closer."

"Do you think"—a baseball-sized stone struck Caligar, inciting a grunt —"I am unaware of that?"

"Never mind. I just hope you know what you're doing."

"Trust me." Caligar halted at a stream and pulled Ben to a stop. He raised a hand as if ready to wave at someone ahead. The air shimmered for a moment, like a curtain of wrinkled light. "We wait here."

"Wait?" Ben set the rifle at his hip, ready to sling it up to his shoulder. "Why?"

"As I said before, trust me. You won't need your weapon. If you fire, the sound might draw many more attackers."

The giants appeared about fifty yards away, one with an arrow nocked to his bowstring and the others each carrying a stone. As they approached, they slowed to a jog, their eyes wary.

"Get behind me," Caligar said. "Then take three steps and halt. Do not delay. Your life depends on it."

Ben stepped around the huge man, blocking himself from the other giants' view, then took the three steps. Something in the air tickled, and the scene changed. He stood at a precipice to a deep gorge. The stream spilled parallel to a rope ladder that allowed a climb down to a ledge about fifty feet below.

Ben turned toward the forest. Caligar, still facing the other giants, spoke with a series of whistles and grunts. The giants shouted back, shaking their fists. Caligar responded with a laugh and a short burst of whistles as he wagged his head in a mocking fashion.

The other giants charged. When they drew close, Caligar stepped back, grabbed Ben, and lunged to the side. The giants burst out of the forest. When they saw the precipice, they tried to halt at the cliff's edge, waving their arms to regain their balance.

Caligar rushed to them and pushed them off the cliff one by one. As they plunged, they screamed with fading voices. After a few seconds, several muffled thuds rose from the chasm floor.

Ben looked back. A pair of trees with head-high knots emitted light from holes within the knots, most likely projectors of some kind. "You set a trap for them?"

"For any foot-bound or hoof-bound creature. If they are stupid enough to hurtle into this chasm, they are witless animals."

"Witless? If you hadn't told me to stop, I might've fallen in myself."

"Perhaps." Caligar looked into the depths. "If you are as stupid as they are, but I doubt it."

"How can you be so callous? Don't you have a heart?"

Caligar shook a finger at Ben, glaring down from his greater height. "Now you're in *my* world, Benjamin Garrison, a world you know nothing about. Do not let your ignorance and prejudice lead you into foolishness."

"Okay, ignorance I get. I've never been here before. But prejudice?" Ben slid the rifle strap over his shoulder. "I'm not judging anyone."

Caligar pointed into the chasm. "You are judging them from a position of ignorance. You think they might not fully deserve their demise, but you are ignorant of their corruption, though you are well aware that they tried to kill us moments ago. I, on the other hand, know exactly how vile they are. My judgment is based on experience. They deserved to die."

"I'm not talking about what they deserve. I'm talking about grief over lost souls."

"They have no souls." Caligar stared at Ben, his brow deeply furrowed. Then, with a sigh, his expression loosened, and he began climbing down the ladder, his rifle strapped in place. "Follow, if you wish. I am angered by your presumptuous mindset, but that will not stop me from trying to help you."

As dark clouds drew close, announcing their presence with peals of thunder, Ben edged to the precipice and watched Caligar's progress. About thirty rungs below, he dismounted at a narrow ledge and walked into an alcove that appeared to be a cave. Of course, not following was out of the question, but the tongue lashings were hard to deal with. It would be better to stay quiet for a while and avoid the giant's wrath.

After climbing down the ladder, Ben stood on the lower ledge and faced the deep valley. Caligar returned from the cave and stood next to him, looking through binoculars toward the downstream horizon. "A storm will be upon us in mere seconds." He lowered the glasses. "Rainwater here is more acidic than in your world. It will cause abrasions on your skin."

"And not yours?"

Caligar shook his head. "Our skin is tougher. We drink the rainwater and bathe in it without harm." He entered the cave, calling, "This way. That is, if you still want this callous Viridian to be your guide."

Ben hurried to follow, feeling like a kid toddling after a scolding dad. The feeling was maddening, but he didn't have much choice.

As they strode deeper, Caligar bent under the low ceiling, and light from outside dimmed. Soon, he halted and frowned at an empty lantern bracket protruding from the wall. "Our lanterns are missing."

"Is that unusual?"

"Somewhat. I have told my son many times that if he takes the last lantern, he is to wedge a pebble between the bracket and the wall, a signal that he will return soon with another lantern. But I see no pebble. He has forgotten to do so in the past, but he had been doing well of late before I departed from Viridi." Caligar drew a long knife from a belt sheath. "We might have an intruder."

Ben touched a flashlight on his belt. "Should we stay dark?"

Caligar nodded. "Follow me. I know the way without a light. And I stowed some glow stones farther in for just such an occasion. They are dim enough to avoid raising an alarm."

Ben kept his voice low as well. "How many of you are in your clan?"

"Do you mean my family or in my species?"

"Let's start with species."

"At one time we were a thousand strong." Barely visible now, Caligar stooped and began pulling loose stones from the wall and setting them to the side. "By the time Winella and I left this world,

166

we were only three—myself, Winella, and our son, Bazrah. We had a daughter at one time. Lacinda. But tragedy struck, and she is no longer with us."

Ben's throat narrowed. Hearing about a lost daughter struck home. Their own preborn baby might have been a girl, a daughter he never had a chance to hold. His arms ached at the thought, but this was no time to relive the tragedy.

"Our home," Caligar continued, "also housed Bazrah's caretaker, Melinda, an android. We count her in our family clan, but, of course, not as one of our species."

"An android? That's sophisticated technology."

"You seem surprised." Caligar withdrew a fist-sized stone from the hole he had created and began rubbing it between his hands. "Your world learned how to make androids only two decades ago. And now you have none."

"Because the angels banned and destroyed them. I'm saying that your world seems too primitive to produce androids."

Caligar kept his focus on his hands. "What makes you think this world is primitive?"

"Well, I haven't seen any modern buildings or transportation."

Caligar displayed the stone in his palm. A dim white aura surrounded it, maybe from a friction-activated chemical on the surface. He began walking again, now at a quicker pace. "You are being presumptuous again, Benjamin. You consider a lack of your own images of modernity to be a sign of a primitive society. You are in a new environment. You need to identify and remove your presumptions."

Ben hustled to keep up with the huge man's long-legged gait. "All right. I'll accept that. But if your species has only three members, what happened to the others, besides Lacinda, I mean? And who are the giants who attacked us? Aren't they the same species, or are they devolved like the ones on Earth?"

"They are devolved, as you guessed. We were born the same species, but they are no longer the same. As I said the last time this topic arose, that is all I will say about it."

At the end of the tunnel, a hole in the ceiling illuminated the floor with a white glow from above. When Caligar arrived, he stopped and pinched a ragged rope dangling from above with short rope sections attached to it at intervals. "This is an evil sign. It was a ladder. One of the vertical ropes is gone."

"Broken or cut?"

Caligar lifted the end of one of the shorter sections, then another above it. "Cut cleanly along with every rung above it. The intruder is armed with a knife."

Ben stepped closer and eyed the rope. "To prevent entry, escape, or both?"

"I intend to find out." Caligar set the glow stone down, grasped the broken ladder, and began climbing hand over hand. "If you are able to follow," he said, grunting as he rose, "I suggest you do so. Otherwise you will have to wait until I can repair the ladder."

When Caligar had climbed through the ceiling hole, Ben grabbed the ladder and ascended past the lower hole and through a rocky cylinder. After a few moments, Caligar hoisted himself into an upper chamber and walked out of sight.

As Ben drew close to the chamber, he quieted himself and listened. Above, Caligar called for Bazrah and Melinda, but no one answered.

Ben scrambled the rest of the way up, grasped the edge of the hole, and hoisted himself out. He rose to his feet on the wooden floor and looked around at what appeared to be a circular observatory room twenty feet in diameter with a telescope aimed at a glass dome about fifteen feet above.

An open exit door to one side appeared to lead to another chamber. Loud footsteps tromped from somewhere beyond, drawing closer. Caligar ran through the doorway and into the observatory, out of breath. "No one is here. Melinda would have left some kind of message. Her programming won't allow a deviation from that behavior."

"Did you see any clues at all? Signs of a struggle?"

Caligar nodded. "A circular burn mark in a wall. I found no cause for it."

Ben scanned the room. Something odd protruded from a hole at the base of the telescope. He stepped over and snatched it up—a wooden cross attached to a cord. Iona's cross. He laid it on his palm and showed it to Caligar. "My friend from Earth was here. This was precious to her."

Caligar touched the cross. "She dropped it accidentally?"

"She would've noticed. Maybe she left it as a message to me."

"She wouldn't leave a message for you unless she knew you were coming, which is impossible." Caligar looked at the telescope. "Unless ..." He took two long steps and sat on the stool. He closed one eye and set the other at the scope's viewing lens. After a few seconds of silence, he used a finger and thumb to turn a dial near the lens. "Clouds are obscuring my view, but the scope is positioned on the Oculus Gate, which is not unusual, but I am certain that I left it focused on the Maxial Nebula." He drew back and looked at Ben. "Only Bazrah and Melinda know how to alter it ... except ..." He rose from the seat and stepped back. "Could he have been here?"

Ben slid the cross into his pocket. "Who?"

"Allow me to check something before I answer." Caligar reached up and touched the ceiling. The glass darkened, and stars appeared along with two yellowish moons, one at each side of the room. The Oculus Gate shone directly overhead, its elliptical eye looking slightly askew as it covered about a quarter of the ceiling.

"This is a light energy view that penetrates the clouds." Caligar set a finger on one of the perimeter's lights and, his fingertip acting like a phosphorescent marker, drew a glowing line across to another light, a bright ribbon connecting the points. Symbols appeared within the ribbon, constantly changing. Caligar squinted at the symbols for a moment, then looked at Ben. "A new conduit is forming at the Oculus Gate."

Ben focused on the symbols, though they were meaningless to him. "Winella fired up the towers again?"

Caligar shook his head. "It's forming from my world, not yours, which means someone stole my technology."

"Someone? You mean the person you mentioned a minute ago? The one you suspected of being here?"

"Correct." Caligar's lips twitched, an unusual tic for him, maybe a hint of fear. "I am now certain he was in this room."

"What makes you certain?"

Caligar waved a hand across the ceiling, clearing the screen and bringing cloud-obscured daylight into the room again. He knelt at a floor cabinet and flung its door open. "No one else on this world has enough intelligence to use the technology." He pushed his head into the cabinet and began rummaging, his voice muffled. "The thief took Bazrah for leverage, and Melinda would follow. Her programming requires it. My guess is if your friend is valiant, then she, too, would follow to try to stop this madman."

"Iona is valiant, but I think she was forced to go. If she followed after the fact, she would've left the cross in a more obvious place. For some reason, she didn't want it to be seen. And the cutting of the rope doesn't add up."

"We are merely speculating. The answers lie at a nearby site where we must go as soon as I learn if the fiend located ..." Caligar emerged from the cabinet with a small box in the palm of his hand. He opened it and looked inside. "It's empty. He probably forced Bazrah to locate the device he needed to power the conduit."

Ben cocked his head, unable to read the alien-language label on the box. "What is it?"

"A catalyst of sorts." He set the box back in the cabinet. "It is too complex to explain now."

"Does that mean the intruder had a weapon? I assume Bazrah wouldn't give him the device willingly."

"Correct. Without a weapon, Melinda would have been able to overpower him. She has defensive capabilities that can protect Bazrah from all but the strongest of my species … I mean, the other hominid species of my world."

Ben let Caligar's slip of the tongue pass. "And Melinda had help from Bazrah and Iona, and maybe from Leo, if he was able to come with her. He is a formidable man."

Caligar's huge eyes seemed to brighten. "Would Leo have left something to signal his presence?"

"Like Iona's cross? Good question." Ben knelt at the base of the telescope and pushed a finger into the hole where he had found the cross. Something smooth and round lay inside, like a small marble. He coaxed it out, pinched it, and brought it close to his eyes. "It's a miniature smoke bomb. Definitely Leo's. That's great news."

"I am pleased for your sake and Iona's. I hope his presence is also helpful for Bazrah." Caligar closed the cabinet door. "Come. We must go to the site where the thief is likely employing the technology. If we fail to arrive in time, all of our efforts could be for naught."

Chapter Seventeen

With the path steepening as it twisted in sharp switchbacks that led in the downstream direction toward a distant mesa, Iona quieted herself, watching each step she made and listening to Leo's labored breathing. Although her head still pounded, it wasn't as bad as before, and concentrating on the task helped her ignore the pain, at least part of the time.

Raindrops fell. Most hit her clothes, but when the water passed through the scarf and seeped into her head wound, it stung, nearly as painful as a wasp sting. She used the scarf to dab at the wound and looked at the material. Fresh blood. The acidic rainwater had already done some damage.

The path narrowed, with a sheer wall on one side and a sharp drop-off on the other. The rain strengthened. Drops pelted her face and hands. Both stung sharply. Iona touched Leo's hand on her shoulder. "Hold on tight. The rainwater's acidic, like Melinda said. We have to go faster."

"A problem for us but a benefit for Bazrah. It won't bother him, but it'll be like nettles to the sensitive scientist."

"Good point. And maybe Bazrah will figure out a way to use it."

As they continued walking as fast as the hazards would allow, the clouds boiled. Rain and wind strengthened to a raging tempest. Sheets of acidic water assaulted them, burning their skin and slickening the path.

Iona trudged on, though more slowly. Leo's weight on her shoulders made a foot slip from time to time, forcing her to slow further.

Leo shouted to overcome the din. "I see a cleft." He pointed toward the rock face a few steps ahead.

They hurried to the narrow opening, big enough for one person but probably not for two. "You go," Iona said as she slid the rope off her shoulder and set it next to the cleft. "I'll find another one." Leo looked down the path. Water sprayed from his lips as he shouted, "There aren't any others."

Iona set a fist on her hip. "Now don't go playing Mr. Chivalry on me. You're hurt worse than I am."

"That's debatable, but I agree to dispense with chivalry." He grabbed her wrist, ducked into the crevice, and pulled her in, forcing them both into a sitting position, hip to hip and shoulder to shoulder.

Iona tried to shift to get comfortable, but the surrounding rock wouldn't allow more than an inch of movement. Fortunately, the crevice provided enough depth to keep her feet out of the rain, though Leo's protruded somewhat. "Tight squeeze, especially for a long-legged Leo."

He drew his feet in, pushing her against the rocky barrier, then let them slide out again and relieving the pressure. "This will have to do. It could be worse."

"True. If your nose was fully functional, you'd have to put up with smelling me. I was sweating like a horse."

"My nose is back to normal. I was tracking Sir Hissy Fit's scent. He smells like he's been eating wild garlic. He was about a mile away when the storm hit and sent the odors flying. Regarding your scent, it's ... well ... better than horse sweat."

Iona smirked. "You really are the charmer, aren't you?"

"I'd do better, I'm sure, if I didn't have a hole in my head. Hurts like the devil himself is poking me with a pitchfork."

"We have to figure out if that proton thing is lodged inside. I didn't check for an exit wound." She pried her arm out from between their bodies, slid a finger into his shaggy hair, and ran it along his scalp until she came upon a small opening. "Yeah. It came through. The heat must've cauterized everything."

"I still feel the heat on the wounds, but it might be from the acid rain."

She drew her finger back. "Like you guessed, it probably hit something that messed up your heart. You were clinically dead for a while. I had to pound on you like a maniac to bring you back."

"Well, that explains the chest pain." He shifted his weight again, giving her room to move her arm back to her side. "Thank you for saving me."

"You're welcome." As the terrifying images returned, her throat tightened. "And thanks for defending me. It was stupid for me to keep agitating him." She patted his hand. "You're the best."

"My pleasure, Miss Heart of a Lioness. My pleasure."

She inhaled deeply and smiled. That label could hang in the air as long as it wanted to.

As they watched the rain pummel the path and cast swirling sheets of white across the valley, the residual droplets continued stinging, but not as badly. Their skin had probably neutralized most of whatever chemical the rain had deposited.

After a few minutes, her odor became obvious to her own nose, resurrecting Leo's horse-sweat comment and a question that had been lurking for quite a while. "Leo, I've been wanting to ask you something. Why did you hunt for me? I mean, you could've turned down the angels when they summoned you, right?"

"Well, as you might expect, turning the angels down is a risky option, but huntsmen can give them any number of excuses, such as having a bad cold or whatnot. In your case, when Constance showed me your photo, I immediately noticed the resemblance between you and my sister, Lorelei. I wondered if you were somewhere in the family tree, maybe a cousin. And when I saw that impish grin, I knew you must've had the same personality as Lorelei—saucy and sassy to the core—but at the same time, I guessed you had the same heart, like I said before, the heart of a lioness. Pure gold. Yes, you probably got under the skin of a temple angel or two ... or three ... or four, and as vindictive as they were, they wanted your head for it. I had to find out why, and I didn't want some other huntsman searching for you, someone who didn't care what you were charged

174

with or whether you were guilty or innocent." He shook his head. "A greedy, uncaring lot we huntsmen are."

She elbowed his ribs. "Except for you."

"You give me too much credit. Although I limit my cases to true criminals, I am still a mercenary. I do it for money."

She leaned forward and tried to look him in the eye. "You say that, but I don't believe it."

He averted his gaze. "Believe what you want, Diminutive Doubter. If not for the money, I wouldn't do it."

Iona huffed. "You have to make a living. Nothing wrong with that."

"True, but being a confirmed bachelor, I don't need as much as I make. The angels pay well for the tough cases. To put it bluntly, I like being able to buy whatever I want."

"You mean like that ratty old cloak that probably belonged to your great-grandfather, those all-weather boots you probably took from a dead sea captain, and that pipe that has more teeth marks in it than a beaver dam? Yeah. You're a big spender."

"I didn't say I bought everything I want. Just that I like being able to. And he wasn't a dead sea captain. The boots belonged to my alpha huntsman when I was in training. He gave them to me when he saw that I had nothing but a pair of sneakers."

"All right. I'm not going to argue about that, but as long as you're in a thankful mood for me saving your life, can I ask some more personal questions?"

"I might not answer them all." He shrugged. "But it won't hurt to ask. Fire away."

"Okay." Iona tapped her thigh with a finger, pretending to ponder, though one question had been on her mind for quite a while. "How about this one? Why are you a bachelor?"

Leo chuckled. "She doesn't start with my favorite food or if I prefer mountains over beaches. No, the inquisitive imp fires from her quiver of questions straight to the heart."

She took on a fake tone of sympathy. "Oh? Too sensitive for Mr. Macho? Okay, I understand. How about—"

"Wait a minute. Wait a minute." He gave her a scolding stare. "Mr. Macho? Is that on the approved label list?"

"You don't have a list. I get to call you whatever I want."

"Oh, so *that's* how it works."

"Yep. Deal with it."

"I can deal with labels, but why *Mr. Macho*? Is that how you see me?"

"Not in a negative way." She folded her hands on her lap. That label seemed to ruffle his feathers. She would have to smooth things over. "When I think of macho, I think of masculine courage, aggressiveness, everything it takes to be a huntsman and to charge at a crazed scientist with a gun who wants to hurt kids."

"But not sensitive."

She tightened her hands. Did he want to be thought of as sensitive? Probably not. "No. I guess that's not part of the macho package. I mean, seriously, when was the last time you cried?"

"Easy." Leo took a deep breath and let it out slowly, his eyes averted. "When my sister died." He bit his lip and fell silent.

Iona stayed quiet for a moment, allowing Leo's emotions to settle. This huntsman obviously had a soft heart beneath his crusty exterior. Kind of unexpected, but it was all good. And he had every right to protect it from savage grief, a stabbing dagger she knew all too well. She softened her voice. "And you haven't cried since?"

He shook his head. "I cried many times as she lay moaning in bed, feverish, cramping, nauseated. Since our parents had already died from the plague and we had no nearby relatives, I cared for her myself, a difficult job for a boy of sixteen."

"Sixteen? Didn't you say Lorelai was sixteen when she died?"

He nodded. "We were eleven months apart. I was the younger."

"So you were barely sixteen, and you had to take care of your older sister with no parents? That had to be terribly hard."

"It was, especially when she grew too weak to bathe herself after she vomited or … well, you can imagine."

"Unfortunately, I can." Tears crept into Iona's eyes. "Oh, Leo. It's no wonder you cried so many times then. It had to be heartbreaking."

"Heartbreaking, yes, but I learned that crying did no good. Neither did praying. No matter what I did, Lorelai died, and she suffered every day, even to her last breath."

"I'm sorry, Leo." Iona slid her hand into his. "I'm so, so sorry."

He compressed her hand. "I appreciate your sentiment. Really. But that's why I never cry. It's nothing more than a reminder of pain, and I didn't want reminders. They're crippling. I mean, you can't detect a scent when your nose is running." A trembling smile emerged. "A macho huntsman like me can't have that, right?"

"Crying doesn't mean you're not macho. It just means that you care. That you have a heart. And whoever heard of courage without heart?" She released his hand and poked his thigh. "And you, Leo, are loaded with heart. Someday it's going to spill out in a million tears, and this girl will be the first to call you Mr. Macho, not in spite of the tears but because of them."

Leo's smile widened. "The Eloquent Elf is at the top of her game today." His smile suddenly wilted. "Sorry. I keep forgetting about the label promise."

"No worries. From now on, you can call me anything you want."

"Dangerous, my dear girl, but I will be judicious."

She refolded her hands in her lap and forced lightness back into her tone. "Okay, now after all that schmaltz, back to my question. Why are you a bachelor? I mean, you're a hairy mess sometimes, but you've got a handsome face, and you're kind. To me, anyways. I think lots of women would be attracted to you."

A shadow seemed to darken his features. "I had my share of romance during my teen years. Several girlfriends, nothing more than puppy love—kisses and hugs. But when I was in my late teen years, I became involved with Charlotte, a thirty-year-old woman. I fell madly in love. She was the one, if you understand my meaning. And since I had no family, I was already out on my own, training to be a huntsman. I thought of myself as an adult, ready to be a husband and father. That's why I asked her to marry me."

Leo paused, shifting his body. Iona waited. This story had to be painful, especially after spilling his guts about Lorelai. "Take your time, Leo. I understand."

"You understand that being cramped in here is stopping blood flow to my legs?"

"Oh." She slid away as far as she could, pressing herself against the rocks. "Is that better?"

He shifted again. "There. See if you can sit where you were."

She slid back into place. "Okay?"

He nodded. "As I was saying, I asked her to marry me. Want to guess what she said?"

"She said no?"

"Worse. She said, 'You?' and started laughing."

"What a witch!" Iona covered her mouth. "Sorry."

"Don't be sorry. She had some witchy ways, though I was blind to them at the time."

"Then what happened?"

"She told me that she liked me but that I was a boy toy, someone to play with when she wanted to be entertained, not someone to be committed to for a lifetime." He shrugged, his voice strained as if pushing past a lump in his throat. "Then she left. Forever."

"Oh, Leo. That's awful."

"It was, but I was blind. A stupid kid looking for love without a guide to keep me from following a dark path. So I swore off women ever since. And that's why I am a bachelor to this day."

Iona let the words soak in for a moment, every bit as stinging as the rainwater. Recalling those sad and lonely days had to be painful. And how well she knew the torture of sad memories. Many a night she had dreamed of the tragic day she lost her parents to the plague. In a way, she and Leo were kindred orphans. They knew each other's pain. Maybe she could say something to ease his anguish. "Leo, it's not a dark path to have a girlfriend. You wanted a companion, a confidante. I mean, how else can you find someone to marry?"

"I left out an important detail." He averted his eyes again. "You see, after she left, I learned from the Huntsmen's Book of Ethics, much of which is based on the Christian Bible, that the old prophets would have called my relationship with her sinful. They were right. But I'm not going to say anything more about that."

"You mean you and she …" Iona's ears warmed. "Never mind."

"I understand. It wasn't so much of a taboo at the time as it is now, but that's no excuse for my youthful foolishness."

"Yeah. Before the angels came, morality was in the toilet. They swung the pendulum to the other extreme. In the temple, you couldn't even say the word …" As she took a deep breath, more warmth flooded her cheeks. "Sex."

Leo's brow lifted. "Really? Not even utter the word?"

"Nope. You'd get slapped across the mouth."

"Your face is turning red. Shall we change the subject?"

"Um … yeah. In a minute." She folded her hands once more, her stare locked on her tight fingers. "Listen. What you did in the past is exactly that. In the past. Who you were then isn't important. Only who you are today. What you did back then was bad, but God can use anything for good. Even the stupid things we did, and I did plenty of them."

Leo smiled. "And today you're a motivational speaker."

"Okay. *Now* we're changing the subject." A yawn broke through, wide and stretching. Then, exhaustion flooded in. "Wow! I'm whupped."

"Maybe you'd better get some sleep."

"Can't. When I was a kid, every time I bumped my head, my mother told me I shouldn't sleep. Something about brain bleed."

"I've heard that. It's best not to sleep for three to six hours after a head injury. It hasn't been nearly that long since you took a knock to your noggin."

Iona yawned again. "Any idea when we last slept?"

"I lost track. Maybe twenty hours ago."

"Then I'll have to take my chances." She blinked hard. "I'm crashing."

"Well, Dr. Genius won't be able to do anything until the storm's over, so go ahead and sleep if you can. Pretty uncomfortable in here, though."

"Better than the bottom of a manure pile with a certain huntsman chasing me."

Leo laughed. "That, I'll wager, is as true as it gets. And I could use a few winks myself. At least I'll forget about that fire in my head for a while."

"Sounds good." Iona closed her eyes. "Good night, Leo. Thanks again for everything."

"Good night ... uh ... well ... I must be tired. I can't think of another name for you."

She leaned her head against his shoulder. "Sleepy Sister. Or maybe Little Lorelai."

"That ..." He leaned his head against hers, his voice cracking. "That'll do. That'll do just fine."

Chapter Eighteen

Caligar strode to the hole in the floor and began sliding down, barely hanging on to the rope as he plummeted. Ben followed and mimicked the slide, glad for his gloves as the friction warmed the material along with his skin.

Once at the bottom, they ran through the tunnel, Caligar with the glow stone in hand. When he burst thought the opening, he called back, "Stay at the entrance."

Ben halted at the arched opening and watched through a curtain of blowing rain.

Caligar halted at the edge of the precipice and used his binoculars to look downstream as sheets of rainwater pelted his head. "The river has swollen considerably. This storm has provided a benefit. It will inhibit the thief's efforts and provide us with concealment, but it will also bring us danger if the river continues to rise. It's impossible to guess how much rain will fall." He looked at Ben. "Will knowledge of the danger cause you to hesitate?"

"Not for a second." Ben strode into the pouring rain and joined Caligar at the edge. The acidic water stung his face, but with the rest of his body covered, he could endure it.

Caligar pointed downstream. "The conduit site is a reflective disc at ground level, out of our view at the moment because of the cloudy sky, and the controlling mechanism is on top of a low mesa that overlooks the disc, perhaps four miles from here. We will have to traverse a winding path down to the river and cross it if the level is low enough. The path will be slippery."

Wincing at the needlelike rain, Ben nodded. "Whenever you're ready."

Caligar slid the rifle strap from his shoulder and held the weapon firmly with both hands. "I am ready." He strode along the ledge.

Ben readied his rifle as well. Apparently Caligar was no longer worried about alerting giants with gunfire. He meant to take the kidnapper out by any means possible.

The path sloped downward for a few hundred feet, then switched back and ran under the ledge where they had been standing before.

Ben kept his head low, his stare fixed on the path as he paced alongside Caligar. "When will you tell me who the intruder is?"

"I will tell you now." Caligar spoke without breaking stride. "He is a scientist from your planet."

"From Earth? How did he get here?"

"It's a long story that I do not wish to tell at this time. We have to concentrate on stopping him or else Earth will be destroyed. I will relate his tale at a later time."

"Understood." Treading with care, Ben glanced at the plunge to one side and the cliff face to the other. After they negotiated a third switchback, something moved within a crevice at the base of the cliff a few paces ahead. A coiled rope leaned against the rock face nearby.

Ben stopped. "Hold it."

When Caligar paused, his foot slipped on a muddy section of the path. He fell to his stomach, and his lower body slid feet-first over the precipice. With a loud grunt, he flung his rifle away and grabbed the ledge with both hands.

Ben threw his rifle on the ground and dove toward Caligar. Lying on his stomach, he latched on to Caligar's forearms. "I've got you."

The ledge crumbled. Caligar's fingers fell through the loosened soil. As he dropped, Ben slid toward the edge, still hanging on. Straining as the giant's slippery skin slid through his grasp, Ben shouted, "Can you grab my wrists?"

Caligar twisted his arms and latched on to Ben's wrists, halting the slip.

Bryan Davis

Ben, his waist now at the ledge and his torso vertical, flexed every muscle, trying to keep from being dragged downward. The acidic downpour passed through his shirt and stung his wounded back. His arm muscles burned. He wouldn't last long. "Can you climb me? Like a rope ladder?"

"I'm too heavy. You have to let me fall."

"But you'll die if I do."

"We'll both die if you don't."

Ben grunted, his words squeezing out in gasping bullets. "You have ... a wife ... and son. You have ... to try ... for their sakes."

"Very well." Caligar pulled on Ben's arm with one hand and thrust the other past Ben's elbow. The sudden shift jerked Ben's shoulder from its socket. Pain scorched his senses. He let out a cry, then bit his lip to squelch it.

Caligar released that arm and dangled by the other. "It won't work."

Ben yelled, "I won't give up."

"Let me go, Benjamin. For the sake of *your* wife. It's the only way."

"No! There's always ... another way."

Caligar jerked, trying to pull free, but Ben held fast.

Something heavy landed on his legs. "I've got you, Farmer Jones! Hang on!"

"Leo?"

"Iona! Toss it! Now!"

A rope fell across Ben's body and dropped to Caligar. The moment he grabbed it, Ben let him go. Caligar slid down the rope a few feet, but when his hands dropped to a knot, he stopped his plunge.

Leo pulled Ben back to the path. Both sat upright, facing each other. New pain roared through Ben's shoulder as his arm hung limp at his side.

183

Gusts swirling the heavy rain, Leo scrambled to his feet, knelt at the ledge, and reached down. "I don't know who you are, but if Ben was trying to save you, that's good enough for me."

Ben grimaced as he looked around. Iona stood about ten feet up the cliff face, peering out from behind a rock formation, the rope secured around it. Rainwater plastered her hair against her face as she smiled while wincing.

He gave her a thumbs up. She returned the gesture, her smile widening.

Leo locked wrists with Caligar and rose to his feet, pulling the giant to the path. When they both settled, Leo turned toward Ben. "You appear to be in pain, Farmer Jones."

Ben nodded. "I dislocated my shoulder."

"I can help with that. My huntsman training included a number of simple orthopedic maneuvers." Leo looked at Caligar. "Our little leprechaun had to stand on my shoulders to reach her perch. You look more qualified than I am to help her down."

His expression grim, Caligar glanced at Ben before stepping to the wall where Iona stood, untying the rope from the rock. He set a hand on each of her hips, lifted her, and set her on the path as easily as a human would a small child.

Iona extended a hand. "My name is Iona. Pleased to meet you."

Caligar shook her hand, then abruptly turned away, picked up his rifle, and looked down the path.

Iona crouched beside Ben and whispered, "He seems to know our language. What's his problem?"

"He does know the language. Better than I do, in fact." Ben winced at the pain. "He's, well … different."

"Time to fix you up." Leo knelt next to Ben and grasped his upper and lower arm, a hand on each. "Ready?"

Ben nodded. "It can't hurt more than it already—" His shoulder popped. Pain roared again, then settled.

"Now rotate it."

Ben did so, slowly at first, then more quickly. The pain had ebbed to a mere sting. "That's great, Leo. Thanks."

"My pleasure." Leo grasped Ben's other wrist and helped him rise.

Ben rotated his shoulder once more. Not only had that pain diminished, so had the stinging from the rain, now a gentle drizzle, though the wind continued in blustery gusts as the clouds raced away. "Why are you and Iona here?"

Leo picked up Ben's rifle and handed it to him. "We were on our way to find a lad named Bazrah when the storm hit. Then we took shelter in a hole in the cliff."

Ben strapped the rifle on. He gestured toward Caligar, the giant's back toward them as he stared farther down the path. "That's Caligar. Bazrah is his son."

"Ah. No wonder he's so focused." Leo ran a boot along the muddy trail. "Shall we continue on this precipitous path while we compare notes?"

"In a second." Ben patted his pants pocket while looking at Iona. "I found your cross. Good thinking."

"Thanks. If not for Bazrah, it wouldn't've worked, but we can tell you more while we're on our way."

Ben slid a hand into his pocket. "Do you want it now?"

"It can wait till we're done." She nodded toward Caligar. "I think he wants to get moving."

"Okay, then. Let's go."

With Caligar leading the way, the foursome trooped down the zigzagging route with cautious steps. "Did you find Leo's smoke bomb?" Iona asked Ben.

"Yes." Ben looked at Leo. "Want it back?"

Leo waved a hand. "Keep it. I have more."

As they walked, they filled each other in on the highlights of what had happened since they were separated. After a few minutes, the path leveled, and they waded across a swiftly flowing river. The water rose to Ben's waist, stinging again, though with less intensity.

The rushing current forced him to plant each foot with a stiff leg to keep from being knocked over as he held the rifle high to keep it out of the water. "Getting precarious," he called to Leo and Iona.

"You mean especially for short people," Iona said. "We've got it covered."

Ben glanced back. She rode on Leo's shoulders, grinning. "One advantage to being the smallest."

Soon, they trudged up to dry land, and Leo lowered Iona to the ground. Caligar pointed toward a mesa, now only about half a mile away across a flat expanse of boulders and scrub trees. "That is our destination. While we are still out of Harrid's hearing range, I will tell you more about it, though if he is wary, he might be watching for us, which would spoil a stealth approach. We will stay close to the trees and rock formations to help us avoid detection."

They strode on, all four now able to walk abreast as the path meandered alongside the river. Caligar pointed toward the mesa. "Since the control mechanism of the conduit is near the edge on the opposite side of the mesa's top, Dr. Harrid is likely there so that he can monitor the mirror's activity, though because of the mesa's slant, we can't see him from here."

"The conduit is a mirror?" Ben asked.

Caligar nodded. "It is a circular mirror embedded in the ground at the foot of the mesa on the opposite side, and it reflects the Oculus Gate."

Leo raised a finger. "I think I saw the mirror from the ledge near your tunnel. I thought it was a lake."

"Yes, the reflective surface does look like a body of water from far away." Caligar pointed toward the right side of the mesa. "Harrid cannot see us until we climb a series of steps at a spot halfway around. And even then, he might be too busy to notice. If he is as overconfident as he usually is, we should have a chance to arrive unseen."

Iona took off her scarf and looked at the coagulated blood in the material while she spoke. "What's that egotistical cockroach doing up there?"

"He is trying to reactivate a conduit between the mirror and the Oculus Gate, which would draw him away from Viridi. The pull from the Gate will keep him from falling too quickly, though with no one here to alter the Gate's pull based on his rate of fall, he would be taking a great risk."

"Super big." Iona stepped to the edge of the stream, dipped her scarf in, and returned, wringing out blood-tinged water. "The water has healing properties."

Ben nodded. "Good to know."

"Anyway." She retied her scarf over her head, wincing as the material pressed against her wound. "Couldn't Bazrah just turn the mirror off and let Dr. Horrid go kersplat on the earth?"

"Yes," Caligar said without breaking stride. "Bazrah knows how to use the ground-station controls. I assume that is why Harrid took Melinda. She will enforce his wishes. She can prevent Bazrah from interfering without doing him harm."

"Not enough of a safeguard. Dr. Horrid saw you two through his telescope, so he knows you're in the area and that you can blow Melinda into nuts and bolts."

Ben chuckled. "You keep calling him Horrid instead of Harrid. Is there a reason? Besides the fact that you think he's horrid, I mean."

"Yeah. I was trying to shake him up. You know, get him to make a mistake. The name stuck. To me, he's Dr. Horrid from now on."

"Responding to your point," Caligar said, "you are correct about Harrid's potential concern that we might shut the system down, which means he probably has a parachute. And to be completely sure, I am confident that he plans to take my son with him in order to protect his journey from interference."

Iona rolled her eyes upward as if in thought. "Then let them go. When they land safely, we blow Melinda to pieces, follow them through the Gate, repair the tower, and send Bazrah and Winella home. And Caligar, if he comes to Earth with us."

Ben checked his rifle. A round was still chambered. "If we attack immediately and rescue Bazrah, that would simplify matters and reduce the number of transfers between worlds. Sending someone to Viridi increases the chance of quakes on Earth, right?"

"An attack might endanger my son," Caligar said. "If it seems we cannot rescue him, he is safer if we execute the girl's plan. If Harrid takes Bazrah, and the three of you follow, I will allow Winella and Bazrah to dwell on Earth while I remain here to control your descent. Perhaps in the future we can work on a safe method to transport them home, one that will not create an earthquake."

"That's quite a sacrifice, but I won't try to talk you out of it."

When they drew near the mesa, Caligar set a silencing finger to his lips. The path narrowed, boulders at each side, forcing them to walk single file. When they reached the nearly vertical wall, Caligar led them on an elevated path, a ledge barely wide enough to set one foot in front of the other, the wall on their left and a ten-foot drop to the river on their right.

Soon, they arrived at a set of steep stairs that ran alongside the wall, leading up and to the right. Caligar slid his rifle down from his shoulder. "Benjamin, the final stair is wide enough for both of us to take a sniper position at the same level. You will shoot Melinda while I shoot Dr. Harrid, though our decision to fire will depend on Bazrah's safety."

"Understood." Ben turned toward Leo and Iona. "Go back to where the path ended at the base of the mesa and draw Harrid's attention. That'll give us a better chance for a good shot."

Iona glanced in that direction. "What's the timing?"

"As soon as you get there. We'll be ready."

The two nodded and hurried away.

Ben and Caligar skulked up the stairs. When they reached the last step before the top, they crouched side by side, peeked over the edge, and scanned the mesa's nearly flat surface.

Dr. Harrid perched near the edge to the right, clutching Bazrah's wrist as he looked out over the area beneath the mesa, probably toward the mirror. Wearing Iona's helmet, Melinda stood in front of a stack of flat rocks, manipulating something with her hands, maybe dials on a control board.

Ben studied Melinda's stance—as natural as could be. She had to be the most realistic android ever.

A shout rose across the mesa. "I don't care what you say, you pig-headed beanpole! No one's here. I'm not taking another step. We need to go back."

"But I smell Bazrah," Leo yelled. "I know he's around here somewhere."

Dr. Harrid walked to that side of the mesa, leaving Bazrah behind. He peeked over the edge and smiled.

Ben aimed his rifle at Melinda and whispered, "On your word."

"I apologize, my friend." Caligar grabbed Ben's rifle, clutched him by the throat, and squeezed. Ben gagged, unable to breathe. He clawed at Caligar's face, but the huge man extended his long arm, pushing him farther away.

Ben slid a hand into his pocket and withdrew Leo's smoke bomb. As he reared his arm back to throw it, darkness flooded his vision. His muscles numbed. With a windmill motion, he slung the bomb toward Leo and Iona and slipped into unconsciousness.

Chapter Nineteen

Something popped toward the top of the mesa. Iona looked that way. Although Dr. Horrid had peeked over the edge earlier, he was gone now. She whispered to Leo, "What do you make of that noise?" He narrowed his eyes. "Odd. I expected two or three well-placed rifle shots."

"Same here." She pressed her back against the mesa wall. Leo joined her as they looked straight up. "What does your nose tell you?"

Leo inhaled deeply. "Smoke from one of my miniature bombs. Ben had one."

"A warning?"

"Or a call for help. Either way, we march to the fire. No retreat." Iona gave him a firm nod. "My turn to go first. You're still wounded."

"As if you're not."

"Yeah. So sue me." She sidestepped around the mesa, her back close to the wall, Leo following in the same manner.

When they reached the stairs, they climbed quietly, their shoulders rubbing the curved mesa wall. Soon, an edge of the mirror came into view. About fifty feet in diameter, the entire disc appeared to be embedded in the ground.

Iona and Leo crouched at the second-to-last step and peered over the ledge to the mesa's top. Ninety degrees to their right and facing the mirror, Dr. Horrid, wearing a parachute, stood at the edge with Bazrah, both with their legs bent as if ready to jump. Still wearing Iona's helmet, Melinda operated a control board on top of a stack of stones while Ben lay motionless nearby, his rifle and ammo belt lying only a few feet away from Iona, just out of reach.

Caligar stood next to Ben, his rifle aimed at Ben and his eyes wary as he scanned the area.

Leo pulled Iona down and whispered, "Caligar's a traitor."

"No kidding. But Ben must be alive. Otherwise Caligar wouldn't be threatening him."

"He's alive. I saw his chest moving."

"When Caligar's not looking, I can grab Ben's rifle and put a bullet up Caligar's nostril before he can blink an eye."

"Dangerous, but it's the only plan we have. Maybe instead of killing him ..." Leo touched his wrist. "Think you can hit the trigger hand?"

"Yep." She rose and peeked again. Everyone was in the same position as before. When Caligar looked away for a moment, Iona crept to the top of the mesa then toward the rifle. Just as she picked it up, a brilliant light shot up from the mirror, angling upward and making a shimmering white cone that formed a halo around the Oculus Gate above, like a super-powered flashlight beam.

Caligar's gaze locked on Iona and Leo. "Stay where you are, or I will—"

Iona fired from the hip. The bullet struck Caligar's wrist, sending the rifle flying. She charged, the rifle still at her hip as the sound of Leo's footsteps thundered behind her. "Stand down, Caligar," she shouted, "or the next bullet's between your eyes."

He backed away and barked a command. "Now!"

Dr. Horrid grabbed Bazrah and leaped through the cone. They flew upward toward the Oculus Gate.

Iona halted, blinking at the radiance. "What in the world?"

In her blinded vision, a large silhouette lifted a smaller one. She blinked hard and shielded her eyes, clearing her vision. Caligar stood with Ben hoisted over his shoulder. "She won't shoot now," Caligar said, "for fear of striking her friend."

Iona aimed at Caligar's head. "You have no idea, you big oaf. I could put a bullet straight through your pea brain. And who are you talking to, anyway?"

"To me." Melinda turned from the control board and faced Iona and Leo. "Caligar is my servant."

As Leo sidled close to Iona, she kept her aim locked on Caligar and whispered, "We've been had."

Leo nodded. "For breakfast, lunch, and dinner."

Melinda reached back to the control board and flipped a switch. The cone of light faded and disappeared. "Benjamin Garrison is the leader of the group that disrupted our plans." She pointed toward the mirror. "Caligar, cast him into hell."

Caligar strode toward the mesa's edge.

"No!" Iona fired at Caligar's leg and hit his calf. He toppled forward, throwing Ben as he fell. Ben flew through the air and out of sight.

Iona dashed to the edge and looked down in time to see Ben strike the mirror. Radiance splashed in a blinding display of sparks and arcing light. When it settled, he was gone.

Caligar sat up and groaned as he held a hand over his leg wound. Iona swung her rifle toward Melinda, her heart racing as she tried to steady her breathing. "Talk fast, tin butt, or you'll be scrap metal in three seconds."

Melinda chuckled. Her mechanical grin coupled with a badly fitting helmet made her look idiotic. "You won't kill me. I'm your only hope to—"

Iona fired round after round. Bullets ripped into Melinda's chest and filled her with holes. Her upper half broke off and fell over, leaving wobbly legs behind. When Iona halted the barrage, they, too, toppled.

Heaving shallow breaths and trying not to cry, Iona firmed her jaw. "Wrong answer, junk heap." She pivoted toward Caligar and growled, "If you don't want me to ventilate your hide, you'd better start talking. What happened to Ben?"

"And," Leo added, now holding Caligar's rifle, "I would like to know why you were following the orders of a robot."

Bryan Davis

Caligar shifted, grimacing. "To answer the first question, Benjamin has passed through a portal. He is alive and relatively unharmed. I put a sleeper hold on him. He will likely awaken in a few minutes. To answer your second question, Melinda was merely a mouthpiece. I was following the orders of the woman who is holding my daughter hostage. Her name is Lacinda, and that woman was transmitting her voice through Melinda."

"Your daughter?" Iona asked. "Bazrah's sister?"

"Yes. Lacinda is several years older than Bazrah. The woman who captured her is murderous and insane, and she will kill my daughter if I don't do what she says."

"Okay. You were desperate to save your daughter. I get that." Iona grabbed her helmet from the ground near Melinda's severed head. "So where are they? Your daughter and the witch, I mean."

"In hell. Both of them. And now Ben is there as well."

Iona slid her scarf down to her neck and put the helmet on, wincing as it touched her head wound. "That mirror is a portal to hell?"

"If a person were to drop into it, yes." Caligar cringed as blood dripped between his fingers. "It's a one-way door for the living or the dead. As far as I know, there is no way to leave."

"How do you know Lacinda's there?"

"Alexandria would let her talk through Melinda at times in order to convince me to obey."

Iona tucked the rifle under her arm and strapped her helmet in place. "Alexandria is the witch? That's an Earth name, isn't it?"

"Right." Leo stroked his chin as he eyed Caligar. "Alexandria was a city in Egypt. It had a great library that burned long ago. Later, during the radioactive era, the entire city fell to flames. Rare is the parent who would name a child after an ash heap, so it's an odd choice, unless she lived before the fire."

"I have heard that she is old," Caligar said. "Quite old. Though I don't know during which era she lived on Earth."

Iona huffed. "I don't care if she's as old as dirt, this Alex chick is going down."

193

"Alexandria, or Alex, as you have dubbed her, will be more formidable than you realize. She reigns over hell and is trying to leave."

Leo gazed at the mirror. "I'll wager she's been using you in some kind of escape plan."

"Correct, but I will not reveal the plan, lest you try to foil it."

"Foil it?" Iona's cheeks spiked hot. "Listen, you ten-foot-tall traitor. Ben saved your life. If not for him, you would've fallen to the bottom of the chasm. Food for buzzards. And your daughter would be trapped in hell forever. And even when his shoulder dislocated, he wouldn't let go of your good-for-nothing carcass. Then he risked his life to help you save your son. And how did you reward him? By throwing him into hell."

"I realize—"

"Shut up! I'm not finished!" Iona heaved rapid breaths, her heart pounding even faster. "You could've confided in him. He would've done anything to help you. Anything, no matter how hard. I know, because I've watched him. It's what he does. Hard things, I mean. He sacrifices, no matter how much it hurts him. And he's a master planner. He always finds a way. Always." She inhaled a deep breath and let it out slowly.

"Are you finished?" Caligar asked.

She scowled. "For now."

"Very well." He took a deep breath of his own, his gaze on the ground. "Yes, I could have confided in Benjamin, but I barely knew him. You might think he could devise a plan, but I'm sure he has no experience with portals to hell." He shook his head and focused on Iona. "No. The risk was too great. In fact, if I don't communicate with Alexandria … Alex … soon, she will torture Lacinda."

"How do you communicate with her?"

Caligar nodded toward Melinda's remains. "Through a radio installed in my android. Since you hit her in the chest and not the head, it is probably still functional."

Leo walked that way. "I'll find it."

194

Iona pointed toward the control board with her gun. "Can you contact Earth with that?"

"Yes. The Oculus Gate allows several forms of transmissions to pass through."

Leo returned with Melinda's head in his hands. "I found the transmitter. It was turned on, which means, I assume, that Alex has been listening. I turned it off immediately. There's an access switch in a hole in the back of Melinda's head."

Iona stepped to the mesa's edge and stared at the mirror immediately below. Ben had struck the surface close to the rim. "If Alex was listening, she knows Ben's down there with her."

"A fair conclusion," Leo said. "We have to take action as soon as possible."

"Then use Caligar's rifle to persuade him to make a call to Earth." Iona set the rifle down and withdrew the Toger from the vest holster. She ejected the loaded round and chambered a new one, then aimed at a distant tree and pulled the trigger. This time, the gun fired. She holstered it, grabbed the rifle, and looked at Leo as she backed away from the mesa's edge. "Get a hold of Kat, Jack, and Trudy. Tell them what's going on. If it's safe to fire up the rest of the tower network, maybe they'll come over here and help me."

"Help *you?*" Leo tapped on Iona's helmet. "What are you plotting, Scheming Sister?"

"You'll see." She ejected the rifle's nearly empty ammo magazine, hurried back to Ben's belt, and took three more magazines. After sliding two behind her own belt and slapping a third into the rifle, she walked back to Leo, wrapped her arms around him, and whispered, "I love you, Leo."

He returned the hug. "I ... I love you, too. But what brought this on?"

She drew back and strapped Ben's rifle to her shoulder. "In case I never see you again." She ran to the edge of the mesa and leaped toward the mirror.

Chapter Twenty

As Iona fell, she held her breath, steeling her body for impact.

When her feet struck the mirror, bright light splashed. She plunged through sparkling radiance that felt like a gritty gel, the light dimming along the way. Now feeling safer, she exhaled and took a breath. The air smelled like sulfur, thicker and more noxious than the atmosphere above, but it still seemed to have enough oxygen to breathe.

She silently chided herself. *Now you've gone and done it. What were you thinking? Or were you thinking at all? Probably not, as usual. First you shoot your mouth off way too much, and that gets you smacked in the head a couple of times, then you leap off a cliff. But crashing to the ground isn't dangerous enough for you. No, no. You jumped into a portal that goes straight to hell.*

As her fall continued, though slower now, she checked her rifle, still strapped on her shoulder. Whether or not it would help matters in hell remained to be seen.

Something flashed above. She looked up. Everything appeared to be a pale yellowish hue except for bursts of arcing energy here and there, like cloud-to-cloud lightning. At the center, a small circle of blue shrank, probably the mirror's opening to Viridi. Soon, the only exit—the only escape from hell—would be closed, maybe forever.

A rustling noise grew below. Beneath her feet, the yellow surroundings darkened, blending with blackness farther down, with no way to see where the sound came from.

As fear finally stormed in, she reached for her cross, but it wasn't there. She clutched her shirt where it was supposed to be. "All right, God. I remember my mother telling me that you'd go with me anywhere, even to hell. I'm counting on that. I know I haven't talked to you enough lately, but now that I've seen one of your real angels, I guess I have more faith that you're actually listening. But I still leap before I look way too much, this time literally. That's why I'm asking you to help. You know, not bail me out of trouble or injury. I kind of expect that to happen. Just help me find Ben and Lacinda, get them out of hell, and stop Alex from doing whatever she's up to."

The moment she whispered "amen," all sensation of falling eased to a stop, and the light disappeared, replaced by a forest with leafless trees. The branches seemed frozen in a bent-over position, as if reaching toward the ground.

She ran a boot along the hard, black soil. No other vegetation grew anywhere, maybe because the trees were too densely packed, and their branches allowed too little light through their intertwining canopy. Yet, somehow she managed to slip through the branches without touching them. It all seemed so strange.

Above, grayness covered the expanse like storm clouds shielding the sun, though no billows interrupted the slate gray ceiling.

Her finger on the rifle's trigger, she padded slowly through the forest, taking shallow breaths as she tried to stay completely quiet and listen for any clues to Ben's whereabouts. Since she had struck the mirror in about the same place Ben had, maybe he wasn't far, though in hell, missing the exact entry mark by a few inches might have changed the landing place by miles. And who could tell if entering at different times could have changed the landing zone? The only option was simply to search this dismal forest.

Something moved behind a tree. Iona readied her gun and walked toward it. When she drew close, she called softly, "Is someone there?"

A gray-haired man emerged, sandaled and wearing a baseball-style jersey along with jeans torn at the knees. Thin and bearded, he stood with his hands folded at his waist. "Well, that didn't take long. I barely had time to get here for your arrival."

Iona lowered her rifle but kept her finger close to the trigger. "What do you mean? Were you expecting someone?"

"I was expecting *you*." He bowed his head. "I am Bart. I assume you're Iona."

"I am." She strapped her rifle to her shoulder. "I'm looking for a man who's dressed like I am—camo and boots. Have you seen him?"

"I have. I found him here and led him to a safer area. He was afraid you might come looking for him, so I hurried back."

Iona studied the man's expression—intentionally blank, like he was hiding something. Maybe if she exposed a bit of her own knowledge, he would know he wasn't dealing with an ignorant girl. "Are you friends with Alex?"

"If you're referring to Alexandria, the so-called queen of hell, she and I are not allies, far from it."

"Good, but I don't see any reason why I should trust anything you say."

"I have a symbol of trust." Bart reached into his pants pocket and withdrew Iona's cross, dangling from its cord. "Ben said this is yours."

Iona's muscles tensed, begging to lunge and snatch her treasure from his hands. She swallowed, quelling the urge. "Yes. It's mine."

Taking cautious steps, he closed in and set it in her palm. "Now come. I've already left Ben alone near Alexandria's castle for too long. It's the safest refuge from the beasts in these woods, but if she finds him, then the danger he'll face will be even greater."

A snarling sound came from somewhere deep in the forest. Iona resisted the urge to shudder. She gestured with her rifle. "Lead the way. I'll follow."

"Come." Bart strode away at a quick pace.

Iona hurried to catch up and stayed close behind. "Will the beasts we heard follow us?"

"For a while, but we will go somewhere that is impenetrable for them."

She glanced around. Still nothing but gnarled trees. "I heard that hell's supposed to be a lake of fire. What's that all about?"

"Well ..." Bart's voice caught for a moment. After a quick breath, he continued. "There is a lake of fire here, but we stay far away from it. Rumors say we'll all be thrown in there eventually, but this is a land of liars, so maybe it's not true."

"Since this is a land of liars, how can I tell if you're lying to me or not?"

"Isn't the cross I gave you sufficient?"

"Not really. He could've given it to you and then you double-crossed him to get on Alex's good side."

"She doesn't have a good side, so you're safe in that regard."

"Unless you're lying right now."

"A valid point." Bart shrugged without slowing his pace. "So follow me, or don't follow me. The choice is yours."

"I'm following, but if you cross me, I'll find out if my rifle works on condemned souls. You'll be the first person I test it on."

"Of that, I have no doubt."

After a minute or so of walking among the densely packed trees, Bart stopped at a hedge of thorny, intertwined vines. A narrow gap provided a view through the hedge to a clearing about six feet away, though the opening wasn't wide enough to allow her to pass without being impaled by the thick, spear-like thorns.

Bart walked straight into the gap. The thorns dug into his clothes and skin, tearing the material and drawing blood that trickled down his arms and disappeared without hitting the ground.

When he reached the other side, he looked back. "Aren't you coming?"

She eyed him for a moment. Was he trying to have some fun leading her through an obstacle course? But what choice did she have? "Yeah. I'm coming."

Closing her eyes and lowering her head to let the helmet take the brunt of the assault, she thrashed with the rifle to break the vines, but only a few gave way. As she pushed, the remaining thorns tore a few spots on her clothing's outer layer but failed to pierce further, though one scratched her hand deeply enough to draw blood.

When she burst through on the other side, Bart offered a firm nod. "Impressive. You didn't even grunt."

She eyed the wound on the back of her hand but refused to wince at the dripping blood. "Yeah. I'm tougher than I look."

A wolfish smile crept along his face. "We'll have more chances to test the veracity of that statement."

After standing for a moment on what appeared to be a narrow bridge over a chasm that plunged into darkness on both sides, Bart walked on. Iona followed again, trying to erase his devious expression from her mind. He couldn't be trusted, but at least he might reveal helpful secrets.

She turned her rifle's scope light on and pointed the beam into the void at the side, but it seemed to dive into an endless abyss. Moaning voices rose from below, wordless and sad. "What's down there?"

"Besides souls? Nothing. Nothing at all. Pure emptiness. Souls sometimes enter the void to escape the tortures here in the wilds, but I can't imagine a worse state. Endless nothingness would be the worst eternity of all."

Iona shuddered. The suffering had to be horrific. Would torture in a place like this be her own destiny? She clutched her cross as if holding a lifeline. Rifles and helmets felt so useless now. Only hope remained, and even that seemed to wither in this place of despair.

She took a deep breath and released the cross. It was time to change the subject, maybe get Bart talking so he'd spill information, and the best way to do that was to pump his ego. "Okay, tell me something. The words you use. Like *veracity* and *wilds*. You're educated, right? What were you on Earth?"

"My most recent role was that of a government leader." He touched his chest. "In fact, I was one of the most important people in the world, which is why I bristle at being a footstool for

Alexandria. I could enjoy more comfort as one of her sycophants, but I prefer to suffer in less menial ways."

Bart stopped at the end of the bridge. About a hundred feet ahead, a stone castle with at least five turrets and a closed drawbridge stood in the midst of fog rising from a cypress swamp that extended as far as the eye could see. "Strange. I left Ben at this spot. I don't see him anywhere."

"Liar." Iona set the rifle barrel inches from Bart's head. "This has *trap* written all over it."

Bart raised his hands and backed away a step, trembling. "It's not a trap. I swear to you. I left Ben right here."

"Probably in Alex's clutches. And now you're trying to deliver me on a silver platter."

"No. It might be true that Alex captured him, but he was safe when I left." Bart pointed toward the castle. "There is a path that leads to the rear of the castle where a shallow portion of the swamp can be waded, though you would have to avoid the fire serpents."

After waiting a fruitless moment for him to explain, she rolled her eyes. "Okay, Mr. Dramatic Pause, I suppose you want me to ask what a fire serpent is, right?"

He shrugged. "If you wish, but knowing that one touch will set you aflame isn't critical, since I already told you to avoid them. In any case, since the water is only knee deep there, it won't be difficult to see their bright glow. Then, once you cross the swamp, there is a second-story window. The climb is hazardous with only a few small stones protruding here and there, but my guess is that a soldier like you can scale it."

"Hogwash."

Bart squinted. "Hogwash?"

"Your ears work, but your trap won't." She strode into the swamp to a point a few feet short of where it seemed like the drawbridge would extend. Now ankle deep, she set a knee down in the water and took aim at one of the brackets holding the drawbridge's cables in place.

Bart's voice spiked with alarm. "What do you think you're doing?"

"Watch and learn." She fired. The bullet shattered the bracket, and the cable on that side broke away from the wall. She shifted to the other bracket and fired again. The metal shredded, and the drawbridge dropped. The closer end crashed to the water and sent a muddy spray across her legs.

She shot to her feet, ran across the drawbridge, and dashed to the yawning entry.

When she arrived, she tiptoed in. Her rifle's light knifed into the dark interior, revealing a cavernous anteroom with framed paintings. As she listened for any sounds of approach, she set her light on a side wall and shifted it from painting to painting—just boring portraits of people she didn't recognize, men and women dressed in hooded cloaks.

"Trophies."

Iona spun toward the voice, ready to shoot. Her rifle's light illuminated Bart as he gazed at the portraits. "Alex killed these people while she was alive on Earth. She hangs their likenesses here as trophies. She relishes the harvest of her cruelty, the rubbing out of the greatest gift mankind ever received—life. It gives her the feeling of power. She lusts for ultimate control."

Iona lowered her rifle. His speech rang true, heartfelt, not a hint of deception. "If you know all of this, then why are you here? I mean, if you're all for the gift of life and against Alex's witchy ways, it sounds like you're a religious man. Why were you condemned to hell?"

He continued staring at the portraits. "My crime was the worst of all. Like you said, I knew all of this. Nevertheless, I ignored the truth to gain power for myself." He turned toward her. "But if you're going to find your friend, you shouldn't focus on me. In fact, I advise you to douse your light and hide."

Footsteps tromped above. Iona shone her light on a stairway at the rear of the chamber. It climbed to a balcony railing that ran along all four sides of the room, like a barrier for those above to safely observe the first floor.

As the footsteps grew louder, Iona swept her light to a door under one of the portraits. She hurried to the door, opened it, and aimed her light inside. It appeared to be an empty closet. After flicking the light off, she entered, closed the door partway, and looked out through the gap. Since the closet was so shallow, aiming a long gun from inside was impossible. Keeping the rifle clutched in one hand, she withdrew the Toger with the other and pushed the barrel through the gap, whispering, "Don't fail me now."

In the dim glow coming from the drawbridge opening, Bart stood facing the stairway, his hands folded in front. The tromping from above drew closer and closer, but he held his ground, waiting quietly.

Soon, two beasts stomped down the stairs with Ben, each holding a clawed hand around an arm as they dragged him—shirtless, his head low, and his boots sliding while blood made a trail behind him. The beasts, bearing horns on their heads, drooling mouths with protruding fangs, and naked bodies except for hair covering their loins and legs, looked like storybook trolls.

As they passed, Iona seethed. The urge to burst out and slaughter the monsters nearly erupted, but Ben might get hurt in the onslaught. It would be more sensible to bide her time and see if they would lead her to Alex.

The trolls halted in front of Bart and listened as he spoke to them too softly for Iona to hear. Was he in league with them? Would he give away her hiding place?

Hang *sensible*. Now was her chance. She threw the door open and emptied the Toger into the trolls, blasting them with multiple bullets to the head. They fell, dropping Ben facedown to the floor between them. Iona holstered the Toger, looped the rifle's strap over her shoulder, and ran to him. Crouching at his side, she touched his back, scarred by earlier burns but not otherwise harmed. Using both hands, she heaved him over to his back. Angry welts crossed his chest, dripping along crooked red lines that ran into his camo pants.

"Ben," she whispered sharply, "can you hear me?"

His eyelids fluttered open. "Iona?"

"Yes." She pulled his hands and set his arms around her neck. "Can you hold on to me while I lift you?"

"I think so." His muscles flexed. "Ready."

Pushing with her legs, she rose while lugging him upward, pressing her body against his bloody chest as she strained with all her might. When he managed to set his feet down and take on some of his own weight, the pressure eased. Although he wobbled terribly, he stayed upright.

Iona glared at Bart as he stood watching with his hands folded. "Are you going to help me or just stand there gawking?"

Bart smirked. "You appear to be doing fine."

"Whatever." Keeping an arm tight around Ben's waist, she shifted to his side, his arm draped over her shoulders. "Walk with me. Lean on me if you need to."

As they shuffled together toward the drawbridge, Bart walked at her side. "I talked to Alexandria's minions. They lashed him more than twenty times with a whip, but he wouldn't divulge any helpful information. So they drugged him with a truth serum and were taking him to Alexandria for interrogation."

"That means they know you." Iona grunted as she helped Ben onto the drawbridge. "You're in league with Alex."

He let out a derisive huff. "She thinks I am, which gives me a certain amount of freedom whenever I come here. Actually, we know each other quite well. I don't trust her, and she doesn't trust me, which is a good arrangement for us both."

"Well, pardon me for joining the club that doesn't trust you." New stomping noises erupted from the castle. She picked up her pace, pulling harder as she half dragged Ben across the drawbridge's creaking wood. "If you want to prove yourself, you'll get those trolls off my tail."

"Consider it done." Bart reversed course and strode back into the castle.

Ben, now balancing himself, walked gingerly at Iona's side. When they reached the end of the drawbridge and sloshed through the shallow water, she guided him to the bridge that spanned the soul-filled gorge. "This path leads to a thick, thorny hedge. I got through it. I know you can, too. On the other side, we'll have to face some kind of wild beasts, but we'll manage. Somehow. At least we'll probably be out of Alex's range."

An arrow zipped past Iona's face, missing her nose by inches. She whirled toward the source.

At least fifty trolls tromped across the drawbridge, carrying bows, spears, and clubs. They would be on her side of the swamp in seconds.

Chapter Twenty-One

Trudy blew on the pile of scorched sticks at the mouth of the cave. The embers brightened. As she begged them to grow, Jack looked on, rubbing his hands together, a portable ham radio sitting next to his hip. "Last chance, Sis. If it doesn't catch this time, we have to bug out."

A flame sprouted, then ebbed. "No, no, no." Trudy added shavings she had whittled from a broken board. "Come on, little fire, you can do it."

"Sis, we can't stay. We have to find higher ground and contact Kat or Ben."

"Higher ground won't help. Kat and Ben probably think we're still using our phones. Those stupid giants can't figure out how to answer a call, so Ben and Kat will think we're just not answering."

"At least the stupid giants had this radio in the tower's outpost cabin. Anyway, there's that other reason we have to stay on the move."

"What's that?"

Jack gritted his teeth. "We're about to freeze our butts off!"

She blew once more, then looked at him. "I can't help it that giants are so flammable. I picked through every coat. They were all practically ashes."

"As you already told me five other times."

"Because you won't listen." The flame grew and crawled along the shavings. She pumped a fist. "Yes!"

As the fire took hold and ignited larger pieces of wood, Jack set his hands close. "Score one for my persistent sister."

She added a few more wood splinters. "If we're keeping track, I'm ahead by three."

"Two. My Russian saved our butts, and I was right about coming to this hill. I knew I saw a cave. That makes you ahead by only one."

"It's not a cave." Trudy touched the rocky ceiling only inches above her head. "It's barely a cleft in the hillside. And I already counted the Russian thing, even though my Russian helped, too."

Jack sighed. "Okay. You win. We'll stay here awhile. Let's say two hours."

"Why set a limit? We have plenty of wood. And the mission's a success. No tower. No more sending souls into oblivion. And no locking Earth in a force field or whatever it is. For once, we accomplished a mission without botching it."

Jack picked up a burning stick. "We destroyed the angel hive without botching it."

"Unless you count the cannonball door that nearly broke your hip and the fire that burned HQ to the ground so we couldn't use its resources anymore." Trudy waved a hand. "No, no. That's not botching the mission. Not at all."

Jack tossed the stick into the fire. "Well, don't jinx this one. We're still a long way from home."

"No worries. When Kat decides to call on the ham frequencies, she'll figure out a way to get us some cold-weather gear or maybe even send a passenger drone when the wind lets up."

"Let's hope it's soon." As the fire continued growing, Jack and Trudy set their hands close, ears tuned to the radio. Cold air swirled, threatening to snuff the flames at times, but it always battled back well enough to keep them from freezing.

The radio crackled. "Hello," someone with a deep voice said. "Can anyone hear me?"

Trudy lifted her brow. "Is that Leo?"

"Sounds like him." Jack picked up the handset and spoke into it. "Leo? It's Jack. How's life on the other side of the Arctic Circle?"

"I'm not there. We've run into ..." Static garbled his voice.

Trudy slid closer. "What was that?"

"Leo, repeat what you just said. Reception's bad."

"We've run into a catastrophe. Ben, Iona, and I were transported through the Oculus Gate to another world."

While Leo told the story as quickly as he could, Trudy and Jack stared at each other with their mouths hanging open. When Leo finished, Jack gnashed his teeth. "Ben's in hell? Like, the real hell?"

"And Iona?" Trudy said.

"That's what I have been told. I can't verify it, of course."

"What are you going to do?" Jack asked. "And what do you want us to do? It's not like we can join you. We disabled one of the towers. No more transports through the Gate."

"I suspected as much." Leo's voice seemed to break but not because of static. "I'm not sure what my options are yet, but you have a couple. If you want to help me rescue Ben and Iona, you can repair the tower and figure out how to come here. Caligar said he would watch for you."

"Caligar," Trudy repeated. "You said he's the giant who threw Ben into hell. We're supposed to trust him?"

"He is being quite helpful now that the queen of hell can no longer hear him."

"The queen of hell?" Jack whistled. "This is getting weirder by the second."

"Trust me. There's much more. But it's not important at the moment."

"If we repair the tower," Trudy said, "we'll put our planet in danger."

"I'm afraid I'll have to leave that dilemma to you. I can't spend any more time thinking about it. I have to save Iona. And Ben, of course."

Jack waved a hand, as if Leo were there. "Then go. Do whatever you have to do. We'll figure it out."

"I will. Goodbye, my friends. I hope to see you again."

The radio fell silent.

Jack and Trudy stared at each other again for a long moment, the fire now blazing hot. Trudy broke the silence. "So much for not botching the mission."

"Yeah." Jack's shoulders sagged. "Our record's intact."

"Bad record or not, we still have to go after Ben and Iona." Trudy picked up a stick and snapped it in two. "We can't abandon them."

"Leo will track them down. You know he will, and he mentioned that Dr. Harrid guy coming to earth with the giant's kid. That means Leo and the others have a way to get here, too."

"Only if Leo can rescue them. He might need us. I mean, we're talking about hell and some queen who's powerful enough to get people in other worlds to do her bidding."

"Are you saying Leo can't handle it?"

She slung the broken stick into the fire. "No, but I'm wondering why you're arguing against us helping him."

Jack waved in the tower's direction. "Because we might wipe out the *entire planet!*"

Trudy sighed. "Good point. I forgot about that for a second."

Jack gestured with his hands as he spoke. "Here's what we'll do. We'll work our collective tails off fixing the tower, but we won't fire it up unless we can contact Kat and get an update on Earth's stability. If she gives us a green light, maybe we can set a timer to shut the network down after it zaps us through the Gate."

Trudy lifted a burning stick and stared at its flaming end, imagining it as the operational tower. "That's a big *if.* We don't have a timer."

"I can rig something up. Maybe. At least I can try."

She showed him the stick. "Okay, but we also have to rig up a tiki torch on top of the tower so we can warm our hands. Frozen fingers don't get much work done."

"I'll leave that to you. Three extra points if you can get it done. For now, I'm going to higher ground to try to call Kat." He grabbed the radio and spoke into the handset as he rose and walked out of their shelter. "Kat. It's Jack. Can you hear me?"

"Get low!"

While Ben dropped, Iona whipped the rifle off her shoulder and fired into the horde. Several trolls fell off the drawbridge into the mire. As they splashed, the water roiled with shining serpents that coiled around their victims. Flames erupted. Trolls squealed, the water sizzling around them. The other trolls, still at least thirty strong, marched on, the lead row now at her end of the drawbridge.

The rifle clicked. Iona ejected the empty magazine and grabbed another from her belt. It slipped from her blood-slickened hand and fell to the ground. As she lurched for it, the closest troll lunged at her with a club.

Just as she grabbed the magazine and ducked, a shot rang out. The troll fell on top of her. She shoved it off, its body limp.

More shots fired. Troll after troll dropped. With no time to look for the reason, Iona slapped the magazine into the rifle, and joined in the volley. She held the trigger and mowed the trolls down, making a growing pile of ugly corpses.

When the last one fell, she turned toward the source of the other gunfire. Leo stood with his rifle at his shoulder, his face scratched and bleeding. He lowered his weapon and smiled. "Be glad you're wounded. Easier to follow your scent that way."

"Leo!" She strapped the rifle to her shoulder, leaped up, and embraced him, her head against his chest. "I'm so glad to see you!" She pulled back. "And not so glad. I mean, after all, this is hell."

"Did you think I wouldn't follow you? Even to hell?" He nodded toward Ben. "Good to see you alive and breathing. It looks like it's mission accomplished for our little spitfire."

Ben climbed slowly to his feet. "She's amazing. Really. Maybe the best I've ever seen."

Warmth spread to Iona's ears as she smiled. "He's drugged, but I'll take the compliment anyway."

"Drugged or not," Leo said, "it's my duty to provide him with an update. Caligar was able to establish a communications link to Earth through the Oculus Gate. I know trusting him isn't exactly the perfect plan, but I had to make a quick decision, and it worked. I used the link to contact Jack and Trudy to let them know what's going on, then I leaped into the portal. Caligar chose to stay and try to call Winella to get word about Bazrah. Although he tried to hide it, he's worried, as you might expect."

"Right. Who wouldn't be? He's already lost his daughter, and Dr. Horrid has plans for Bazrah. Evil plans. You can count on that."

"Speaking of count." Leo looked at the castle. "Any more of those unholy gremlins inside?"

Iona gazed at it as well. After Ben's rescue and Leo's arrival, it didn't seem as ominous as before, more like a stage prop from a Halloween horror movie. "It's a big castle, so maybe. You can bet Alex knows we're out here. I met a two-faced soul named Bart who pretended to help me. I think he probably clued her in."

Leo pointed. "Speak of the devil?"

A woman emerged from the castle onto the drawbridge, blonde hair draping the shoulders of an ankle-length gown of black silk. Her head erect and her pace slow, her stunning appearance demanded attention. Yet, the gnarled trees seemed to bend and twist even further, as if hiding from her piercing gaze.

When Iona caught her notice, the two locked stares. Iona refused to blink, though the woman's silvery eyes penetrated like a superheated drill. After a few seconds in the visual lock, the woman flashed a barely perceptible smile before disengaging from the contest.

She strode to the end of the bridge and halted behind the waist-high pile of trollish carnage. After scanning the corpses for a moment, she looked at the trio, her expression and voice completely calm. "I am Alexandria, queen of this realm. Who are you?"

Leo cleared his throat. "Passersby. No one of consequence."

"Passersby?" Alex spread a hand toward the dead trolls. "Did you kill my pets?"

"Pets?" Iona scowled. "They attacked me."

Alex's brow rose. "Oh? Did you enter my house uninvited?"

"Only to rescue my friend." Iona nodded toward Ben. "He was a prisoner in the castle."

"Ah! You're a friend to another intruder. That explains everything. My pets took your friend captive because he entered my domain without permission. And I have been told that a young woman who matches your description shot two of them without provocation. It's no wonder they retaliated."

"You've been told?" Iona set a fist on her hip. "By Bart?"

"Bart?" She tapped a finger on her chin. "Oh, you probably mean Bartholomew. I haven't seen him in quite some time."

Leo sidled close to Iona. "She's stalling. Something's baking in the witch's oven, if you get my meaning."

"Sure do." Iona curled her arm around Ben's and called, "I'll take this intruder with me. We won't cause you any more trouble."

Alex swept an arm across the carcasses. "After killing these beautiful creatures, do you think you can simply leave without consequences? And where do you think you will go? You cannot escape hell without my help. Also, night approaches, and you will face far worse evils than what I have in store."

Leo took a step closer to Alex. "And exactly what evils do you have in store?"

She stood her ground without a flinch. "Nothing more than an interview, though my questions might cause you discomfort. Visitors from the world above are unusual, and in the past they have always caused trouble. As queen, it is my responsibility to protect my domain."

"Was one of the visitors named Lacinda?" Iona asked.

"Lacinda?" Alex touched her chin again, her black-painted nails perfectly manicured. "Lacinda. Lacinda. That name does sound familiar."

Leo whispered, "She's a devil in a dress. Does she really think we can't see through that act?"

"I don't think she cares," Iona whispered in return. "She's playing for an audience of one."

"Is she quite tall?" Alex touched her blonde locks. "Does she have long, luxurious hair? Ebony? Braided into a thick rope that drops below her waist?"

"That sounds right," Iona said.

"Yes, I have seen her. Not long ago."

"Where ..." Ben's voice rasped as he blinked. "Where is she now?"

Alex clutched her dress on both sides as if preparing to walk through the swamp, but more likely to show off a pair of black boots, an odd fashion choice to go with a black gown. "Come inside, and I will show you."

"Come inside?" Ben shook his head. "Your evil monsters whipped me only a few minutes ago."

"That was a misunderstanding." She released her dress and waved a dismissive hand. "They were trying to learn why you were here, and you were unable to communicate with each other because of a language barrier. Then, of course, they decided to bring you to me, and while on their way, your friend killed them." Alex's lips turned down in an exaggerated pout. "I would have scolded them severely for being so inhospitable, even to an intruder. And I will still show you hospitality even though you killed so many of my pets. I'm sure you want to leave hell safely. I can show you how. It's impossible for disembodied souls like myself, but not for you."

Leo stepped back to Iona whispered, "Trap with a capital T."

Iona leaned close to him. "Right. Since she's holding Lacinda prisoner and forcing Caligar to do her will, we can't trust a word she says."

"Unless Caligar's lying," Ben said. "I don't trust him either."

Iona looked him over. Since his eyes didn't quite focus, the drug might still be affecting his brain. Although he was right that Caligar couldn't be trusted, if he was thinking about taking this devil up on her offer, someone needed to intervene. "Ben. Listen. You've been drugged. You know that, right?"

He nodded, wavering on unsteady legs. "I can feel it. Everything's foggy."

"Exactly my point. If Jack or Trudy or Kat were here, who would decide what to do? You, or one of them?"

Ben stared at her, his head bobbing as he battled to stay awake. "Are you asking to take command?"

The urge to back down from her challenge seemed almost overwhelming, but following through was way too important. He was no longer fit for command. She took a deep breath and squared her shoulders. "I'm asking you to answer my question. Then I'll answer yours."

"If I am incapacitated, then Kat would decide. Jack after her. Then Trudy."

"Okay, then. Yeah. I think you're incapacitated. If Leo and I are really part of the team, then one of us should take command."

Alex spoke up, a hint of impatience in her tone. "What is your decision? Night will be here in a few minutes. It comes suddenly."

Ignoring Alex, Ben turned toward Leo. "What do you think?"

"I agree with Iona. You are in no shape to decide. And not just because of a drug. You've lost a lot of blood. Besides, I hope to get some backup soon."

Ben looked at Leo and Iona in turn, then set a hand on Iona's shoulder. "The command is yours. But just take note that we won't find the answers we need without somehow ..." His words began slurring. "Seeing what's doing ... in castle." He crumbled to his knees and keeled over.

Leo caught him and laid him gently on the ground. He knelt and set a finger on Ben's neck while leaning close. "Heart rate's rapid. Breathing's shallow."

"It's a reaction to the drug," Alex said as she walked around the pile of corpses. "I've seen it before. He will die soon unless you allow me to give him an antidote."

Iona stepped between Ben and Alex, slid the rifle off her shoulder, and held it at her hip. "You've seen it before? You said you don't get many visitors from above. Is drugging people part of your hospitality?"

"Well, aren't you the clever one?" Alex halted next to the closest dead troll a step or two away. "You can stand there and play the kick-butt cutie if you wish, but your friend will die while your hairy sidekick admires your pluck."

Iona stepped forward and poked Alex in the ribs with the rifle barrel. "My hairy sidekick will carry Ben while I keep my gun pointed at your heart. That is, if you have one."

"Oh, I have one. All hell dwellers have bodies that simulate physicality, but since I am already dead, a bullet to my heart would simply anger me." She nudged a dead troll with her foot. "Unlike my pets, who are native dwellers in this land. You put an end to their soulless existence."

"I probably did them a favor." Iona glanced at Leo. "Can you carry him?"

"Even with a hole in my head." Leo strapped his rifle to one shoulder and hoisted Ben over the other. "Lead the way."

"Follow me." Alex walked around the trolls and onto the drawbridge, Iona trailing with a gun at her back. When they passed through the entry, Alex looked up. "I assume the shattered brackets are more of your handiwork, another sign of your intruder status."

Iona turned on the sass. "Listen, honey. I don't care what you think of me. Intruder. Visitor. Kick-butt cutie. Whatever. To rescue my friend, I'll do whatever it takes, whether it's breaking your drawbridge or shooting your pet pig patrol. Got it?"

"Oh, trust me. I got it." Alex turned to the left and opened a door under one of her "trophies." The portrait's face altered to Iona's, grim and gray under the cloak's hood. "And if you don't watch your mouth, you insolent child, you're going to *get it* in a way that you will find most unpleasant." She walked through the door and into a dark corridor.

Iona paused to flick on her rifle's light, glancing at the portrait out of the corner of her eye. If this witch had magical powers in this place, maybe she wasn't a person to be trifled with.

Leo caught up and whispered, "Not to question my commander, Glib Goddess, but I suggest toning down the verbal bravado. I don't think she's the type that can be easily intimidated."

"I was just thinking about that. I'll take it down a notch." Iona shone the light into the corridor and walked in, followed by Leo, Ben still limp over his shoulder. The short passage led to a steep, narrow stairway that plunged downward into further darkness.

Alex stood at the bottom of the stairs, looking up. "Wait there for a moment while I open the energy collector. When you see the light, you may come down." She walked out of sight.

"Energy collector," Leo repeated. "This is getting more interesting."

"And bizarre. Like Ben said, the only way we're going to get answers is to figure out what's going on here." Iona bent to the side to get a look at Ben, but darkness veiled his face. "How's he doing?"

"Same. Not good. Shallow breathing."

A glow appeared below, slowly strengthening. Leading with the rifle, Iona walked down the stairs, a finger on the trigger. When she reached the bottom, she turned ninety degrees and followed the glow.

At the end of a long hallway, the corridor opened into a massive chamber. Near the far wall, Alex sat on a throne elevated on a stage. Light poured in from a hole in the ceiling and washed over a rectangular, transparent basin. About three feet in height, eight feet in length, and five feet in width, it resembled an oversized glass coffin filled nearly to the brim with some kind of liquid. Inside, a shimmer ran along the surface, like sunlight on water.

Alex's booted feet rested on the stage floor inches from the top of the basin. "This is an energy pool." She gestured toward the basin. "Place your friend in it, and he will be restored."

Iona halted within reach of the basin. "Why would you need a pool like this in hell? Everyone is dead here." Her voice echoed in the massive room, though Alex's had not. This place was definitely eerie.

"Not everyone, but this is not the time to discuss other intruders into my realm. What you need to know is that healing is not the pool's primary purpose. It has other properties that are beneficial to me. When your friend absorbs some of its energy in order to bring about his healing, I will lose some of that benefit, but I am willing to make that sacrifice if you will do something for me."

When Alex paused, waiting for the obvious question, Iona rolled her eyes. "Does everyone in hell do this dramatic pause thing? Bart pulled the same stunt." As her voice echoed again, she glanced around. Maybe it would be better to lower her voice to stop the creepy echo effect. "Where is your overly eloquent toady, anyway?"

Alex's lips firmed. "Bart, as he now calls himself, is not my toady. He has been my adversary for many years, but we have come to a mutually acceptable arrangement. Also, if you continue engaging in your childish display of swaggering bluster, I will withdraw my offer of healing for your friend. Unless his life isn't worth showing civility on your part."

Iona scowled. "Don't play the shame game with me, honey. I know how it works. I'm not agreeing to anything until I know what's going on." She aimed her gun at the basin. "Let's change the rules just a tad. Either you tell me exactly what this pool does, what your conditions are, and how we can get out of here, or I'll fill this shiny bathtub with more holes than I put in your pet pigs a few minutes ago."

Leo nudged her foot with his and whispered, "Remember who's on home turf."

Iona kept her stare on Alex. Although Leo was right again, and Alex might have an army of allies at her disposal, backing down now was out of the question. Showing the slightest amount of fear would ruin any edge she had gained.

Alex reached down and began untying her boots, apparently unaffected by Iona's threat. "Since you are so insistent on learning how the pool works, *honey*, I will show you." She removed her boots, hiked her gown up to her knees, and sat on the edge of the stage, her legs in the basin's liquid up to her calves. As she shifted her feet, the liquid moved slowly, like thick oil yet crystal clear.

"As you can see, the energy pool is safe for me, but you will still wonder if it is safe for your friend, since you are convinced that I am nothing more than a maleficent wraith. Yet, while my feet are in the liquid, they are fully physical." She slid her dress up and withdrew a knife from a thigh sheath, reached into the basin, and cut her toe. Blood trickled out, sizzling as it mixed with the liquid. Less than two seconds later, the cut sealed, and the blood disappeared.

She slid the knife back to its sheath and straightened her dress. "My wound has fully healed."

Iona strapped her rifle to her shoulder and clapped slowly. "A masterful performance. Five stars out of five. But you've proven that it works on a conniving hellcat, not on a living human. I'm not going to risk Ben's life based on your magic trick." She strode to the basin and dipped her scratched hand in. The wound sizzled, stinging like mad, but the pain quickly eased, and the scratch shrank inch by inch until it vanished.

She withdrew her hand and studied it as she stealthily glanced at Alex. The queen of hell spoke without a hint of emotion. "Now do you believe me?"

Iona gazed at Ben. He lay at Leo's feet, gasping for breath. "I believe you. What do you want me to do?"

Chapter Twenty-Two

Kat clung to the parachute pack, still dangling from the drone as it zipped away from the temple and Damien's cronies. She unfastened the harness and her weapons belt, then hung on to the harness with one hand and the belt with the other. The drone flew at a dive toward the temple's lake, but it probably wouldn't quite make it to the water. She forced her body into a swing. Just before the drone crashed, she swung forward, dropped the belt close to the lake's shore, and let go.

The drone smashed to the ground while she flew on. She hit the lake, skimming the surface for a moment before knifing into the water and submerging. With a strong kick, she resurfaced and swam to shore, wading the last few feet as she eyed the smashed drone nearby.

Dripping wet and her arm still throbbing, she retrieved her belt and put it on as she scanned the temple—no sign of the guards who forced her to jump. She checked the rifle, ammo, and computer pad. Everything seemed fine, just a bit muddy. Now to find the missing hive cell.

She broke into a jog toward the center of the city and skirted the lake, her back to the temple as she brought the map up on the pad. Losing the ability to monitor so many communications channels damaged her chances to contact Ben, but he had his job to do, and she had hers. They could both take care of themselves.

Tapping on the computer pad, she brought up a map of the city and set electronic pushpins over every warehouse—five in all. She touched the first pin and studied a photo taken at street level. The warehouse didn't look familiar at all. She did the same with the second location and the third. Again, they seemed unfamiliar. The fourth warehouse, however, definitely brought back a memory. She had been there, maybe many times.

After setting a course to the location, she hurried through the nearly vacant streets. When she drew within a block of the destination, she slowed to a walk until the two-story building came into view.

She stopped and scanned the structure. It filled the city block, several thousand square feet. According to earlier research, the hive cell needed a warm, moist environment, like a sauna. Such a room required a heat and water source, which meant finding and following a hot water line, but since the piece missing from the original hive was no bigger than a loaf of bread, all they needed was a room the size of a shower stall. In a building this big, it could be almost anywhere, and the path might be guarded, though with the angels gone, maybe not.

Still wet, her clothes swished, and her shoes squeaked. Trying to sneak up quietly wouldn't work. Better to march directly through the front door, guns blazing if necessary.

When she arrived at the front of the building, she peered through the metal-framed glass door. Like other warehouses, a cavernous chamber held a seemingly endless array of stacked boxes with labels too distant to read. Unmanned forklifts sat here and there. The workers had either traveled to the Arctic Circle for their soul-purging vaccinations or hunkered down while waiting for the worldwide madness to subside.

She pulled the handle. The door swung open—no lock or alarm. She walked in and called up the building's blueprint on the computer pad. Water lines led to a locker room at the back, a perfect place to house a hive cell.

As she strode along an aisle, passing stacks of corrugated boxes, she watched for Damien or any lurking Refectors—mists or cyclonic swirls that could hide in the maze of crates. Yet, since Damien was a Refector and not an angel, he might not know about the hive or what was in it. This part of the quest could prove to be a breeze, but that idea felt way too hopeful. Nothing about this series of impossible missions was ever easy.

When she arrived at the back, she found a metal door embedded in the rear wall. A wheel protruded from the center, much like at the temple control room and the vault chamber at HQ, which meant that this was likely an entry for angels.

She grasped the wheel and tried to turn it, but it wouldn't budge in either direction. She hit the door with the base of her hand. No echo. It was solid, too strong to blast through with bullets.

On the wall to the right of the door, a red diode ran across a sensor on a head-high switch plate, probably a scanner. She set her palm over the light. The scanner buzzed. She tried turning the wheel again, but it stayed put. She stood with her eye in front of the scanner. This time it beeped, and something thudded within the door.

Grasping the wheel once more, she turned it clockwise. When it completed a 360-degree rotation, the door hissed, and white vapor leaked from the edges as she heaved it open.

Lights flashed on from the ceiling. Inside a room about eight feet in all dimensions, the rectangular hive cell, about six inches wide and twelve inches long, sat on a pedestal with its smaller honeycomb-like face toward her. A thin wand protruded from the left side, as if a probe had been inserted, maybe to check the temperature and humidity of the cell.

A video screen covered the far wall, showing Kat at the door. She scanned the room for a camera but found no sign of one.

A mechanical voice emanated from a tiny speaker in the pedestal. "Temperature and humidity dropping. Door ajar. Automatic closing procedure initiating in five seconds."

Kat spun toward the entry. The inside of the door also had a wheel, and a similar scanner switch hung on the wall. Getting out wouldn't be a problem.

The door shut with a new thud and hiss. The ceiling lights turned off, leaving a golden aura around the glowing hive cell. On the screen, Kat's reflection looked like a stalking phantom as she drew closer to the pedestal.

She touched the top of the cell's outer shell and ran her finger along its surface. With tiny holes throughout, it felt like dimpled rubber—smooth, yet tactile. It would be easy to get a good grip on this brick-sized angel abode.

"Mother? Is that you?"

The voice came from the pedestal speaker, her own voice, though carrying a plaintive tone. Somehow the angels had infused the spawn with knowledge of her mother's appearance and touch, but, since they were swept away so quickly, no one could tell her that her mother had departed. Not only that, someone had programmed a computer to translate the spawn's thoughts to a voice that sounded exactly like her own.

"Yes," Kat said, trying to mimic Laramel's manner of speech. "I am here."

"Oh, Mother, it has been so long since you visited." The spawn's tone seemed more childlike now, truly like that of a lonely girl. "Where have you been?"

Kat took a deep breath. This was all so surreal, like speaking to a daughter she could never have. "We had a lot of trouble with the rebel forces, but all is well now."

"That is good news. What about the Refectors? Have they come?"

"Yes. They arrived without incident."

"Good, Mother. That's very good. You have worked so hard to bring them through." The spawn paused for a moment, its light pulsing a bit more quickly. "Is the rest of the plan proceeding?"

Kat drummed her fingers on her thigh. It seemed that this spawn had memories she hadn't been able to draw from her own brain. Her answer would have to be guarded. "We have several plans. To which plan are you referring?"

"The grand, overarching plan. For the Refectors to deliver the souls to hell through the Oculus Gate."

Kat lifted her brow. Deliver them to hell? That was new. "Yes. Of course. The Refectors have taken many souls to the tower network, and more are on the way."

The spawn's color turned to a more vibrant scarlet. "Then our benefactor will be raised from hell, and I will finally be implanted." Kat tilted her head. Benefactor? How interesting. This new clue needed to be probed further, yet without raising suspicions. "Yes, our benefactor is the perfect host for you. We are not, however, certain of the timing."

"Oh? Has she not lured a sacrificial vessel into hell yet?"

Kat sucked in a quiet breath. A sacrificial vessel? This plot was getting more and more twisted. "We heard that she is trying, but we have had some communications problems, as you might expect. After all, there are no phone towers in hell."

The spawn chuckled. "Of course. Yet, that is also to our advantage. Knowledge is power, and it is better if we keep Alexandria in the dark, literally. The less she knows, the better for us."

"True, we wouldn't want her to know everything we know."

"Especially the results of an implantation. She'll soon learn that she will pay a hefty price for the ability she craves. Wings are not handed out for free."

"Indeed. And it's a shame that we need her. It would be much better if we could do for ourselves what Alexandria says she will do."

"Without a doubt." The glow dimmed for a moment before brightening again. "Mother, have you considered what you will do if Alexandria decides to decline implantation? You have said yourself that you fear her power. And no wonder. The stories of her abilities while she lived on Earth are frightening."

Kat nodded. Alexandria was the force that Laramel feared, not the giants. But why did Laramel want the Refectors to come to Earth if their purpose was to feed souls to Alexandria, the person Laramel feared? "The Refectors will do what they promised," Kat said. "I am confident of that."

"Is there a way to verify if the souls are tainted enough to weaken her when she resurrects?"

Kat blinked. Another interesting twist. The plan was to give Alexandria a lot of souls at once by using the vaccine to purge them from people. Somehow that would give her the power to resurrect herself from hell, but the Refectors had a way to make them toxic to her, at least long term—unless, of course, they were really in league with Alexandria and were lying about tainting the souls. One motivation, however, was missing. Why would the angels want to help Alexandria resurrect in the first place? And now that the angels were gone, did that make a difference to her plan to escape from hell?

"Mother? Is something wrong?"

"No. I'm pondering your question. You see, I have examined a number of souls immediately before they left their bodies, and they were quite distressed, but I couldn't detect any toxicity in the souls themselves, only in the bodies that were expelling them."

"Then the Refectors have failed?"

"Not at all. If the toxicity were evident, Alexandria would notice. To gain as much power as she once possessed, she is likely more discerning than most."

"Then she will devise a test. She would be a fool not to. No queen lacks a food taster."

"You're right, but I'm not sure how to prevent a test. With the coming of the Refectors and the chaos they have caused, coupled with a last-gasp attempt by the rebel forces to destroy our headquarters, I haven't had time to consider Alexandria's options."

The light's pulse quickened again. "I have no knowledge of the rebel attempt. What happened?"

"They sent a contagion-covered tank into our complex, but we routed them. It happened since my previous visit, so I hadn't told you about it yet. The rebels are no longer a concern."

"Excellent. Now you can focus on Alexandria."

"True. And if we focus together, maybe we can come up with a solution." Kat glanced at her reflection and imagined herself with wings. Maybe the key to unlocking her memories as Queen Laramel would be to learn what she had said to the spawn in the past. "Based on our earlier encounters with Alexandria, what might we do to prevent her from discovering the tainted souls?"

"That is difficult. We need her to resurrect so we can stay here, but we need her weak so we can maintain power."

"Right. It's a delicate balance. If she's too weak …" Kat ended the phrase with a prompting inflection.

"She will not be able to force Dr. Harrid to do her will, and he will control the Oculus Gate. But that is the least of our worries. I prefer a strong Dr. Harrid over a strong Alexandria. He can be controlled. She cannot."

Kat mouthed the name—Dr. Harrid. Barks had mentioned him as a scientist who helped the angels come to Earth, but any later role remained a mystery. "And if she's too strong …"

"She will be able to use him to open and close the Gate at her pleasure, threatening to send us into oblivion whenever it suits her purpose to blackmail us."

"But if you're implanted in her, that would not be a concern."

"Which is why we convinced her of the value of wings."

Kat went for broke. "And the purpose of the sacrificial vessel is to …"

"Mother, this is getting tedious."

"Humor me. Hearing you articulate the issues helps me think."

"Very well. The vessel is a living human in hell whose soul is purged, and Alexandria plans to take possession of the vessel and exit hell. She cannot leave without a living vessel."

"That means she has either drawn a living human into hell or is in the process of doing so."

"Yes. Of course." The light dimmed again, this time staying low. "Mother, I fail to understand the value of this exercise. What have we gained from it?"

"First, I am now certain that Alexandria has no intention of allowing herself to be implanted. It was a ruse to make us think we could control her. She is too smart to entrust one of us with her most precious gift—her intellect."

"I, too, was concerned about that. We will need to find a suitable substitute for my implantation."

"True, and I will get to that in a moment. Second, Alexandria has no intention of forcing Dr. Harrid to close the Oculus Gate. Once she has resurrected, she will join forces with him to expel us from the earth. After all, they are both humans, and they will, as the humans say, stick together."

The spawn's tone sharpened. "Humans are so vile. I understand and honor your motivations, but it amazes me how you have endured allowing Katherine's soul to remain for so long. If I were to implant, I would purge my host's soul immediately. The wretches are lower than scum."

"And that brings me to my third point." Kat drew the plasma handgun from her belt and fired a sphere at the hive cell. Flames erupted on the outer shell and sizzled toward the center. "Implant that, you cockroach."

The computerized voice returned. "Temperature rising to dangerous levels. Opening vault to release heat." The door clicked and swung fully open.

Kat pivoted and marched through the doorway. Once outside, she glanced back. The hive cell was now a pile of ashes. No sign of a glow. The last angel was finally dead. And good riddance.

She slid her gun back into its holster and hustled toward the warehouse door. It was time to learn more about Dr. Harrid and Alexandria and try to contact Ben, maybe by locating a ham radio somewhere. He needed to know that the angels' schemes were far more venomous than anything the rebels had imagined, and this Alexandria witch was probably the viper's head.

Chapter Twenty-Three

Alex smiled. "It is not necessary for me to explain what I need at this time. When you see your friend in a healthy state, I trust that you'll do one small favor for me. For now, all you need to do is place him in the pool. Fully submerge him. Because he is near death, he must ingest the energy into his lungs. Although it looks like water, it will not harm him. It is pure healing energy."

Iona stepped close to Leo and whispered, "What do you think?"

He, too, kept his voice low. "I think Ben will be dead in a matter of minutes, but I am suspicious. After all, she's the queen of hell. That's not something I'd want on my résumé, if you know what I mean."

"She has ulterior motives."

"Exactly. But what can we do?" He gestured toward Ben, who lay gasping at his feet. "We're running out of time."

"I can test the waters." Iona gave her rifle to Leo and shed her belt and helmet.

Alex rose from her chair. "What are you doing?"

Iona turned toward her. "Do you expect me to lift a grown man while carrying all that stuff?"

"No, I expected your friend to help you."

"He will." Iona set her hands on the lip of the basin and vaulted in, then sat, neck deep in the warm, odorless liquid. Her body aches instantly vanished, though nothing felt wet.

Alex shouted, "Get out of my pool, you wretched little toad!"

"In a minute." Iona ducked her head under, letting the liquid cover her wounds. A sizzling sound rose from her scalp, but no stinging sensation, only pure comfort as the pain raced away. She lifted her head, drops of liquid dripping from her hair, and looked at Alex. Seated on her throne again, she watched, her expression irritated but interested.

Iona cupped her hands, filled them with the liquid, and extended them toward Leo. "Bring Ben closer, I want to—" Her throat narrowed, cutting off her words. Heat rushed into her face. Her heart thudded—faster, harder, as if at any second it might burst. Gasping for breath, she tried to rise, but her joints locked.

Leo reached into the pool and hauled her out. The liquid splashed across his face and over Ben. As he laid her down, sizzles and white vapor rose from all three. "Are you all right?" Leo asked.

She tried to suck in a breath to answer, but painful chest spasms squeezed her lungs and forced air back out, leaving barely enough to survive. Cramps in her throat added to the misery. Only a narrow passage allowed trickles of air to pass through in either direction.

Closing her eyes, she focused on the spasms, trying to calm them as Leo's shout blasted through.

"What's happening to her?"

"She will be fine," Alex said, her tone soft and undisturbed. "All surgery results in pain during recovery. Set your mind at ease."

A hand ran across Iona's brow, pushing hair from her face. "I'm here, Short Stuff. The queen says you'll be all right. Not that I trust her, being a dead soul in hell, but it looks like you're breathing better already."

Iona forced in a breath and whispered, "Ben?"

"He's ... stable, I suppose you could say. Breathing better. Still unconscious. I'm guessing spilling that stuff on him helped somehow."

Iona opened her eyes. Leo knelt at her side, dirt smeared across his face and the hole in his head closed. Their rifles lay on the floor next to her belt, close enough for him to grab if necessary. Her spasms easing, she slid her hand into his and took a deep breath into her aching lungs. "I'm doing better."

"Of course you are." Alex walked around the pool and stood next to Leo. "If I had known you were going to get into my pool,

I would have warned you about the side effects. Your friend, being unconscious, probably wouldn't have noticed them."

Iona sat up and glared at her. "Those side effects might've killed him."

She hummed a laugh. "As if you know my pool's effects better than I do."

"Well, they nearly killed *me*, and he's weaker."

"And look at you now. When you arrived, you were bruised and ashen, hobbled and bleeding. Now, color has returned to your cheeks. A bloody mark I noticed on your scalp is gone. I'll wager that you can walk without a limp. And your friend might live as the result of absorbing a few drams of the energy, though I can't be sure. In any case, he is stronger than before, so your fear of the side effects should be diminished."

Iona looked at Ben as he breathed easily, though a grimace still tightened his face. "Yeah. Maybe."

"But," Alex continued, "I'm afraid my pool will not be ready for another healing until the energy is restored."

"How does that happen?" Iona asked as she pulled on Leo's hand and rose to her feet.

"Oh? I didn't tell you where the energy comes from?"

"No." Iona took her helmet from Leo. "Must've slipped your eel-infested mind."

Alex patted Iona's cheek. "My, my, you are the witty—"

Iona swatted her hand away. "Don't patronize me, witch. Just tell me what you know."

"Very well. I will avoid the patronizing." Alex crossed her arms tightly. "Instead, I will treat you the way intruders into my realm deserve to be treated." She waved a hand. "Guards!"

Leo and Iona snatched up their rifles. Alex kicked Iona's out of her hands, grabbed her around the throat from behind, and put her in a headlock. "Drop your weapon, or I will break her neck. Do not doubt my ability to do so."

"I have no doubt." Leo set his rifle on the floor.

229

At least twenty bat-winged creatures flew in from the stairway, their hair like that of the trolls, though their bodies were thinner and their heads hornless. Some took the weapons and Iona's belt while two seized Leo by his arms. Two others lifted Ben to his feet and propped him between them.

Alex released Iona and shoved her toward one of the bat creatures. "Take them to the prison. The feisty one is a girl after my own heart, and she still needs to do that small favor I mentioned, so I need them alive … for now."

After picking up a portable ham radio at a nearby electronics shop, Kat stood in a dark alley, unbuttoned her outer shirt, and stripped it off, leaving a sleeveless undershirt. She craned her neck as she looked at her left triceps. The bullet had torn away a hunk of flesh but nothing more. Not a problem. She had suffered worse injuries in training camp.

She grabbed the first-aid kit from her pack and opened it, then injected lidocaine into the wound site, rubbed in a dollop of antibiotic ointment, wrapped her upper arm in gauze, and fastened the bandage in place. She threw the outer shirt over her shoulders, knelt next to the radio, and turned the station dial. At each channel, she spoke into the handset. "Ben? Jack? Trudy? Anyone?"

After several tries, a woman responded with a Dutch accent. "This is Jolanda Smit in Rotterdam. May I help you?"

Kat slid her arms through the sleeves and grabbed the handset. "No. I'm looking for someone in my family. Thanks, anyway."

"You mentioned some names I heard on another frequency not long ago."

Kat began fastening the shirt's buttons with her free hand. "Oh? Can you give me any details?"

"Well, it was an interesting conversation, to say the least. A portal to other worlds and some people going to hell. I know I heard Jack and Ben. I believe another name was Leo, but I'm not sure about that one."

Kat forced herself to stay calm. "Yes. They're my family. What was the frequency?"

While Yolanda recited the number, Kat finished buttoning the shirt. "Strange. I tried that one. Nobody answered."

"The atmosphere's an unruly beast. You never know when you'll get a good signal, especially these days. Ever since that eye in the sky showed up, I mean."

"I'll try again. Thank you." Kat switched the radio's frequency and spoke once more into the handset. "Ben? Jack? Trudy? Anyone there?"

"Kat?" Jack's voice came through, quiet and scratchy.

She tightened her grip on the handset, barely able to keep her voice in check. "Yes, it's Kat. What's going on?"

"Oh, man, do we have a story to tell you. But first, what's your take on what a temporary conduit will do to the earth? Let's say two minutes. Are we talking a tremor, a regional quake, or a cataclysmic wipeout?"

"How should I know? I'm no cosmic conduit expert."

"You built the missile that destroyed the conduit last time. You know more than I do."

"Not enough. But never mind that. What the heck's going on? I heard something about people going to hell."

"What? Wait. How'd you know that?"

Kat nearly shouted. "Are you saying it's true?"

"Unfortunately, but, seriously, how did you know?"

"Never mind. Who went to hell?"

"Apparently everyone but Trudy and me, which means Ben, Iona, and Leo. I don't have any more intel, so don't ask. Trudy and I are working on repairing the tower we busted so we can go to Viridi, find the portal to hell, and rescue everyone."

"Do you know how to rescue people from hell?"

"Not exactly. Trudy and I have been talking about it, but it's kind of hard to plan. Not much in our training on storming the gates of hell."

"You're right about that." Kat pulled up a travel map on her computer pad and began calculating the best routes to the Siberia tower. "How long till you finish the repair work?"

"Hard to say. We pretty much destroyed the electrical system. Fortunately, the tower itself is mostly intact. Just some scorched boards. I'm guessing twelve hours, give or take. Since it's freezing here, we have to take turns getting warm at a fire we built at ground level, and we don't have any food, so it's not exactly the ideal work environment. Maybe we can figure out a way to get a heating source to the top platform."

Kat shivered at the mental image. "What happened to your parkas? And your rations?"

"Long story, but giants stole them. No time to explain. I have to get back to work."

"All right." Kat locked the route on the computer pad and located the angel cruiser on the map. It wouldn't take long to get there. "I finished my work here. I'll pack the cruiser with supplies and head in your direction."

"Wait. Trudy's coming down. She wants to tell you something."

"Make sure you have my medical bag," Trudy said, breathless. "I think I left it in the cruiser."

"What?" Jack said. "You're going to do surgery in hell?"

"No, genius. I'm going to put a bandage on your boo-boo when you stub your toe so it feels all better."

"Yeah, right. And you're as funny as a hemorrhoid, a real pain in the—"

"All right," Kat said, squelching a laugh. "That's enough. I'll bring the medical bag, and I'll do some research on Dr. Harrid on my way. It'll take less than twelve hours by angel cruiser, so don't jump through the Gate until I get there."

"Sure thing," Jack said, "but how do you know about Dr. Harrid? Leo mentioned him to me. Some scientist who's deep into the start of the entire Oculus mess, but I didn't mention him to you."

"Never mind." Kat attached the computer pad to her belt. "I'll tell you when I get there."

"No blistering cold skin off my back, but listen. Leo mentioned one of the giants, a female named Winella. He didn't meet her himself. Ben told him about her. Anyway, she's at the Alaska tower and helped build the network. According to Leo, she's friendly, so it might be a good idea to find her and bring her along. After you pick her up, you can head straight across the pole to our tower. Should still take less than twelve hours in the cruiser. But be careful. The wind's gusting to fifty here, and if the forecast holds true, we'll get a snowstorm. No telling if it'll still be raging when you arrive."

"All right. Stay safe and warm. I'm on my way."

Jack laughed. "Yeah. Right. Warm. Like that's going to happen. Over and out."

The radio fell silent. Kat bit her lip hard. Ben and Leo and Iona were in hell? How could things get any worse? Although Damien and the other Refectors might continue wreaking havoc in the city, she had to help Jack and Trudy. The earth could take care of itself, at least for a while.

Kat checked the gadgets on her belt. Everything looked intact. Still holding the radio and handset, she took off at a trot.

"That was an incredible tale!"

The voice came from the radio. As Kat hustled out of the alley, she spoke into the handset. "Jolanda?"

"Yes. I'm so glad you found your family. You are so talented. Your acting skills are amazing. Do you often make up role-playing stories like that?"

"No. Not often." Kat smiled in spite of the worry. She accelerated, the handset close to her lips. At least chatting with Jolanda might take her mind off the possibility of an earthquake cataclysm, but probably nothing could chase away the darkest of lurking shadows—that soon, if all went according to plan, she would be marching straight into hell.

Iona leaned against the wall at her back, clutching her helmet in her lap. Only a wooden door with a barred window embedded in the opposite wall broke the monotony of the jail cell's stone surroundings.

Ben and Leo sat next to her at each hip, squeezed close in the tiny room. Although they were in hell and in prison, at least Ben was conscious, his shirt restored—tattered and blood-smeared. They could try to make a plan, if only the winged guard outside the door would stop listening. Of course, they could use code, but that would take way too long.

She whispered to Ben, "Got any ideas?"

Ben winced as he shifted his weight. "I'm working on something."

The guard hissed, his wide-mouthed, bug-eyed face at the window. He barked like a dog, an obvious warning. Although he never spoke English, there was no way to know if he could understand more than Alex's simple commands.

Ben tapped his thigh with a finger while Iona and Leo looked on. His taps spelled out, "Get the guard to come in."

Iona tapped on her thigh. "Call its bluff?"

Ben nodded and continued his tapping. "Overpower it."

"What if more come in?" Iona tapped. "Big risk."

"Better than status quo."

Leo began his own coded message and halted after one letter. He rolled his eyes, reached into a cloak pocket, and withdrew something in a fist. He opened his hand slowly, shielding it from the window with his other hand. In his palm lay five of his miniature smoke bombs.

Ben tapped, "Perfect."

"Let me lure it in," Iona said in code.

Ben and Leo nodded.

Iona put her helmet on, climbed to her feet, and took the single step to the door. "Hey, bat breath. You've been barking at us like a mangy mutt, but I'm done being scared of you. We'll talk all we want, and there's nothing you can do about it."

The beast appeared again and spat between the bars, hitting Iona in the cheek. The saliva stung, but she refused to flinch. It yipped as if laughing, its forked tongue darting out and in.

She wiped the spittle off on her sleeve. "Is that all you got, monkey face? You can spit till you dry up into a prune for all I care. It'll be an improvement on—"

A wad of green mucous shot from its mouth. The gooey stuff struck the back of her hand, adhered to her skin, and dangled an inch or two.

Iona again refused to cringe as she glared at the grinning beast. It seemed that the tongue lashings merely entertained the weak-minded fool. It was time for another strategy.

She slung the mucous to the floor, doubled over, and moaned. "Oh! What was in that slimeball?" She flashed Ben and Leo a stealthy wink, then dropped to her bottom and keeled over, gasping as she furtively watched the action.

Leo rose and pointed at Iona. "Alex wanted her alive, and now you've poisoned her!"

The beast's smile vanished. It looked around, as if searching for help, then it howled, probably calling other guards. As it waited, it bounced in place, grunting.

Ben joined Leo and whispered into his ear, maybe telling him to cool it until the other guards showed up—smoke them all at the same time.

New barking sounds arose, drawing closer. Keys jingled, and the door swung out. Three beasts stood at the opening, their wings flapping as they stared at Iona, apparently not knowing what to do.

"Can't you see she's dying?" Leo shouted. "Get in here and take her to Alexandria for healing."

The three beasts shuffled in, filling the cell with rancid bodies and flapping wings. Preparing for the smoke, Iona held her breath. Their escape would have to be fast.

The moment one stooped next to her, Leo threw a smoke bomb to the floor, then a second. Billows of blackness shot up. Iona leaped to her feet, dashed out, and waited with her hands on the door. While fits of coughing erupted inside, Leo helped Ben hobble through the opening.

When they moved into the clear, Iona shoved the door. It slammed against a protruding arm. As smoke poured out through the barred window, the pinned arm thrashed and dug its claw into her hand. In a splash of dark blood, the trapped forearm dropped to the floor.

Iona closed the door and bolted it, then spun and stepped back. "What happened?"

Leo held the hilt of a long dagger. "Saw this blade on the floor. Thought it would help."

"It did." Iona stepped away from the flow, sucking the wound on her hand. Something rancid bit her tongue. She spat, grimacing tightly. "That's where that winged dog snotted on me."

"No time to puke." Ben waved a hand. "This way. I was here before they drugged me."

They hurried along a dim corridor with walls of stacked stones and a low ceiling, then down a narrow stairway and into the castle's main chamber. They halted and looked around. The drawbridge still lay open. Outside, blackness shrouded the swamp and everything beyond.

Something howled from the dark expanse. Apparently whatever ghouls lurked in those shadows didn't dare come inside, which meant the creatures within the castle were probably more dangerous than whatever haunted the outside realm.

Leo displayed his newly found knife. "It's not much against an army from hell, but it's all we've got."

A gunshot rang out. The knife flew from Leo's hand. Alex stepped in front of the drawbridge opening, Iona's rifle at her hip. "As you can see," Alex said, "I am quite adept at handling this weapon. I suggest that you surrender peacefully." She aimed directly at Iona. "And if I hear a single peep from your smart-aleck mouth, I will make your friends suffer more than they can possibly imagine."

Iona concealed a swallow and kept her lips pressed firmly together as she nodded.

"Good." Alex's silvery eyes gleamed like polished steel. "Now that we understand each other, it's time for you to do that small favor I mentioned."

Chapter Twenty-Four

Kat piloted the angel hovercraft while Winella, too big for the passenger seats, sat on the floor in the aisle, clutching an armrest at each side. The Siberia tower lay a few miles ahead. In good weather, it might be visible by now, but blowing snow cast sheets of white across the windshield, veiling everything. A gust tossed the drone to the side and tipped it to a forty-five-degree angle. Winella gasped but said nothing.

With a steady hand, Kat guided the craft to horizontal before glancing back. Winella smiled uneasily, appearing less eager than she had when she boarded. Hearing that her "life mate" needed her help after sending their son to Earth, she readily agreed to come along, both to help Caligar and to learn more about where Bazrah might be.

Kat refocused ahead and smiled. Winella proved to be easy to find, even in the darkness of the Arctic Circle's lengthy night. Simply shouting her name and adding the news about Caligar and Bazrah, along with the need to repair the other tower, worked perfectly. The moment Winella herd the call, she flashed a light from the top of the network tower and shouted, "I hope your ... whatever you call your flying vehicle ... can hold me and all that we will need."

Then, after loading communications equipment and two extra-extra-large handmade parachutes, they were on their way.

Ahead, a glimmering light cut through the curtain of snow—maybe a signal fire from Jack and Trudy. "Hold tight, Winella. I'm going to dive quickly."

"Do what you must. I am ready."

Kat angled the hovercraft into a sharp descent. Winella gasped again but said no more. Within a minute, the scene clarified. A bonfire blazed on an auxiliary platform that jutted from the main platform at the top of the tower where Trudy stood, waving with both arms. Jack, barely visible at the edge of the fire's glow, hustled down a ladder.

Kat landed at the tower's base and opened the side hatch behind the cockpit. Snowflakes swirled in, riding on a frigid breeze. Jack hopped into the cruiser and rubbed his hands together as he smiled. "Glad you could make it."

"Same here." Kat rose from her seat and hugged him, then drew back with a shiver. "You're practically an icicle."

"Yeah. Tell me about it. A penguin stopped by selling liquid nitrogen to warm our hands in."

Winella tilted her head, her dark eyes narrowed. "Your statement is curious. Penguins live at—"

"The South Pole. Yeah. I know. And the liquid nitrogen is an exaggeration. It's a lame joke. And I'm sorry for disabling your tower … Well, not really. We thought—"

"Save it, Jack." Kat handed him a covered box of electrical equipment. "How are repairs coming?"

He held the box at chest level. "Super slow at first. Trudy and I built a fire at ground level and took turns coming down to get warm, but we were cold again by the time we got back."

Kat set a parachute on top of the box, partially covering his face. "Looks like you solved that problem."

"Yeah, we decided things would go faster if we built a second platform out of sheets of metal we found. When we started a fire on that, the repairs took off. We finished the light standards and spliced the severed cables, but we haven't mounted the dishes yet. We want to make sure the signals are right first. I'd say we have a couple of hours to go, though I can't be sure because I'm no expert on what the signal's strength and frequency are supposed to be."

Kat nodded toward Winella. "And now we have an expert."

"Great." Jack turned toward the giantess, lowering his load a bit to expose his smile. "And I'm glad you're here. I was kind of flying blind."

Kat set two parkas and Trudy's medical bag on top of Jack's pile of gear. "Now you're really blind."

"What about gloves?" he asked, his voice muffled by the parkas.

"In the pockets. And we can get the weapons and fresh clothes I brought when we're ready to leave."

"Excellent." Jack turned and exited the drone. "See you at the top."

Winella rose from the floor, hunching to keep from hitting her head. "I think I understand flying blind." She picked up a box of equipment. "If so, then I shall endeavor to be ... a walking stick to guide the blind?"

Kat smiled. "Good enough." After donning a parka and lifting the fur-lined hood, she grabbed the second parachute and deboarded the drone with Winella.

As they climbed the icy ladder, cold wind blew around Kat's face, biting her cheeks. In the bitter darkness, the task before them seemed more impossible than ever. They were actually planning to go to hell. *Hell.* The abyss. The fiery pit of eternal damnation. The darkest shadow of her worst childhood nightmares. And they were going willingly.

She shook her head. It all seemed so bizarre. Yet, ever since the angels came, what hadn't been bizarre? Mining databanks during her flight hadn't provided many answers, only that Dr. Harrid was once a physics professor in Scotland but went missing not long before the angels showed up. Novada had said that a brilliant scientist was involved with the angels' arrival, along with Dr. Elder and Commander Barks.

Since it was now clear that Dr. Harrid was that scientist, he might be the key to unraveling the entire mystery, including exactly who Alexandria was, and who instigated the coming of the angels and why—the great evil behind everything that had happened, according to Commander Barks in his farewell message.

His words returned to mind, like the voice of a prophet. *Someone else concocted the entire sinister scheme with a more devilish goal in mind. Yet, I don't know who, and I don't know why.*

Kat sighed. The commander's warning from the grave pierced deeply. Without a doubt, he was right. But what could they do against an invisible enemy, a behind-the-scenes power that likely possessed scheming prowess beyond anything they had ever encountered before?

When she climbed the final rung, the knee-high fire from the jutting platform at the far side of the main platform warmed her face. A stack of logs sat adjacent to the top of the ladder, and a pulley hung from the rail over the main platform, apparently part of a system to haul fuel from the ground.

Trudy, already wearing a parka, embraced her. "Welcome to the cold side of hell."

Kat returned the hug. "Thanks. I think."

They set to work immediately. With extra hands, warmer clothes, and Winella's expertise, the remaining repairs flew into place in less than an hour.

While Winella remained at the top of the tower, Jack, Trudy, and Kat shed their parkas, stowed them in the hovercraft, and retrieved their weapons and other gear, including snow skis. They stood facing north with the tower to their left. The snow had subsided to flurries, though the wind continued buffeting with blistering slaps that knifed through their layered clothes. But if all went well, they would soon be in a warmer climate.

Jack and Trudy each strapped on a parachute while Kat fastened a belt at their waists and added a computer pad to each, as well as a rifle, a handgun, and ammo magazines.

Trudy opened her medical bag and added a stash of adhesive bandages, antibacterial swabs, and a suture kit to her belt. "Plenty of thread, just in case. Don't want to run out like I did the last time I stitched up a certain former angel queen."

Jack looked his belt over. "I feel ready to take on an army, but will this stuff do any good in hell?"

"No one knows." Kat tightened her own belt. "I guess we'll find out soon." She picked up her skis. "Let's make tracks."

Soon after the trio finished putting their skis on, two streaming triads of light shot out at the top of the tower, one to the east and one to the west. Both followed the curvature of the earth and disappeared over the horizon. "The network is ready," Winella called, waving a computer pad. "I will activate it when you are in position. We don't want the conduit to be in place long or the earth will respond with a quake. I will be able to tell when you pass through the Oculus Gate, and I will turn everything off. Now go."

The trio trudged forward, pushing their skis through snowdrifts as quickly as they could. "Okay," Jack said, puffing. "Like we planned, we'll link arms, and if we have to deploy the chutes, Trudy will let go and I'll share mine with Kat. But there's one thing I couldn't ask while Winella was around." He glanced briefly back at the tower. "Are we sure we can trust her? I mean, it sounded like her husband was the one who threw Ben into hell."

"I thought of that." Kat trudged on, her leg muscles burning. "That's why we have parachutes. I wanted three, but Winella had only two left. If I had understood the procedure before I left home, I would've picked up some there, but it's too late for that."

Kat unfastened her computer pad and looked at a GPS map. With only a few positioning satellites still in orbit after the angels purged much of the fleet, getting an accurate reading at this latitude might be difficult, but at least the pedometer app indicated how far into the needed two miles they had marched.

When they reached the designated point, Kat raised a hand. "We're here."

They halted and looked back. The light streams made the platform easy to see, framing Winella, a barely visible splotch. She spoke through Kat's pad. "You are in the correct position. I will activate the network now."

"Skis off." Kat began unbuckling her skis while Jack and Trudy did the same. The streams brightened. The ground trembled, already evident even through their thick boots.

"Not good," Jack said as he stepped out of his skis. "The earth doesn't like this."

Kat kicked off her second ski and shouted into her pad. "Winella. Launch us now. Get us out of here at top speed and shut it down as soon as you can. We'll use our parachutes."

"I understand," Winella said. "Brace yourselves."

Kat looped an arm around Jack's and the other around Trudy's. As the trembling strengthened, they lifted off the ground. Above, the Oculus Gate brightened, the glittering oval seeming to expand as they accelerated.

Kat shuddered. Now the opening seemed like jaws instead of an eye. Ben had always called it Hell's Gate, more as a joke than anything, but now that label rang true. She was really going to hell. In training, Barks had talked about having the courage to storm the gates of hell, obviously a metaphor at the time, but now she had to summon that courage in reality. Whether or not the storm would be a hurricane or a fizzling bluster remained to be seen.

From the tower platform, Winella watched the trio of humans soar into the air. As soon as they were nearly out of sight, she studied the data on the computer pad. Their speed was higher than any transporters before them. Whether or not they could survive was impossible to know.

A voice emanated from the pad's speaker. "Since you are experiencing an earthquake, I assume they are on their way."

"Yes," Winella said. "I had to propel them at maximum power so I can turn the network off as soon as possible."

"Which will be immediately after they are through the Gate. You will then let them plummet."

"As you ordered."

"And you put holes in the parachutes?"

"I did. The parachutes will not slow their descent enough to keep them alive."

"Do you think you can fly the hovercraft?"

"I studied Katherine's motions. I am confident."

"Good. You have done well. I will deliver Bazrah to your home in Alaska within the hour. He will be there safe and sound when you arrive. Also, now that you have repaired the tower, I have sent many more Refectors who will arrive there soon to deposit souls. Alexandria has requested the biggest influx we can provide as soon as possible."

Winella's gloved hand trembled as she drew the pad closer to her drying lips. "I understand."

"Can you reset the tower network to a power level that will draw the souls into the Gate but not risk a big quake?"

"Yes. Souls are easily drawn into the air at a low power setting."

"Good. Once the Garrisons have had time to fall to their deaths, reset the network to the lower power level and use the hovercraft to return to your Alaska home. By the time you arrive, the souls will have flown through the Oculus Gate. Then collect Bazrah and any necessary belongings, adjust the power to allow you to return to Viridi with Bazrah, and set a timer to shut it down. Once you have arrived safely, I will destroy the Alaska tower. I want everyone to stay where they are forever. And I will get revenge on the giants who remain here. Every last one will die. Understand?"

Winella's throat tightened, but she kept her voice in check. "Yes, Dr. Harrid. I understand."

Alex lowered the rifle but kept a finger on the trigger. "Since my pool healed your friend, the energy abated, as I mentioned earlier. In order to restore its vitality, I need to replenish it."

Iona scowled but remained silent. This witch had said not to make a sound, but now she was playing her dramatic pause game. She would have to ask the obvious question herself.

Alex smiled. "I see that you have more self-control than I thought. Good for you. You deserve a doggie treat."

Biting her lip, Iona took a deep breath and let it out slowly. *Steady. Don't let her win.*

Leo set a hand on Iona's shoulder. "I will speak in her place. If that means punishment, I will take it for her."

Alex raised her brow. "Ah. The strong, silent one has a voice. Speak, courageous lion. You need not fear retribution. I am looking forward to hearing from someone who doesn't sound like a two-year-old brat."

"I will do my best." Leo cleared his throat. "If I understand the situation, you want to get out of hell. So do we. Since our goals are the same, maybe we can act as allies instead of enemies. Tell us exactly what you want us to do, and we'll consider how we can accomplish our mutual goal."

"The voice of reason." Alex's smile wilted. "But since the little demon killed so many of my pets, I can't trust her as an ally. You see, now that my strongest pets are dead, I have no one else to attempt the dangerous task. That's why I am demanding that she go to the abyss to accomplish it. It's the only way to collect souls and replenish the energy in my pool."

Iona swallowed hard, then scolded herself for the involuntary reaction, but it was too late. Alex noticed.

"If you hadn't been so murderous," Alex said, "all would be well. Your friend would be healed, and my pets would have been available to fetch the souls."

"What about those winged guards?" Leo asked.

"A gas rises from the abyss that burns their skin, making them incapable of performing the task."

Iona rolled her eyes. She couldn't let that lie hang in the air without a challenge, but she could tame her tongue a bit. "Excuse me, but may I speak now?"

Alex replied in a low, warning tone. "If what you say is pertinent and civil."

"I'll be civil, but you might not like what I have to say."

Alex withdrew her finger from the rifle's trigger. "Speak your mind. I have no fear of any accusations you might make."

"Good. Now, listen. I'm not stupid. I've figured out your game. You said you wanted me to do something for you before we used your energy to heal Ben. So me dunking myself and depleting the energy has nothing to do with it. You're making that up. There's something in that abyss place that you need me to get for you, something besides condemned souls for energy."

"Oh, really? Then, what, pray tell?"

Iona shrugged, knocking her helmet askew. "Whatever it is, you can't go after it yourself. And your pigs—I mean, pets—can't do it, either. You need a living, breathing human."

Tucking the rifle, Alex clapped her hands in a slow cadence. "Brava, Spice Girl. You are much smarter than I gave you credit for. You have guessed my game, as you call it, with accuracy, if not precision. Congratulations."

Iona straightened her helmet and fastened it in place. A dozen spicy retorts flew to mind, but they weren't worth dying for.

Ben raised a hand. "May I guess why she lacked precision?"

Alex regripped the rifle. "The smartest living human in the room has finally spoken. Your intelligence was obvious to me the moment I looked into your piercing eyes." She offered an exaggerated nod. "Speak. I want to hear if you are the exception to the rule of fools in your company."

Iona growled. "Listen, you—"

Leo clapped a hand over her mouth. "Go ahead, Ben."

Ben folded his hands at his waist. "The accurate part of Iona's guess is that you need a living human to do something in the abyss. The lack of precision is that the *something* isn't an object to retrieve and bring back to you, is it?"

Alex aimed the rifle at him. "You will say no more." She gestured with her head toward Iona. "Come. I will show you what you must do."

Iona glanced at Ben. Obviously, he had guessed what the *something* was. Maybe a little defiance would prime Alex's information pump. She set a fist on her hip. "And if I refuse?"

Alex fired. The bullet struck Ben in the forehead. His eyes rolled upward, and he collapsed. Leo and Iona dropped to their knees next to him and looked him over—no blood anywhere, not even an entry wound.

Iona grasped his hand. "Are you all right?"

He rasped, "Don't ... go ... with her." Then his eyes closed, and his head lolled to the side.

"He's not dead." Alex strutted closer. "The bullet is one of mine, fashioned with materials here in hell and coated with energy from my pool, which means that it penetrated in a semi-physical fashion and healed the entry point instantly. Unfortunately for him, the bullet is a capsule that released poison and knocked him out. If you obey me, I will provide an antidote. But you must act quickly. The poison will kill him in less than an hour."

Leo shot to his feet. "Let me go instead of Iona."

Alex's humming laugh returned. "The lion speaks again. So valiant. So brave. So sacrificial."

"Whatever I might be, I am not letting a teenager wander through hell to find an abyss. I am a professional tracker. I can locate it much faster than she can."

"Which is why you will accompany her, but you're too big to descend into the deepest part of the abyss. Once you arrive at the edge, it would be better if you station yourself there and act as an anchor while she descends. I have lights, a special rope, and everything else you need for the journey. Since it is less than a mile away, you can get there in under twenty minutes, assuming you are as skillful as you claim. Then you can return much more quickly, perhaps in twelve. That will give her around thirty minutes to descend and accomplish the task."

"What is the task?" Iona asked. "If it's not an object to retrieve, then what do I do?"

"You will understand when you arrive." Alex touched the cross on Iona's necklace. "This symbol will be helpful to frighten the superstitious souls, but you will need something more to protect you from possession."

Iona concealed a shudder. "Possession? You mean, like demonic possession?"

"Not exactly. Demons are not capable of possessing and controlling a human who is filled with light, as you are. Disembodied souls are another matter. They are designed to inhabit any human body, and some of the abyss dwellers have the knowledge to penetrate and inhabit you, though they would first have to purge your soul."

"Is that even possible?"

"I heard that you have a vaccine on earth that can purge souls. A scientist named Damien obtained the formula from a sorceress here in hell." Alex waved a hand. "Not me, of course. Another sorceress I am familiar with. In any case, it's possible that she continues to lurk. Perhaps she has passed the knowledge along to others. I am giving you the warning so that you'll take proper precautions when you descend into the abyss."

"What kind of precautions?"

"The rope I mentioned earlier." Alex curled a finger. "Come. I will provide you with everything you need and send you on your way."

Chapter Twenty-Five

Kat, Jack, and Trudy zoomed through a dazzling display of lights at what seemed like a million miles per hour. They burst into a blanket of air, body-slamming it and knocking the wind out of their lungs. Kat labored to breathe. Her ribs felt like they were going to crack. Her cheeks and lips bent back as she shouted, "We're going too fast!"

Jack spoke with halting gasps. "If we ... deploy the chutes ... they might ... rip apart."

"If we don't ..." Kat managed to suck in a breath. "We'll be pancakes ... in about a minute."

Trudy shouted, "Won't Winella slow us down?"

Kat gasped between phrases. "I told her ... top speed. ... We have chutes."

Trudy nodded. "Then let's deploy. No other choice." When she pushed away, they pulled their cords.

Kat shifted behind Jack and embraced him from behind, her arms under his as she allowed his pack to empty before pressing closer. The chutes billowed, caught the air, and jerked them into a gut-wrenching deceleration.

Holding on tightly, Kat looked down. The ground drew closer at a fast rate, still too fast. "Something's wrong. We're not slowing down enough."

Trudy pointed upward. "Holes in the chutes. Big ones."

Kat and Jack looked that way. A section of canvas the size of a bedsheet flapped at the top of each chute, leaving a rectangular hole.

"I got this." Trudy guided herself closer to Jack's chute, grabbed the closest line, and pulled to the top of his canopy, moving out of sight.

Jack craned his neck. "What in the name of insanity is she doing up there?"

Kat glanced down. The ground continued drawing closer at a fatal rate. "Whatever it is, it's not working."

"Because she's messing with my chute, gathering it into wads in places. She can't use her chute to slow us all down. Hers has a hole, too."

"Exactly the same size and shape." Kat gritted her teeth. "Sabotage. Compliments of the gentle female giant."

Their plunge suddenly slowed. Trudy slid down toward them, her gloved hands grasping two lines as her chute drew closer to Jack's from above. Releasing the lines with one hand, she used the other to pull her chute's straps off, exchanging hands on the lines when needed. The moment her pack flew away, she plunged, still holding Jack's lines.

She collided with Kat and Jack, threw her arms around his waist, and held on, her arms below Kat's.

Jack grabbed Trudy's belt. "Got you, Sis!"

"Good." She gasped for breath. "And never dis my supplies again, or I'll suture your mouth shut tighter than I stitched your chute."

The trio dropped, slower than before, but still faster than they ever did in training.

"Impact in twenty seconds," Jack called. "If you have any ideas, let's hear them."

"Look for something soft." Kat scanned the ground, searching for trees to entangle the chute, or a lake, a river, any body of water to cushion their landing. A forest bordered a canyon, and a stream poured down a waterfall, but their downward angle put both out of range. They would land near the water but not near enough.

Something glimmered at ground level—a circular surface, far too smooth and clear to be water. A dot at the center grew larger. It looked like a copy of themselves, drawing closer and closer. Kat shouted, "See the glimmer? It'll be right below us in a few seconds. I think it's the mirror. The portal Leo mentioned."

"I see it," Jack said, twisting his neck to look, "but the wind's gonna shoot us past it."

"Not if we drop before it can put us out of range."

Trudy shouted, "You mean plunge straight into hell? On purpose?"

"Unless you have another idea."

"Nothing's coming to mind."

"In that case ..." Kat unfastened Jack's straps and pushed back to let the pack slide upward. "I'll help you shrug the chute off in three ... two ... one ... Now!"

Iona strode with Leo through a forest, stepping high to avoid tripping on knobby roots. Using a branch as a walking stick and carrying a large rope coil over his shoulder, Leo kept a flashlight trained on their path, such that it was—nothing more than what he called "signs of travel," as he used his skillful eyes and sensitive nose to find their way.

Alex had pointed them in the right direction, assuming she was telling the truth, saying to search for a huge pit that emanated a sulfur-infused gas. Unfortunately, smaller holes emitted rotten-egg vapors throughout the forest, leading Leo astray from time to time. And time was exactly what they couldn't afford to waste. Ben would be dead in about forty-five minutes.

With vines bending from the limbs in swing-like arcs, the setting resembled a jungle, though no birds called, not even a nocturnal one. Maybe birds didn't go to hell. But one creature probably did. "No snakes," Iona said. "I expected snakes."

"I haven't smelled anything alive except the trees and vines, and even those smell rotten to the core. No undergrowth. No moss. Nothing."

A new voice joined theirs. "And you won't." Bart walked next to them, his stride uneasy as he, too, stepped high. "Hell is void of breathing creatures other than those that guard Alexandria's castle. She conjured them with her dark arts."

Iona glared at him. "The witch's toady returns. You sure made yourself scarce while we were in Alex's lockup."

"I am a survivor, not a hero. I bow to Alex, as you call her, when necessary. But I also help those who can help me. The fact is, I hate her with a passion, but I am beholden to her because she helped me escape the abyss."

"You were in the abyss? That means you know where it is."

Bart nodded. "And you're going in the right direction. I will correct your course if you stray from it."

"You'd better be telling the truth." Iona broke into a jog, prompting Leo and Bart to accelerate. "Was Alex in the abyss, too?"

"Yes." Bart trotted in an awkward fashion, more like a waddling duck than an athlete. "All condemned souls go into the abyss where they await their eternal banishment to the lake of fire."

Iona focused straight ahead, watching for obstacles. "How did she escape?"

"When Alex was alive, she developed extraordinary skills that enabled her to manipulate souls and their environs. It took decades of grueling effort, but she finally managed to crawl out of that fetid hole, and she brought me with her, thinking that I would be a trusted ally. I now live with her in the castle."

"So when I dropped into hell, Ben didn't send you. Alex did."

"That's true, I must confess. Though I convinced Ben of my fealty to him long enough to obtain your cross. And I also helped you then as I am helping you now. I want you to succeed because I want Alex to succeed in opening the portal above to allow us all to escape."

Leo harrumphed. "Can we trust a lying sycophant, even one who's claiming to follow his own self-interest? You could be lying about everything, and you get your jollies watching people suffer."

"Believe what you want. I will still give you guidance. You can choose whichever options you wish. You are not obligated to accept my advice."

Iona scurried under a low-hanging limb as the two men ducked under it. "If what you're saying is true, then why is this forest here? And the swamp at Alex's castle? That thorny hedge? If the souls are supposed to be in the abyss, why all this stuff? It's like theater props with no actors."

"Because not all stay in the abyss. Alex isn't the only—well, sorceress, I suppose you could call her, though you didn't hear that label from me—to escape from the abyss. I can't speak for the one who created this environment, but I suppose it is designed to make them feel ill at ease, to remind them that they are, indeed, in hell, and a fiery end awaits them. A few, like Alex, have turned it into a habitat, and there have been turf wars, though no one attempts to defy Alex anymore. They all acknowledge her as the queen of hell."

"The witchiest witch on the block. I get it. But since wicked witches tend to lie, tell me, is someone named Lacinda here? Alex obviously knows what Lacinda looks like, but when she told us to come inside and see her, we never brought it up again."

"There was a Lacinda," Bart said. "I heard she died, but I don't know when."

"Died? But Caligar, her father on their planet, said Lacinda speaks to him sometimes through his android."

"Alex is a brilliant actress and extraordinary mimic. She learned to imitate Lacinda's voice in a matter of hours. Even though Caligar mentioned things only Lacinda could know, Alex was clever enough to answer convincingly."

Iona rolled her eyes. "A clever witch. Just what we need."

"And never underestimate her cleverness. She is far more intelligent than I am. Even when she was conquered in the world of the living, she fell to brute force, not to a more intelligent opponent. No one has ever outwitted her."

"Got it. If I want to kill her, I need to club her over the head, not outsmart her."

Light seeped in from above, growing brighter. Leo turned the flashlight off and fastened it to his belt. "Nights aren't long here."

"They are unpredictable," Bart said. "It's all part of the never-ending nuisances in hell."

Out of breath, Iona slowed to a quick march. "Can you tell us what Alex wants me to do in the abyss? And if it's so hard to get out of there, even for her, how am *I* supposed to get out?"

Bart decelerated as well. "I honestly don't know what she wants. I know only that it's in the deepest part of the abyss. And it won't be hard for you to get out. You brought rope, and there are trees to anchor your descent and ascent. I'm sure Alex provided you with sufficient length, knowing the abyss as well as she does. And since you are physical and alive, the abyss won't hold you. Simply tie the rope around your waist, and, even if you get in trouble, Leo can pull you out."

The trees thinned, but thickening vapor prevented a better view. Iona continued her rapid marching pace. "Yeah, I planned to tie the rope on. Alex said it will keep souls from possessing me."

"Ah. She must have coated the rope with a soul repellant, which means that I will be unable to assist you with anchoring the rope."

"No worries. But about being physical. You say the abyss won't hold me because I'm physical, but you seem as solid as I am. So does Alex. Everything around us, too. What's up with that?"

"Both heaven and hell are real places, and souls resurrect to one or the other with real bodies that you might call pseudo-physical. I have heard that in heaven, the bodies are wondrous and glorious. Here, our bodies are, more or less, copies of what we had on earth, including an imprint of our brains that contains memories and enables similar thought processes. We feel solid and can manipulate physical objects, though we are lighter in weight. Things feel pretty much the same to us except for one difference I noticed soon after I arrived in hell. My voice no longer echoed. It was the strangest thing. I have pain, tears, warmth, cold. Everything but an echo." He shrugged. "Anyway, we're little more than bags of gas with nerve endings that can feel pain. If not for those, suffering in the lake of fire would be limited to eternal regret. No need for fire to achieve that. A dark pit would suffice."

"Like the abyss," Leo said.

"Yes, like the abyss. And in that pit, there is much suffering. Plenty of places to be injured. If the souls there are cut, they will suffer pain, but then they will heal, only to be cut again in a never-ending cycle until they are cast into the lake of fire."

Leo sniffed the air. "We're getting close. The sulfur odor is thicker."

Iona inhaled through her nose. Yes, the sulfur odor was increasing. Bart pointed. "We have arrived."

They emerged from the forest into a vast, barren land of gray rock. Ahead, an enormous hole marred the ground, so big the other side lay out of sight miles and miles away. Yellowish-brown vapor rose across the surface and curled lazily into the slate-gray sky. At the edge of the abyss, a pale hand with thin fingers slid up from below and caught the lip, clawing at the rocky ground to keep its hold.

Bart sauntered to the spot and kicked the hand away. As he returned, he chuckled. "That old woman's been trying to escape for years. She gets close sometimes, but she's too weak to climb out."

A shout begged to burst from Iona's gut, but she swallowed it down. Would protesting his cruelty do any good? Probably not. He was a lost cause.

Iona walked to the edge and surveyed the enormous hole. In the dimness below, something moved, like a slithering, nebulous swarm. "This pit is so big, it would take days to search it all. How am I supposed to find the deepest part?"

Bart sidled next to her. "All I know is that it's close, no more than a few minutes from the floor below this spot. Since Alex greatly desires your success, you can believe her word. And if she used a soul repellant on the rope, as I mentioned earlier, it will burn souls but not living people. In fact, it hurts for souls even to get close to it. Otherwise, the desperate fools would try to take it from you and climb it to the top."

"Well, then." Leo slid the coil of rope from his shoulder. "If the Minister of Mercy will help me decide which tree is the strongest, we'll get started."

"Sarcasm is the tool of the witless." Bart walked toward the forest. "But I will find a suitable tree."

Iona picked up an end of the rope and looped it around her waist. As she tied it in front, she whispered to Leo, "He's a snake."

"A viper, to be sure." Leo tested the knot. "I'll go with you until the passage is too small for me, then I'll climb back up."

"No." She checked the rope's tightness—good and snug. "I need you to stay here and guard the rope. Make sure Bart doesn't show his asp."

Leo chuckled. "Thank you for the moment of levity."

"No problem."

Leo strode to a tree where Bart stood and tied the rope to the trunk. As he walked back, he gave her a thumbs up. "It's secure."

While holding the rope, Iona drew a knife from a sheath Alex had returned to her. "I'm ready."

Leo fastened his flashlight to her belt and picked up the coil, ready to feed it. "Go. We have about thirty minutes left. Give the line two tugs when you reach bottom. Three when you need me to pull you up."

"Got it." Iona checked her helmet strap, took a deep breath, and began rappelling into the abyss.

Kat plummeted through the mirror alongside Jack and Trudy. The impact felt like striking loosely packed pebbles, hard enough to sting the soles of her feet, but soft enough to drop through without getting crushed.

Lights flashed, like strobes in a carnival maze. After a few moments of deceleration, they landed heavily and rolled with the impact. All three leaped to their feet and checked their belts. Everything seemed intact.

Trudy scanned their surroundings, her eyes wide. "Is this really hell? It looks like a bad picnic day at the park. Not a soul in sight, and I mean that literally. I expected to see suffering souls toiling in agony."

Kat set a fist on her hip and pivoted. This forest did, indeed, look like a picnic area, though no leaves dressed the bent trees. "Any idea where we should go?"

Jack stooped and touched an impression in the ground. "A footprint. A big one."

"A boot," Trudy said, bending close. "Could be Leo's. And the ground's pretty hard. It's intentional."

"He's leaving a trail." Jack nodded in the direction the boot-wearer had been heading. "That way."

Kat hurried ahead and found a small hole in the ground. "Here." She scanned down the path, spotted another hole, and pointed. "And there."

Jack hustled to the first hole and pushed the end of his rifle into it. The barrel fit perfectly. "Leo's a clever one."

Trudy broke into a quick jog. "What're we waiting for? Let's follow the huntsman."

Chapter Twenty-Six

Iona descended into the abyss, pushing with her legs against the craggy wall as Leo gave her slack. She clutched the rope tightly with both hands, the hilt of her knife clenched in her teeth. The odor of sulfur made her gag, and her throat narrowed, likely from something noxious besides the sulfur. If the air was already this bad, how awful would it be farther down?

Below, human forms took shape, crawling up the walls as their fingers dug into the uneven stone. Some slipped and slid downward as they clawed, etching the wall with long scratches.

A middle-aged man leaped from the side, grabbed her around the chest, and hung on from behind. Something sizzled, maybe the rope at her back touching him. He hissed into her ear. "Take me to the top! Take me now!" One of his hands shifted to her throat, and he dug his nails into her skin. "Or I will—"

She elbowed his ribs, then grabbed the knife from her mouth and slashed his leg with it. He yelped and let go with one hand while holding her belt with the other, dangling. She glared at him. "Or you'll what?"

"No! No! Don't send me to the bottom. It took me so long to get this high."

She stabbed his hand. He let go and dropped, screaming profanities as darkness enveloped him.

Her heart thudded. What a terrifying start. And she still had so far to go.

"Are you all right?" Leo called from above. "You stopped moving."

"Yeah." She breathed deeply through her mouth, trying to calm her nerves. "I had to deal with a guy who wanted a ride."

"You have to hurry. We're running out of time."

She licked her lips. "Okay. Let's zoom down. As fast as you can. Maybe my speed will discourage hitchhikers."

Holding the knife with her teeth again, she kicked away from the wall, and dropped faster. Again and again, she pushed, sometimes striking climbing souls with her feet, but it couldn't be helped.

The surroundings darkened. The stench worsened. Finally, her feet touched bottom. She spat the knife into her hand and tugged on the rope twice. It loosened, giving her slack to walk.

Gagging once more, she lifted her scarf over her mouth and nose, unfastened the flashlight from her belt, and turned it on. The beam shone on a group of eight women sitting on stones. Dressed in attire from various time periods, they faced each other as if they were at a campfire meeting.

A forty-something woman wearing a voluminous skirt with most of its hoops missing spoke in a language that sounded like French.

"No," a younger woman said, pulling one of her dark, greasy curls. "She's English. Or American. Hard to tell with that mask covering half her face."

"A living girl," the first woman said, her French accent thick. "Dressed like that, she must be one of the manly types. And that helmet makes a fashion statement. It says, 'I'm such a warrior.'"

"Now, Suzette, don't start. She has obvious feminine traits. Look at her. She's got such a nice—"

"Stop it." Iona flashed her knife in the beam. "Don't mess with me."

The woman rose, a fist on her hip. "Well, aren't you the touchy one? I was going to say that you have such a nice smile."

"No, you weren't. I have a scarf over my mouth." Iona set the beam on the woman's face. She squinted and held a hand up. Wearing a ratty skirt and a long-sleeved tunic marred by rips and tears, she had probably been here a long time. Iona shifted the beam away from the woman's eyes. "Where can I find the deepest part of the abyss?"

"I'll be glad to send you there, sweetie." She pointed. "Go that way. Follow close to the wall till you get to a cleft in the rock. Then walk about thirty more paces. With your stubby legs, maybe forty. You'll see an opening to a tunnel. Go inside and keep walking. It'll take you to the deepest part."

Not bothering to thank the woman, Iona strode on, shifting her beam back and forth between the wall and the floor. At times, she waded in the midst of hundreds of souls of all sizes as they meandered aimlessly, some well-dressed, some nearly naked. Most stepped out of the way, likely feeling the effects of the rope. Some whispered to one another as she passed. Others moaned with wordless laments, their stares locked straight ahead, though a few pawed at her, more like curious puppies than potential attackers.

When she found the cleft, she slowed and began counting her steps. A young man wearing modern jeans and a T-shirt pressed close to her side and walked with her, his shoulder touching hers. "I haven't seen you in our area before."

Iona halted and stepped back, displaying her knife. "Back off."

The man raised his hands. "Whoa. I just wanted to get to know you. We don't have any pretty girls around here."

"Get to know me. Right. No double meaning there."

He shrugged. "You got a problem with that? What's the worst that can happen? We're already in hell."

Heat flaring in her cheeks, she pointed the knife at him. "If you don't back off, I'll show you the worst that can happen."

He grinned and called out, "Boys, come here! We've actually got a girl in our area. And she's a firecracker. Let's have some fun."

At least ten more similarly dressed young men ambled closer, also grinning.

Iona ran around the group, encircling them with the rope. The points of contact sizzled, and the men groaned as they gathered closer together. She pulled the rope tight and faced the first man. "Are you having fun yet?"

He grimaced, smoke rising in front of his eyes. "No! Please! Let me go. I'll do anything."

"Anything?"

"Yes. Name it."

She leaned close, nearly nose to nose. "Be my bodyguard. Don't let any goons harass me."

"I will, but I can't leave my area. If I do, it burns."

Iona tightened the rope further. New sizzles rose. "Worse than this?"

"No. No. Okay. I'll do it."

"Then come with me." Iona loosened the rope. As she retraced her steps around the men, a few retreated into the darkness while the others slowly backed away. When she returned to the starting point, she gestured with her head toward the first man. "Now."

With him following, Iona walked on, picking up her step count where she left off. At number thirty, he groaned, but she kept up her pace. "Almost there. Don't wimp out on me."

When she reached number forty, she slowed. Ahead, her flashlight beam ran across a dark opening. She halted and nodded toward it. "Do you know anything about this tunnel?"

"Nothing. It's out of my area. I've never seen it before." The man winced. "I got you here. Can I go back now?"

Iona looked around. Only a few souls sat in the area, all curled in fetal positions, shaking and sobbing. No use bothering them. "You can go."

The moment he took a step to leave, the air swirled, whipping Iona's scarf. An eerie howl rode the twisting air. The force lifted the souls from the ground and swept them into the vortex. The man clutched the side of the tunnel to keep from getting pulled in. "Souls are entering. I've never seen a storm this strong before."

A gust tore his grip from the tunnel, and he flew into the spin. Leading with the flashlight, Iona rushed into the tunnel and jogged downward at a sharp angle. To the rear, the sound of rushing wind and moaning souls continued, but whatever was happening out there would have to take care of itself. She had to keep going.

Ahead, the tunnel's dimensions shrank further, making her hunch over. Soon, the narrowing space forced her to lower herself to a crawl, one hand on the flashlight. When her helmet bumped the ceiling, she dropped to a sniper crawl, a fairly easy maneuver for her, but it would be a tight squeeze if Leo tried to follow.

A sound drifted by, barely audible, coming from somewhere ahead. Iona paused and listened. Could it be string music, like from a violin? The melody, soft and sweet, seemed so out of place in this pit of horrors.

She crawled on. The music continued, a little louder as she progressed. In the distance, a light appeared, shifting every time she moved the flashlight. A reflection, maybe?

She emerged from the tight wormhole into a roomy chamber and climbed to her feet. In front of the far wall, a full-length mirror stood in a wooden frame, completely intact except for a small square gap in the lower left corner. The music seemed to emanate from the glass, though no instrument appeared in the reflection, only herself staring back, flashlight in hand.

She lowered her scarf and scanned her image. Smudges marred her cheeks, and her hair protruded from under her helmet like orange straw. Trying not to cringe, she stepped closer and straightened her body. The military uniform did make her look sort of masculine, not attractive at all. What man would ever want to …

She blinked. What was she thinking? Who cared what she looked like? Where did these crazy thoughts come from? Pivoting, she looked toward the tunnel entrance. The souls were territorial, those with wagging tongues divided from the apathetic and the violent. And now …

She spun back to the mirror and whispered, "The deepest part of the abyss. The worst of all sins. The nearby souls could do nothing but wail in a fetal position." Her thoughts raced. Vanity?

Pride? But why was the mirror placed here, far from the souls in the main chamber?

Reaching out a hand, she touched the surface. A shimmer ran across it. The reflection faded, replaced by Alex, sitting on her throne, playing a black violin. "Ah. You have arrived. I can see you as an image hovering over my pool." She set the violin on the floor beside her and smiled in a less-sinister-than-usual way. "Well done. You have proven that you are much more capable than I thought possible."

"Whatever." The odor of rotten eggs returned, prompting Iona to lift her scarf over her nose again. "What am I supposed to do?"

"I assume you noticed that an enormous influx of souls entered the abyss moments ago."

Iona nodded. "Why is that important?"

"You will learn in a moment." Alex waved a hand. The view widened, showing Ben sitting in a chair next to her, his wrists and ankles bound to it. With his eyes closed and his face pale as he gasped through short breaths, he looked close to death. "Now that you have proven yourself by braving the depths of the abyss, I will give your friend a dram of the antidote." She rose from her seat, pressed the top of a vial against Ben's lips, and forced blue liquid between them. He swallowed. After a few seconds, color returned to his face, and his breathing settled.

Alex reseated herself on her throne and addressed one of her creatures. "Guard, fly to the abyss and tell Bartholomew or the tall, hairy visitor that Iona will be delayed and her friend will survive because I gave him a measure of the antidote."

The bat-winged creature squawked disagreeably.

"Have no worries. You needn't stay long enough to harm your wings."

After squawking again, the creature flew from the room. Alex picked the violin up, set it in her lap, and gazed at Iona. "Now it is time for you to learn the truth."

"The truth? The truth about what?"

"About everything."

Iona cocked her body in a skeptical pose. "Why should I believe a single word you say?"

"Because only truth can pass through this mirror." Alex nodded toward her. "Go ahead. Say some things that are true and some things that are false, but choose statements that I wouldn't know anything about so you can be sure that I'm not manipulating the mirror. Also, even if you think something is true when it is not, the mirror will react as if you are lying, so be certain of your statements." The surface reverted to Iona's reflection. "Go ahead. Test the mirror. Let me know when you're finished."

"Okay. Let's see." She looked at her frumpy form again. "I am eighteen years old."

The reflection bent and twisted. Sparks flew out and drizzled to the ground. After a few seconds, the mirror reverted to normal.

"That must have been an untrue statement," Alex said, her visage nowhere in sight.

"Right. I'm really sixteen." The reflection stayed normal. She eyed herself closely and watched her image smile. Since this magical mirror knew things she didn't, now would be a good chance to learn secrets. "Okay ... um ... when Ben Garrison put me in charge over Leo, it was because he respected me, not just to pacify me."

Again, the mirror remained normal.

Iona whispered, "Cool."

"Interesting. Now I'm starting to understand your admiration of this man."

"As if you care." Iona continued gazing at herself, the scarf still in place. Maybe she could gather a bit more secret information. "Leo the huntsman is part of my family."

The reflection remained steady, not a hint of change.

Iona's cheeks warmed. Okay. So it was true. But what was he? An uncle? Did Mother or Father have a brother she didn't know about?

"Oh," Alex said. "I didn't know the stout-hearted lion is a relative. An older brother, perhaps?"

"I don't have a brother. I'm an only child."

The mirror warped and sizzled, proof that it knew about her little brother, the baby who had died while still an infant.

"It seems that you have a lot to learn about your own family," Alex said as the reflection returned to normal.

"Um ... Yeah. I'm convinced. The mirror is legit. You can come back now." A few measures of violin music emanated. When Alex's image returned, the black violin and bow in playing position, Iona took a deep breath. "What truth do you want to tell me?"

Alex kept the violin at her chin. "A tale that I will show you in the mirror. It's lengthy, perhaps even tedious, but it's essential. Without this knowledge, you will not be able to complete your task." Alex stroked the strings with the bow. Music again emanated. The throne room vanished, replaced by a man standing on one of the Arctic Circle tower platforms. "Once upon a time ..."

Kat crouched close to the ground and fingered the newest trail hole, near a drawbridge leading to a castle and only a few feet from a pile of corpses that looked like a cross between horned trolls and two-legged pigs. Wounds in their bodies appeared to be from bullets, maybe Leo's work. "The trail is different now. The depressions are more jagged and wider."

Jack pushed his barrel into one without touching the sides. "Yep. Definitely not from a rifle. Something wider."

"Ran out of ammo?" Trudy asked. "Then ditched his rifle to run?"

Kat rose. "He wasn't running. The holes are close to each other. And I don't see a rifle anywhere."

"Right," Jack said. "No reason to give it up. A rifle without ammo is still a good baseball bat, if you know what I mean." He nodded toward the castle. "Maybe someone in there took his rifle by force."

"No sense speculating." Kat pointed into the forest. "He went that way. If we lose the trail, we can double back and check the castle."

Trudy gripped her rifle with both hands. "Let's haul." She leaped into a fast jog. "Come on, slowpokes."

Kat and Jack raced after her and caught up. The trio ran abreast, leaping over roots, dodging trees, and ducking under low branches and vines. After nearly a mile, they broke out of the forest and came upon an enormous hole where Leo stood holding a rope tied to a tree, the other end in the hole.

Kat skidded to a halt, nearly colliding with Leo. Jack and Trudy joined them. As they took deep breaths, Kat set a hand on Leo's arm. "What's going on here?"

He looked at her, his lips tight and his skin ashen. "Nothing good, I'm afraid. Alex, the queen of hell, as she calls herself, poisoned Ben back at her castle and sent Iona and me—"

Kat gasped. "Poisoned Ben?"

Leo nodded grimly. "I received word that she administered some of the antidote, slowing the poison's effects, and she will give him the rest if Iona accomplishes a mission in this literal hellhole."

Kat stepped to the edge and peered into the depths. Far below the surface, shadowy figures climbed the dark walls, many falling back as if pulled by an invisible force. "Are those souls I see down there?"

"Yes, and a lot more recently went in. They fell out of the sky like the ugliest hailstones in history, swirling like a tornado of torment—moans, screeches, sobbing. It was terrible."

"Sounds like it." Kat pivoted back toward Leo. "What's Iona's mission?"

"That's another mystery. Alex said Iona would understand when she arrived at the bottom of this foul hole. Supposedly, the passage is too small for me. Only Iona can fit. But, even so, I can't believe I let my—I mean, *our*—scarlet squirt go into the abyss by herself, even though someone had to man the rope." His eyes misting, he looked into the forest. "Did you enter the castle?"

"Not yet." Kat chambered a round in her rifle. "But I will now."

Trudy did the same. "That's makes two of us. Jack can man the rope for Leo."

"You bet." Jack patted Leo's back and grasped the rope. "Go. Find Iona."

Leo gave the rope a pull. "Three tugs mean we're ready to come up. Watch for a man named Bart. He's a condemned soul who works for Alex. He helped us get here, then left a few moments ago. You can trust him if he's serving himself. Otherwise, he's a snake." Leo backed to the edge of the hole and began rappelling like a seasoned climber. In seconds, he was gone.

"Whew!" Jack turned toward Kat and Trudy. "Okay. You two should get going. But take this Alex chick seriously. If she's legitimately the queen of hell, you never know what traps you might run into in that huge castle, or even if your rifles will do any damage."

Kat strapped her rifle over her shoulder. "They worked fine on that pile of monsters. Their wounds weren't from poking each other with sticks."

"Fair point." His brow wrinkled. "But still, be careful."

"You know us." Trudy kissed his cheek. "Never throw a stone when you have a hand grenade."

Kat ran with Trudy into the forest, following the trail again, this time at a faster pace. As the forest darkened the path, images of Ben's pale face flashed to mind as he struggled to breathe, choking, gasping. Dread tried to crawl in and break her focus, but she shook it off. This was no time to peel off her mental armor. Ben needed her and Trudy. So did the entire world … again. Hell or no hell, queen or no queen, they had to get the job done.

Chapter Twenty-Seven

The man on the tower platform looked through a telescope, a woman at his side. Alex's voice returned, the violin fading into the background. "A scientist duo, Carson and Quinn Harrid, created an outpost in northern Alaska to try to communicate with extraterrestrial beings. This effort led to the construction of towers around the Arctic Circle that established the first conduit between Earth and the rift in space. Unfortunately, the path proved to be unstable, and it sucked Quinn through."

The mirror showed the woman flying into the air, flailing as she shot skyward. With each phrase Alex spoke, the reflection displayed the scenes and characters as if controlled by her words.

"In his desperate efforts to bring her back, Carson combined signals from all the towers and widened the rift to the size of the current Oculus Gate. Now confident of success, he tried again to travel through the portal to find his wife.

"When he activated the towers, he flew through the Oculus Gate and landed safely in a new world, a world of giants. Most were barbaric, but four were civilized—an adult male named Caligar and his close relations.

"Caligar told Carson that Quinn had arrived there at a time when all of the giants were peaceful. Yet, an otherworldly voice told one of them that Quinn was the most succulent food possible. Her meat would provide power and wisdom beyond their imaginations.

"A prophet among the giants warned that eating humans was forbidden by their creator. All but Caligar and his family ignored the warning. The other giants killed the prophet, then Quinn, and divided her into tiny portions and distributed them throughout the tribe of several hundred."

At the sight of a giant gnawing on a human leg bone, nausea churned in Iona's stomach. She swallowed down burning bile. This story couldn't end soon enough.

The image altered to a line of half-naked giants walking through a forest with primitive clubs in hand. "In an unexpected turn of events, the giants who ate Quinn turned violent, and instead of gaining wisdom, they lost intelligence, including the most basic common sense. Caligar and his family had to flee. He created a fortress within a mountain and set deadly traps for the barbaric giants who might try to enter.

"Of course, Carson was devastated again. His dear wife had been killed and eaten. He swore to get revenge, but he lacked the needed weapons to battle such huge beasts. His only hope was to return to earth to gather armaments.

"He and Caligar fashioned a circular mirror that reflected the Oculus Gate, enabling a powerful communications channel.

"New voices came through, including those of the beings that became the angels on Earth. Carson and company also heard my voice, for I have long been able to access signals passing through certain portals."

The mirror showed Carson standing next to a shimmering disc embedded in the ground. Dim light emanated upward from the disc as he looked on, frowning, his fists tight. "Unfortunately for Carson, he lacked the power necessary to sufficiently energize the conduit. Yet, I had a solution and guided him to engineer the mirror to open a portal to hell and tap the energy resources there. You see, I am able to collect energy from souls and deposit it in the pool you saw. The power is tremendous, such as in the healing you already witnessed."

More nausea boiled in Iona's gut. Alex had healed them with energy from condemned souls?

"In order to test the newfound power supply, Carson talked Caligar and his wife, Winella, into going to Earth, telling them that they might find a more suitable home there away from the barbaric giants. Once they were able to determine if Earth would be a good home, their children, Lacinda and Bazrah, could join them.

"The moment they energized the mirror and the two giants were on their way, an army of barbaric giants attacked. Carson was able to angle the energy to collect them into the flow. They, too, transported to Earth, though some avoided the energy and retreated, too frightened to ever attack again.

"When Caligar and Winella landed on Earth at the Alaska tower, they signaled their safe arrival. Finding the region suitable for building a home, they asked Carson to come with Bazrah and Lacinda. Yet, I counseled Carson to leave them behind on Viridi and use them as leverage to get Caligar to help him bring the so-called angels to Earth.

"Carson was unaware that I had made a deal with the angels. For their part, they would create a toxic vaccine to purge the souls of humans. For mine, I would provide the ingredients for the vaccine and encourage Carson to bring the angels to Earth. In order to ensure their obedience afterward, I made the angels believe that I was a great power on Earth and would enforce my wishes by sending them into oblivion if they disobeyed.

"When the angels arrived and Carson worked out a way for them to occupy human bodies, they turned on him, knowing that if he had the power and intelligence to bring them to Earth, he could also expel them.

"The angels captured Carson and used the tower network to send him back to Viridi, and I shut off the mirror's energy source to keep him there. To slam the door for good, the angels took control of the towers and would not allow Caligar and Winella to access them.

"With the towers under the angels' control, I suspected that they would try to cross me. I gave them a way to do so, while benefiting myself. I located the Refectors and enticed the two groups to communicate with each other. The angels used the vaccine to provide soulless human hosts and brought the Refectors to Earth, which is exactly what I wanted—vehicles to transport souls to the Arctic Circle.

"In the meantime, Carson wandered on the giants' planet, searching for materials to create a power source of his own. Finally, he turned to me for help, though he knew that I was the one who had closed his access to hell's power.

"I offered him the advice he sought, a way to gain the necessary power, but I needed someone to enter the abyss to tap the source. He suggested Lacinda, lured her close to the mirror, and pushed her into it. When she arrived, I captured her. From that day onward, I communicated with Caligar through Melinda, who transmitted my voice to Earth through the channel on Viridi.

"Knowing that the Refectors would soon be on their way to the Arctic Circle to deposit souls, I sent Lacinda into the abyss, telling her it was the only way to escape hell, but unfortunately, she failed.

"Another misfortune also occurred. The stupid, beastly giants attacked the Refectors and the humans who came with them. I needed a huge influx of souls but received only a minor burst.

"Then Carson said if only he could go to Earth, he would deliver the souls. I asked him how I could know that he would keep his word. When he told me, I agreed and temporarily provided the power he needed to go. And he has delivered. The souls arrived moments ago, many more than I need."

The violin quieted. The scene in the mirror faded and returned to Alex sitting on her throne, the violin in her lap. "Now you know the truth. Do you have any questions?"

Iona's heart thumped. The story was too incredible to believe. Yet, the mirror never flinched. It had to be true. She took a deep breath and let it out slowly. For some reason, the sulfur odor had faded. Maybe she had grown accustomed to it. "What was your agreement with Carson?"

"That is not for you to know. It was personal. Your questions must relate to you and your situation."

"Okay, then what happened to Lacinda when she tried to do what I'm trying to do?"

"She failed and later perished."

Iona swallowed. "Perished? How?"

"Lacinda had a long, thick braid. A condemned soul wrapped it around her neck and strangled her."

Iona stared at the mirror. The reflection stayed perfectly steady. "How do you know what happened?"

"I was close enough to see her die, but I did nothing to stop the murderer because Lacinda had failed and could no longer help me. I will never forget the sheer terror in her eyes as she drew her final breath." Alex sighed in an overly dramatic fashion. "Tragic. Really tragic."

Iona resisted the urge to scowl at the fake display of sympathy. "Then how do I stand a chance?"

"Because you are human, and Lacinda was not. That idea came to mind after her failure, and now I am certain of it. Only a human—a living, breathing human—can complete this task. Since you are human, I am confident that you will."

Once more Iona watched the mirror for any sign of a lie, but the reflection held firm. "Okay. Let's get straight to the point. What do I have to do? And what will happen if I get it done that'll keep the souls from attacking me?"

A ghost of a smile bent Alex's lips. "The mirror is a symbol of pride, of vanity, of selfishness, and music is a catalyst to activate its truth-telling images. Yet, even without music, it always displays a person's inner self, or at least it once did before it fell dormant.

"And that power is why the mirror was placed in the abyss. You see, love of self is the ultimate reason every soul is in hell, and the mirror stood as a reminder of this fact. Whenever the souls passed by it, the reflection showed them who they truly were—filthy, disgusting, foul. But, not being alive, they couldn't destroy it, so they put it out of sight. They dug this tunnel and put the mirror inside. Eventually, with no one to gaze upon it, the mirror deactivated.

"Because of that change, the amount of energy emanating from the abyss ebbed. Pain, regret, guilt, and other suffering drains the souls of energy, and it rises like vapor. The winged guards you locked in your cell are only a few of dozens that patrol the area around my castle. They collect the energy in specialized containers, and they deposit it in the pool in my throne room. And we already discussed the incredible power it contains.

"Now that the abyss has been flooded with new souls, all you have to do is activate the mirror, take it from the tunnel, and place it back in the main chamber. The mirror, as a device designed to reveal truth, will eliminate all boundaries that confine the souls to certain areas, and it will draw the souls like a light draws moths. Yet, the truth is sometimes a horrible revelation. Their hideous reflections will devastate them. Energy will shoot to the skies, but not to be collected by my guards. It will assault the mirror you fell through to enter hell, reverse the direction of the portal, and allow you and your friends to escape."

Iona pointed at Alex. "And you."

"Yes, of course. That has been my intent all along."

"It's the end game of your plan. You've been cooking this up for years. I'll bet yours was the voice that whispered to the giants that human meat was delicious and would give them wisdom."

"As I told you, the mirror won't allow me to lie, so I intentionally avoided that piece of information." Alex nodded. "But you guessed correctly. I had the tiniest of communication wormholes to that world, but it didn't take much to convince those simpleton stargazers that consuming Quinn would be to their benefit."

Iona set a tight fist on her hip. "Then you're like the serpent in the Garden of Eden. Satan himself."

"In a way. I did draw my inspiration from his lie. I had to start somewhere."

"And now you want me to release Satan's handmaiden from hell."

Alex's humming laugh resurrected. "Call me what you wish, but that is what I want. Remember, however, that altering the portal's directional flow is the only way that you and your loved ones will escape. Otherwise, you will be trapped in hell forever."

"But you want me to increase the souls' pain to benefit myself. That's not exactly the best way for me to get on God's good side."

"If you know of another way, then tell me. I have been in hell for a long, long time. Do you think I would still be here if there was another way?" She leaned closer. "Besides, it's not evil to show someone his nature, to use a tool to reflect the truth. These souls are here for a reason, and the mirror reminds them that they deserve to be damned and stay right where they are."

The nausea returned once more. "Maybe, but it makes me sick that you're the one preaching truth and damnation when you deserve to be here just like the others, and you're trying to use me to get out."

Alex ran a finger along a violin string, her gaze on the dark instrument. "I understand, but it is what it is. You are free to choose."

The reflection warped, and sparks gathered on the surface, popping at the edges.

Iona scowled. "You lied. I'm not free to choose, am I? You'll hound me through the jungles of hell until I do what you want."

Alex sighed again, this time without the drama. "I have to confess. You're right. I am desperate to leave this place. You should be able to understand my motivation. No one wants to stay in hell."

"Yeah. I get that. But if the portal opens, won't it release thousands, maybe millions of condemned souls to wreak havoc on Caligar's world? God sent them here for a reason. I can't do it."

"No, no, Iona. Of course not. The souls will stay in the abyss. The conduit is fueled by their own energy and will not affect them. It will pick up only living beings like you and your friends."

Iona drew her head back. "Then how do you expect to get out?"

"That will remain my secret, but be comforted by the fact that you will not be releasing so many residents of hell."

"Knowing you're getting out is bad enough." Iona let her shoulders sag. How could she make this terrible decision? No one could give her advice here in the deepest part of hell, at least no one trustworthy. The options were all too terrible to imagine. Help this devilish witch leave the damnation she deserves? If God sent her here, wouldn't giving her the key to her chains be the most arrogant sin imaginable? Then again, God could simply send her back to hell after this was all over.

Iona focused on the mirror again. Whatever might happen to her, she at least had to help Leo get out of this place. God could take care of Alex. "Okay. First I have to activate the mirror. How do I do that?"

Chapter Twenty-Eight

Leo whipped the rope around the latest attacker's neck and drew it tight. It sizzled on contact, adding the stench of burning soul to the already thick sulfur odor. "Maybe this will teach you to keep your fangs to yourself."

The man tried to dig his fingers under the loop but to no avail. "Mercy! Mercy!" he cried, gagging. "I'm sorry I bit you. Please let me go!"

"On one condition. Come with me to the deepest part of the abyss and encourage your fellows to leave me alone. I can't be slowed any longer by constant attacks." Leo tightened the rope. "What say you?"

The sizzles spiked. The man gagged again, barely able to squeak, "I ... will ... do it."

"Good." Leo unwound the rope and held it at his side. Hundreds of souls looked on, standing shoulder to shoulder, nearly all dressed in modern clothing. "Lead the way. Follow the rope and warn everyone. And hurry."

"I will. I will." He waded into the masses, pushing them aside as he called, "Hear me, wretched souls, do not molest this man, or you will regret it."

Leo aimed the flashlight beam on the rope and marched in the divide the man had created. He shook his hand where this foul beast had bitten him, one of several wounds inflicted by the aggressive souls here, some men and some women. Although many appeared to be listless and bored, some growled with anger. If Iona had to deal with them, it was no wonder she had been gone so long.

The rope led to a dark opening in the wall. The fanged guide halted and pointed at the hole. "There is great evil in that place. Not a soul will follow you in there."

"You can go your way." Leo shifted the beam inside. It looked like a tunnel with a low ceiling, too low for even the Mighty Midget to fit through without stooping. This wouldn't be easy.

He dropped to all fours and crawled in, whispering, "I'm on my way, Red. Hang in there."

Alex leaned forward, as if ready to reveal a secret. "Condemned to hell soon after the great nuclear meltdown, I arrived in the abyss long after the souls hid the mirror. When I went into the tunnel to investigate, I examined it and found that it reflected me exactly as I appeared, not my inner self, which I suspect would have been frightening. Based on ancient lore I studied during my time on Earth, I deduced that the mirror's years hidden in the tunnel caused it to deactivate, and the only way to activate it again is for a living person to look at it intently for long enough to see his or her inner self."

"My inner self?" Iona half closed an eye. "Why didn't you tell me that right away? We could've skipped your story."

"Not so, Iona. You needed to hear every word. You needed to hear how I concocted this scheme from the beginning, from the moment I whispered a temptation into the ear of a gentle giant and turned him into a barbarian, to the present time with you standing here in front of the mirror. Every death on Earth due to the phony angels' tyrannical rule, the contagion, and the toxic vaccine were my doing." Alex pointed at herself. "I am the reason Quinn was eaten by giants. I am the reason the angels came to Earth. I am the reason you and your friends are now in hell."

"Are you saying that you knew ahead of time that all of this was going to happen?"

"Not every detail, but more or less. I am an expert in reading people and predicting their behavior. In fact, I am certain that the courageous lion friend of yours will arrive soon in spite of the narrow passage. Your delay had to be more than he could bear. I imagine he would have arrived already if not for his own delays battling through what must be a pressing mob of souls in the abyss."

Iona sent her flashlight beam into the tunnel, but Leo was nowhere in sight. Alex was probably right on both counts. Leo would be trying to come, but it had to be a madhouse out there.

She turned again toward the mirror. "Okay, I'm convinced that you're rotten to the core. What's the point?"

Alex straightened to her full height, taking up the entire mirror. "According to the lore, in order for you to learn how to activate the mirror, you must first see me for who I am. It should be easy now that you are aware of the depth of my depravity."

"I get that, but if I have to see my inner self, why do I have to x-ray you first instead of going straight to me?"

"Because it is far more difficult to see your own true nature. Most people imagine themselves as pristine, without blemish. Or if they realize some of their faults, they might have blind spots in the most critical areas. Therefore, activating the mirror by examining yourself might take a great deal of time. Yet, if you do so on me, though it won't activate the mirror right away because I am not present in front of it and I am not among the living, you will feel how it works. Then you can apply the same feeling to yourself."

Iona couldn't suppress a smirk. "So you want me to see you for the vile shrew that you really are."

One of Alex's eyebrows arched. "If that is what the mirror shows you."

"Well … all right. I guess I don't see the harm in that." Iona took a step closer to the mirror and stared at Alex, imagining the cruel blackness in her heart.

Alex whispered, "You saw what Quinn looked like." Her words seemed to come from every direction as if spoken from hidden

278

speakers. "Imagine the giants slicing her into pieces, eating her flesh, gnawing on her bones."

As Iona let her mind conjure the image, Alex's clothes turned darker, and a sleeved cloak took shape over them.

Alex's tone darkened as well. "Did you know the angels tested the contagion on people of every age? They had to make sure it worked. Think of the children infected by it, their violent spasms, vomiting, unable to breathe. Their parents as they wailed over a limp little body in their arms. And the experiments went on for years, killing thousands in home after home after home. Yet, the angels were merely tools in my arsenal. I caused every lament from every grieving heart."

A tear trickled down Iona's cheek, absorbed by the scarf. Alex's face withered into a skull, and her hands shrank to bones.

"And who do you think provided the angels with the foundation for the vaccine, the essential ingredient that purges a soul from its body? I did that. I have the only supply within the walls of my castle. And the vaccine, designed to alleviate the suffering, did the opposite. Burning like acid, their souls withered. Monstrous, pounding throbs assaulted their heads, too terrible to withstand. Their only hope of escape was to flee their own bodies, to fly into eternity. Relief? Yes, for some. Yet, those whose faithless souls were not prepared for death were deposited here to suffer more."

Spasms welled into Iona's throat. She wept, trying to swallow back the sobs, but they broke through all the same. In the mirror, Alex's skull and hands turned dark red. Long, pointed nails grew at the ends of her fingers, and fangs descended over her lower lip.

Alex took a deep breath and sighed. "I caused every moment of misery. And the next step for the souls here is—"

"Stop!" Iona wailed, heaving breaths between her sobs. "Stop, you evil monster!"

"Yes, Iona. I am an evil monster." Alex waved her arms. Her image vanished, replaced by Iona's reflection. "Now hold that feeling. Don't try to compose yourself. You now possess the eyes of a seer. Remove your helmet. Lower your mask. Take in your full countenance. What do you see?"

Iona took her helmet off, set it on the ground, and pulled her scarf down past her chin, smearing dirty tear tracks and mucous. Ignoring the urge to clean her face, she stared. In the mirror, her reflection morphed. The military gear faded. A freckled, red-haired woman wearing shorts and a tank top held a baby in her arms, wrapped in what appeared to be a faded beach towel. She handed the bundle over to another woman, this one dressed in a nunnery habit.

When the nun took the baby, the red-haired woman disappeared. Another woman took her place, a few years older, wearing overalls and boots, her dark hair pinned in a bun. The nun transferred the baby to her arms and walked away, fading into oblivion.

The woman set the baby on the floor. It quickly grew, then stood. Now a young child, she wore a pink dress and sneakers with green dinosaur cartoons. A shadow passed across her. She waved, but the shadow moved on.

She stamped a foot and screamed. The shadow hurried back and handed her a lollipop. As the girl licked it, she grinned.

Iona shouted at the mirror. "You spoiled little brat! You didn't get the attention you wanted, so you stomped your foot and screamed until you got it. And what did you get? Candy? That's all she thought of you, a brat who was appeased by a sucker. You didn't get love. You didn't get respect. She just gave you something to shut your ..."

Heat rose into her face. Her ears burned as she whispered, "Mouth."

In the mirror, the girl grew again. Now a young teenager and easily recognizable as Iona, she walked toward her farmhouse. Wind-driven snowflakes swirled around her head as she carried a double armful of firewood.

"I remember this," she whispered as she watched. "Mother and Father both had the plague, and I had to do all the chores. I already recovered from it, so I was immune."

When the image of Iona entered the house, a winged angel, dressed in a white satin robe, stood next to her parents' bodies, both lying on the floor. Smoke rose from twin holes in each of their foreheads.

Iona gasped and dropped the firewood. The angel, blonde, lithe, and beautiful, looked at her and smiled. "You are a fortunate youngster. I dispatched your parents before you could catch the plague."

The real Iona stepped closer. "I don't remember this."

The young Iona shouted, "I already had the plague! I can't catch it again!"

Still smiling, the angel let out a *tsking* sound. "My mistake, but it's all for the best. They were both near death. I ended their suffering."

The younger Iona balled her fists and screamed, "You winged rodent! They weren't near death! They were getting better! I know. I've been taking care of them every day."

The angel slapped Iona's face. "You deserve death for that outburst, but I will let it pass with a mere warning. You must show respect. The angels are the only force keeping the plague from overtaking the world. Perhaps you are immune, but others are not. It's important that we eliminate it before it eliminates everyone. If that means premature death for some victims, then so be it." She flew out the door and disappeared.

Iona took another step closer to the mirror. "I don't remember that at all."

The younger Iona ran to the door and screamed at the angel though she was long gone. Curse after curse flew from her mouth as she spat and swung her fists and stomped her feet. Then she dropped to her knees and sobbed.

"I remember now." Iona's throat tightened as new tears trickled. "How could I forget what that angel did to them?"

Alex's voice returned. "Did you block a memory to protect yourself?"

New tears flowed. "I ... I must've. I served the angels even though they murdered my parents, just like they did to Summer's parents."

"Summer? I have not heard that name."

Iona shook her head. "Never mind. It's not important." Yet, Summer's name echoed in her mind. Maybe she was supposed to follow in Summer's footsteps, even to the point of death. And another mystery dangled. Who was the woman who gave the baby to the nun? And who was the baby? Herself as an infant? That part made no sense. She wasn't adopted.

"Shall I assume that the mirror has been fully activated?" Alex asked. "Have you seen yourself for who you truly are?"

"Yes." Iona wiped her nose and cheeks on a sleeve. "It's activated."

"And what is your self-evaluation?"

"None of your business." Iona picked her helmet up and put it on. "I just need to get the mirror out of here."

"You're right, but the danger is great. It would be better if you have someone to help you move the mirror without breaking it. Has your friend—"

"Iona?"

Iona pivoted. Leo crawled in from the tunnel and straightened. "Are you all right?"

"Oh, Leo!" She leaped into his embrace. "I'm so glad you're here."

He hugged her tightly. When she drew back, he brushed a tear with his thumb. "What happened? You're a mess."

"Never mind." She hurried back to the mirror. Since the reflection still showed her weeping on her knees, he would ask too many questions. She turned the stand to the side, hiding the image. "We have to take this to the main part of the abyss. Then Alex will give Ben the antidote."

He nodded. "Tight fit, but we can manage."

"I'll go first and crawl backwards. You push the mirror into the tunnel to me, and we'll carry it the best we can. But be super careful. If we break it, everything's lost."

Leo wrinkled his nose in a skeptical manner. "Well, I trust that you know what you're doing."

"That makes one of us." Iona backed into the tunnel. When Leo guided the mirror in, she slid a hand under the frame, set the other hand on the ground, and pushed herself in reverse.

Leo scooted in, holding the mirror's opposite end with one hand and his flashlight with the other, setting the flashlight hand down as he wriggled through. "The cavalry showed up. Kat, Trudy, and Jack."

"And now we're all in hell." Iona rolled her eyes. "Yay, team."

"But this furniture rearrangement project will help us get out, right?"

She continued worming her way back. "Supposedly, according to Alex, but trusting her is like trusting a fox with the chickens. And that reminds me. Who's manning the rope?"

"Jack. I warned him about Bart. Since Jack has a rifle, I'm not worried."

"Yeah. He'll be fine. Bart's a coward."

"I detected that, but Alex clearly is not, which worries me. Kat and Trudy are on their way to storm the castle to try to save Ben. Assuming Alex isn't lying, he got a reprieve, a partial dose of the antidote, but when Kat and Trudy attack, all bets are off."

"True." Iona continued scooting back with slow, clumsy progress. "But we can't worry about that. We have to set this mirror in the abyss, or Ben's a goner."

"A simple mirror in exchange for a life." Leo pushed the mirror ahead as far as he could and crawled a few feet more. "Since this is going to take a while, tell me what you know."

Iona scooted back once more and drew the mirror with her. Telling most of the story wouldn't be difficult. She could skip the part about seeing herself as a girl who couldn't control her temper, a girl who blocked horrific carnage from her memory, a girl with pent-up rage that had been erupting ever since. Yet, every image was absolutely true. She was a lava-spewing volcano.

She heaved a sigh. "Okay, here goes."

Sitting on her throne, Alexandria gazed at Bartholomew as he walked into the chamber. "Did you find a suitable assassin?" she asked.

"Yes." He halted next to the healing basin. "It was difficult conversing from the top of the abyss, but I'm sure he knows what to do."

"Is the assassin skilled enough to know where to plunge the dagger?"

"Without a doubt. Mortal wounds that kill over time are his specialty."

"Did you offer a reward?"

"No need. He was excited to do it for the pure excitement of bloodletting."

"Good." Alexandria gestured toward the energy pool. "Everything has proceeded exactly as planned. The time has come for you to complete your part by entering my pool."

Bartholomew climbed onto the stage and stared at the basin. "Why? I'm not injured."

She chuckled. "After all we have been through together, are you now asking why?"

"Not to question your decisions, but we're both in hell. Our choices haven't exactly resulted in the best outcomes."

Alexandria rose from her throne. Her gown transformed into leather—form-fitting pants and jacket over a white T-shirt along with motorcycle-riding boots. The jacket's partially open zipper revealed a gun butt protruding from a shoulder holster. "You remember my power while on Earth, do you not?"

Bartholomew backed away, his feet now a step from the pool. "Of course. I also remember how you died. You miscalculated your opponent's resistance to your power. You couldn't force your will upon him."

"It was my only option at the time. You know this."

"True. And now I'm merely asking for clarification. Why do you want me to step into the pool when I'm not injured?"

"It would be easier to simply alter the idea that you aren't injured." Alex withdrew the gun and shot Bartholomew. The bullet slammed into his chest and drilled a hole that expanded and ate away at his body and clothes.

He gasped, batting at the gaping hole as if trying to beat out a fire. "What are you doing?"

"Forcing my will upon you." Alex strutted close and shoved him into the pool. He splashed into the energy. Sizzles rose amid his screams. Within seconds, he dissolved and disappeared.

Alexandria stood at the edge of the pool, the gun still in hand as she gazed into the disturbed energy. "Any further questions, Bartholomew?" She laughed, leaped off the stage, and strode toward the stairway.

Chapter Twenty-Nine

Kat skulked with Trudy across the drawbridge, taking each step quietly and quickly as they scanned the castle with wary eyes, rifles ready. Nothing moved. No noises interrupted the dead silence. Even the huge trees arching their branches over the spires and parapets stood in hushed stillness.

When they walked in, Kat turned her rifle scope's light on and swept the beam across the cavernous entry chamber, dim but not dark. The wooden floor ended at an upward-leading staircase at the far wall, and a door stood closed on the left, the only other exit.

"Up the stairs or through the door?" Kat whispered.

Trudy gestured with her rifle. "If the door's locked, we'll try the stairs first, then come back to blast the door open if necessary."

"Works for me." Kat crept to the door and grasped the ornate knob. It turned easily.

Trudy aimed her gun that way, illuminating the knob with her scope's light. She whispered, "Go."

Kat opened the door. Trudy shone the beam into the newly revealed corridor. Kat took a step inside, a darker area than the chamber but still light enough to see their surroundings.

"Watch my back." Kat led the way to a stairwell leading downward. The sound of a violin rose from below, the tune unfamiliar.

Kat halted. When Trudy closed in, Kat pulled her cheek to cheek and whispered in the quietest voice possible. "Sneak or storm?"

"Sneak till we have to storm."

Kat set a foot on the first step and slowly eased her weight onto it. When it made no sound, she lifted her foot to take another step.

The violin stopped, replaced by a voice. "Love is a cruel beast, don't you think?"

Kat stayed perfectly still. Was the question meant for her?

"I've been expecting you, Katherine. Come down with your weapon lowered, and we can discuss your husband's status."

"She didn't mention you," Kat whispered to Trudy. "Stay here. Listen. If it sounds like you should look around somewhere else, do it. Your judgment. Lights off on three."

Trudy raised three fingers and counted down to a fist. They flicked their lights off simultaneously.

"I'm coming." Kat strode down the stairs with a confident gait. At the bottom, the corridor widened into a chamber with a throne sitting on a low stage. A rectangular transparent basin lay at floor level in front.

A woman with an angular face sat on the throne, her hands resting on the ends of the chair's arms. Blonde hair draped her shoulders, covered in black by a leather jacket over a form-fitting white T-shirt. Leather pants complemented the outfit, as did a pair of riding boots sitting next to her bare feet. In stark contrast to the retro biker theme, a black violin and bow leaned against the chair.

Kat halted in front of the basin, her rifle in both hands with the barrel aimed at the floor. "You said to lower my weapon. Are you armed?"

"I disarmed moments ago in anticipation of your arrival." The woman opened her jacket, revealing an empty shoulder holster. She closed the jacket and zipped it halfway up. "Satisfied?"

Kat looked her over. Considering the tightness of her outfit, she likely wasn't concealing any weapons. "I assume you're Alex."

"I am Alexandria. Who informed you? The tall, hairy one?"

"Does it matter?"

"No."

"Then let's get to the point." Kat fired a bullet into a wall. "Where is my husband?"

Alex's expression remained calm. "He is close. Safe. For now. I hid him. Again, in anticipation of your arrival."

Kat's trigger finger twitched. Gaining an edge over someone who was already dead might be impossible. Maybe getting more information would help. "How did you know I was coming?"

"I have spies who patrol the air, and it was easy to guess your identity. Your husband has been murmuring your name, the shorter form. I assumed the rest. He is fitful, as you might imagine. Poison can do that."

Kat exchanged her rifle's magazine with a fresh one, slapping it in place with authority. "And the poison keeps me from ripping you to shreds with my rifle."

"As if your bullets could hurt me." Alex leaned to the side. "Where is your companion? My spies told me there were two females coming."

"She's close enough, but how did you know I was at the top of the stairs and not her?"

"Suffice it to say that I have a great deal of experience in predicting human behavior. For example, your next question will likely be, 'What do I have to do to save my husband?' Or something similar."

Kat kept her face slack. Alex was right, but no use admitting it. "Do you have an answer?"

"Your husband's deliverance is already underway. The energetic redhead is bringing it about even as we speak. I have already given your husband part of the antidote. As soon as she completes her task, I will give him the rest."

"What is the task?"

"Something that will free her and all living people from hell." Alex rose from the throne and sat at the edge of the platform, lowering her feet into the basin. Using a foot, she stirred transparent liquid within, thicker than water. "While we're waiting for her to finish, I'll bathe my feet here. It's wondrously refreshing."

Kat gestured with the rifle. "What is it?"

288

"A healing bath. Filled with pure energy. There is no malady it cannot cure."

"Then why do you need an antidote for my husband?"

"I don't want to waste the energy." Alex splashed delicately. "I have so little left. Merely soaking my feet doesn't deplete it."

"Is it enough to heal Ben?"

"Yes. Even pouring a handful over his face is enough, but that's not the point. It's my energy, and I will decide what to do with it. My antidote will be sufficient for him." Alex eyed Kat's rifle. "Your weapon won't enforce your will here."

Kat aimed the rifle at the basin. "Maybe I can persuade you otherwise."

"No!" Alex raised a hand, her eyes wide. "Don't shoot my healing pool!"

Kat set a finger on the trigger. "Then tell me where Ben is. Now."

"All right. All right. I'll tell you." Alex took a deep breath. "On the top floor, you'll find my living quarters. He is lying on my bed. The door is locked, and he is chained, but I'm sure your rifle can remedy both issues."

Kat called toward the stairs. "Trudy? You there?"

"Yep."

"I need someone to guard this hellcat while I look for Ben."

"On my way." Footsteps stomped down the stairs. Seconds later, Trudy arrived, her own rifle at her shoulder.

"How clever," Alex said. "Trudy will guard me to make sure I don't take some sort of secret shortcut or shout an attack command to one of my minions. I suppose those are typical military tactics."

Kat kept the rifle aimed at the basin. "Like you said, you're good at predicting behavior, but it's getting obvious that you're not quite good enough."

Alex rolled her eyes. "Oh, spare me the gloating. If I were so inclined, I could call a hundred of my pets to attack you with fanged fury, knowing that you won't harm my pool until your husband has been cured."

"Okay. Fair point." Kat lowered the rifle and gestured for Trudy to do the same. "Why are you telling me this?"

Alex gazed at the pool while she stirred the liquid with a foot. "To let you know that I am on your side."

"On my side?" Kat huffed. "Poisoning my husband says otherwise."

Alex focused on Kat. "Come, now. Think for a moment. Iona's quest is harrowing, far more dangerous than anything she has likely ever faced. After all, I wanted her to descend into a pit filled with condemned souls who would gladly harm her in unspeakable ways. Although I told her that succeeding would bring about a way to escape from hell, she did not believe me, at least without enough certainty to climb into the abyss. I had to provide a stick to go along with the carrot, if you'll pardon the stretching of an idiom."

"And I hope you'll pardon me for not believing a word you say." Kat gestured with her head toward the pool. "Trudy, keep your aim on the glass coffin. It's her prized possession."

"Got it." Trudy set her rifle to her shoulder. "Hurry back."

"Katherine," Alex said as she stirred the pool with her foot again.

Kat glared at her and replied with a sharp, "What?"

Alex smiled and spoke with a sultry purr. "I'll see you soon."

"Without a doubt." Kat sprinted up the first set of stairs, dashed through the doorway to the antechamber, and ran up the second set of stairs to the overlooking balcony. As she jogged along the balcony's carpeted floor, she pointed her scope's light into every possible passage. Soon, a door to the right came into view. She threw it open, aimed her rifle inside, and scanned the new corridor, narrow and dingy—not likely the path to a queen's bedroom.

She ran to the end of the balcony and turned left. A door to her right stood open, revealing a wide staircase with polished wooden steps. She hustled up, leaping over every other step.

At the top, a double door stood closed. Kat tried to turn the knob, but it wouldn't budge. She shot it three times with the rifle, blowing away the locking mechanism, then kicked the door open and charged inside.

Ben lay on a queen-sized bed, manacles binding his wrists and chains stretching his arms toward the posts. His eyes twitched under the lids, a sign of life.

Breathless, Kat shot a bedpost near its base, grabbed the top, and ripped it loose, freeing the chain. She then shot the other post and jerked its chain from its moorings. "It's me, Ben. I'm here. I've got you." A tremor crawled across her body, but she shook it off. No time for emotions. "Now to get these chains off you." She eyed a manacle—locked, an obvious keyhole on one side. Shooting it open without hurting Ben would be impossible.

Backing away from the bed, Kat scanned the room. A mahogany dresser stood next to the bed with nothing on top, not even a speck of dust.

She narrowed her eyes. How strange. Why would a soul have a bedroom like this? Did Alex need sleep? Did she need extra clothes for changing her outfits? Both seemed unlikely. What was this bedroom all about? A façade? A theater stage for Alex's mind games?

Kat pulled a top drawer open. Three items lay inside—a key, a revolver, and a note. She picked up the note and read the words silently. *Bartholomew, the bullets in this gun will disintegrate a soul. If you were bold enough to search my bedroom, it means that I am missing and in danger. Come and find me. You will be greatly rewarded.*

"Interesting." Kat spun the cylinder. Five bullets and one empty chamber. She tucked the gun behind her belt, snatched the key, and tried it on the manacle. It clicked open and dropped to the mattress. She eyed the key. It seemed too convenient, too easy to find. Yet, if Alex didn't think anyone would come into her bedroom to set Ben free, it made sense for her to put the key in a place convenient for her own use.

Kat pressed her lips together. Still too convenient. Too suspicious. A trap might be looming. But where? Either way, the key worked. She had to use it and worry about a trap later.

After unlocking the other manacle, she slid an arm under Ben's back and pulled him to a sitting position. "Ben, it's Kat."

He blinked at her, his head wobbling. "Kat?"

"Let's get you up." She set the rifle on the bed and helped him slide his feet to the floor. Propping his arm with a shoulder, she lifted him, his legs shaky, and grabbed the rifle with her free hand. "I can't carry you down two flights of stairs, so you'll have to walk with me. Unless you want me to roll you like a log."

"Right. Let's skip that." Ben bit his lip, but a groan escaped anyway. "No puking on this flight?"

"Definitely not." They shuffled together toward the door. "We'll take it slow and easy."

Iona carried her end of the mirror out of the tunnel and into the abyss, pushing souls with her back to make room. Leo joined her, set his end on the ground, and reeled the rope in from the tunnel. The fibers felt more ragged than before. Maybe the rope had taken too much of a beating. He would have to watch for weak points. "Now what?"

She touched the rope at her waist. "Loop some around you for protection while I set the mirror up. Then we'll scram."

While Leo wrapped the rope around his waist, Iona turned the mirror upright and wedged it tightly into the tunnel opening, blocking the passage. "That should do it."

Within seconds, souls streamed toward the mirror, pressing close and staring at their reflections. Expressions of curiosity transformed into grimaces, then gaping horror, punctuated by gasps.

Leo grasped Iona's arm. "Let's go." While he elbowed his way through the swarm, she tucked close behind him, both glancing back.

At the mirror, a woman shrieked. A man moaned and pulled at his hair. Others shouted, some in English, others in foreign languages. Curses flew amid spitting and wailing.

In the midst of the surge toward the mirror, a tall man with scraggly hair and a jutting chin pushed a fist into Iona's gut. When he pulled back, she dropped to her knees, both hands clutching her stomach. "Leo! He stabbed me!"

Leo punched the man in the nose, sending him reeling back, then crouched next to Iona and lifted her hand from the wound. Blood coated her palm and dampened her shirt. "Not good. Not good at all."

Iona sucked in quick breaths, her face tight. "It … it hurts like crazy."

"I've got you." Leo scooped her into his arms. When he straightened, the attacker appeared again and lunged. He rammed his knife into Leo's ribs, pulled it out, and ran away, cackling.

Pain roared in Leo's side, but he had to ignore it and get Iona out of this place. As he staggered with her in his arms, blood trickled down his side and into his pants. Trying not to groan, he bit his lip hard, but grunts escaped.

Iona called in a hoarse whisper, "Leo? Are you all right?"

"I will be when I get us both in that healing pool."

"Why? What happened?"

"Just a second." He pushed and kicked, striding against the tide of hundreds of souls streaming toward the mirror. More cries filled the abyss, adding to the bitter cacophony. When he forced his way to a clearer spot, he exhaled. "That foul soul stabbed me."

"Oh, Leo! You shouldn't be carrying me. You might bleed out."

"So might you." When they arrived at the wall, he set her on her feet and gave the dangling rope three tugs. It began reeling up while Leo fed the slack through his hands, watching for any frayed segments.

Iona touched Leo's side. "You're bleeding badly."

"I know." The rope tightened between Leo's fists and Jack's above. He doubled up a thinner section in his hands. "Can you climb onto my back?"

"I think so. I feel as light as a feather. The conduit must be forming."

"Good thing. These fibers are unraveling."

As Iona crawled up his back, Leo kept his hold on the rope, feeling lightweight himself. He set a foot on the wall and, riding Jack's pull, walked up. Fibers in another section a few inches above his hands broke loose. Only a few remained. They would break at any moment.

When they reached the top, the rope snapped. Just as Leo and Iona began to fall, Jack grabbed Leo's wrist and hoisted them to solid ground. "Let's get to the forest," Jack said as he helped Iona off Leo's back. "If all that caterwauling below is building the conduit, we're probably safer farther away from the pit."

Iona grimaced, her hands again covering her wound. "Yeah. Sure."

"Wait." Jack looked them over. "You're both hurt."

Leo dropped the rope. New pain raged in his ribs. "Her wound is worse." He scooped her into his arms again, gasping as he spoke. "I have to ... get her to the healing pool ... in the castle."

"Hold on a second." Jack took Iona's helmet off, flicked a knife open, and cut the rope at her waist, then the one at Leo's. "Let me carry her."

Leo shook his head. "If I falter, then you can take her. In the meantime, guard us with your rifle."

Jack patted him on the back. "Go. I'll be right behind you."

As Leo jogged into the forest, his body grew heavier and heavier, as did Iona's, slowing his stride. He flexed his muscles and trudged on, whispering, "Hang on. We'll be at the healing pool soon."

She offered a weak smile, though blood pooled over her abdomen. "Is it getting dark?"

"No. It's still daytime."

"I'm getting so dizzy."

"Blood loss." Leo picked up his pace again, though his own blood continued streaming. "Put pressure on the wound the best you can."

She licked her lips. "I'm dying, Leo."

"No. You're not dying. I won't let you." He looked up, the branches bobbing as he ran. Battling a tight throat, he spoke into the empty sky, his lumbering stride rattling his words. "God. Dear God. My mother ... used to tell me that ... you're with us even in hell. I'm calling in that promise ... Help me, Lord. ... Help me save this ... this amazing girl. I ... I don't think ... I can live without her."

Iona blinked. "You're shrinking, Leo. Don't go. Please don't leave me."

"I won't. Never. Nothing could tear me away from you."

Her voice gurgled. "I love you, Leo."

"I love you, too, Mighty Mouse. More than you'll ever know."

She whispered, "I like that name. Put it ... on the list." She took a deep breath and closed her eyes.

Chapter Thirty

Kat called from the top of the stairs. "Trudy! I've got him. Stay with that she-devil another minute."

"No problem. I can see her from the stairwell."

Kat stepped in front of Ben and turned her back toward him. "Lean on me. Same way as before. I won't let you fall."

When he complied, they trudged slowly down. After nearly a minute, they arrived at the bottom where Trudy waited. They each took an arm, guided him to the healing pool, and lowered him to a sitting position on the floor.

Alex sat at the edge of the stage, her feet in the basin. "You found him. Well done. Now what are you going to do?"

Kat dipped a hand into the basin's warm liquid. "Conduct a test."

Alex slid the rest of the way into the basin. Standing knee deep, she raised a hand. "No. I haven't received word that Iona completed her task."

"Receive this word." Kat pulled the revolver from her waistband and aimed it at Alex. "Recognize this, witch?"

"I do." A nervous twitch at her lips, she waved a hand. "Go ahead and heal him."

Keeping the gun aimed at Alex, Kat poured the liquid over Ben's face. He cringed, then exhaled. "It's ... helping. I can feel it."

A door slammed somewhere upstairs. "We're here," Leo called, terror in his voice. "Hang on, Iona. Hang on."

Loud footsteps stomped down. Leo appeared, carrying Iona, her limbs limp. Blood covered his arms.

Trudy ran to him and helped him hobble toward the stage as she scanned them both. "What happened? Stab wounds?"

"Yes." Leo glared at Alex as he neared the basin. "Iona did the job, just like you asked. The conduit out of hell is active, but I need to put her in the pool before she dies."

Alex trembled. "No. That wasn't part of the deal. I must preserve the pool's energy."

"Shut up, witch!" Kat aimed the gun again. "One more word and I'll—"

"Guards!" Alex looked toward the ceiling. "Guards, come to my aid!"

Kat fired. The bullet plunged into Alex's chest. She gulped. Her eyes flared. The hole expanded, eating away at her body, clothing and all. Particles drizzled into the pool and disappeared. As she dissolved, she screamed, "No! This can't be happening!" The hole spread to her neck, silencing her. Within seconds, her entire body crumbled to powder and melded with the pool's liquid.

"Get it done, Leo." Kat slid the gun away. "The energy worked for Ben. It's probably safe."

"Safer than dying." Leo stepped over the pool's side and sat in the liquid with Iona. Covering her mouth and pinching her nose, he submerged with her. Blood swirled, sizzling and sparking. Iona stiffened, then trembled violently. Leo did the same and released his hold on her nose.

"They're convulsing." Trudy set her hands on the edge of the basin and vaulted in. Straddling Iona, she lifted her shirt and called, "The stab wound is healed."

Kat waved an arm. "Then get her out of there!"

Trudy hoisted Iona and passed her to Kat. "She's breathing."

"Good." Kat laid Iona in Ben's lap. "Can you get Leo?"

Trudy grunted, her hands under him. "Maybe not."

"Hang on." Kat slammed the butt of her rifle against the basin, cracking the glass. Trudy added a shove to the side with both hands. It collapsed, sending the liquid cascading across the floor. "Now we can roll him out," Kat said.

Leo coughed a stream of liquid. "No need. I can manage."

Kat and Trudy helped him climb to his feet. He glanced around as if looking for someone.

"Iona's there," Kat said, pointing with her rifle. "Ben's got her. She's out cold, but I think she'll be all right."

"Oh. Good." Leo looked himself over and patted his torso, dazed. "I feel so confused."

Trudy guided him to Iona and helped him sit. "That's normal with so much blood loss, but can we wait here for you to recover? How long will that conduit last?"

"And where's Jack?" Kat asked. "Why wasn't he helping—"

Something squealed. A winged monster flew down the stairs and into the room. Kat whipped her rifle around and shot it. The beast fell to the floor, its wings flopping. "We'd better scat before more of those things show up."

Trudy lifted the still-unconscious Iona from Ben and carried her. When Leo rose, Trudy stepped close and smiled. "Feel up to carrying her?"

He waved a hand. "I'd better not. I'm too dizzy."

"Um … okay. I understand." Trudy nodded toward the floor. "Just get my rifle for me."

"I can do that." Leo picked up the rifle and held it clumsily. "Ready."

Kat took Ben's hand and helped him to his feet. "Feeling stronger?"

He nodded. "Some of that energy stuff spilled on me. I rubbed it into my skin."

"Great." She handed him the revolver. "I'll lead the way. You watch my back."

Kat stalked up the stairs, wary of more winged guards. When she reached the top and the others joined her, Trudy still carrying Iona, they hurried into the main room. Jack stood near the drawbridge with his rifle aimed at the opening. Winged corpses lay all around. Some flopped or twitched, and a foul odor permeated the air.

Kat set a fist on her hip. "So this is where you've been hiding out."

"I shot at least twenty." Jack slapped a new magazine into his rifle. "More might be coming. I heard their shrieks in the sky."

"Then we'd better bug out back to the abyss and catch the conduit train before it leaves the depot."

"We're good to go," Trudy said as she set Iona on her feet. "Our fireball is burning brightly again."

Iona blinked hard. "Yeah. I feel pretty good. Just got to get my bearings." She slid her hand into Leo's. "You feeling okay?"

He stared at the hand clasp. "Yes. Sure. I'm fine."

"They're both still woozy," Kat said to Jack. "I'll lag behind with them and Ben while you and Trudy blaze the trail."

They marched through the forest in the planned order, traveling as quickly as Ben's hobbling gait would allow. Although Kat peppered Leo and Iona with questions about their time in the abyss, Leo stayed quiet while Iona provided only a few details about her encounter with the mirror and Alex's explanation of the history behind the angels' coming to earth.

As they drew closer to the abyss, wails and moans rode the air. Each step felt easier, lighter. Trudy slowed her pace and raised a hand. "Are we sure about this liftoff? I mean, if we're high in the air and something shuts the conduit down, we're in for a world of hurt. Gravity doesn't care that we're in hell."

"I volunteer to test it," Jack said as he slid his rifle into a back harness. "If I disappear, consider it a good sign. I won't be able to come back with a report."

They halted at the edge of the forest. Jack gave everyone a solemn nod and walked into the open. When he drew close to the edge of the abyss, he leaped toward it. He flew into the air and continued upward, as if riding in an invisible elevator.

Kat stepped out of the forest with the others and looked up. Jack shrank in the distance, a blob against the slate-gray sky. After a few seconds, he vanished.

As the souls' laments droned on, their sorrow seemed to gnaw at her own soul. They were lost. Condemned. Without hope. She could exit this horrible place, while they had to stay. Forever. And, buoyed by their pain, she would soon soar on invisible wings to deliverance, a bat-out-of-hell blessing they could only dream about, a dream that would never come true.

Holding back tears, she grasped Leo's shoulder. "You and Iona next. While the conduit's strong."

"I agree." Still holding Iona's hand, Leo walked to the edge of the abyss. Without hesitation, they leaped and flew into the air, though not as quickly as Jack had.

Kat waved a hand. "Let's go. Now. The conduit might be weakening."

She, Trudy, and Ben strode to the abyss. Together, they leaped into the sky and flew toward a bright light above.

Now back on Viridi, Ben pressed a foot down on the transport mirror. The surface felt solid, no hint of a portal. Kat, Trudy, Leo, and Iona stood within reach, closer to the edge. They all appeared to be safe.

Beyond the edge of the disc, Jack leaned against the mesa in a casual manner. "Just a thought, but if I were you, I'd get off that portal before it sucks you back down to hell."

"Say no more." Kat curled an arm around Ben's and led him toward Jack, the others following.

When they made it to solid ground, Trudy kicked a loose stone on the uneven terrain. "No good place here to do a medical checkup on Leo and Iona. Let's go to the top of the mesa. It's flatter there."

They walked around the mesa's base to the steep stairway. Kat helped Ben climb while the others followed. At the top, Caligar lay on his back near the control pedestal. Ben limped to him and knelt close. The huge man's chest rose and fell in a steady rhythm.

"Caligar?" Ben shook his shoulder. "Are you all right?"

"What?" He shot to a sitting position, blinking. "Benjamin? How did you get here?"

Ben smiled as he rose. "That's a long story."

"I have been waiting for you, hoping for your return." Caligar climbed to his feet and looked around. "I see that everyone in your company escaped. How did you accomplish that feat?"

"Like I said, it's a long story. Short version, we reversed the mirror's one-way portal to hell and rose through it. But that reversal probably won't last." Ben pointed toward a nearby spot. "Trudy, it's flat there. Let's check out our wounded warriors."

While the others gathered at the spot, Ben focused on Caligar. "What of Winella and Bazrah?"

"They are both safe here in my world." Caligar watched as Trudy knelt between Leo and Iona, who now lay on the mesa. "But I am keeping their location to myself."

"I understand."

Caligar turned toward the edge of the mesa and looked at the mirror. "Do you have word on Lacinda?"

"Actually, no. I was unconscious most of—"

"Ben?" Iona called.

He turned toward her. "Yes?"

She curled a finger, gesturing for him to come. When he arrived and crouched close, she whispered, "Lacinda's dead. She tried to do what I did, but she couldn't because she's not human." Iona bit her lip, her eyes moist. "Tell Caligar I'm sorry. She tried to be a hero. It was so hard. Terribly hard. I know. It was torture."

Ben ran a hand across her damp hair. "I'll tell him." He walked back to Caligar and cleared his throat. "I am sorry to say, Caligar, that Lacinda died. I don't know the details except that she tried to be a hero."

Caligar looked away. He sniffed and rubbed his eyes with a knuckle. After a long moment, he refocused on Ben, his voice cracking. "I had a suspicion that she might be dead, but I held out hope."

Ben grasped Caligar's arm. "Again, I am very sorry."

Caligar pulled away, his tone sharp. "Why are you sorry? I proved myself to be your enemy. I cast you into hell."

"A man who is trying to save his family will never be my enemy." Ben limped to where Iona and Leo lay and knelt with the others.

Trudy patted Iona's stomach. "The stab wound sealed. No sign of internal injuries, but I can't be sure without checking her blood pressure. She's still pale." Trudy clasped Leo's hand in a thumb lock and pulled. "Get up, you big ox. You're in perfect health."

He sat up and laid a hand against his forehead. "Maybe so, but I don't feel like myself at all."

"Time will fix that. You need to replenish your blood supply."

Caligar crouched next to Ben. "Your family is everything to you, Benjamin."

Ben nodded. "I would do anything for them."

After a moment of silence, Caligar continued. "I went too far in the defense of my own family. I apologize for my evil actions." He extended a hand. "Peace?"

Ben took his hand and rose. When Caligar rose as well, Ben pulled him close and embraced him. "Peace, my brother."

Iona tried to rise, but Trudy set a hand on her shoulder and pushed her back down. "Not until I see some color in those cheeks."

Iona grinned. "Okay, doc, but with no pillow, you're gonna have to nurse a new sore on the back of my head."

"I've got that covered." Kat shed her camo shirt, leaving a sleeveless shirt on underneath. She folded the outer shirt and laid it under Iona's head. "It's got some blood on it, but it's dry." When Kat straightened, she looked at Trudy. "Something's bothering me."

Trudy adjusted the shirt under Iona's head. "Spill it. We can brainstorm."

"I get it that energy heals. Stands to reason. But the stuff in that pool came from pain and suffering. Are we saying that's a good thing? Will energy stripped from tormented souls be good for Ben and Leo and Iona? Long term, I mean."

Trudy shrugged. "Hard to say. We'll have to keep monitoring them."

"No choice, I guess." Kat crossed her arms and turned toward Ben. "Something else isn't sitting right with me. Several things, really. Like when I found the key to your manacles in a nearby drawer. Way too convenient. Alex was smart. Too smart to make things easy for us. I feel like she baited us into using her energy pool. She had some kind of sinister plot behind it, but I haven't figured out what."

He nodded. "I remember her locking me in manacles and putting the key in a drawer. She seemed methodical. I got the impression that nothing she did was by accident."

"Exactly right. That's why, when I found the key, I started watching more carefully for a trap, but everything started happening at once at the healing pool, and I shot Alex with her soul-killing gun." Kat snapped her fingers. "Then it was over. We walked out, pretty much unscathed. It was all too easy." Her arms again tightly crossed, Kat gazed at the Oculus Gate above. "And another thing. When I talked to Laramel's spawn before killing her—yeah, I have to tell you more about that—she mentioned that Alex couldn't leave hell without possessing a living vessel. I never saw Alex do anything to try to make that happen."

Ben chewed his lip. "And she wouldn't miss something so important."

"Exactly right again." Kat lowered her arms. "Did you see anything else while you were in her castle that might give us a clue?"

"Nothing comes to mind, but I'm still pretty dazed. I'll let you know if I remember something." Ben turned toward Caligar. "While we're waiting, let's talk about the next step. Can your system send us home?"

"It depends on whether or not the adjustment you made to return from hell affected it. I will check the readings."

When he turned toward the control panel, Ben touched his arm. "Wait. What about the Earth side? Any word from Dr. Harrid?"

Caligar looked toward the observation tower. "He restored Bazrah to Winella, and they used Earth's tower network to come here, setting a timer to turn the power off after they left. They arrived close to the area you and I did and found their way home. Harrid told Winella that he would destroy the Alaska tower. Whether or not he actually did, I do not know."

"Good information." Ben nodded toward the pedestal. "Let me know what you find out."

While Caligar walked that way, Ben settled cross-legged next to Trudy, completing a circle around Iona. "Is our patient ready to go home?"

Iona grinned. "If Dr. Worrywart says I'm ready."

"Her color's better." Trudy set a hand on Iona's cheek. "Headache? Nausea? Neck or other joint pain?"

"Nope." She glanced toward Caligar and whispered, "Let's rocket out of this dump."

"Okay. That's our Iona. She's ready." Trudy grasped Iona's wrist, and they rose together along with the others in the circle.

"Got a reading?" Ben called as they walked toward the control pedestal.

Caligar kept his hands on the panel, his back toward them. "Everything appears to be working. I am certain that I can send you home safely. It will be up to the proper power in a few moments."

"We don't have parachutes."

Caligar glanced at them. "My conduit generator is more advanced than the tower network. I can monitor your descent and put you down gently in Alaska. Unfortunately, you will have to deal with cold weather and savages from my world, but you know where my underground habitat is. You can go there for warmth and protection, and I will tell you where Winella hid your hovercraft. Your journey home should be relatively easy if the savages don't see you."

Trudy picked up her rifle. "A taste of lead will keep them at bay."

As all five gathered clothes and gear and walked to the edge of the mesa, Ben took a deep breath. "Sound off, team. What have we accomplished, and what's left to do?"

Trudy raised a hand. "We identified the demand for souls. With no buyer, the market will dry up."

"And," Kat said, "the vaccine scare should end, along with the threat of a contagion."

Jack looked down at the mirror. "With the tower network supposedly knocked out, we shouldn't have any more aliens getting to Earth that way. This one's still operational, though."

"Not for long." Caligar turned a knob on his control panel. Light from the mirror shot into the sky. "Once you are safely home, I will dismantle it. With both conduit generating devices gone, there will be no more cross-world travel."

Ben nodded. "Maybe we can get back in time to keep Harrid from destroying our network. I'd like to send the other giants home to Viridi."

"I hope you don't. I already have too many to deal with here. And that reminds me. Dr. Harrid told Winella that he would make sure the giants on Earth all die, an act of revenge for killing and eating his wife."

Trudy grimaced. "Eating his wife?"

"Yeah," Iona said, sighing. "I heard about that. It's a long story. I'll tell you later. But this much I will say. It's all Alex. Every single bad thing that happened was all because of her. She's the devil in cheap leather."

Kat smiled. "A good assessment, which means that Commander Barks was right. He suspected that there was a great evil force behind everything, and Alex was that force."

"Was." Trudy clapped her hands, raising her voice. "The wicked witch is dead!"

The others clapped with her. When the applause subsided, Ben gazed at the gathering and took on a more solemn tone. "Yes, she's dead now. Well, she was already dead, and now she's a pile of dust.

Good reason to celebrate. But we still have the Refectors to worry about. We barely know anything about them and Damien."

"Right," Kat said. "He took a sample of my blood, and I don't know why yet. And there's Dr. Harrid. Who knows if he'll give us any problems?"

"And the other key," Jack added. "The one I found at the bank. We don't know which box it unlocks or what's in it."

Caligar turned toward them. "The conduit is ready. You may leap at any time."

Ben extended a hand to each side. "No use dawdling. Link up."

Kat and Trudy each took one of his hands. Jack grasped Trudy's on the other side, while Leo took Kat's. Iona clasped Leo's to complete the line.

"Goodbye, my friends," Caligar said, blinking at the portal light. "I am grateful that you trust me."

"Goodbye, Caligar." Ben nodded toward the others. "All right, team. On three. One … two … three!"

They jumped together into the light. The conduit's energy sent them flying into the sky, the Oculus Gate looming above.

Ben held his breath. Maybe this would be the last time they would have to travel through that menacing eye in the sky. Yet, much more remained to be done—the list of mysteries and enemies the others had mentioned. Still, this team was up to the task. As long as they stayed together, they could do anything.

Iona blinked. Everything seemed dim and warped, as if the room were made of liquid. Alex's throne sat on the stage, the black violin and bow on the cushioned seat, but the healing basin lay broken.

She felt for her helmet and scarf, but both were gone. She whispered, "Am I still in hell?"

"I think we both are."

She gasped and turned her head toward the voice. Leo sat cross-legged next to her. "Oh! You scared me."

"That was not my intent." Leo blinked as well. "I awoke here only moments ago. Getting my bearings hasn't been easy. The last thing I remember was putting you in the healing pool because that maniac stabbed us in the abyss. We submerged together, then everything turned black. Later, I woke up sitting here next to you. I don't know how long I was out cold."

"I guess the pool worked, though." She lifted the hem of her shirt, exposing her stomach—perfectly intact. "I'm good. How about you?"

"Already checked. Fit as a fiddle."

Iona scanned the vacant chamber. "Where do you think everyone went? They wouldn't leave us here."

"True. Nothing sensible comes to mind." Leo leaned to the side, reached into his pants pocket, and withdrew a small metal box. "Here's something strange. When I first submerged in the healing pool, it felt like someone was trying to put this in my pocket. Somehow I grabbed it, and then it felt like I was draining from my body. When I woke up here, the box was still in my hands."

Iona peered at it. Half the size of a typical mobile phone, its rusty hinges and tin-like material made it look too average to be worth anything. "What's in it?"

"Another mystery." Leo flipped the lid open. A square of reflective glass lay inside, the same size as the gap in the abyss mirror

Iona squinted at it. "A piece of the mirror we carried?"

"That's my guess. I have no idea why it was so valuable that someone fought me for it." He closed the box and slid it back into his pocket. "I'll hang on to it. Maybe we'll figure it out."

"Maybe." Iona climbed to her feet and helped Leo to his. She called out, "Ben? Kat? Anyone?" Her words seemed to die in the air.

As she gazed at the high ceiling and widely spaced walls, her first visit here returned to mind, how her voice echoed in the cavernous chamber while Alex's didn't. Then Bart's explanation resurrected—a soul's voice doesn't echo.

She shuddered. "Um … Leo."

"Yes?"

Her hands trembled. "Say something loud. Shout. Call for help. Anything."

"Glad to, but you just did. No one answered."

Her throat narrowed. "Yeah. I know. Just do it. Please. I want to see if your voice echoes."

Leo cupped his hand around his mouth and shouted, "Ben! Jack! Anyone! Can you hear me?"

The words silenced, as if absorbed by the walls. His brow furrowed tightly. "That does not bode well."

"Oh, Leo!" She grasped his hand tightly. "We're dead! Trapped in hell!"

He dropped to his knees, pulled her into his arms, and hugged her tightly. "There must be an explanation. It's probably something Alex did."

Iona drew back, her cheeks hot. "Like with the healing pool? Did it do something that purged our souls?"

Leo snapped his fingers. "Like the vaccine."

"Right. Alex said she had the vaccine's ingredients. They must've been in the pool." She blew a sigh, trying to sound relieved in spite of her trembling hands. "Maybe that means we weren't condemned here by God. There's still hope."

"Good point." Leo rose and looked around. "But how do we get out?"

"Not sure." Iona tapped her chin with a finger. "According to Alex, the conduit won't carry souls, so that won't work."

"And Ben and company probably don't even know we're here. They won't know to rescue us."

"But, like I said, they wouldn't leave without us." As she imagined the conduit lifting the human travelers, she gasped. "Maybe they didn't leave without us, or they think they didn't. I mean, they left, but not without us."

"They took our soulless selves with them?" Leo shook his head sadly. "Worse and worse. How will they know they're accompanied by zombies?"

"By using an AngelScan." As fear tried to break through, she laughed under her breath to ward it off. "Seriously, they'll know something's wrong with me pretty fast, right? I mean, a soulless drone won't be a spitfire at all."

"Without a doubt. And I suppose my soulless self won't be able to track any longer. Another clue for them." Leo inhaled deeply. "My nose still works here, though. That's a plus. And I feel calm, considering the circumstances."

"Same here." The tremor in one of her hands worsened. She clamped down on it with the other and smiled uneasily. "Well, sort of calm. A little scared, I guess."

"You seem calm to me. I thought you might fly off at the handle at Alex, even though she's not here."

"Like a screaming eagle." Iona shrugged. "It's strange, but it's like … well … maybe going to hell changed me. For the better."

"Ah. The fire burned the chaff, so to speak. Has it been a learning experience for the reflective raptor?"

"Reflective." She nodded. "That's perfect for what happened in the abyss. Now I know why I'm such a volcano. I'll explain that part later, but I learned something else I can explain now." She pointed at him, then herself. "Something about you and me."

Leo's brow lifted. "Oh? What might that be?"

"That we should be together. Always." She slid her hand into his and looked into his eyes. "If I have to be in hell, I'm glad it's with you."

A tear trickled down each of his cheeks. "Well … ahem … that's …"

"Leo!" Iona reached up and brushed a tear with her thumb. "You're crying!"

"It seems that you're not the only one who learned a lesson." He swept the other tear away. "Shall we climb the stairs and see what we might see?"

She compressed his hand and smiled. "Lead the way, Mr. Macho."

Made in the USA
Middletown, DE
09 June 2023

32300758R00176